Praise

Praise for The Hollow Boys (The Dream Rider Saga, #1)

Winner of the 2023 Aurora Award for Best Young Adult Novel
Winner of the 2023 juried IAP Award for Best Young Adult Novel

"This arresting series kickoff grips from the start as it introduces its inventive milieu, its flawed but fantastically powered hero, its playful worldbuilding, and a host of tantalizing mysteries. ... [A] vigorously imaginative scenario. ... Takeaway: Thrilling YA fantasy" —*BookLife* (Editor's Pick)

"An assured, confident novel ... A must-read story for YA fantasy fans."
—*Blueink Review* (Starred review)

"Inventive, engaging, and boundless fun." —*The Ottawa Review of Books*

"A fun supernatural tale with well-developed characters and a touch of romance." —*Kirkus Reviews*

Praise for The Crystal Key (The Dream Rider Saga, #2)

"The richly inventive *Dream Rider* adventure continues in this second appealing entry...of Smith's epic YA series. ... An exciting plot...always enlivened by the Smith hallmarks of crack dialogue, fun sleuthing and puzzle-solving, a strong through-line of emotion, a swift pace...and a principled refusal to settle for the familiar. ... This thrilling superpowered urban fantasy series continues to grip."
—*BookLife (Editor's Pick)*

"Smith continues to demonstrate an ability to expertly weave multiple complex fantasy elements into a cohesive whole. ... This fast-paced story delivers in a big way—and Smith has all his ducks lined up for an explosive conclusion that readers won't want to miss." —*Blueink Review (Starred review)*

"Smith's take on superheroes and serials is both modern and original, but it recreates the same energy, the same yearning for superpowers, the same subconscious fear of dark places and boogeymen as the best stories of our own remembered youth. High adventure leavened with romance and mystery. ... *The Crystal Key* has everything that made *The Hollow Boys* work and turns it up a few notches. I can't wait for the conclusion in *The Lost Expedition.*" —*Ottawa Review of Books*

"A fun and engrossing superhero sequel." —*Kirkus Reviews*

Praise for Douglas Smith

"One of Canada's most original writers of speculative fiction." —*Library Journal*

"The man is Sturgeon good. Zelazny good. I don't give those up easy." —*Spider Robinson, Hugo & Nebula Awards winner*

"A great storyteller with a gifted and individual voice." —*Charles de Lint, World Fantasy Award winner*

"His stories are a treasure trove of riches that touch your heart while making you think." —*Robert J. Sawyer, Hugo & Nebula Awards winner*

"Stories you can't forget, even years later." —*Julie Czerneda, multi-award-winning author and editor*

How to Read This Series

The short answer to the above question is, "In order (please)!"

There are two types of series: those meant to be read in order, and those where the reader can dip into the books anywhere along the line. *The Dream Rider Saga* is the first type. It is one large mystery, one single story, told over the course of three books (*The Hollow Boys*, *The Crystal Key*, and *The Lost Expedition*), with each book building on what went before.

Reading *The Dream Rider Saga* out of order will lead to confusion and disappointment, two things I take great pains to avoid for my readers. After you read *The Hollow Boys*, I hope you will want to continue the series. If so, please read *The Crystal Key* next and finish up with the exciting conclusion to the series, *The Lost Expedition*. This will let you enjoy *The Dream Rider Saga* as I intended.

Buying links for all *The Dream Rider Saga* titles can be found at the back of this book. Thanks for listening and for your interest in my writing.

— Douglas Smith

THE
HOLLOW
BOYS

THE DREAM RIDER SAGA

BOOK 1

DOUGLAS SMITH

A Spiral Path Book

The Hollow Boys
(*The Dream Rider Saga*, Book 1)

ISBN 978-1-928048-27-5 (trade paperback)
ISBN 978-1-928048-32-9 (hardcover)
ISBN 978-1-928048-26-8 (ebook)

Published by Spiral Path Books
Toronto, Canada
smithwriter.com

First edition

Cover design and artwork by Jeff Brown

Disclaimer

To my family.

Because, at their heart, that's what these books are about—family.

The family we're born into. The family we find.
The family we make. The family we choose.

And the family we stitch together from all those pieces.

Act I

City With No Children

Chapter 1

When I Live My Dream

At seventeen, Will Dreycott was a superhero.

In his dreams.

Happily for Will, right now, he *was* dreaming.

To start his night as the Dream Rider, he "awoke" as usual on the Bed of Awakening in the House of Four Doors. Will knew he wasn't really waking. He was asleep. But entering Dream always felt as if he had finally woken up. As if his time spent in the "real" world was time spent asleep, waiting to return here.

To return to Dream. To be the Dream Rider.

Brian, his favorite Doogle, waited for him. The creature sat beside the bed, its head on the covers, staring at Will.

Doogles were dog-shaped—sort of. Kind of like a Dalmatian, white with black splotches, or the other way around. But with a snout like an anteater, ears like a koala, and eyes like an owl.

Big nose, big ears, and big eyes. The better to smell, hear, and see you with, little girl. Or old man. Or middle-aged woman. Or whoever or whatever Will set his Doogles to search for in Dream.

Okay, so they weren't much like dogs at all. But they were his creations, his logical constructs in Dream, and he thought of them as his dogs.

Dogs that *searched*.

Doogles.

Will stood and looked around. The House changed each night. Tonight, it was a round, domed chamber of white marble with dark wooden doors of varying shapes—rectangular, round, oval, and square. The four doors were carved with writings in Latin. Or Greek. Or something. Languages weren't his strongest school subject.

He scratched Brian behind his ears. "Evening, Bry. I missed you, buddy." In reply, Brian curled his long, whip-like tail into a spiral, a Doogle display of happiness.

Will tugged at the costume hugging his slim frame, again regretting the form-fitting spandex. But by now, hundreds of millions of people recognized the Rider—and that recognition gave him power in Dream. Too late to change his appearance.

Besides, the costume looked cool. It was black as the night sky, its surface speckled with blazing red comets with silver tails. Gray clouds drifted over his chest, obscuring then revealing the moon behind them. The moon, which changed phases like the real one, was full and bright tonight.

A black cloak, its hood currently thrown back, completed the look. A jeweled clasp in the shape of a twelve-pointed crystal star fastened the cloak at his neck.

Yeah. Cool.

He considered the four doors the House presented tonight. Which to choose?

"Nyx!" he called.

A cloud of gray mist the size of a beach ball formed before him. Inside the cloud, a woman's face appeared—blue skin, violet eyes, and long, purple hair floating around her head. She was striking, but too sharp-featured to call beautiful.

Seeing Will, Nyx rolled her eyes. "Really? You again?"

"Uh, since you're *my* subconscious, who did you expect?"

She pursed dark blue lips. "Someone better looking? I mean, a girl can dream, can't she?"

"You *are* dreaming."

"Have you ever wondered why your subconscious appears to you as female?"

"I'm in touch with my feminine side. Just give me the data file I prepared on the missing little girl, please."

"Lisa Carter? Well, at least you bothered me for a good reason. Here."

He held out his hand. A crystal sphere the size of a baseball appeared with a "pop," dropping into his palm. Inside the sphere, words, numbers, and images scrolled and tumbled, appearing and disappearing.

"May I go now, oh Great Master?"

"Please. And lose the sarcasm," he said. Nyx made a rude sound and disappeared.

He offered the data ball to Brian. "Here you go, boy. It's everything I know about Lisa."

The Doogle bent his snout up to sniff at the sphere. A long black tongue shot out, wrapping around the ball and sucking it into his mouth.

Brian swallowed the ball. Sparks of light danced in his black eyes. He began a circuit of the House. After sniffing at each door, he returned to the oval one, cocking his round ears forward. His tail sprang straight up, then bent into an arrow shape pointed at that door.

Will walked up to him. "You sure?"

Brian's tail whipped out, smacking Will on the leg before forming the arrow again.

"Okay, okay. Don't get grouchy." He patted Brian's head. "We have to be sure, pal. Tonight may be our only chance to find her before..." He didn't finish. Before it was too late. Before Lisa Carter was dead.

He pulled up the hood of his costume. Now anyone meeting him in Dream would see only blackness where his face should be. A blackness no light could penetrate.

He grabbed his skateboard from beside the bed. Across its black surface, constellations spun behind a thin veil of cloud. He touched the door. It swung open, and he stepped into Dream, Brian at his heels.

They emerged into rambling green parkland glowing under a mid-day sun. And a full moon. And a crescent moon, too. Dreamers liked moons, even in daytime scenes. A paved path cut through the park. In the distance, a cityscape of tilted towers loomed. Will turned. Behind him, the white dome of the House of Four Doors vanished with an audible pop.

Brian's tail curled into a question mark as Will scanned the Dreamscape. "Well, she disappeared from a park, so this is promising." He touched Brian's head.

A glowing silver cord appeared, running from Brian's collar to Will's wrist. Brian quivered in anticipation, his tail now pointing straight up.

Dropping his board onto the path, Will put one foot on it. "Go!"

Brian sniffed the air, then set off in a determined trot, his silver leash playing out behind him. Will kicked off, following the Doogle. The path wove through the park and the trees, all lit in bright sunlight.

Bright sunlight that in the next eyeblink died to murky twilight. From behind them, faint and far away, came a squeal like fingernails on chalkboard.

Crap. Nightfall and that sound meant only one thing. "Look sharp, Bry. They're coming."

Brian's tail shot straight up, an exclamation point of understanding. Will had given his early Doogles the ability to bark and howl like real dogs. Which they'd loved to do. A lot. And loudly. Hard to track things in Dream when your trackers kept waking up the dreamers.

The squealing came again, much closer this time. Will tugged on the leash, stopping Brian, then stepped off his board to face the coming danger.

"They'll be on us soon. We won't make it in time."

Brian's tail curled into another question mark.

"You keep going. Find Lisa. Dream led us here, so she must be close." He touched the leash, and it disappeared.

Snapping his tail straight up, Brian sped off along the trail he'd been following.

The squealing grew louder, and a tingle like electricity prickled Will's skin. "Nyx!" he called. No response.

Over a distant hill in the park, a dark swirling mass appeared. As it grew closer, the individual creatures comprising the mass became clearer. Each was a black rotating jumble of spikes and points and knife-edges, the size of a basketball. Electricity sparked and leaped over their surfaces.

Dream was built from the dreams of sleepers around the world, dreams that carried the *feelings* of their dreamers. When those feelings were strong enough, they created a life form existing only in Dream, creatures born from the emotions of dreamers. Emotional djinn. Or, as he called them...

Emojis.

Emojis changed depending on the emotion creating them. The ones bearing down on Will were the most dangerous. Fear emojis.

Gritting his teeth against their noise, he called again. "Nyx!"

Nyx's face appeared, hovering in a cloud of mist beside him. "Seriously? Again?"

He nodded toward the approaching black mass. She sighed. "Is that all? It's not as if they'll kill you. If they touch you, you'll just wake up."

"And lose what might be our last chance to find a little girl before she's killed."

"Hmm. All right, I forgive you. The usual?"

"Please." He held out both his hands.

A glowing crystal ball dropped into each of his palms. The ball in his left flattened, expanding into a round crystal shield attached to his arm. In his right hand, the other ball flowed into the hilt of a sword from which a crystal blade grew. Both sword and shield glowed silver in the darkness. Across their surfaces, equations, mathematical theorems, and numerical series flowed in a never-ending cycle.

He dropped into a fighting crouch, shield raised, sword ready to strike.

Just in time. The cloud of emojis swooped down on him like a tornado on a Kansas farmhouse.

And crashed into his shield, exploding in a cacophony of snaps, crackles, and pops. Those that hadn't struck the shield pulled back. Ten steps away, they clumped into a smaller swirling mass, bobbing and screeching at him.

If they split up and attacked him from all sides, he'd have no chance. But fear emojis were cowards, only attacking in mobs.

The mass of creatures shot forward again. This time, they feinted a strike against the shield, then swirled behind him. But he was ready for that. Pivoting to face them, he spun and swung his sword, cleaving the dark cloud.

With a shriek like rending metal, the survivors scattered, forming into an even smaller clump at a much greater distance. He waited, muscles tensed, shield up. The remaining emojis gave one last squeal, then sped off into the darkening twilight to haunt someone else's dream.

He tossed the sword and shield into the air where they disappeared with a popping sound. He touched his wrist, and the silver cord reappeared.

Back on his board, he followed the glowing leash along the park path. On the top of the next hill, Brian sat waiting. When the Doogle saw him, it flipped its tail into an arrow, pointing down the hill. Grinning, Will stopped beside Brian.

Below, a playground of crystal slides, swings, and jungle gyms rose shimmering from silver sand. He patted the Doogle's head. "Good dog." Brian's tail curled into a happy spiral. "Okay, your work here is done, Bry, but I have one more job for you." Brian's tail formed a question mark as he waited. "Nyx," Will called, "I need that second data ball."

Nyx didn't appear, but he heard her sigh. A second crystal sphere materialized and dropped into his open palm. Across its surface scrolled names of companies and corporations, some well-known, some not. He held it out to Brian.

The Doogle sniffed it, then sucked the morsel into his mouth. White lights danced again in his eyes, and his tail shot up. He tilted his head at Will.

"See what you can find on those. Meet me back at the House."

Turning, Brian sped off into the trees of the Dreamscape on his new search.

Carrying his board, Will walked down the hill toward the playground. As he approached, children appeared. Some sprouted up from the sand. Others emerged from behind posts and poles too slender to have hidden them. Still more popped into existence from thin air. The children ran and played together, yelling, laughing.

All except one.

One little girl with long, straw-colored hair huddled alone under the slide. She was maybe eight years old. He recognized her from the news reports. Dirt smeared her blue overalls and her white and pink striped t-shirt, the outfit she'd been wearing when she disappeared. He breathed a sigh of relief. She was dreaming—so she was still alive.

Tears streaked her face. She sat hugging her knees to her chest, rocking back and forth. Staying invisible, he wove his way unseen through the playing children toward her. The girl was humming, the tune soft and sad. He stepped forward.

Into *her* dream.

As his shadow fell over her, she stopped humming and looked up.

"Hi, Lisa," he said.

Her eyes ran over his costume, and a huge smile broke across her face. She jumped up. "I *knew* you'd come. I *knew* it!" Her smile ran away, fear replacing it. "Are you going to save me?"

"Yes, I am." *I hope. If I'm in time.* "Can you show me where you are?"

She pointed towards the city in the distance...

And the scene rushed towards them.

Gone was the playground, the park, the children. The tilted towers of the strange cityscape now surrounded them on an empty street lined with low-rise apartment buildings. He read the signpost.

Lanville Street.

One by one, the streetlights winked out until only one remained. A light at the far end of the street. A light shining on a red-bricked building with "1021" over its doorway.

A building they now stood before.

Inside of.

On the third floor.

Before a door with the number "327."

Lisa looked up at the Dream Rider with big, sad eyes. "Save me." Turning from him, she walked toward the wall...and through it into the apartment.

"Nyx," he called. "I found her. Record."

"Ready to record," Nyx's disembodied voice replied, all business this time.

"1021 Lanville Street, apartment 327. Tag that with 'Lisa Carter'."

"Recorded."

Outside on the street again, he tapped his wrist, and Brian's silver leash reappeared. He gave it a tug. "Nyx, bring the House."

The House of Four Doors appeared with a "pop." From the outside, it showed only one door—the oval one by which he'd entered Dream. He opened it. Inside, Brian sat waiting. Lowering his long snout to the marble floor, the Doogle spat out a data ball.

Will picked it up, wiping off Doogle spit on his arm. "I seriously need a better metaphor for communicating with you guys."

He tapped the code ball with a finger. It collapsed into the names of two companies from the original list, hovering above his palm, a pulsating red arrow, pointing down, beside each.

Memorizing the names, he patted Brian. "See you tomorrow night, Bry."

He closed his eyes. He touched the jeweled clasp at his neck.

He opened his eyes.

And sat up in bed. His large, round, real bed in his penthouse suite in the real world. He now wore a pair of boxers. Dream Rider boxers, mind you.

"Hallie," he called out in the dark.

"Yes, Mr. Dreycott?" a computerized female voice replied from the room speakers.

"Call Adi."

"Calling Adrienne Archambeault."

Ring. Once. Twice. Three times. *Click.*

"Oh, god, William," came Adi's sleepy voice over the speaker. "What time is it?"

"Found her, Adi. She's still alive."

A rustle of bed sheets. When Adi spoke again, she sounded wide-awake. "Give me the details."

He repeated the address. "Call Harry Lyle at the Standard. Have him give the cops the tip right away."

"I'm on it."

"One more thing."

"Yes?"

"Sell everything we have in these stocks tomorrow." He spelled the two company names. "Don't know why, but their shares are about to tank."

"I'll place the sell order after I contact Mr. Lyle. And William?"

"Don't call me that, but yeah?"

"Good work."

He grinned in the dark. "Hey, it's what superheroes do. See you in the morning."

He lay back in bed. *Yeah, good work.* Rolling over, he fell back to sleep. Normal, dreamless sleep.

Chapter 2

In the Streets of the Jungle Toronto

Yes, at seventeen, Will Dreycott was a superhero.

In his dreams.

Unfortunately, right now, Will was *not* dreaming. Right now, it was the next morning, and he was trying to do the hardest thing in the world. Well, the hardest thing for *him*.

He was trying to go outside.

Just go outside. Just step out of a car and meet a friend for coffee.

He sat rigid in the back of his limousine. Across from him on the opposite seat sat Adrienne Archambeault, business-like as usual in a navy pantsuit and crisp white shirt, short-cropped, blonde hair framing a round face. Adi—his confidante, legal guardian, and surrogate mother. And CEO of his company. She watched him, wearing an expression that managed to be both worried frown and sympathetic smile.

He gripped the car's door handle as if it might detach itself and leap for his throat. Beyond the car's tinted windows lay a typical street scene for a June lunch hour in downtown Toronto. That is, he assumed it was typical. He didn't get out much.

As in, not at all.

A broad sidewalk spread before him, a concrete canyon beneath looming office towers. People filled the sidewalk—office workers with morning coffees, tourists with cameras, food vendors with carts, couriers with bikes, students with backpacks, street people with their hands out. Some scurried, some strolled. Some stood, some lounged on benches. Some looked happy, some angry. Or bored. Or lost. Or whatever. But none of them looked the way Will did in his reflection in the tinted window.

None of them looked terrified.

Sweat glistened on his lean pale face, plastering his long dark hair to his forehead. His mouth was a thin tight line. He trembled. His heart pounded. He was breathing so fast he wondered if he'd hyperventilate.

He tore his eyes from his own image. That brought his attention back to the hordes of people separating him from his goal. Ten steps away, in a row of street level retail shops, a Starbucks beckoned. Ten steps that might as well have been ten light years. Ten steps outside. Through all those people. All those people, all those—

"William..."

He turned, his fingers still locked on the door handle.

"You don't need to do this," Adi said quietly.

"Wrong. I do, but..." He slumped back against the black leather seats, releasing his death grip on the handle. "But I can't." He couldn't get out of the car. He couldn't cross a sidewalk into a coffee shop to meet a friend. Nothing wrong with his legs. Nothing wrong with his *body* at all.

Adi pulled out her phone. "I'll call Mr. Lyle."

His pulse and breathing had slowed again. He wiped his sweating forehead on the sleeve of his David Bowie t-shirt. "It's okay. Here he comes."

The barrel-shaped figure of Harry Lyle emerged from the shop. Short legs pumping, he headed straight for the limo.

"And wearing that awful plaid jacket again," Adi said, shifting over to make room.

Harry opened the door. A blast of hot, humid air laced with car fumes and street vendor hot dogs hit Will in the face. *The air normal people breathe*, he thought.

Harry sat beside Adi, opposite Will, his battered leather briefcase on his lap. Will dropped his eyes, embarrassed.

Adi tapped the glass separating them from the driver. The partition lowered. "Take us back to Mr. Dreycott's tower, please, Jimmy."

Jimmy nodded. The partition rose again, and the car pulled into traffic.

Once they were heading home, Will's tension began to fade. His tower was only three blocks away.

"At least you keep swinging, kid," Harry said.

"And striking out. Oh-fer this season." *Past eight seasons*, Will thought. "Well, I'm trying to kick my coffee habit, anyway."

Harry grinned. "They're way over-priced."

"Far too crowded and noisy," Adi offered.

"And you'd make Adi here—" Harry began.

"Ms. Archambeault to you," she said.

"—Adi here mix with the common hordes. That'd never do."

Will laughed despite himself. "Yeah, I couldn't handle a common Adi."

"A problem you will never face," she said. "We will continue, Mr. Lyle, to rely on your daily scribblings for our regular dose of *common*."

Harry laughed. "Ouch. Well, I *am* the champion of the people."

People, Will thought, glancing outside again. *Too many people*. He shivered.

Harry nodded to where several copies of *The Dream Rider #94* lay in plastic slip covers beside Will. "Hey, is that your new issue?"

Will picked up a copy. The costumed figure of the Rider battled a swarm of giant beetle creatures. Behind him, a nightmare version of Toronto City Hall loomed against a red-tinged night sky.

Killer cover. Great issue, too. Still the one thing he could do right in the waking world. He handed the comic to Harry. "Yep. Here, take one for Dylan. Final issue in the *Infestation* series. Big reveal of who the Cockroach King is."

Harry held up a hand. "Don't tell me. No spoilers."

Will raised an eyebrow. "You read them, too?"

"Uh, yeah. I get Dylan on weekends, so this gives us something to talk about. You know, something we share."

"Sure. You're just being a good dad."

"Exactly."

Will grinned. "Just let Dylan read it first."

The limo slowed in front of a brilliant white skyscraper, the tallest in the city. Jimmy lowered the partition. "We're home, sir."

"Do you want to continue with Mr. Lyle inside?" Adi asked. "I'll get us a conference room."

He shook his head. Close to home again, he felt much better. "I'm fine in the car. At least this way I can pretend I'm outside. Jimmy, just keep circling our block, please?"

Jimmy nodded and raised the partition again.

Adi turned to Harry. "I assume you have a reason for meeting William beyond scoring a free comic."

"Thanks for this, Will." Harry tucked the comic into his briefcase. "Yeah, sure I had a reason. Two reasons. First, to thank you for the Lisa Carter tip. Police found the creep this morning at the address you gave. The kid's safe and back with her parents." He eyed Will.

"We heard. And you're welcome," Will said, ignoring Harry's unspoken question. "And your second reason?"

Harry considered him, then shrugged. "I'm working on a new series. On street kids. What their lives are like. How they survive. Why they're there. Find new ideas to get them a chance for a better life."

"Sounds like a great series. Are you hitting me up for a 'Give Street Kids a Chance' fund?"

"Actually, I'm hoping you'll help in my investigation."

"Because of my deep and intimate knowledge of the streets? In case you didn't notice—we're not exactly best buds." Will glanced at the crowded sidewalks.

"No," Harry said. "I need you to do…" He shrugged "…whatever you do."

Adi gave the slightest shake of her head. *Say nothing.* Like he needed to be told.

"C'mon, kid," Harry said. "How many times have you tipped me off? Given me a lead, a name, a place, something that cracked a case that'd stumped the cops for months? Or…" The reporter leaned forward, his eyes narrowing. "…even told me about a crime *before* it happened."

"You've done rather well, Mr. Lyle, from those tips," Adi said. "How many journalism awards is it now?"

Harry held up his hands. "Hey, I'm not complaining. Neither are the cops. They've even stopped grilling me about my mysterious source—who remains mysterious, I'll add. At the paper, I refer to you as 'Galahad'."

Even Adi smiled at that. "The virtuous knight of Camelot."

Harry turned to Will. "You like it?"

"I'd have gone with Merlin, personally."

"Anyway," Harry said to Adi, "you know damn well I've never mentioned Will."

"Which is why William still contacts you. The first hint of his involvement is the last time you will hear from us."

"I get it. Golden goose and all that. I'm not asking *how* you know this stuff. I figure you can afford a cracker-jack private investigation team." Harry eyed Will again.

Will nodded, happy to let the reporter believe that. "You're right. I have my own PI team. When you're famous, somebody always wants to sue you or use your stuff without permission or just cause trouble." Which was true. But he also used his team to find information on cases the Rider investigated, giving him more to use in his Dream searches.

"Sure. You're playing the good guy." Harry nodded at the pile of comics again. "Like the Dream Rider."

Will forced a smile. "Yep, that's me. Just your everyday superhero—who can't go outside."

Harry laughed. "Hell, you'll lick that someday, kid. Anyway, I don't care how you play cop better than the cops…"

Yeah, right.

"…but I need *that* kind of help."

"What's up?"

Harry waved a hand at the street scenes passing by outside. "I've met with lots of these kids. Took a while before they'd talk to me, but now some of them even sort of—well, I wouldn't say, trust me. More like tolerate."

"I can relate," Adi said.

"Hey, you love me, and you know it. Anyway, recently I noticed a few weren't around anymore. When I asked about them, most of the kids stonewalled me. But then two of them—a brother and sister act—told me kids were disappearing."

"Disappearing? As in...?" Will asked.

"As in disappearing. Poof. Gone overnight. No trace. It's a tight community. Even if kids aren't friends, they know each other, keep track of who's where. Each has their own turf. Corner for panhandling. Place to crash. Very territorial. If a kid disappears, it's noticed." Harry hesitated. "I think someone's taking them."

"Why would they?"

Adi and Harry exchanged a '*Should we talk about this in front of the children?*' look. Harry shrugged. "Well, it's tough to say—"

"Human trafficking. Drug mules. Pornography. Prostitution. Thrill killings," Adi said, her face set in hard lines.

"—or maybe not that tough," Harry finished.

"Alien abductions," Will said. They both stared at him. "Oh, c'mon. You can't leave *that* out."

"William, be serious," Adi said.

"Hey, just trying to lighten the mood after you low-balled the human condition."

Harry sighed. "Unfortunately, the real reason is probably on Adi's list."

"Okay. Sorry. You think Lisa Carter's abduction was related?"

"Nah. She's no street kid, and she's happy at home. Plus, all the missing kids are boys. Not one girl so far, from what I've found."

"You told the police?"

Harry snorted. "Yeah, but they've been no help. In their defense, it's hard to prove these kids are missing. None of them has any fixed address. Most don't have parents—or don't want the ones they have. A lot are on the streets because of problems at home. If they have parents, those parents never see or hear from them. And most don't care if they do."

At Harry's mention of "parents," Adi gave Will a worried look, which he ignored. Harry caught it though. "Sorry, kid. Didn't mean to stir up bad memories."

Will shrugged. "They've been gone eight years. Long time ago. I'm over it." *Yeah, right. Totally over it.*

An embarrassed silence fell. He stared out the window, hoping the topic of his parents would end. From a poster on a bus shelter, the hooded figure of the Dream Rider stared back at him while wrestling a giant winged snake on the top of a skyscraper. *Last month's issue. Better make sure Marketing changes those to the latest cover.*

Harry nodded at the poster. "You're everywhere."

You have no idea. "The Rider's everywhere. My range is a little smaller."

"Dylan has Rider pajamas, sheets, comforter, even underwear," Harry said. "You ever figure it'd get this big?"

Will shook his head. No, he'd never expected it would. He'd never expected his little comic creation would become—as *Time* had called it—the "most recognizable popular culture creation in history." He'd never expected to be a billionaire at seventeen.

But then, he'd never expected to be an orphan at nine, either.

"So..." Harry said, pulling him back to the moment.

Most of these kids don't have parents, Harry had said. "I'll help. At least, I'll try. Give me what you have. But no promises."

Harry grinned. "Thanks, Will." He pulled out his phone and tapped a few times. "Just sent Adi my notes. Pretty well organized if I do say so. Call me with any questions."

"May we drop you at the *Standard*, Mr. Lyle?" Adi asked.

"Nah. I can use the walk." Harry rapped on the partition, motioning Jimmy to pull over. The limo stopped. Shoving his battered briefcase under his arm, the reporter considered Will for a moment. "I know I shouldn't check out mouths on gift horses..."

"You're mixing your metaphors. I'm a goose, remember?"

"I've always wondered. Why me? Why'd you pick me for your tips?"

Will thought back to when he first realized his powers in Dream. He'd wanted to use those powers to help people. He shrugged. "I liked your articles. You're smart. You're honest. And you care about people." Plus, he and Adi had figured Harry would ask fewer questions than the cops. Questions about how Will knew the things he knew. But he didn't tell Harry that.

Harry smiled. "Thanks, kid. I like you, too. And I'm not saying that just because you could buy our paper with your spare change." He squeezed Will's arm. "You're good people."

The reporter got out, then leaned back in. "You could ask the Rider, you know."

Adi shot Will a look he ignored. He swallowed. "Sorry?"

Harry grinned. "About these missing kids. If we were in your comics, you could just ask the Rider to find them in Dream. The Carter girl said that's who found her."

Will forced a smile. "Hey, great idea. Yeah, I'll get DR on the case."

Harry laughed and slammed the car door. Will watched him walk away.

"Well, we wondered when he'd start asking questions."

"William—"

"Will."

"Be careful. Harry Lyle is smart."

"You don't think we should help him?"

"No. We should. These poor kids..." She shook her head. "But he's been an investigative reporter longer than you've been alive. Don't let that buffoon image he cultivates fool you. He knows a lie or a cover-up when he hears one. It's his job. He knows we're hiding something. Something bigger than any story we've given him so far."

"I know he does. But I trust him. And I like him."

"That's why I'm warning you."

"Adi, if I listened to all your warnings, I'd never leave home. Oh, wait..."

"Very droll."

"Send me Harry's notes. Looks like I have homework before Dream tonight." He tapped on the glass. Jimmy lowered the partition. "Jimmy, take me home, please."

Chapter 3

My City of Ruins

C ase wandered past the food stalls inside the St. Lawrence market carrying an empty plastic bag. Fader, her younger brother, trailed behind her. They weren't shopping. Shopping required money, and panhandling had not gone well today. Case was saving what little cash they had for when they were desperate.

No reason to pay for dinner when they could get it for free.

The merchants behind the booths eyed her as she passed. Not surprising. She knew how she looked. Black teenager with a torn t-shirt two sizes too big. Dirty, baggy jeans with more holes than denim. Running shoes that didn't match. And a mass of tight curls that badly needed a cut. She might as well wear a "Street kid / No money" sign.

Fader was the shorter, younger, boy version of herself. He wore a sleeveless hoodie and dirtier jeans. At least his sneakers matched. But merchants didn't look at Fader. Nobody noticed Fader. That was why this worked.

Because Fader was Fader. And because Case heard voices. Well, one voice. Her Voice.

The sights and smells of fresh produce made her hunger almost unbearable. Their only meal that day had been half of a bran muffin scooped from a garbage can outside a Starbucks.

"What do you feel like?" she asked Fader.

"Cheeseburger."

"Nice try. Fruit and veggie-wise, I meant."

"Cheeseburger with lettuce."

She stopped, glaring down at him. Fader was twelve to her sixteen and a head shorter. He grinned back, then shrugged and scanned the stalls. "Apples. Pears. Tomatoes. And burgers."

"Funny. Pick two. I don't want to push our luck. And one better not be burgers."

He sighed. "Fine. Forget the tomatoes."

"I'll forget the pears. Tomatoes are better for you. We'll get some bread, too."

He made a face but fell in beside her as she approached a fruit stall. Stopping at one end, she pretended to inspect the merchandise. Fader stood at the opposite end beside a crate of apples. The man behind the booth kept his eyes on Case, paying no attention to Fader. Crossing her arms, she flashed a finger signal for Fader to get ready.

She waited. And watched.

Guy in the stall opposite glancing at her. Shoppers passing by looking this way. Lady with a flowered bag walking up to the stall.

She continued to wait. For her Voice. For her Voice to say when the right moment—

Now, it whispered.

She dropped her arms—the signal to Fader.

The next second, the guy in the opposite stall turned to a customer. The people passing by glanced away. And the woman with the flowered bag asked the fruit merchant a question.

In that same second, Fader's hands flashed out. Grabbing two apples, he stuffed them into the pockets of his hoodie, unnoticed by anyone.

Case sauntered away from the booth. Fader caught up and dropped the apples into her bag. "Cheeseburgers next?"

"Tomatoes, smart ass."

Case and her brother strolled from the market into the heat and humidity of the street. They'd repeated their act at a vegetable booth then a bakery stand. She glanced back as they walked west along Wellington toward the downtown core.

No angry merchants in hot pursuit. They'd pulled it off again. Relaxing, she started to turn away when two men in the crowd exiting the market caught her attention.

One man was over six feet tall, the other shorter than her. Both had long white hair and wore identical all-black outfits. Black suits with black shirts. Black bowler hats and leather gloves.

Pretty freaking hot for the Goth look, she thought.

Both were rail-thin with sharp features and faces so pale they almost glowed in the sunlight. Each wore black goggles that hid their eyes.

The men stopped on the sidewalk. Tall Boy stared east, Shorty west. Shorty's gaze fell on her and Fader, hesitated for a heartbeat, then kept scanning the street. His lips moved, and Tall Boy spun around, looking in their direction. His gaze also seemed to pause when it passed over her and Fader. Then Tall Boy turned to Shorty. They stood talking, not looking Case's way again.

She shivered despite the heat and humidity. Something...

Fader looked back. "S'up? Somebody see us?"

I'm getting paranoid. "Nah. Nothing. Let's rock."

They continued weaving along congested sidewalks as the office towers spewed out end-of-day commuters. Crossing Yonge Street, she glanced behind again. Half a block back, Tall Boy's black-hatted head bobbed above the crowd. Shorty might have been there, too, but she couldn't tell. She shivered again.

Left, her Voice said.

The lights changed. "This way," she said, turning left, crossing Wellington and heading south down Yonge.

Fader shrugged, used to the erratic routes she often followed. They walked past the stores of the retail plaza beneath the office towers of BCE Place. At a bookstore window, Fader grabbed her arm. "Look! It's the new issue!"

Case glanced behind them. No sign of creepy guys in black. She *was* getting paranoid. She turned back to Fader, knowing without looking what had seized his attention. He had his nose pressed against the window. Behind the glass, copies of a Dream Rider comic she hadn't seen before lay beneath a poster with the Rider's famous tagline: *He only comes out at night.*

"Bugs?" she said. "He's still battling bugs?"

"This is where he finally faces the Cockroach King!" Fader turned pleading eyes up to her. "Can we?"

"No."

"Please, Casey!"

"Don't call me that."

"Please, Case!"

"No. We're not blowing nearly five bucks on a comic. You can wait till the library gets it."

He started to protest but stopped. His shoulders slumped. He gave the display a last look. "Yeah. Okay."

She swallowed. Good kid. The best. And she couldn't even get him a freaking comic. She put her arm around him. "Sorry, bro."

He shrugged. "Can we go home now?"

Home. Perhaps the saddest thing in their lives was her brother thinking of their current crash spot as home. A church on King Street closed to the public. Part of the ceiling had fallen, injuring three of the congregation. Not the message from on high they'd been expecting, she bet.

Hearing about it, she'd checked out the building. Locked up, but she'd found a basement window just big enough to fit through after breaking the glass. An advantage to being underfed.

A construction crew worked there during the day but never came downstairs. At night, the entire church was empty. The basement was dry—and cool, too, a rare treat on these hot summer nights. But best of all, they were alone. On the streets, alone was safer.

Especially this summer. Too many of their kind going missing. Rumors of kids being snatched. Thinking of those disappearances, she checked behind them again.

Tall Boy and Shorty stood at the intersection she and Fader had just left, turning their goggled heads in all directions. She sucked in a breath. Paranoid? Maybe not.

"Yeah, sure. Home. But let's hit the can first." Grabbing Fader by the arm, she pulled him through the sliding doors and into the retail mall of the office complex.

"Okay, okay, jeez, you can let go now," he said, pulling his arm free when they were inside.

"Sorry."

He glanced back to the street through the glass doors. "Something wrong?"

"Nah. Just being careful. Go to the can. And wash your face, too. I'll meet you back here."

Fader headed for the men's room. She watched as his tiny figure disappeared into the throng of adult workers and shoppers. *Disappeared*. Shivering at the thought, she checked the entrance from the street again. No sign of Tall Boy and Shorty. If the creeps had been following, she'd lost them.

A fountain sat encircled by the stores at this end of the mall. She walked over to it. Probably only small change as usual, but sometimes a dumbass would toss—

There. A toonie. And another. And there. A loonie. Five bucks. Worth the trip.

Sitting on the edge of the fountain, she slipped off her shoes and rolled up her jeans. She scanned the area. No mall security. Lots of people, but she doubted anyone would kick up a fuss. They had enough money to shop and still throw away more in a fountain. When the fewest people were looking, she swung her legs into the water. Wading over, she grabbed the coins, scooping up three quarters as well.

She waded back, ignoring the stares of passersby. Sitting again, she struggled her wet feet into her mismatched runners. Her score bumped their kitty up to twenty-two dollars and fifty cents, if she'd done the math right. Not much of an emergency fund, but better than zilch.

She reached for the makeshift cash pouch she wore under her t-shirt. Then stopped. Jiggling the wet coins in her hand, she considered the bookstore. Fader still wasn't back. *Good kid*, she thought again. *The best*.

Hard Case. That's what they called her on the street.

Getting up, she walked to the bookstore.

She shook her head. *Hard Case. Yeah, right.*

✺

She was sitting by the fountain when Fader returned. "Sorry," he said. "Had to take a dump."

"TMI, bro." She reached into a plastic bag and handed him the Dream Rider comic, still in its slipcover.

His eyes went wide. His mouth opened, but no words came out.

"So you want it, or do I take it back?"

Grabbing it from her, he gaped at the cover. Then he pressed it to his chest and looked around. "You steal it?" he whispered.

"Bought it." She jerked a thumb at the fountain. "Somebody made a wish for you."

A huge smile lit his face, and his eyes devoured the cover again. Case had to swallow away a lump in her throat.

"You're the best, Case."

"So true."

He jumped up. "Can we go home now? I want to read it."

Outside, she held Fader back before they stepped onto the sidewalk again. Peering around the corner, she checked up and down the street. No sign of their two creepy followers.

"C'mon, what's wrong?" Fader asked. "You're acting weird. Even for you. Your Voice?"

She let herself relax. "Told you. Just being careful. Let's roll."

They followed a winding route back, finally turning west again on King. As they headed for the church, they passed the brilliant white tower with the image of the Dream Rider on top.

Fader waved his comic at the building. "He lives there."

"He? Who he?"

"The Dream Rider guy."

"He's made up, dude. You know that, right?"

"Duh. I mean the guy who writes the comics. They say he lives there."

"In an office building?"

"That whole place. It's, like, his house."

Case stared at the white tower, trying to imagine such a life. How could anybody be that rich? "Sounds like an asshole."

Fader glared at her. "He's not an asshole."

She shrugged. "Well, I doubt he'll invite us to visit, so we will never know, little bro."

Chapter 4

Welcome to the Jungle

The limo eased down the ramp to Will's private underground garage beneath the Dream Rider building. As Jimmy placed his hand on the palm reader to raise the heavy security door, Will's gaze ran to the giant artwork atop the white tower. There, the hooded head of the Rider watched over the city. Harry had been right. The Rider *was* everywhere.

Will was certain no other person on the planet would define "home" as he did. A seventy-five-floor skyscraper covering an entire city block might appear a tad excessive on the available living space spectrum. But when going *out* wasn't an option, then staying *in* better be as good as it gets.

In the garage, Jimmy drove past the cars of staff and building visitors. He stopped at the elevators. Adi and Will got out. "Won't need you any more today, Jimmy," Will said. "You can take off."

Jimmy touched his chauffeur's hat and grinned. "Thanks, Mr. Dreycott." He drove away.

"Why does no one call me Will?"

Adi pressed the *up* button on the elevator. "You are aware we pay him full-time?"

Will shrugged. "Am I running out of money?"

"Hardly. Between your parents' fortune, the Dream Rider franchise, and your stock tips from Dream, you have nothing to fear..." She stopped.

Nothing to fear. Except going outside.

"Sorry," she said. "I didn't mean..."

He shook his head. "It's okay. Glad I still have money."

"I should say you *are* running out. Perhaps then you'd take more interest in the business. It is yours."

"Not till I'm eighteen. That's why I have you. And that Board thingy with all those old guys."

Sighing, Adi shook her head. "How do you know I'm not robbing you blind? Your parents would want you more involved."

Putting an arm around her, he gave her a hug. "Look, my parents trusted you..." He swallowed. His parents were in too many conversations this morning. "...and so do I. If you're robbing me blind, well, I'm just going to let you. At least until I need glasses. Much like my current romantic life."

She gave a small smile. "I thought you were seeing that young lady you met at our New Year's staff party. The daughter of our controller?"

He grimaced. "Siobhan? She got tired of staying in for date night after we ran out of new floors to visit." He didn't tell Adi the real reason—that Siobhan was more interested in his money than in him. Another problem not likely to disappear anytime soon. "Speaking of romance, how are things with you and Laura?" he asked, wanting to change the subject.

"On-again, off-again. Currently on." She bit her lip. "I think."

"Good. I like Laura."

An elevator arrived. Its doors opened on dark wood paneling, and they got on. Each floor button displayed words instead of numbers. *Musée d'Orsay. The Louvre. Tibet. AGO. Egypt. Restaurants. Concert Hall.* And many more. Each button glowed red.

Will placed his palm on the glass plate of a hand scanner beside the array of floor buttons. Every floor light switched to green. His finger hovered over the button marked *Egypt*. "Are the latest sculptures in yet?"

Adi tapped her phone screen. "Due tonight. But they installed a new van Gogh yesterday."

"Paris it is, then." He pressed the button labeled *Musée d'Orsay*. The elevator accelerated upwards. Seconds later, they stepped out into the Musée d'Orsay in Paris. Or at least, what his art curator assured Will was a faithful recreation of the famous museum.

The ceiling above had been removed, allowing the replica Musée to better simulate the two-story original. He walked through the central sculpture hall, Adi at his side, towards the van Gogh gallery at the far end. "Do I own this one?"

"On loan. Although, you could afford to buy it." She nodded at the array of painting and sculpture reproductions. "You could replace several of these with originals."

"Kind of surprised you told me that."

"Fine art is a smart investment—unlike your manga collection."

"Manga *is* art."

They entered a smaller room. On its walls hung reproductions of paintings by Vincent van Gogh. Adi checked her phone again. "The new one is—"

"*The Church at Auvers*," he said softly, walking to that painting.

In it, a small stone church seemed a thing alive. Its stone walls writhed upwards to a blue sky so dark, it was almost black. Its windows framed that same deep blue, as if the church, too, contained the darkness haunting the sky.

Darkness inside. A darkness that haunted.

Adi came to stand beside him. "Why is Vincent your favorite?"

Because he was as lonely as I am. Lonely and haunted. But he just shrugged. "Because his paintings are beautiful. And he was my dad's—" He caught himself. "He *is* my dad's favorite."

He felt her eyes on him, but she stayed silent. They stood staring at the picture.

"William…"

"What?"

"There's a new bloom in the greenhouse."

A surge of hope. And fear. *Speaking of haunted.* "Is it segregated?"

"Yes."

"Where'd they find it? Bolivia again?"

She hesitated. "Peru. Arequipa."

His heart jumped. "Arequipa? That's the closest in over two years. I thought we'd found all the species in Peru."

She didn't look at him. "Apparently not."

"This is great. I gotta check it out." He turned to leave.

"Aren't you going to read Mr. Lyle's notes? To get ready for tonight?"

"I have time. This won't take long."

"Don't you think…?" Her voice trailed off. She still didn't look at him.

He knew where this was going. "I won't stop looking, Adi. I won't give up."

"It's been *eight* years," she said quietly. "You've found no trace of them. Not even in Dream."

"They're my parents. I have one clue, one link to what happened to them and…" He stopped. *And to me.* He shook his head. "I won't give up."

She pursed her lips but didn't reply. They walked to the elevators in silence. Adi pushed *down* while he pushed *up*, symbolic of their respective attitudes on his pet project.

"I miss them, too," she said. She stared straight ahead, but her eyes glistened.

He swallowed. "I know."

"Your parents were my best friends. They…" She hesitated. "They did a *lot* for me. More than you know. Much more."

"And look what that got you. Stuck with raising their screwed-up little kid."

She hugged him, an uncharacteristic show of affection. "Well, that kid has exceeded my expectations." A down elevator arrived. She got in.

"Are you saying you're proud of me?"

She smiled. "Or maybe my expectations were low." The doors closed.

"Hey, no fair," he called. "No chance for a comeback." His elevator came. Inside, he scanned his hand and punched the top button: "Roof / Jungle."

As the car accelerated upwards, he leaned against the wall and closed his eyes. Maybe this would be the one. Maybe he could finally stop searching.

Will stepped from the elevator into a green sunlit world.

The roof was both his most and least favorite floor in his high-rise home. Here, under a retractable glass dome, he could stroll through a grassy park or lie in a wild meadow. He could wander a small forest or tour tended gardens of plants from around the world. Here he could see clouds swimming across the sky. Hear birds singing and squirrels chattering. Feel the heat of the sun, the breath of the wind, the cool sting of rain.

Here, he could go outside. Or, rather, pretend he could.

But the roof also held the Jungle. And the Jungle held both his greatest hope and darkest fear. He wondered which it would feed today.

He took a yellow-bricked path through a park of trimmed lawns. His target was a sprawling greenhouse in the northwest corner of the park.

The Jungle.

Reaching the greenhouse, he hesitated at the double doors. Maybe Adi was right. Maybe it was time to let go. To admit his parents were dead. Admit he'd never find them, never learn what had happened to them.

Or to him.

A corkboard hung to the left of the doors, protected by glass. A collage of yellowed newspaper clippings covered its surface.

It had been years since he'd even glanced at those clippings. He'd first put them there to remind his younger self why he kept coming here whenever a new flower arrived.

He walked over to the corkboard display. Time to quit? Or time to remind himself again?

In the center of the display, a headline blared from the largest clipping:

Controversial Art "Collectors" Vanish in Peruvian Jungle

Below, his parents' faces smiled at him, cropped from publicity photos for their last lecture tour. He could never figure out which one he resembled.

His dad, Jonathan "Jon" Dreycott. Handsome, angular features. Neat van Dyke beard. Blond hair combed straight back from a high forehead. His mom, Dr Theresa "Terri" Yurikami. She'd been a medical doctor. Will never knew why she gave it up. The dark to his dad's light, with her black eyes and long black hair and mischievous smile. They looked more like movie stars than the affluent dealers in rare antiquities and art that they were.

Or the thieves that they were, depending on what stories you believed. Smugglers who'd built a financial empire on cultural grave robbing.

He preferred art dealers to thieves and smugglers. The hardest part of his search for answers had been discovering, at nine years old, the rumors about his parents.

He scanned the articles on the board, hoping for a puzzle piece to at last jump out at him. Something he'd missed. Something the Peruvian police—and Adi's team of investigators—had missed as well.

Nothing. No "aha!" moment. No bolt of mental lightning. The mystery remained a mystery.

Eight years ago, his parents had mounted an expedition into the Peruvian high jungle in the Andes. Normally, Adi had said, such trips had clear goals. Retrieve a specific artifact. Investigate legends of a lost city. Confirm rumored ruins.

But this time, wherever they were going for whatever purpose, they'd shared it with no one. Not their regular outfitter. Not the Peruvian authorities. Not even Adi, their closest advisor and friend.

And certainly not their nine-year-old son.

Or maybe they had, and he couldn't remember. Just as he couldn't remember anything of the expedition. Not one memory from before he'd left home to when the Peruvian army had found him alone, dazed, and half-dead in the jungle.

A different jungle. Hundreds of kilometers and a journey of several weeks on foot from where they'd supposedly started.

Yeah, they'd taken him along.

He always came back to that. He'd had a fairly normal childhood until then. Public school, friends, and loving parents. Parents with the typical look-both-ways-before-crossing-the-street-and-don't-talk-to-strangers care and concern for him. Sure, he'd gone on expeditions before, starting when he was seven. But he also remembered disappointments of being left behind with Adi whenever his parents decided a trip was "too dangerous for the boy."

Which meant, he reasoned, they hadn't expected the Peru trip to be dangerous.

So what had happened?

No clue had ever been found of them. Or any guides or bearers they might have used. Nothing. The entire expedition vanished without a trace.

Except for him. And he'd returned with only two things, apart from a sudden inability to go outside.

One was a ragged scar on his chest below the hollow of his throat. A scar in the shape of the twelve-pointed star known in South America as the Incan Cross. A scar that became his inspiration for the Rider's jewel.

His other souvenir was a memory. His *only* memory from that trip. And one he would not give up. Just as he would not stop using it to search for answers.

His resolve renewed, he turned away from the yellowed clippings and pushed open the doors to the greenhouse, humming "Welcome to the Jungle." Heat, humidity, and the thick, cloying scent of flowers hit him as he entered. The greenhouse's climate control simulated high-altitude Peruvian jungles. He hadn't gone ten steps before his t-shirt and jeans clung to him, wet and clammy.

He passed rows of wooden tables covered in explosions of plants in soil-filled trays. Plants from the jungles where his parents may have disappeared and from where he was found. And growing in their native soil.

Flowering plants. Different colors, different species. But all plants with flowers.

All with a *scent*.

But—for eight years—not the *right* scent.

He stopped outside a smaller, self-contained, glass room, a greenhouse within the larger greenhouse. A sign labeled "Isolation" hung over the door.

Lately, the plants had been coming from points farther and farther away from where he'd been found. But Adi said this newest bloom came from near Arequipa, where the expedition had supposedly started.

Maybe this time.

Opening the door, he stepped into the sealed entrance to the isolation room. The air here was cooler and dry, devoid of any scent. The door behind him closed with a click. A soft hiss sounded as the compressors started. Jets lining the airlock blew warm air at him from all sides, drying his damp clothes and removing scents of flowers from the greenhouse.

The jets died. A click sounded, and the inner door swung open. Taking a deep breath and holding it, he stepped inside.

The isolation room was empty except for a wooden table with a ceramic flowerpot. In the pot, under the overhead bulbs that simulated sunlight, a plant grew with broad, thick, dark green leaves. From its leafy center rose a single white orchid, brilliant in the light, its petals tinged with yellow.

Walking to the table, he let out the breath he'd been holding. He leaned over the flower and breathed in through his nose. Slow and deep.

He straightened. He stared at the orchid, fighting an impulse to fling the plant and its pot against the wall. Slumping to the floor, he hugged his knees to his chest.

No. Not the one. Again.

Eight years ago, after being found in the jungle, he awoke with one clear memory. And only one.

A smell.

A sickly sweet scent that could only be a flower.

When he returned home, he'd begun his search. A search that grew as his resources grew. Those resources included this facility and a team of botanists who scoured the Amazon jungles for new flowers to send to him.

Flowers like this one. Flowers that were never the *right* one.

Would he *ever* find the right one?

And if he did, would it lead him to his parents? Adi wasn't wrong. He'd never found a trace of them in Dream in eight years. Did they never dream? Had he just not found them yet?

Were they dead?

He wouldn't think about that today. He had work to do, reading Harry Lyle's notes on the missing street kids before tonight's Dream Ride.

As he left the Jungle, his eyes fell on the faded newspaper clippings again.

Missing street kids. Missing parents.

Sometimes, the world just sucked.

Chapter 5

Man at the Top

L eaving the Jungle, Will descended a stairway from the roof to the floor below, the floor called "Will's Room." Several rooms, actually, covering the entire top level, two stories high. This was his living space, so it contained everything he included in a daily routine. To him, this was home.

When his parents had disappeared, they were leasing these two floors. One level had been their home apartments, plus their business offices. The second level had contained a restoration lab and a gallery for selling "recovered" artifacts to top-end buyers. An offsite warehouse had held any finds not on display or awaiting restoration.

As Will's Dream Rider empire grew, so had his holdings in this tower. Eventually, he'd bought the entire building and converted floors as he wished. He'd started with this level, then moved the warehouse onsite, using those artifacts to build out his themed floors.

A wooden track, complete with skateboarding ramps and obstacles, circled this level beside floor-to-ceiling windows. He walked along the track, passing his dojo where he practiced *kendo*, Japanese sword fighting, a skill useful as the Rider.

A traditional Japanese theme ran throughout, a nod to both his mom and his love of manga. Wood hallways divided the floor into quadrants. Each room had sliding walls of wood and paper, letting him reconfigure spaces as needed. Doors of thinner paper let light in, and rooms beside the track were open to the windows to maximize natural light. His tower was the tallest in the city, so nosey neighbors weren't a problem.

He reached his main living area on the south-west corner of the floor. The lower level here included his design studio where he worked on the Dream Rider comic. This room also served as his crash space. Big black leather couch, comfy chairs, low tables, floor pillows. And a big screen TV and access to every video game ever made.

The studio walls rose halfway up the two-story height. Bookshelves lined those walls, filled with graphic novels. Warm and bright, this was his favorite place to be. An open staircase led up to his bedroom from his studio.

A large computerized graphics design table with a slanted top dominated the middle of the studio. Sliding into its tall chair, he tapped the screen. The last panel he'd done for the next Dream Rider issue appeared, magnified. He stared at his costumed creation.

It had all started with a dream. A dream he'd had after returning from Peru. A dream of the Rider.

As he'd slowly discovered his powers as the Rider in Dream, he started drawing the comics. He posted them on social media, just for fun. Short comics became graphic novels. A cult following grew. And grew. Cult became phenomenon. Phenomenon became unprecedented.

Unprecedented became the Dream Rider.

As more people came to know the comic Rider, the more power the real Rider gained in Dream. The more the Rider appeared in people's dreams, the more they thought of him. The more they thought of him, the more popular the Rider became in real life.

Each Rider, the comic version and the real one, made the other stronger.

Rereading the script for the new issue, he started the next panel. He sketched issues in black and white, marking areas where he wanted a specific color. Using his draft, his team would finish the final version for his review.

He threw himself into the art and the story. His disappointment with today's flower still lingered, and he couldn't have those thoughts follow him into Dream. Working on the comic—the one thing he was good at in the real world—helped calm his mind for his journey that night.

He worked into the late evening, breaking only to make himself a sandwich in the small kitchen attached to his studio.

Finally, he saved his work on the issue. "Hallie, you there?"

"At your service, Mr. Dreycott," came the immediate computerized reply.

He sighed. Even his computer wouldn't call him Will. "Email from Adi, forwarded from Harry Lyle. Received today. Display attachments, please."

Harry's research files on the missing street kids appeared on the table's screen. He scanned the material, then went through it again more slowly. Finishing, he leaned back in his chair, considering what he'd found.

Not much.

No legal names for the missing boys, only their street names, plus where they usually panhandled or slept. And two fuzzy pictures, which he guessed Harry sneaked during interviews. Not much to work with. Only four kids had enough information to support a search for them in Dream.

Fine. Four searches at one time was his limit, anyway. He went through Harry's research again, tagging anything on those four boys into a separate file. He memorized the information for each boy as four search sets for his Doogles.

Doogles plural. To run four searches at once, he'd need four trackers. He couldn't waste any time. If Harry and Adi were right, something terrible was happening to these kids. If any of the four dreamed tonight, he'd find them. And hopefully, in time.

Ready for Dream, he climbed the open staircase to his bedroom. Enclosed by a waist-high railing, the room overlooked his studio and extended over the running track to the windows. It was large but sparsely furnished. Just a round bed with a low semi-circular headboard that functioned as a bookcase and side table. The walls, carpet, comforter all featured the comet-filled night sky and clouds of the Rider's costume.

Walking to the windows, he gazed down at the scurrying patterns of late-night pedestrians and traffic in the streets below his tower home. People going places he could never go. People living where he could never live.

He turned away. Enough. He couldn't live in the real world like normal people, but he had his own world. He had Dream. And in Dream, he ruled.

"Time to be a kick-ass superhero," he muttered.

He undressed except for his boxers and jumped onto the bed. Settling into a lotus position, he closed his eyes. And began his meditation. He slowed his breathing. He relaxed his muscles. He emptied his mind of any thoughts, focusing on his breath.

Once the calmness came, he continued his meditation, switching his focus from his breath to the search data he'd memorized for the four missing boys.

When he'd first entered Dream eight years ago, he could only walk around and observe. But night by night, he'd learned to grow his powers and to interact with Dream and dreamers. He found if he could imagine an item, no matter how fantastic, he could bring it into Dream.

First, he had to visualize it while awake. He used his artistic skills to create 3D designs of anything he needed. Doogles, his skateboard, his sword and shield. Whatever. He then memorized that design down to the last detail and gave it a name. In Dream, he could then retrieve any item by calling it from his subconscious. By calling Nyx. Tonight, he'd do that with the search sets for the four boys.

Finally prepared, he stretched out on his back on the quilted comforter. Before Peru, he loved sleeping under heavy blankets with even his head covered. Now, that guaranteed he'd wake screaming from a nightmare of drowning in a raging river. Just one more mystery from that trip.

Closing his eyes, he whispered his mantra, his subconscious cue to fall asleep—and into Dream.

"He only comes out at night. He only comes out at night. He only..."

"...comes out at night," he said. And awoke. As the Dream Rider.

He sat up on the Bed of Awakening. This time, the House of Four Doors resembled a child's nursery. Blue and pink teddy bear wallpaper, with each of the doors a different bright color. He'd given up wondering what the House's decoration each night meant, if it meant anything at all.

At the foot of the Bed, Brian waited with three other Doogles, all staring at Will. "Evening, Brian, and, uh..." Will said, trying to remember their names. He was never sure how he could tell them apart, but he could. "And evening, Lassie, Toto, and Snoopy." Each Doogle's tail curled into a spiral of pleasure. Getting up, he walked to them.

"Nyx. The search sets for tonight, please," he said, cupping his hands before him. Four crystal data balls dropped into his hands, one for each missing boy he was targeting.

He held the balls out. Each Doogle shot out a black tongue, sucking in a separate data ball. Lights sparkled in their eyes, then all four trotted to the closest door. In unison, four tails snapped into arrow shapes pointing at that door.

Interesting. Each Doogle had sensed either their target kid dreaming or someone else dreaming of the kid. And each Doogle had sensed them in the same neighborhood of Dream. Hence, the same door.

If the Doogles were sensing the missing kids, then the boys were still alive. Which was good. But if they were in the same place, it also supported the kidnapping theory.

Only one way to find out. Pulling up the hood on his costume, he grabbed his skateboard and tapped the door. It opened, and the Dream Rider stepped into Dream, the four Doogles at his heels.

Chapter 6

Chasing Something in the Night

C ase guessed their crash space in the church basement was a storage room. Folding tables and chairs sat stacked along one wall. Hymnbooks and flyers about summer choir practices (now canceled, she assumed) lined another. The books and flyers had once been in cardboard boxes. She'd emptied and collapsed the boxes to give her and Fader something softer than the floor for sleeping.

Brooms and mops stood waiting beside one of the room's two doors. The extra door was why she'd picked this room. She liked having two escape routes, and the room's sole window was too small and high for a quick exit. Both doors locked from the inside, and she kept them locked when they were in the room.

They ate their meager dinner of apples, tomatoes, and bread, washed down with tap water from the basement washroom. Fader read and reread the Dream Rider comic until the light through the window grew too dim. Case wouldn't use the overhead light for fear of attracting unwanted attention. They both washed up in the washroom, then settled down on their cardboard beds for the night.

"Night," Fader called in the darkness from beside her.

"Night."

"And thanks, Case."

"For the comic? You're welcome. Glad you liked it."

"No, I mean...for taking care of me."

She swallowed, guilty again for the life she'd pulled him into. But this place still beat foster homes. And at least they were together.

"Shit, dude, go to sleep," she managed to mumble before her throat constricted.

Pause. "Love you, Case."

She had to swallow again. "God, you're a pain. Go to sleep."

A few moments later, Fader was softly snoring.

She lay awake, guilt still gnawing at her. In many ways, her brother was old beyond his years, handling their daily struggles without complaint. The street did that.

But in others, he was still a kid. Younger in many ways than she'd been at his age. Too trusting, blind to risks she saw right away—sketchy people to avoid, bad places to crash, cops and security.

Did she protect him too much? In a fair world, they'd have parents, friends, and schoolmates to learn from. Instead, all they had was each other. The only role model Fader had was her. If he wasn't growing up right, she was to blame.

She clenched her jaw. No, she wasn't. Their mom was.

Enough. Pushing thoughts of their mom away, she closed her eyes. *I love you, too, little brother*, she thought just before sleep took her.

Something was wrong.

Case fought to wake up. How did she know something was wrong?

Her Voice. Her Voice was screaming. Screaming at *her*.

WAKE UP! it screamed.

Her eyes opened. Darkness. Where was she? Right, church basement. What was happening?

WAKE UP!

Fully awake now, she listened.

The soft shuffling of feet sounded outside the farthest door. Fear seized her. She held her breath. Someone tried the doorknob.

Oh, shit.

As silently as she could, she sat up. A throbbing golden light glowed through the crack at the bottom of the door. That wasn't the hall light, and it didn't look like a flashlight.

Who cared what type of light it was? They had to get out of there.

She reached over in the dark until she found Fader's sleeping form. She shook him, gently at first, then harder when he didn't respond. What was the matter with him? He was a lighter sleeper than she was. Crawling closer, she put her mouth right beside his ear. "Fader," she rasped as loudly as she dared. "Wake up."

Still no response. Near panic, she grabbed him with both hands and shook him so hard she was afraid she'd hurt him. He still didn't wake. She drew her hand back, preparing to slap him.

The door flew across the room.

Later, she would remember no sound of an explosion, just a sharp scream of splintering wood as the door burst from its frame then slammed into the far wall with a deafening concussion.

At that moment, she was dazed and terrified. She knelt frozen beside

Fader, ears ringing, eyes locked on the open doorway. The doorway through which the strange golden light now poured into the room.

A figure appeared in the doorway, a short thin silhouette against the light. A second silhouette appeared behind the first, taller but just as thin. They stepped inside, and the radiance from the hall fell on the sickly white and goggled faces of Shorty and Tall Boy. They saw her, and something like surprise flickered over those faces.

Seeing her pursuers from that afternoon let her shove her panic aside. This was just another street rumble. Fight or flight.

Flight worked.

The other door. If Fader would wake up, they could escape. But even the door's destruction hadn't stirred him. Shit, what was wrong with him? What was happening?

RUN! cried her Voice.

Not without Fader! she shouted back. If she could pick Fader up, maybe she could carry him. Jumping up, she grabbed him under the armpits and heaved. She could barely lift his shoulders off the floor. Asleep and limp, he was dead weight. She'd never be able to carry him.

RUN!

Ignoring her Voice, she lowered Fader, putting herself between the two men and her brother. Pulling her knife from her back pocket, she flicked the blade open in one smooth unconscious motion. She dropped into a crouch, knife hand back.

Flight was out, so fight it was.

Tall Boy and Shorty both looked at her knife, their heads moving in unison. Their looks of surprise vanished. They smiled, revealing rows of pointed yellow teeth. To Case, those smiles were more frightening than anything so far tonight. Those smiles said her little knife was amusing. Those smiles said they would enjoy this.

But they didn't try to close on her. Still smiling, still moving in unison, they looked back towards the hallway.

A woman stepped into the open doorway. Unlike the men, the woman did not appear as a black silhouette, framed by the strange golden light from the hall.

She *was* the light.

Despite her terror, Case lowered her knife. Straightening, she stared in awe at the most beautiful creature she'd ever seen.

The woman was nearly as tall as Tall Boy, with long legs, narrow waist, and full breasts. The clothes she wore only emphasized her figure. Stiletto heels, narrow slacks, and a tight, low-cut, sleeveless top. A gold medallion on a chain lay below her throat. A cape hung from her shoulders. Her clothes were differing shades of dark green, the perfect complement to her hair.

Her hair. Red. Flaming red. Red so red it seemed on fire, flowing in rivers of wavy lava to her waist, framing her face like a burning halo. Her face. Full lips, high cheekbones, wide eyes, delicate nose and chin. It was, Case thought, the most perfect face in the world. Until she looked into the woman's green eyes, and only coldness stared back.

Case shivered. Those eyes broke the spell the woman's beauty had cast on her. Those eyes brought her back, not just to the danger she and Fader faced, but to the strangeness, too.

The woman *glowed*. Glowed with a golden light that now filled the basement room. The glow seemed to come from inside her, shining outward through her skin.

Case stepped back, suddenly wanting more distance between her and this woman.

Shorty spoke. "Mistress, the boy sleeps. But the girl—" His voice gurgled, as if liquid filled his throat.

"I have eyes, fool," the woman said, her voice rich and husky. She raised her left arm, pointing it at Case.

Case jumped back, expecting a gun. But the woman's hand was empty, her fingers open. Staring at Case through lidded eyes, the woman began muttering unintelligible words—low, guttural noises. Case thought they must be commands to the two men, but then her words took on a singsong, rhythmic quality.

As the woman chanted, her skin changed.

Strange symbols appeared on her face. Vague outlines at first, then golden shapes shining brighter than her inner glow. The symbols shifted across her features, rearranging themselves. They stopped moving for a heartbeat, then swam down her neck, filling her bare left arm from shoulder to wrist. Once the last was in place, the shapes seemed to settle into her skin, like golden tattoos.

The woman straightened her arm as if flinging something away. The symbols flew from her, straight at Case.

Nothing happened. Aside from Case almost peeing herself.

The woman stepped back, her eyes wide, her lips parted. She repeated the action. Still nothing.

Tall Boy and Shorty exchanged glances. "Mistress?" Tall Boy asked. His voice gurgled, too.

Ignoring them, the woman frowned. Lowering her arm, she stood with hands on hips, considering Case with those cold green eyes. Then she shrugged and turned to Tall Boy and Shorty. As she did, the symbols faded from her skin as her inner light died. The room fell into darkness again, lit only by dim outside light from the single high window. "Take the boy to the Master."

"And the girl?" Shorty asked.

In the darkness, Case felt more than saw the woman's eyes on her again.

The woman's voice was low and chill. "Kill her."

Run! screamed the voice in Case's head.

"Fader!" Case sobbed.

Stay and die. Run and live. You're his only hope.

Still Case didn't move. Tall Boy's arms dropped to his sides. Something long and shiny appeared in each hand, glinting in the faint light. He glided forward, still smiling. Behind him, Shorty pulled something from his coat pocket.

Run!

Sobbing, Case broke for the other door.

Duck!

She ducked. Something whistled past her as she dropped and rolled. On her feet again, she wrenched the door open and dashed into the hall.

Right!

She dodged right. Something flew by her head, nicking her left ear. Reaching the stairs leading up to the ground floor, she took them three at a time, not looking back.

Left!

She jumped sideways. Something whistled by her again, thunking hard into the top step. She reached the door at the top of the stairs. Shoving it open, she dashed along the church's back halls. Footsteps sounded behind her as she flung open the door to the main part of the church. She tore down the outside aisle, pews to her right. To her left, stained glass windows glowed with electric light from the street.

At the end of the pews, she turned hard towards the center doors. She chanced a glance back.

Shorty stood at the door she'd just come through. He stood sideways, his left arm raised and extended towards her. His right hand was back as if he aimed an invisible bow and arrow. Then she noticed his left hand *was* holding something. What...?

His right hand opened.

Stop! cried her Voice.

She pulled up, stumbling, almost falling. Something flew past her head, cracking into the stone wall. A round metal ball fell to the floor and rolled across the tiles. Regaining her balance, she slammed into the doors, shouldering them open.

A slingshot? The freak was hunting her with a slingshot?

She crossed the church foyer in two bounds, shoving down the bar to open the door, praying for no more locks. The door opened, and she was outside and leaping down the broad stone steps.

She stopped, heart pounding, gasping for breath on the sidewalk. Which way?

Right.

She started east along an empty King Street, snatching a look over her shoulder. She expected to see Shorty with his slingshot or Tall Boy with his knives.

At the top of the church steps, the flame-haired woman smiled down at her.

Case stopped.

Run! her Voice screamed in her head.

Case didn't run. Trembling with adrenaline and fear, she stared at the woman, again under the spell her presence seemed to cast.

The woman raised her left arm. The strange golden symbols danced again on her skin, dimmer now under the streetlights. Her arm straightened, and her hand opened, again as if she threw something at Case.

Case's skin tingled. *Run!* her Voice screamed again.

She ran, this time not looking back. At University Avenue, she ducked down the stairs into the subway. It was past two in the morning. The trains weren't running, but she wanted to hide her route from her pursuers. Dashing through the empty station, she pushed open the doors on the opposite side. She sprinted into the PATH system, the underground maze of corridors connecting the retail malls below street level in the downtown core.

Which way? she asked in her mind.

No answer. Her Voice was silent.

She kept running, taking turns at random. Running, running. Winding past closed retail shops and food courts. Passing beneath one office tower after another. Running, running. Just wanting to put more space between her and the red-haired woman and Tall Boy and Shorty and...

She stopped running.

And Fader.

She sank down to the gleaming floor of the mall. There, alone and frightened, surrounded by stores where rich people shopped, the reality of what she'd done sank in.

She'd left her brother. She'd run away and left him. Left him with those...people. If they were people.

You'd be dead by now.

She couldn't tell if that was her Voice or her own thoughts. "So what?" she whispered. She buried her face in her hands. So what? What could she do? How could she find Fader now?

Click...click...click...

Her head snapped up from where she sat on the floor. Footsteps. Nearing the corner she'd just come around. Her silent prayer for a night security guard vanished when a black-clad goggled figure appeared. Tall Boy's gaze fell on her, and even from twenty steps away, she could see him smile. Where was Shorty? Tall Boy straightened his arms, and the long knife blades appeared once more in each hand.

She was running again before he'd taken his first step towards her, hoping Shorty wasn't waiting for her around the next corner.

To the street! cried her Voice.

Almost shouting with joy at the return of her strange protector, she bounded up a stationary escalator to street level. These street doors opened from inside even at night. She sprinted to a door and shoved it open.

Outside, she scanned King Street, six lanes wide with broad sidewalks, praying for a cop for the first time in her life. Or for anyone who might help her. King, the heart of the financial district, was jammed by day. But at this time of night, not a car or person was in sight. Following her Voice, she ran east, turning left at Bay Street, whose four lanes and sidewalks were just as empty.

She was halfway up the block when someone appeared around the far corner ahead of her. Case skidded to a stop. The red-haired woman stood with arms folded, smiling at her down the length of the wide street. Case spun around. Tall Boy waited on the corner she'd just left, also smiling.

This block held no entrance to the underground PATH system and no side streets. She was trapped.

Chapter 7

Blinded by the Dark

"Well, this is cheery," Will said, looking around the Dreamscape. Beside him, Brian's tail drooped in agreement. The other three Doogles regarded him, their heads tilted.

They stood in a dark twisting alley. Overturned garbage cans and empty cardboard boxes littered the space. A filthy sleeping bag and discarded fast-food cartons lay in one corner. The stench of rotting food and unwashed humans almost made him gag.

Above, impossibly tall parodies of office towers loomed, reducing the night sky to a clouded ribbon. The buildings grew larger as they rose, leaning inwards as if they might come crashing down any second to crush him.

This is how it feels to be one of these kids. This is their life. What did they think when they looked up at *his* office tower? His tower where, at that moment, he slept in his penthouse, safe and secure. He tried imagining the lives of these kids—and failed.

He shook his head. Enough. Time to get moving.

The alley dead-ended to his right and slanted down to his left. He headed down, the Doogles falling in behind him. Steam rose from sewer grates along their route, together with scratching, scrabbling sounds. Passing one grate, he glimpsed something bloated, white, and hairless slithering past beneath it. He kept moving.

The route twisted and turned, finally reaching a point where it branched into three even darker, dingier alleys. Two rose, one descended. He glanced back. Even though this route had sloped down, it now appeared they'd just climbed a steep rise. Dream was like that.

Now faced with a choice, he stopped. "Okay, boys and girls. Time to do your Doogle thing."

He touched each dog's head. Four glowing silver leashes appeared, running from around their necks back to his wrist. The search dogs waited, tails pointing straight up, muscles quivering, anticipating his command.

"Go!" he said.

All four tore off down the left alley, running as a pack, their leashes playing out behind them.

Same direction again. Maybe the kids he searched for tonight *were* together. Or maybe the Doogles followed the same dream, the dream of someone who knew all four kids. Or something more sinister—someone who knew where these kids were and why they'd disappeared.

Expecting the Doogles to pick separate alleys, he'd planned to wait here for the first one to report in. But now, he dropped his board and set off after them. He wouldn't catch them. Doogles traveled faster than he could, but he'd follow until they split up.

Every time he reached a side passage, he expected a leash to split off. Expected a Doogle to send him a signal along its leash. But the silver cords stayed together, playing out ahead of him. Together—and silent.

So he followed and waited for a signal.

And waited.

Theoretically, things occurred at the speed of thought in dreams. But for someone in Dream, it didn't work that way. A delay with a Doogle represented not so much time passing as the complexity of the search. A search might take a Doogle through multiple dreams of multiple people, even looping back to the same dream.

Maybe this was a dead end. Maybe no one knew where the kids were. Maybe—

He cried out as pain seared his wrist where the leashes hung. Electricity shot up that arm into his chest. He tumbled sideways off his board, slamming into a wall and dropping to the ground. Another jolt hit him. He tried to rise, tried to force air into his lungs. A third jolt struck him, and he collapsed again. Inside his chest, an invisible fiery hand squeezed his heart.

He fought to move his arm, reaching for the jewel at his neck. His search forgotten, all he wanted was to escape from Dream. The pain stopped. Gasping, he collapsed back to the dirty pavement.

What had happened? His wrist throbbed. He inspected it, expecting it to be bleeding. No blood, but what he saw sent a chill down his spine.

Only one silver leash now hung there, trailing down the alley.

Struggling to his feet, he reached for his Doogles with his mind, calling to them. He reached. He called. He waited.

Nothing.

Wait. There. A tingle came from the remaining leash. A tingle that, if he described it as a sound, he would've called a whimper. He recognized the Doogle who'd made it—Brian.

He'd sent out four Doogles. Three times the pain had hit him. Three leashes gone. Only one reply.

He knew now what his pain had meant—but he couldn't understand how it was possible.

Three Doogles had just died.

Not died as things die in the real world, but they were alive as anything could be in Dream. His Doogles were his creations. He made them. And something had just destroyed three of them.

But Brian was still alive. Reaching again, he called to him. "Come to me, boy. Come home, Brian."

A faint tingle came in reply, but even weaker than before. Brian was dying.

Hopping onto his board, he kicked off, following the last silver leash. He took turn after turn in the nightmare maze of alleys, calling to Brian, telling him to hold on, that he was coming. But around each corner lay only another alley. He'd almost lost hope when he finally emerged into a tilted parking lot, its broken asphalt choked with gray weeds.

The scattered corpses of derelict cars flanked him on either side. At the far end, a black building towered, stretching to touch the night sky. Boarded windows, scattered at odd angles, scarred its face. A sign hung askew on the roof. He could make out only the first letter. An "H."

Another faint tingle on his wrist pulled his attention back. The glowing leash disappeared into a darkened doorway in the building. From it, a limping black and white four-legged figure emerged.

Brian.

Seeing Will, the Doogle limped faster. Will ran forward, catching the dog just as it fell into his arms in the middle of the lot. Laying Brian gently on the dream pavement, he examined him.

He shuddered. Brian's right front leg was broken. His tail, now half its normal length, lay lifeless on the ground. One ear was torn off. Fur and skin were ripped away in patches. Masses of ones and zeros swirled in each wound as underlying algorithms worked to repair the damage.

What had done this to him? Fear emojis often attacked his Doogles, sometimes burning them, but never causing injuries like these. So what had the Doogles run into?

Coding a healing program in his mind, Will fashioned it into a quilted comforter. He wrapped Brian in it. Dim lights sparkled again in the dog's eyes. Brian whined and licked Will's face.

"Hang in there, Bry-guy. We'll go back to the House, then—"

"Is that your dog?"

Will's head snapped up. A figure stood in the doorway where Brian had appeared. A male figure with a face caught between child and adult. A face strangely expressionless.

And gray.

The boy was all gray. Gray clothes, gray hair, gray skin.

No. Not all gray. Not the eyes.

The eyes were black. All black with no whites. But not black as in the absence of light—black as in the absence of anything. If he gazed too long into those eyes, he would fall into an abyss. A bottomless pit where he'd fall and fall and fall and...

With an effort, he wrenched his gaze from those empty eyes. Rising, he put himself between the gray figure and Brian. "Who are you?"

"Is that your dog?" the boy repeated in a voice as dead and lifeless as his eyes. Something moved behind him. Three more gray figures emerged from the doorway. All were boys. All appeared to be in their late teens. And gray except for the same terrible blackness of their eyes.

The three new figures each carried something. Something black and white hanging limp in their gray arms. Three dead Doogles.

"Are these your dogs?" the new boys intoned together in the same flat, empty voices.

"Is that your dog?" the first boy repeated.

As one, the four gray figures took a step toward him.

He realized something else, something he'd overlooked, shaken by the fate of his Doogles. These boys could see him. No one he met in Dream knew of his presence until he stepped forward and let them see him. But these boys, if they *were* boys, were aware of him.

He moved back, still keeping himself between the gray boys and Brian. "Stay where you are," he commanded.

The four strange boys took another step.

"Is that your dog?" the first boy asked again.

"Are these your dogs?" repeated the others.

Step.

"Not much on conversation, are you?" Will replied. "Nyx!"

Nyx's ghostly face appeared, hovering in a cloud of mist beside him. "Really? I was having such a nice dream— Ooh!" she said, noticing the boys. "Now *they're* different."

"They can see me."

"Curiouser and curiouser..."

"And they killed three of my Doogles."

Her features creased into a hard frown directed at the gray boys. "Naughty! Rider will punish."

"Wall shield, please," Will said.

"Catch!"

A ball popped into his hand, rough and heavy, like a round brick. Which it was. He threw it.

It struck the ground in front of the boys, exploding with a loud crack. A clear crystal wall sprang up, rising a story in the air. Spanning the parking lot, it separated him and Brian from the strange boys.

The boys stopped. The three holding the dead Doogles dropped the dogs with sickening thuds. All four stared at him through his crystal barrier.

Breathing a sigh of relief, he knelt beside Brian. "Okay, boy. Let's get you back—"

"Uh, DR?" Nyx said.

He looked up as the four boys stepped through his shield wall as if it wasn't there.

"Is that your dog?" they asked together.

"Nyx! Bring the House!" he called.

"Run, run, run in fright," Nyx crooned. "Live to fight another night."

"Just bring it!"

A loud "pop" sounded behind him. The House of Four Doors appeared, ten steps away in the parking lot. He turned to pick up Brian so they could escape.

And looked at the approaching gray boys.

They were five paces away now, shuffling closer. This close, their dead black eyes stood out clear and stark against their gray faces. And behind those eyes, the unfathomable depths. The abyss into which, if he gazed too long, he would fall.

And if he fell, he would fall forever. Forever and ever and ever...

The gray boys drew closer, but still he didn't move. Some part of him knew he should look away, knew that he was in danger. That he mustn't let these strange creatures touch him.

But another part of him didn't care. That part wanted to keep falling.

And as he fell, he saw a dark thread connecting these boys, like the silver leashes between his Doogles and himself. But this thread was black and ran from each boy to plunge down the dark abyss into which he fell.

Down to the thing that lived there.

The gray boys stepped closer, reaching for him.

Chapter 8

Over the Wall We Go

T rapped on the street between Tall Boy and the red-haired woman with no place to hide, Case agonized over which way to run. Both were bigger than her. She guessed Tall Boy was very good with those knives, but when she thought of running towards the woman, something in her recoiled. Tall Boy then. She took a step in his direction, hoping Shorty and his slingshot didn't suddenly join him.

Wait! her Voice called.

What the freak for? But she waited.

A rumbling grew from the end of the street where the red-haired woman stood. A moment later, a tractor-trailer turned the corner past the woman, heading towards Case. She crouched behind a recycling bin.

The truck stopped, then backed into a ramped driveway beside her, halting before a huge metal door. Lowering the window, the driver punched buttons on a keypad on a post beside the ramp. The door rolled up with a loud clanking. The truck backed inside.

She checked her pursuers. The woman and Tall Boy were running toward her, no longer smiling.

Hurry! Careful!

"How do I hurry carefully?" she muttered as she ran to the door. She peeked inside. The truck had backed up to an elevated receiving dock. Four men in white coveralls wheeled wooden crates from the truck to a freight elevator. The elevator was at the rear of the dock but on her side. Maybe these men would protect her. She started forward.

Wait!

I can't wait! she shouted back in her head. But she did. Besides Fader, her Voice was the only thing she trusted in this world.

Elevator! Now!

She sprinted to the dock, not even surprised that all four workers had their backs to her. Rolling onto the raised platform, she ran quietly to the elevator and slipped inside.

The car was half-full with the wooden crates, most taller than her. Now what? She saw nowhere to hide. Voices from the dockworkers came closer.

Hide! In the back.

She scrambled over the front crates labeled "Do Not Stack." Sure enough, the crates behind were shorter. She dropped to lie hidden just as someone wheeled another crate into the elevator. She lay still and waited.

The men continued to fill the car, until someone called, "That's it. We'll take it up."

"Need help unloading?"

"Nah. We can handle it."

They exchanged more words she didn't catch. She heard the doors close, and the elevator shuddered into motion.

She'd never ridden an elevator in a skyscraper. The acceleration caught her by surprise, as if an invisible hand had grabbed her guts and pulled down hard. She doubled up, stifling a groan. A few seconds later, her stomach caught up with the rest of her, and she lay panting quietly.

I'm safe. Then she realized which building she was in.

The tall shining white one. The one with the picture of the Dream Rider on the top.

And that made her think of Fader again.

The red-haired woman, known for the past two centuries as Morrigan the Bright, last of the white coven of Ellan Vannin, stood under a street light outside the white tower. Beside her, the tall figure of Mr. Stayne waited, using the tip of a gleaming knife blade to clean his fingernails with the delicacy of a surgeon.

Morrigan was not happy. No, not one bit. The evening had not gone well. This girl had seen their faces. This girl had escaped. This girl was a problem.

And a mystery.

First, the slumber spell had failed on her. They should have found her asleep, the same as her brother. But she had been awake. Awake and ready to fight.

Then Morrigan had cast another spell, one that should have exploded the waif's heart inside her. That spell failed too. And then this urchin had evaded the slingshot of the usually reliable Mr. Stryke. She'd never known the little man to miss, not even once, let alone several times.

At least the tracking spell she'd thrown from the church steps had worked, allowing her to trap the girl on this street. But then Fate interfered again (Was it Fate? She didn't believe in Fate. She hated even the concept), and the street rat had escaped where no escape was possible.

And now, another problem. The tracking spell had stopped working after the brat slipped into the white tower. A hiss escaped between her teeth. Beside her, Mr. Stayne shifted nervously.

Morrigan closed her eyes. Forget that spell. She had others. The girl was in this building and could not hide from her.

Muttering, she composed a search script. As the runes crawled down her arm, she thrust up her hand. The golden shapes poured from her fingertips, coalescing into a glowing phoenix above her. She flicked her hand, and the bird shot toward the white tower.

Now I will find you, girl. I will search this tower, floor by floor, until...

She frowned, sensing something. The girl? No. Something different. Something unusual. Something...

The phoenix touched the outer wall of the tower. And exploded.

She gasped, taking a reflexive step back. Mr. Stayne stared at her in wide-eyed surprise. Composing herself, she shot him her most withering glare. He dropped his eyes to his feet. She turned back to the tower.

She knew what she'd sensed. An astral force. One that had repulsed her, slapping her away like a fly. She hadn't found the girl. She'd found something much better.

A power lived here. An astral power that approached the Master's.

Was this the one they had sought for so long? They knew he was in this city. He was why they were here. Was their search finally over?

She smiled. Perhaps this night was a success after all. They had another boy of the right age. And now, possibly, much, much more.

Their prey. At last, their prey.

She frowned, realizing the extraordinary coincidence. A random street stray flees to a random building in one of the largest cities on this continent. A building that shelters their long-sought prey? Improbable to the point of disbelief. Unless...

She smiled again. Of course. The power hiding here was behind the strange happenings tonight. He had touched the girl's mind as they'd hunted her and her brother. He had awakened her, guided her escape from the church to here.

Yes, that was it. He was playing the hero. Again.

She considered her options. They needed the girl. The heavy door to the loading dock had closed. She did not know the magic numbers to the door's spell box, and such modern technology always resisted her spells.

She called up a rune script for contacting Mr. Stryke. When the letters arranged themselves on her arm, she touched the script. The contact with the little man was immediate. From the sensory picture she pulled from his head, she knew he was back at the hospital. *Is the new boy safe?* she asked.

Yes, Mistress.

And how is the Master?

A hesitation. *He sleeps.*

She bit her lip. Marell. Her lover, her mentor. The man to whom she'd tied her life and hopes. The reason for this quest. Marell slept more and more in past days. They must do the next transfer soon, before it was too late.

Come to this place. She sent a mental map to her location, then broke the contact, not waiting for a reply.

"I've sent for Mr. Stryke," she said, not bothering to look at Mr. Stayne. "You two will watch this building. If the girl leaves, my tracking spell will activate again, and I will contact you. You will then follow her."

"And kill her?" Mr. Stayne asked, a grin twitching a corner of his mouth.

"I want her alive."

Stayne's face fell.

"You will follow and capture her. Discreetly. Bring her to me." She nodded at the white tower. "This building hides a power, perhaps the one we seek. I have questions to ask this girl. You can help with that."

Mr. Stayne's smile returned, as she knew it would. Mr. Stayne liked asking questions, especially to women. He ran a white fingertip along the edge of his blade.

With that, she turned and walked up the street. Chanting under her breath, she raised her left arm. Her skin glowed. Golden runes swam down her arm, arranged from shoulder to wrist in the rune script she desired. Opening her hand, she flung the spell ahead of her. The glow and the runes disappeared from her skin.

A few seconds later, a taxi appeared at the corner and stopped. Getting in, she threw a control spell to ensure the driver didn't call his dispatcher. She wanted no record of any trips to their location. She gave the man an address in the east end.

"You're lucky gettin' a cab this time of night, lady. I was headin' home," he said, eyeing her in the mirror.

"Luck," Morrigan replied, "had nothing to do with it."

Weary, she laid her head back, her thoughts still on the white tower. Even if their prey was not inside, this building held a power. For centuries, she had sought such powers, to make them her own, to ensure no one could ever hurt her as they'd once hurt her mother, her coven...

She swallowed. Her brother.

Enough. One spell remained before she could sleep. The most difficult—and important—spell she would cast today. A spell that must wait no longer.

The spell to keep Marell alive.

And then, she and Marell would turn their attention to this tower and what hid within.

The freight elevator slowed, and Case's stomach did another flip. She heard the doors open, followed by the sound of crates being wheeled off. Creeping to the front of the car, she peeked out.

A wide hallway with a floor of rough stone stretched to her left and right. Towering carved blocks of smoother stone covered with drawings formed the walls. The drawings showed people with animal heads in strange stiff poses. She'd had enough schooling in her pre-street-kid years to recognize Egyptian hieroglyphics. Giant vases and statues lined the hallway in both directions.

Where the freak was she? In a museum?

To her left, the two workers wheeled crates toward the end of the hall. She slipped out to her right, looking for a place to hide. Ten steps along, she squeezed between two statues of elongated cats as tall as her and crouched behind them to wait.

The men continued to unload the crates. She needed to pee. Just as she decided to sneak out to search for a washroom, their voices approached again. Moments later, the elevator doors slid shut.

Silence settled onto the strange floor, and with it, fear and despair settled onto her. Freaky people had kidnapped her brother and were trying to kill her. She was alone with no idea of what to do. She wanted to cry, but after one heaving sob, she got control of herself again.

Screw it. Hard Case didn't cry. Crying wouldn't help Fader. Besides, she still had to pee.

Pee. Get out of here. Find Fader.

Emerging from her hiding place, she began exploring.

Chapter 9

Lady Midnight

In Dream, the gray boys stepped closer to Will. They were two paces away now, their arms raised, reaching for him. Another step, and they would have him.

Still he didn't care. He fell and fell into the dark depths of their eyes.

A sharp pain stabbed his leg. Gasping, he stumbled back, landing hard on the ground. Lying beside him, Brian had his jaws locked on Will's left ankle. Will looked back at the gray boys, their hands grasping for him. If the Doogle hadn't done that...

He scooped Brian up in his arms, kicking his skateboard at the nearest boy who lunged for him. Avoiding their eyes, he backed away from the strange figures until he reached the House of Four Doors. From the outside, it was the House of One Door, the door through which they'd entered Dream.

"Nyx! Open the door! I've got my hands full."

Nyx's disembodied, mist-shrouded head appeared, floating beside the House. "Now why should I pay attention to *you* when you've been ignoring *me*? I've been screaming and screaming at you to stop the Creepy Boy Stare Fest."

"Sorry! Got a little distracted."

"Humph."

The gray boys drew closer.

"Nyx!"

"Oh, fine."

The door swung open. Jumping through, he kicked it closed behind him. Inside, he gently laid Brian on the Bed of Awakening. He lifted the healing quilt enough to check on the progress of the Doogle's wounds. Satisfied Brian would recover, he stroked the dog's head and commanded him to sleep.

Nyx's face materialized over the Bed. "Will he be okay?" She sounded worried.

"Yeah, but make sure he stays asleep until my next Ride." He looked back at the door, half expecting the strange boys to walk through the walls. "What's happening outside?"

"They're standing like statues, staring at the House. What *are* those things?"

"No idea. Did I create them? Without knowing it?"

"Even *you* aren't that weird."

"Humor me. Run a search on my subconscious, will you?"

"Meaning I should search myself. And if I *don't* find them snuggled between your id and super-ego?"

Will bit his lip. "Then someone else created them. Someone with powers like mine in Dream."

"Even greater powers."

"Well, I wouldn't say—"

"They kicked your butt, right? They won, you lost. Then you ran away, like a Doogle with its tail between—"

"Yeah, okay. Point taken. I was there, remember? Just run the search, please. Tell me the results tomorrow night."

"Touchy, aren't we?" Nyx's face disappeared with a "pop."

Even greater powers. He didn't need his subconscious to tell him that. He'd figured it out himself.

Touching the jewel at his neck, he woke up.

Will got out of bed, shaken and confused by his Dream encounter with the Gray Boys, as he now dubbed them. An encounter that had cost three of his Doogles their unreal lives.

It was three AM, but he felt too wound up to sleep. Throwing on his sweats and grabbing his phone, he walked barefoot along the running track to his kendo dojo.

He selected a *shinai*, a bamboo practice sword, from the wall rack. In the middle of the room, he moved through several katas, formal series of strikes and blocks, letting his muscle memory perform the movements. It felt good to attack something and win, even against imaginary opponents. Because Nyx was right. He'd had his butt kicked. His subconscious knew the truths he didn't want to accept.

But what could do that to his dream constructs? Both to his Doogles and the shield wall? And how could the Gray Boys see him in Dream before he stepped forward? That implied they could enter the dreams of others—as he did.

And why had they interfered with his search for the missing street kids?

He stopped, letting the sword drop to his side.

Duh.

He'd sent four Doogles to track four missing kids. Those Doogles had met four Gray Boys.

Four.

A shiver ran down his spine. The Doogles had done their jobs. Too well. Those four boys were the Dream spirits of the missing kids he'd been looking for.

What had happened to them? And who'd done it to them? He was now convinced Harry Lyle was right. These disappearances were all connected somehow.

Connected...

The black thread. The black thread he'd seen running from each Gray Boy. Running from them into that abyss. Connecting all four boys to something—the *same* something.

Something or someone? The someone behind the disappearances?

The good news? Those kids were dreaming, which meant they still lived.

The bad news? Something was horribly wrong with them.

So now what? He'd planned to find the missing kids in Dream, hoping they'd know where they were in the real world. That plan had assumed they'd want to cooperate with him—not destroy him.

He had nothing. Normally, his Doogles would report on what happened during their searches. But three were destroyed, and Brian was so damaged Will doubted he'd recover much from him.

Wait. He remembered a sign on the building from where Brian and the Gray Boys had emerged. He'd only seen the first letter, the letter "H," but he could still have Adi run a search for companies starting with "H."

Yeah, right. How many could there be in a city of over six million people and the business heart of the country? But what else did he have to go on?

Now wide-awake, he had no thoughts of sleep. Adi had said the latest Egyptian sculptures were due tonight. Maybe the workers had uncrated them. He walked to the elevators. He was about to press the button when his phone buzzed.

It was his security app. The building locked down after hours, and elevators required proper authorization to access any floor. But since he enjoyed wandering his tower at night, Adi had insisted on this system. The app alerted him if anyone was above the office floors after midnight. It used motion detectors. Or infrared sensors. Or something. He hadn't paid attention.

He tapped the alert. The floor name popped up on the screen: Egypt.

Excellent. Probably the dockworkers setting up the new sculptures. He pressed the down button.

On the Egypt floor, Will checked the labels on the still unopened crates. Yep, these were the expected sculptures. The workmen must have left them to open tomorrow.

Then who's on this floor? he thought with a sudden chill.

He smiled. They were probably taking a break. That Dream encounter had made him paranoid. He continued to explore. Turning a corner, he stopped.

About twenty steps away, a figure moved along the hall, examining the statues and hieroglyphic-covered tablets. A woman. Or a girl. He couldn't tell from this far away. She had her back to him but had an obvious (and attractive) female shape. She had tight-curled black hair, a dirty white t-shirt, dirtier jeans, and mismatched running shoes. And from the cross-legged way she walked, she was searching for a washroom.

His dockworkers wore matching uniforms. An intruder? If she was, he wasn't worried. She appeared more anxious than dangerous. Besides, meeting some-one new was a rare treat for him.

Moving quietly, he approached her, wondering if this night could get any weirder.

Chapter 10

Crush on You

After almost a full circuit of the strange floor, Case began worrying it didn't even have a washroom. She'd need to try another level, hoping the elevators weren't alarmed or set on service. And that another floor would have a freaking washroom.

She stopped. Or she could improvise.

An alcove to her right held a vase with hieroglyphics on its sides. Slightly wider at its top, the vase sat at a convenient height, a little below her waist. The vase's lid, topped by the head of a bird, lay beside it.

With a shrug, she stepped into the alcove. Life on the streets taught practicality over modesty at an early age. Besides, it served them right. Who designed a building without washrooms?

For that matter, who designed a building with a floor like this? It was like a museum. Fader claimed the creator of his beloved Dream Rider comic books lived here. This was his home—an entire skyscraper.

Shaking her head, she unzipped her jeans and pulled them down over her hips. "What kind of weirdo lives in a place like this?" she muttered aloud. She hooked her thumbs into the top of her panties, ready to pull them down too.

"Actually, a weirdo like me."

"Holy freaking goddam shit!" she screamed, yanking up her jeans and spinning to face the source of the voice.

In the hallway, a guy stood watching her, his arms casually folded. He looked her age, a little taller, with long, unruly, straight, black hair falling over one eye. He was barefoot and wore gray sweats—and an amused smile.

Snatching her knife from her back pocket, she flicked it open. She thrust it at him while she tried to zip her jeans with her other hand.

The guy seemed unfazed by her weapon. "Hi."

She kept jabbing her blade in his direction, still tugging at her unresponsive zipper.

He continued to ignore her knife. "Were you going to *pee* in my canopic jar?"

"*What?* Your what?" she said, still waving the blade while battling her zipper.

He pointed at the vase. "That's a canopic jar. A funerary jar. The ancient

Egyptians used them when they mummified their dead. To store the internal organs for the afterlife. Late eighteenth dynasty—you can tell by the image of Horus on the lid." He frowned. "I always wondered what they expected the mummy to *do* with the organs in the afterlife. I mean, were you supposed to unwrap your bandages and, you know, stuff your organs back inside? Not sure they really thought it through." He smiled at her.

A part of her brain she tried to ignore said he had a nice smile.

"I won't hurt you, so if you want to use *both* hands to, uh, zip..." He nodded at the knife.

She thrust the knife at him again, shooting him what she hoped was a menacing glare. A grin still played at the corners of his mouth. *Screw it*. He seemed more weird than dangerous. Giving him another glare, she flicked the knife closed, returning it to her back pocket. She zipped and stepped out of the alcove, keeping two steps between herself and her surprise visitor.

"Will," he said.

"Will I what?"

"Uh, no. Will. That's my name."

She didn't reply, suddenly remembering her urgent problem.

"And now is where you tell me your—"

"I need to pee!"

His grin widened. "Hah! Knew it. Just around the corner to the right. You were almost there."

She started in that direction, then stopped to look back at him. "You going to call the cops?" she asked, jiggling where she stood.

"Would you like me to?"

"No!"

He shrugged. "Then I won't."

The guy's weird. Half walking, half running, she turned the corner. Finding the washroom, she dashed into a stall to finally answer nature's call. As that urgency faded, one dark thought returned.

Fader.

The night's horror gripped her again. She had to get back to the streets and search for her brother. But where could she look? Lots of street kids had vanished lately. She figured the creeps who'd taken Fader were behind those disappearances, too. She swallowed. And none of those kids had been found.

Because no one was looking for them. The cops didn't give a shit. Nobody did. Except her. Fader had that one thing going for him. Her. She wouldn't quit until she found him.

Safe, she added in her thoughts. Until she found him *safe*.

But she'd need help. And she'd just figured out where she might get it. She washed up in the sink, splashing cold water on her face. She'd need to sleep soon, but not yet.

The guy Will was sitting cross-legged on the floor where she'd left him. He jumped up when he saw her. "Better?" he asked with that same infectious grin.

She pointed at the urn where he'd found (and embarrassed) her. "You said that vase thingy was yours?"

"Do you ever, you know, *answer* a question? Yes, it's mine. And it's a canopic jar, not a 'vase thingy'."

"Whatever. What do you mean by 'yours'?"

"Um, as in *mine*. I own it."

"What else do you own?"

He shrugged. "A bunch of stuff. And that's kind of personal, considering you broke into my building, and I don't even know your name."

"*Your* building." She'd been right. "You're the Dream Rider comic guy."

Will brightened. "Graphic novels. But, yeah, I am. Do you read it?"

"No."

His face fell.

"But my brother does." She swallowed. "His name is Fader. He's twelve. And he's been taken. Kidnapped. Grabbed." She shook her head. "I don't know." She sank to the floor, trying not to shake.

Will sat again, across from her, his grin now gone. "What happened?"

She studied him. The streets had taught her how to read people. She wasn't always right, but she was never badly wrong. This Will guy seemed okay. He seemed kind, even concerned. Weird, but not scary weird—just *different* weird. And sort of cute. *Stop it. Focus on Fader.* And he hadn't called security or the cops, at least as far as she knew.

She needed help. If he was telling the truth, then he had money, maybe even people who could help look for Fader.

She decided. "Case."

"In case of what?"

"No. My name. It's Case."

"Oh. Will." He held out his hand.

She smiled despite herself, shaking his hand. "Yeah. You told me."

"Right. Yes. I did."

"Um..."

"What?"

"My hand." Will still held her hand, which another part of her brain told her felt nice.

"Ah, sorry." He released her hand and blushed.

Yes, definitely cute.

His smile disappeared. "Tell me about your brother."

Fighting to keep the fear from her voice, she told Will about that night.

***

Will stood at his design table in his studio. He held a creased and faded photograph Case had provided. In it, a Case with shorter hair stared back at him, alongside a younger, smaller, boy version of Case. Fader, her brother.

Case wandered the studio, looking at art from Dream Rider issues hanging on the walls.

What was he doing? And why? This girl had broken in—well, snuck in—in the middle of the night. And with the craziest story. A glowing woman with weird tattoos and her creepy helpers, one with knives and the other with...a slingshot?

But, he admitted, not as crazy as the story he could tell her. Besides, if she wanted to lie, why make up such a wild one? And kids *were* disappearing from the streets. Her brother might be the latest.

"So this is where you do your comic thingy?" she asked as she wandered.

"Serialized graphic novels," he replied. She raised an eyebrow. He shrugged. "Yeah, comics."

She paused on her tour, eying his long leather couch.

"Why don't you lie down? You look beat."

She shook her head. "Can't. Gotta find Fader first."

"You need to sleep sometime."

Shooting him a glare, she turned her back on the couch and walked over to him. "You gonna help me or what?"

Not exactly Ms. Congeniality. "Is this the best picture you have of Fader?"

"Yeah, cuz it's the only one. Not too many Kodak moments on the streets."

"Oh. Yeah. Right. So where'd you take this?"

"Photo booth in a mall. I wanted a shot of each other in case we ever—" She swallowed. "—got separated." She turned away.

Tough on the outside, he thought, *but she loves her brother.*

He placed the photograph facedown on the drafting surface. Summoning a command screen with a finger swipe, he tapped on the scan symbol. The photo popped up, magnified, on the table display.

Case stared at the enlarged image of her and Fader. She rubbed her face with both hands. "Oh god, oh god, oh god."

"We'll find him," he said, trying to sound more confident than he felt.

"How?"

"I have private investigators who work for me." Tapping the screen, he enhanced the picture.

"You have your own detectives?"

"Uh, yeah," he said, giving her the explanation he'd provided Harry about the downsides of being famous.

She brightened. "So they'll look for Fader?"

"Yep. I'm sending this picture to a reporter friend, too. Harry Lyle. He's investigating street kid disappearances."

"The guy from the Standard?"

"You know him?" he said, surprised.

"We call him 'Bad Plaid' cuz of his jacket. He's been talking to kids out there. Most don't trust him, but some talked to him. Me and Fader did. He seemed okay. He gave us his card. Couldn't tell him much." Her face went hard. "At least not then."

"Harry has a network of sources who feed him tips. He might turn up something, too."

She hugged herself. "*Might*. Great."

"We should also report this—"

"No!" Case interrupted, shaking her head.

"—to the police."

"No freaking way."

"They're your best chance of finding Fader."

She snorted. "They won't give a shit. Kids have gone missing for months now. The cops have done nothing. They wouldn't listen to me, even if I went to them."

"They'd listen to me."

She stared at him. "Because you're rich. And white. Because you're *somebody*."

He felt himself flushing. "They'd know my name, anyway. And I'll say Fader is a friend, not just—" He stopped.

"Not just some street kid?"

"That's not what I meant."

"Yeah, it was." She shrugged. "And it's true."

An uneasy silence fell between them.

"So...can I call the cops?"

She bit her lip. "There's something else."

He raised an eyebrow.

"I kind of busted Fader out of the foster home they'd stuck him in."

"Kind of?"

"They separated us after I got sent to juvie the last time. When I got out, I found him and snuck him out of the house one night. We've been on the streets since."

He understood. "You're afraid if the cops find him, he'll go back to a home. Without you."

Her expression was unreadable, but she nodded.

"Case," he said, as gently as he could, "we have to find Fader first. The cops are your best bet. I'll help you with the foster home stuff later."

Her face went hard again. "Why are you helping me?"

"Um...you asked me to?"

"You know what I mean."

He felt himself reddening again. "No, I don't. You're in trouble. And you seem...nice."

"Oh, right. Nice. Yeah, I get that a *lot*. Uh huh. And you like my butt."

"What?"

"And my tits."

"What? No!"

"You don't like them?"

"No. I mean, yes. I mean..."

"Cuz you keep checking them out. Is that the deal? Is that how I'll pay you for being nice to me?"

His face burning, he fought to keep his voice calm. "Look. *You* broke into *my* home. *You* are the one in trouble, not me. I could've called the cops on you. Instead, I'm doing everything I can to help you. And no, I'm not expecting you'll...*do* anything for me in return."

She crossed her arms, her face impassive, studying him.

Stepping back, he lifted and dropped his arms in frustration. "Case, I don't want anything from you." *Yeah, that's it. Start by lying to her.* "I only want to help find your brother. If you don't want my help, just tell me."

She continued to stare at him. Finally, she shrugged. "Sorry."

"Sorry, you don't want my help?"

She shook her head. "Sorry for what I thought. You seem like a nice guy." She rubbed her face again, and he remembered how exhausted she must be. At least he'd grabbed some sleep during his failed Dream search.

"Yeah, I want your help," she said. "I'm just not used to people offering it. People on the street... Everybody's working an angle. Everybody expects something in return." She waved her hand around the room. "I've never met anyone like you. You're just so...different."

You have no idea. "Then you're okay if I contact my people and Harry?"

"Yeah."

"Cops, too?"

She grimaced, but nodded.

He sat back down at his table. "Then let's do this." He addressed an email to his head investigator, attaching Fader's photo. "How old is Fader?"

"Twelve."

"And you?" he asked, as casually as he could.

"Why?"

"Just wondering."

She hesitated. "Seventeen."

He just nodded, fighting a smile. She was his age.

Turning away, she walked to the leather couch, then half sat, half collapsed on it. "Gotta get back on the streets. Look for Fader." Stretching out, she yawned. "Tell me when you're done. Then I gotta..." Her voice trailed off.

He looked over.

She was fast asleep, her head cradled in an arm. Asleep, her face lost its hard lines, and a softness touched her mouth and the long curve of her neck.

Sighing, he turned back to his screen. Nope, he didn't want anything from her.

Yeah. Right.

Chapter 11

Darkness on the Edge of Town

The cab pulled onto the hospital grounds as the sun tinted the eastern sky. As she got out, Morrigan touched the driver's shoulder. The man grinned at her, believing he'd received payment plus a handsome tip. He drove away, also convinced he'd dropped his fare in a completely different location.

She scanned the abandoned psychiatric facility and its grounds. Boards covered the windows, a precaution she and Marell had taken after moving in. A private road cut through the forty-acre property. An expanse of lawn, overgrown with weeds, stretched from the building to a thin forest edging the entire property. The hospital grounds perched atop high bluffs overlooking the lake on which this city sat. Beyond the trees, the land fell off sharply to the water below.

She searched the area, sensing for any human presence but expecting none. The hospital, abandoned for five years, sat isolated from its suburban neighbors. A simple repulsion spell helped it remain so, inducing people to avoid the place. No one must see her, or any of their group, entering or leaving. The street people who'd once squatted here had served as Marell's early and unwilling hosts in this city.

Satisfied, she climbed crumbling steps flanked by two weatherworn stone lions. At the entrance doors, she prepared to throw a spell to open the lock but stopped. Better to save her dwindling energy for what lay ahead. She retrieved a ring of keys from an inside pocket of her cape. Selecting one, she unlocked the door and entered the darkened foyer within. She locked the door behind her, looking around as her eyes adjusted to the dimness.

An abandoned reception desk occupied the center of the foyer. Behind that, a hallway ran left and right for the length of the building. Beside the desk, a figure stood still and silent, arms at his sides as if guarding the empty gift shop behind him. In one hand, he held an unlit taper. He showed no reaction to her entrance.

She approached him. Which one was this? His hoodie and baggy jeans didn't differentiate him. Perhaps eighteen. Taller and older than most of them, so one of the first Marell had used when they came here. Started with an "L." Lance?

Lloyd? No.

Link.

Brushing his unkempt brown hair back from his face, she tucked it behind his ears. She stroked his cheek with the back of a long-nailed hand. "Hello, Link. How are you?"

Link did not answer. He did not move nor give any sign he was aware of her.

She smiled. Her boys. Her Hollow Boys. So many now. Well, even if they could no longer serve Marell as they once did, at least they were still of use.

"Candle, please." She was always polite to her boys. Adults must set a proper example.

Link held out the taper. Runes danced down her arm. A simple spell, not too draining. She touched the wick. A flame leaped up. The city had cut the hospital's power when it closed. No matter. Electric lighting would be visible from outside at night, even through the boarded windows. Besides, she preferred candlelight.

"Lead me to the new boys, Link."

She followed Link through the foyer then up two flights of stairs to the third floor. Another Hollow Boy stood guard at the stairwell. She smiled. Tumble. One of her favorites. She pinched his cheek. "Come with us, please, Tumble."

The hallways on this floor formed a rectangular figure eight. Two long halls on the north and south sides. Three shorter halls, on the ends and in the middle, connecting the two long halls. This stairwell sat at the north end of the middle hall.

Link headed toward the southeast corner, Tumble at his side. Behind the two silent boys, humming a tune from a century ago, Morrigan followed in the candle's flickering light.

Fader's first thought when he awoke was a memory of Case calling to him. A dream? Or a nightmare? Case had sounded scared. Rubbing his eyes, he sat up and looked over to where she slept.

She wasn't there.

He blinked. He was no longer in the church basement. Confusion morphed to fear, a fear that threatened to become panic.

He didn't recognize this place. He didn't know where he was. Worse, he didn't remember getting here. He lay on a mattress on a bare linoleum-tiled floor in a corner of a small room, maybe five paces by ten. It had one door. And a single window with boards on the outside and bars inside. The air was musty and stuffy. He caught a faint chemical smell, too. It reminded him of when Case took him to Emergency once. They'd been crashing at a landfill site, and he'd sliced his leg on some rebar.

Part of him wanted to call for Case. But another part was afraid to break the strange silence. He didn't hear the normal street sounds of the city. He didn't hear anything.

No. He *did* hear something.

Breathing.

He wasn't alone. His eyes had adjusted enough to see two figures lying in the far corners on their own mattresses. They lay on their backs, legs straight, arms folded on their chests as if someone had posed them that way. And neither figure was Case. From what he could see of their features, both were boys, bigger and older than him.

How did he get here? How did they? Were they prisoners? Was he? If he *was* a prisoner, were they his captors?

He realized he was trembling. He wanted to cry. He wanted Case.

Case. That was it. That's how he had to think. What would Case do?

Well, she wouldn't cry or call for help. No way. Not Hard Case.

So what *would* she do?

Get out. She'd get the freak out. With an image of Case in his head, he pushed his fear into a corner and rose as quietly as he could. He tiptoed toward the door, gritting his teeth at each squeak of the floor. But the two sleeping boys remained sleeping. As he passed them, he got another shock.

He knew these boys. Rattle and Slip. Rattle was an asshole. Slip was okay, though. He guessed they were in the same spot he was, but he wouldn't risk trusting them. Case wouldn't. Case didn't trust anyone.

He tried the doorknob. Locked from the outside. Great. At least he had one answer. He *was* a prisoner. But now what? Maybe he could force the lock. Or unscrew the hinge plates. He felt for his pocketknife. Gone.

A sound came from beyond the door. A rhythmic clicking. Footsteps. Footsteps that grew louder until they stopped outside. When he heard the jingling of what he guessed were keys, he decided.

Work with what you've got, Case always said. Well, all he had right now were his wits and what Case called his "superpower."

The reason she called him Fader.

As the key slid into the lock, he moved. Not to his mattress, but into the darkest corner. Pushing back into the shadows, he concentrated on not being there, on becoming unimportant.

On fading.

The door swung open.

"Thank you, Link," Morrigan said, as the Hollow Boy stopped outside a room in the southeast corner, Tumble beside him. Unlocking the door, she entered the room, followed by the two silent boys.

She took the candle from Link in her right hand to keep her rune hand free. Moving to the boys, still asleep under her spell, she bent to examine them. She straightened.

Two? Why only two? "Where's the new one? The little one from tonight?"

Link and Tumble stood like statues in the flickering candlelight. Neither responded.

She sighed. She kept doing that—thinking of her Hollow Boys as real boys. Any activity still occurring in their heads was restricted to obeying simple commands.

So where *was* the new boy? The young brother (she assumed) of that bothersome girl who escaped? Had Mr. Stryke misunderstood her instructions? Had he assumed she'd use the boy tonight? She *had* told him to "take the boy to the Master." If so, the child was in the Weave Room where Marell rested.

She sighed again. Stryke and Stayne had their uses, mostly killing and hurting when required. Their intellects, however, were as limited as their interests.

No, she wouldn't use the new boy tonight. She'd save him. She clenched her rune hand, unable to ignore the enormity of the danger to Marell.

His ability to remain within a host became shorter with each new body. But worse still was the recent need that each host be younger than the one before. Otherwise, Marell could not perform his transfer at all, even with her magicks to assist.

She would save the new boy until later since he was the youngest of the three. Assuming she judged their ages correctly. She frowned. If only they came with "best before" dates. The boys always provided their ages, under a compulsion spell. But sometimes, these strays weren't even sure themselves. That had proved near disastrous recently. Marell had transferred into a boy older than his current host. She'd barely been able to get him back out and into a younger boy before...

Before she would have lost Marell, her lover, her mentor, forever. Before his astral spirit scattered into nothingness. And with it, their plans.

How much longer could he continue this way? How long before he became pre-pubescent, making her sex life the next victim in their long quest? Far worse, how long before she'd be holding a diapered newborn?

Hot wax dripped onto her hand, and she snapped back to the moment. She pointed to the sleeping boys. "Link, pick that one up. Tumble, the other.

Gently."

Link and Tumble complied, with an ease belying their underfed frames. The Hollow Boys all displayed unnatural physical strength.

She started toward the door when something drew her attention. Something in that corner. The darkest corner. Someone hiding?

The runes for a stun spell danced along her left arm. Holding the candle before her, left arm raised, she stepped forward to see what hid in the darkness.

Nothing.

She drew herself up. The runes faded from her arm. She rubbed her eyes. Tired. So tired.

"Come," she said, leaving the room. She walked down the hall, the candle-light performing a flickering dance with each of her steps. Behind, the silent Hollow Boys followed with their unconscious burdens.

When the red-haired woman entered the room, Fader continued to focus on fading. He didn't know how his odd power worked, but he knew it did. People overlooked him. Maybe it came with being a street kid. The way you became invisible to people. The way they walked right past you as if you weren't there.

As the woman bent over the sleeping boys, he edged along the wall to the open door. The woman was beautiful and had a cool cape. He recognized the two boys with the woman. Link and Tumble. Both stood strangely silent and still behind her, but far enough from the doorway to let him slip by.

Outside the room, he found himself in a long door-lined hallway, lit by early morning light sneaking past boards covering the windows. The woman spoke in the room behind him. He padded to the nearest door, praying for it to be unlocked. The handle turned. He slipped inside, closing the door until only a crack remained.

A moment later, the click-click of the woman's shoes sounded on the tiled floor. He peeked out. The woman swept past, disappearing down the hall, candle in hand, cape and red hair billowing behind her. Deciding not to delay in case she returned, he stepped from his hiding place into the hallway.

And into the path of Link and Tumble, each carrying one of the sleeping boys.

Fader leaped aside, and his heart leaped with him. He waited for the boys to call out to the woman, ending his short-lived escape.

But they passed by where he stood pressed against the wall, their eyes straight ahead. They gave no sign they'd seen him. They did not call out. He slipped back into the room, his heart pounding, still expecting shouts that never came.

That made no sense. He'd been right in front of them, barely a step away. Even the dim light and his fade power couldn't explain that.

Something was wrong with these silent boys. He swallowed, thinking of Rattle and Slip, the boys being carried. That could have been him, being carried to...

To what? What would happen to them? He thought of the kids who'd disappeared from the streets since spring. Was this where they'd ended up? And what had happened to Link and Tumble?

More importantly, where was Case? Was she here, too? A prisoner like him? She must be. She would never leave him.

He decided. He'd planned to get away from this awful place as quickly as possible. But not anymore. He had to find if Case was here, trusting in his fade ability to avoid being caught. If she was, they'd escape together. Case would know how to do that. And maybe while he searched for her, he'd find out what was going on here.

This is what Case would do, he told himself. Slipping out of hiding again, he crept down the hall after the silent boys.

Chapter 12

Psychedelic Ramblings of Rich Kids

"And that's all I know," Will said, leaning back in his chair. It was eight o'clock in the morning. He sat on the long side of the huge cherry-wood table that dominated his second-floor boardroom. Floor-to-ceiling windows formed the wall behind him and to his left. A display screen covered the wall at the far end of the room to his right.

Two cops, both plain-clothed detectives, sat across the large table from him. One was young and female, with a round face and short-cropped brown hair. She was taking notes. The other cop was male and heavier, with a gray buzz cut. He'd remained silent throughout, studying Will through lidded eyes. He made Will nervous.

The younger cop closed her pad. "I think that's it, Mr. Dreycott." She tucked the photo of Fader that Will had provided into her notebook.

The male cop finally spoke. "It'd help, son, if we could talk to the boy's sister."

"She's out looking for him," Will lied. "But I'll have her call you."

The cop pursed his lips. "Have her drop by the station instead."

"Sure," Will said. *Right. That will happen.*

The boardroom door opened. Adi entered. When she saw the cops, she hesitated, her eyebrows shooting up. Walking to Will, she bent and whispered in his ear. "William, security caught an intruder attempting to leave the building. A teenage girl. A street kid, by the looks of her. We don't know how she got in, but..."

Oh shit. "Thank you, Adi," he interrupted. "Let's discuss that after the officers leave. I've taken up too much of their time."

"Or," Adi whispered again, "we could hand her over while they're here."

The older cop leaned forward, trying to catch their conversation. Will stood, facing Adi with his back to the cops. "No, that doesn't fit with where I want to take the next issue. We'll discuss this *later*," he said, making his best not-in-front-of-cops face.

Her eyebrows shot up again. He tried to remember seeing Adi surprised twice in two minutes. But she nodded. "Understood...*sir.*"

Will turned to the two officers. "Well, thanks for coming so quickly. Please keep me informed of any progress. Ms. Archambeault will show you out."

Adi glared at him but led the cops from the room. A few minutes later, she returned. "William, would you mind telling me what is going on? And please be brief."

"Her name's Case. Street kid. Brother's been snatched. Helping her find him."

"Perhaps not that brief."

"More later. Where is she?"

"Mr. Bevington is holding her in a conference room down the hall."

Bevington was one of his uniformed security guards. "I need to see her," Will said.

Leaving the boardroom, they walked along the wood-paneled hallway, its black carpet dotted with the comets and clouds of the Dream Rider's costume.

"Why'd Bev grab her?" he asked.

"He was on duty in reception. When she couldn't open the reception door to exit into the building lobby, he explained she needed to scan her hand. When that didn't work, she...assaulted him and ran back to the elevators."

"Which wouldn't take her anywhere except the lobby without a hand scan. Assaulted him? Bev's about six-foot-twenty and built like a rhino."

"She kicked him. In a sensitive area."

He grinned. That sounded like Case.

Adi wasn't smiling. "I'm glad you find having your staff attacked amusing."

"I am so *never* letting him forget this. She's half his size."

Adi indicated a conference room on his left. Pushing open the door, Will entered, Adi following.

Bevington stood near the door, to prevent any exit by Case, no doubt. Eight leather swivel chairs surrounded a black lacquered table. Case sat by the window, arms crossed, chair tilted back, feet up on the table. A denim jacket hung over the chair beside her. She regarded Will then turned to stare out the window.

"Sir," Bevington said, "I told her to take her feet off the table—"

"No worries, Bev." He grinned at the guard. "So, I hear you two met earlier?"

Bevington reddened. "She took me by surprise, sir."

Will pretended to frown. "Don't you have, like, a kajillion black belts? Oh, but then I guess you normally get hit *above* those belts."

The guard looked pained to find a response. Will slapped him on the arm. "Just messing with you, big guy. Look, I know you're doing your job, but this lady is a friend. I forgot to tell her how to get out of here, because..." He turned to Case. "...I didn't expect her to be leaving so soon."

Case swung her legs down and jumped up, pushing the chair back so it crashed into the wall behind her. "Yeah? Well, just what the freak did you expect me to do?"

Bevington's jaw tightened, and he started towards her. Will held up a hand. He walked over to Case, who stood with arms crossed, glaring at him.

"I gotta find Fader," she said. "Remember him? And where the freak were you? You said you'd help me."

Will took a breath, biting back a retort. He had a feeling he'd be doing that a lot around this girl. He held up a finger. "One, I called my investigation team, and they're working on it." He held up another finger. "Two, I called Harry Lyle, and he'll check his sources on the street about Fader. And, three..." A third finger. "I called the cops. I just gave a statement to two detectives, and they're opening a file. You were still sleeping when I left..."

Adi's eyebrows shot up again.

"...uh, on my couch. In my studio. Alone," he added, for Adi's benefit. "*That* is what I was doing. With no sleep. For someone I just met. Someone who broke into my building."

"Then she *did* break in," Adi said, looking hard at Case. Bevington straightened.

Will shook his head. "No. Not really. Yes. Sort of. Look, never mind. I'll explain later." He turned to the guard. "Sorry about this, Bev. You did your job, so thanks. But we're done here."

Bevington glanced at Adi, who gave a slight nod. The guard left the room.

"He knows he works for *me*, right?" Will said.

"We are most certainly *not* done here, William," Adi said.

Case snorted. "*William?* Who's this? Your mother?"

"You will keep a civil tongue in your head, young lady."

Case shrugged. "Sorry, *old* lady. My mistake. Now that I get a better look, I'm guessing *grand*mother."

"*That* does it," Adi snapped. "I'm bringing the police back." She started toward the door.

Will stepped in front of her. "Adi. Please?"

Adi stopped. Something must have shown in his face, for her own look softened. She sighed. "All right, William. I only hope you know what you're doing." Her eyes ran over Case's figure. "And *why* you're doing it." With a final glare at Case, she left the room.

Will turned to Case. "You're not really a people person, are you?"

She dropped her eyes, kicking the carpet with the toe of a mismatched running shoe. She held up three fingers.

"I'm guessing you're using two too many fingers?"

"Your three things. That you did for me. For Fader." She looked at him, and there, for a second, came that softness that had touched her face while she slept.

His heart did a little skip. *Oh shit*. He knew that feeling.

"Thanks," she said.

"You have an odd way of communicating."

She smiled. Just for an eyeblink. Then it was gone. But that little smile had transformed her. "I usually don't. Communicate."

"I shall consider myself lucky, then."

"You should."

A silence fell.

"So...you're going?" he asked.

She nodded. "Gotta find Fader. It's great, what you're doing, but I still gotta look for him myself. Kind of the fourth finger." She grabbed the denim jacket from the back of the chair.

"Is that my jacket?"

She considered the jacket. "Yeah. It sort of is."

"Sort of?"

"Sort of found it. In your closet."

"You were in my closet? Upstairs? Beside my bedroom?"

"Glad you know where your closet is."

"Not quite my point."

She shrugged. "I woke up. You were gone. I looked around. For you. Found the closet."

"Oh."

"And it's raining."

He glanced out the window. "So it is." He turned back. She was holding the jacket out to him. "No. Keep it. I...I don't get out much."

He expected her to refuse. Instead, she flung the jacket over a shoulder, making even her acceptance of his gift a defiant gesture.

They stared at each other for a breath, then he turned to the door. "C'mon. I'll walk you out."

"So I don't kick someone else in the balls?"

"Yeah. Pretty much."

They rode the elevator in silence. At street level, he led her down a short hall to his building's reception area. Security doors and walls of clear, bulletproof acrylic separated the reception from the main public lobby for the tower, another nod to Adi's paranoia about his safety.

The receptionist smiled at him. She sat behind a glass desk with a slanted top that was a display and control console for the building. Opposite her, white leather couches and a low glass table formed the waiting area, empty this morning. Recent issues of the Dream Rider lay scattered on the table.

Bevington stood by the doors leading from reception to the public lobby. The guard eyed Case, but at a nod from Will, he pressed his hand against a palm reader. One door swung open. Case stepped through, ignoring Bevington's scowl. Will followed her.

Case headed across the lobby for the exit to the street.

"Hey!" he said.

She turned back. "You coming?"

He swallowed. Was he coming? He watched the traffic and people streaming by in the summer rain outside his tower home. *Outside.* He shivered. His guts clenched. Sweat beaded on his brow. He stuffed his hands into his jean pockets to hide their trembling. "No. I have...stuff to do. You know, the three fingers."

She considered him for a moment, then shrugged and started toward the street again. She reached the revolving doors. In a second, she'd be out-side—and maybe out of his life forever.

"Will I see you again?" he called. *Really? That's how you had to phrase it?*

She stopped, her back to him. Turning, she considered him from across the lobby. "You're a nice guy."

"Uh, okay."

"You have lots of stuff."

"Yeah?"

"I don't. You have money. I don't. You have a big home. I don't. All I have—*all* I have—is my brother. And I'm going to find him." With that, she pushed through the doors and stepped outside.

Outside. Where he could never go, could never follow. She disappeared into the rain and the crowds, heading west. He stood there, staring at where she'd vanished from his view, staring at passersby scurrying along. Living their lives, lives he could never have.

Outside.

Turning away, he walked back to the elevator.

Adi was waiting for him in his studio beside his design table, one foot tapping a silent rhythm on the carpet. *Shit, she is pissed.* "How'd you know I'd come here?" he said.

"I know you, William. I know your habits. And—"

"Don't start."

"And I know you are buying yourself a mountain of trouble."

"I have money. I can afford to buy stuff. And I've always wanted a mountain."

"I saw how you looked at that girl—"

"Her name is Case."

"—and she'll cost you much more than money."

"You haven't even heard her story."

"Because you didn't tell me."

He sighed. "Fair enough. I'll tell you now. If you'll listen."

She looked hurt. "Of course, I'll listen."

"Okay, let's sit." He collapsed onto the couch. God, he was tired. He'd had only a few hours of sleep on his aborted Dream search. And the rest of the night and morning had not exactly been relaxing. He laid his head back on the cool leather. A faint but now familiar musky scent rose from it.

Case. She'd slept here.

"William, you're exhausted," Adi said, concern on her face. "Get some sleep. We'll do this later."

He rubbed his eyes. "Nah. Let's do it now, while it's still fresh. Even if I'm not."

He related Case's story and the events that followed right up to where Adi had joined his meeting with the cops.

When he finished, she was silent for a while. "Do you believe her?"

"Yes."

She raised an eyebrow. "A woman who glows in the dark with tattoos that move and disappear? A ghoulish man chasing her with a slingshot? Another with knives? And yet, she *somehow* escaped all three *and* broke into this supposedly secure building?"

"Why would she make a lie that weird? Plus, she was scared—for herself and for her brother. And she strikes me as someone who doesn't scare easily. Adi, kids *are* disappearing. I think her brother's the latest."

"Perhaps. What did Mr. Lyle say when you called him?"

"An impressive string of four-letter words for waking him at four AM. But he remembered Case and Fader when I texted him their photo. He'll ask his street contacts, but he doubts he'll get much. He pointed out he came to me for exactly the help I'm asking for."

"An accurate observation. Perhaps Mr. Zhang and his team will have more success."

Winstone Zhang was a former captain in the Hong Kong police force. He led Will's private investigation and security unit. "Hope so. I don't expect much from the cops." He rubbed his face. "There's something else." He related his encounter with the Gray Boys in Dream.

"I'll admit it stretches coincidence," Adi said. "You search for four missing boys and find four strange ones. But you don't know for certain. And you don't know what's happened to them. Perhaps they were having nightmares—understandable if they've been kidnapped. You may have seen how their fears manifested in Dream."

"All four having the *same* dream? All four looking identical, even down to the creepy eyes and monochromatic fashion sense? And talking and moving in perfect unison?" He shook his head. "No. They were the four I searched for. And whatever's happened to them, it wasn't on our list."

Adi got up, smoothing her skirt and straightening her jacket. "You need to sleep. I'll also have Mr. Zhang search for buildings with signage starting with an 'H'. And follow up with the police and Mr. Lyle throughout the day."

His three fingers. While he worried about the fourth one—Case, out on the streets alone. In the meantime, he planned to add a fifth finger tonight. Or was that a thumb?

He stretched out on the couch. "Works for me. But wake me by noon. I need to sleep tonight to go into Dream. No use trying in the day. Not enough sleepers."

"You're going into Dream again? After what happened to you last night?"

"I can handle myself there. It's my world."

"What are you doing tonight?"

He hesitated. "Looking for Fader." *Partly true.*

"Fader? Or his sister?"

He felt himself redden. "Both. Either. If I can't find Fader myself, then Case could help. She'll have memories of her brother. The Rider can access those in Dream, use them to track him. Besides, she's in danger out there. I want her to know she can stay here if she gets in trouble."

"That girl *is* trouble."

"Stop it, Adi. I know what I'm doing."

"I don't like it."

"You mean you don't like her."

"No, I don't. But I'm more concerned she's met you in real life. What if she recognizes you through your Rider costume?"

"The Rider's hood hides his face. Anyway, she'd think it's her dream—that she's making it up from her subconscious. She meets the guy who writes the Rider comics during the day, so she dreams about him that night. Plus, my Rider persona acts different from me." At least, he thought it did.

Adi was silent for a moment "Have you ever wondered why that is?"

Because he's not broken. He closed his eyes. "Adi, kinda tired. Just cuz I'm on a couch doesn't mean you can play shrink."

He heard her sigh as she left the studio. The click of her heels on the running track faded into the distance. Turning onto his side, he breathed in Case's smell from the couch and let sleep take him.

Chapter 13

Monster Hospital

Fader followed the two silent boys, Link and Tumble, along the dark hall, keeping well back. Ahead of them, the red-haired woman seemed to float in a dancing globe of candlelight. Reaching the end of the hall, she turned a corner to her right. The boys followed her. Catching up, Fader peeked around the corner.

At the end of a shorter hall, the woman stopped beside an open door to the corner room. A brightness flickered within. The silent boys carried their still sleeping burdens of Slip and Rattle into the room. The woman followed them inside, pushing the door almost closed behind her. A sliver of light still showed along its edge.

Creeping to the door, Fader listened at the open crack. Two voices—one female, one male. Cautiously, he pushed the door open far enough to peer inside.

The room was large. The tiny room he'd escaped would fit inside many times. Ten steps away stood the red-haired woman, her back to him, Link and Tumble to her left. Link still held Slip in his arms. The other sleeping boy, Rattle, lay on a hospital bed to the woman's right.

Dark curtains covered the windows but torches flamed on the walls, sending shadows slinking around the room. Two high-backed chairs sat in the far corner to the left. In front of the chairs lay a round red-and-black rug. The rug bore a strange design—three bent skeleton legs arranged like clock hands inside a circle, as if they were chasing each other.

On the wall behind the chairs, a painting hung. In it, a thin man with cruel sharp features and long black hair sat on a chair like those in this room. The man's clothes reminded Fader of pictures in history books in the library. Beside the man stood a tall red-haired woman in a blue gown. Around her neck hung a pendant with the same symbol as on the carpet. She looked a lot like this woman.

The male voice spoke again, pulling Fader's attention from the painting. "You're certain of this one's age?"

Just past the woman, Fader saw the end of another hospital bed. The woman faced the bed. Fader realized the man speaking lay there, hidden from view by the woman. The man sounded old and weak but menacing despite that. Fader tried to imagine the face behind that voice, and images rose in his head of street people Case had taught him to avoid.

"Quite certain, my love," the woman replied. Fader found her voice beautiful, too. "Trust in me. Have I ever failed you?"

"The last boy struck close enough to failure, Morrigan. I lack the strength to survive another mistake."

Morrigan. Even her name was beautiful. The woman called Morrigan stiffened. "That boy lied or did not know his age. Marell, all I do is for you and our quest."

"Yes, yes. But how can you be any more certain of this one?" He waved at where Rattle lay on the other bed.

"This time, we will have a second prepared." She indicated Slip. "In case you require another vessel." She glanced around the room. "Where is the new boy?"

"What new boy?" the man replied.

"Did Mr. Stryke not bring a boy to you tonight? A younger one?"

"I have not seen Stryke, nor did he bring me anything. What are you on about?"

Morrigan nodded slowly. "No matter. I believe I understand." Her voice now carried the same hint of menace as the man's. She raised her hands, and her cape fell back to reveal the smooth whiteness of her arms. She chanted in a singsong rhythm, using words Fader didn't understand.

Strange gold markings appeared on her left arm, from her bare shoulder to her fingertips. The marks reminded him of symbols he'd seen on posters for a Hong Kong movie festival, but they weren't quite the same.

The marks began to move, dancing in time to her chanting, sliding into new positions along her arm. She fell silent. The marks stopped moving, sinking into her skin as if they were tats.

Morrigan thrust up her arm. The symbols flowed over her skin, streaming from her fingertips like a writhing sunbeam. Above her, the symbols formed into a glowing bird, with wings wider than Fader was tall. Hovering near the ceiling, the bird flapped once, twice, and then shot forward.

Straight for him.

He ducked back. The bird passed through the closed door, paused in mid-air, and then flew down the corridor to his right. As it disappeared into the darkness, he breathed a silent sigh of relief.

He looked back through the door. Morrigan now stood beside the bed, still hiding its occupant except for his lower legs. The man wore black shoes that shone in the flickering light, black socks, and black pants. He was very short.

Given how close Morrigan was to him, the man's head and shoulders should have been visible.

Gripping the raised side of the hospital bed, Morrigan wheeled the bed around. And Fader saw the man who lay on it.

He shivered. Not a man. A boy. No. Not a boy either. He didn't know what this person was. The man-boy looked like a skeleton. The skin on his face was gray and so thin it showed his skull underneath. His hollowed chest was a crater beneath his black jacket and white shirt. His hands twitched like gray spiders crawling from his sleeves. He was a bit taller than Case.

Morrigan pushed the bed alongside where Rattle lay.

"Hurry," rasped the thing on the bed, "I have stayed too long in this one. I am dying."

"Marell, I will not lose you. You will continue," Morrigan said, "but first I must prepare him."

Turning to the sleeping Rattle, she pulled up the sleeve of his torn t-shirt. She raised her left hand, forefinger extended. The finger glowed, brighter and brighter until Fader could no longer look at it. She moved her finger over his skin as if writing, beginning at his shoulder and ending at his hand. Golden symbols like those he'd seen on Morrigan herself flamed into visibility on the boy's arm. As she moved to trace the next, each symbol disappeared.

When she finished, she took Rattle's hand, the one on which she'd just written. She laid it on the withered hand of the thing she called Marell. Covering their hands with her own, she chanted. Again, the weird symbols danced along her arms. She faced where Fader peeked through the door. The symbols, glowing golden, now covered her face, long neck, and the top of her breasts where they showed above her low-cut top.

She was the most beautiful thing he'd ever seen. Her chanting continued, her voice rising and falling, rising and falling, rising and falling...

Strong hands closed on both his shoulders like twin clamps. He screamed. Wrenching free, he spun around.

A crowd of silent boys surrounded him, staring at him with those awful dead eyes. He recognized more faces but didn't have time to think. The nearest boy reached for him. Fader let out another yell and leaped backwards, crashing into the door. The door swung open, slamming against the wall. He fell into the room. He looked up.

Morrigan stood where she had been, her hands on her hips and her eyes on him. The glowing symbols were gone from her skin. To her left, Rattle sat with his legs over the side of the bed, staring hard at Fader. That look made Fader turn to Morrigan instead.

She smiled down warmly at him. "There you are, little one. I knew you were around somewhere. That's why I sent my Hollow Boys to find you. Thoughtful of them to wait until I finished here." She flicked a finger, and the nearest boy pulled Fader to his feet.

Behind him, the silent boys blocked the doorway. No escape that way. Hollow Boys, she called them. What did that mean?

Morrigan helped Rattle ease himself onto the floor. The boy stood on shaking legs, gripping the table for support, while Morrigan held him on the other side.

"Marell, my love, my life," Morrigan said.

Marell? Morrigan had called the man-boy on the bed that name. Now she called Rattle that. What was going on?

She stroked Rattle's hair with her free hand. "It worked. Again."

Rattle brushed her hand away. He considered the man-boy lying motionless on the bed. "None too soon, it appears."

A jolt of fear hit Fader. Rattle now sounded like the thing on the bed. Stronger, but that same rasping voice, that same hint of menace. Fader didn't know how, but he knew this boy wasn't Rattle anymore.

Morrigan laid a finger on the man-boy's neck. Her shoulders slumped, and the joy on her face faded. "Dead," she said, her voice soft. She turned toward Fader. "He will not join you after all, my children." Fader realized she was talking to the Hollow Boys.

Rattle-Marell's eyes fell on Fader again. "Is this the one you lost?"

Morrigan flinched. "Misplaced."

The boy now called Marell regarded Fader. Marell's eyes seemed to slice layers from him, exposing what lay inside. Fader tried to look away but couldn't. "He's young," Marell said.

"The youngest yet," she replied. "What's your name, child?"

Fader swallowed. "They call me Fader," he whispered.

"Fader," Morrigan repeated slowly, as if tasting it. "Odd."

"Let's hope I won't need him, whatever his name," Marell said. Shaking himself free of her arm, he straightened and then let go of the table. He raised his hands before him, opening and closing them into fists several times. "This one is strong. Stronger than the last."

"The strongest I could find."

Marell considered her, as if seeing her for the first time. A look of hunger filled his eyes. Reaching up, he buried his fingers in the red billows of her hair and pulled her mouth down into a long savage kiss. He released her with a laugh. Morrigan laughed too.

"The strongest you could find? Well, then," Marell said, pushing her onto the now empty bed, "let's see just how strong." He waved at where Fader watched, the Hollow Boys arrayed behind him. "Send them away."

Morrigan raised her arm. The symbols appeared and did their dance. A golden bird materialized, then shot toward Fader, striking him in the chest. His eyes grew heavy, his limbs weak. He collapsed into the arms of a Hollow Boy. The last thing he remembered was Morrigan's beautiful face smiling at him as Marell ripped off her cape.

Naked, Morrigan slid quietly off the bed. Behind her, Marell slept in his latest body, exhausted after their lovemaking. She smiled. His new host was strong indeed and (thank the Goddess) still carried Marell's knowledge of what she liked in bed.

She retrieved her clothes from the floor and dressed. Time to check on her Hollow Boys. Fastening her cape around her shoulders, she left the room and her sleeping lover.

The light of a gray morning lit the corridors, creeping through cracks in the boarded windows. Dust motes swirled in the dim light as she walked. She cast a rune script from her arm to have her Hollow Boys mop again.

Her Hollow Boys. *Hers.* Once, each had hosted Marell. But one by one, he had been forced to abandon them. And then...

Then they belonged to her.

She checked on the newly captured boys in the barred room. They slept again under her spell. Only two now. She'd need to find another. Marell was consuming them faster and faster. She wanted at least three in reserve.

She knelt beside the youngest, the one called Fader. Brushing his curly black hair back from his face, she stroked his cheek. Such a beautiful child. This one, more than any other they'd taken, she wished to keep unbroken. For herself.

Perhaps she could—if their long-sought prey was in this city. She remembered the astral force she'd detected in the white tower where that troublesome girl had fled. Who else could hold such power? It must be him. If so, Marell would finally be restored.

She hadn't told Marell yet. Transferring him to his new body had been her priority, and then her own body had become his priority. She'd tell him when he awoke, and together they would decide how to proceed.

In the meantime, she had her boys.

Locking the barred room, she left Link and Tumble on guard. She descended to the second floor. This floor housed the hospital's wards, each much larger than the private and semi-private rooms on the third.

Walking to the southeast corner, she entered the largest ward. Twenty beds, arranged in two long rows, stretched the length of the room. On each, a Hollow Boy (or in some cases, a Hollow Man) lay immobile, eyes closed, arms folded on their chest.

Morrigan arranged them by age, for no reason other than she liked order. The row to her left held the oldest ones, ranging from twenty-eight years of age down to twenty-one.

The more recent additions lay in the row to her right, ranging from twenty down to seventeen. She moved along that row, brushing her fingers over the feet of seven boys—her favorites of those lying here. At her touch, each boy rose silently and fell into step behind her.

She led them to a smaller ward, empty of beds. In the center of the room, eight metal chairs surrounded a rectangular wooden table. Glass-doored cupboards, some still containing medical supplies, lined one wall. Beside a sink in a far corner, a small refrigerator stood, its contents kept cold by a simple spell.

Seating herself at the head of the table, she smiled at the boys. And nodded.

At once, the boys moved to the cupboards and the refrigerator. Retrieving their assigned items, they carried them back. A minute later, the table was set.

Atop a white and blue tablecloth, eight Wedgwood china teacups sat in eight saucers, each with a tiny silver spoon. Beside each cup lay a matching plate bearing a blueberry scone and silver butter knife.

In front of Morrigan sat a white china teapot with a blue tea cozy. She touched the pot, and steam rose from its spout. Beside the pot sat a jar of strawberry jam and a bowl with clotted cream. When the boys were seated, she smiled at their blank faces. "Who would like tea?"

As one, the seven Hollow Boys nodded. Once. Twice. One by one, each boy passed her his teacup, which she filled and passed back. One boy started the cream around the table, another the jam.

When each had their tea and scones, they turned again in unison toward her. She smiled again. "Shall we begin?"

Again came the synchronized nods—one, two. Lifting her cup to her lips, she took a sip. Each boy did the same. She broke her scone in half. Each boy did likewise. The boys mirrored her every motion.

As she sipped her tea, she wondered again how it would feel to have a child of her own, a family of her own. Long ago, she had hoped she and Marell...

She left the thought unfinished. The past was dead, and that hope had died with it many years ago.

She looked around the table. *This* was her family, the only one she would ever have. A growing family, at least. Since each addition to her Hollow Boys was younger than the one before, that boy became her new "baby."

Which was why the boy's death tonight had hit her so hard. She should have expected it. Marell's bodies were decaying faster each time, and he had stayed too long in that one. But it had still been like losing a son in childbirth. Losing him as he was born—born into the life of a Hollow Boy.

However, given the speed at which Marell was using up hosts, she would soon have another child to care for. She sighed. It would be wonderful to have a real boy, not one of these broken things.

That made her think again of the boy called Fader.

A rune script tickled her arm, pulling her from her musings. She smiled as she recognized the tracking spell from last night. That irksome girl had just left the strange protection of the white tower.

"Now I have you, my dear," she whispered.

Chapter 14

I Know You're Out There Somewhere

Outside the white tower, Mr. Stryke sat on a bench in the light drizzle, killing pigeons. The slingshot the little man used was almost invisible. Two flesh-colored thimbles slipped over the index and middle finger of his left hand. A clear rubber band, with a clear cup that could hold ball bearings of various sizes, connected the thimbles.

By resting his left arm on his knee, hand palm down, he could pick off the birds with no witnesses. He killed without looking at his prey. His peripheral vision was excellent.

After a moment, he'd stroll over to the dead bird, shaking his head as if in sympathy. Like a good citizen, he would carry the pigeon to a garbage can, enjoying the bird's fading warmth in his hand. He'd then move on to another bench.

For four hours, he'd watched the white tower as Morrigan had ordered. In that time, he'd killed twenty-two birds, circling the block three times. And not once had the distracted office workers scurrying by given him more than a passing glance.

Somewhere on the opposite side of this tower, Mr. Stayne kept his own watch, amusing himself in his own way. Looking at girls passing by, probably. Stayne liked to look at girls.

Stryke gasped, crying out from a sudden burning pain on the back of his left hand. The rune characters Morrigan had drawn on his skin now glowed with a faint golden light.

He touched the symbols. "Mistress?" he whispered.

Morrigan's voice sounded in his head, as if calling to him down a long metal corridor. Jumping to his feet, he wove his way west along King Street as she completed her instructions. She broke contact just as Stayne met him at the corner. He had, no doubt, received a similar message.

"Can you see the guttersnipe?" Stryke asked his taller companion.

Stayne peered west along the street, then nodded. They headed in that direction, following the girl who'd escaped them last night, but keeping a discreet distance.

"You received the same instructions?" Stayne asked.

Stryke did not point out he'd no way of knowing what instructions his partner had received. "Follow. Grab her, discreetly. Bring her to the hospital. For questioning."

Stayne smiled. "For questioning," he repeated, as if savoring the word. "Something in this white tower has captured the witch's interest."

"Perhaps our prey?"

"Perhaps. Did she say anything else?"

Stryke's fists clenched. "Not to lose her this time."

Stayne didn't reply, making Stryke think this last instruction had been for him. "Weren't just us what lost her," Stryke muttered. "Her Ladyship's spells failed on the little bitch, too."

Stayne remained silent. Stryke didn't like his failure discussed. And he was quite aware he'd failed. Even now, he couldn't believe it. He never missed (well, that once in Budapest, but his target had stumbled). And never four successive times. Four!

Slipping his left hand into the pocket of his long black coat, he fingered the carved maple curves of his Betsy. His pride and joy. His master slingshot. Through a brief gap in the crowd, he caught sight of the girl ahead. *Well, dearie, I won't miss again.*

Morrigan walked the hospital grounds, arm in arm with Marell in his latest body. A late evening wind blew off the lake cool and crisp, washed clean of city smells by the day's rain.

Marell once again wore his black suit, black shoes, and white shirt, all now a tad large. She wore a pale-green silk blouse with tight black slacks and open-toed white sandals with a low heel. Under her arm, she carried a newspaper.

She had just told Marell of what she had sensed in the white tower last night. The force that had pushed her away.

"Magicks?" he asked, looking up at her.

She shook her head, still not used to his new face and even shorter stature. "I detected no spell. No, it was an astral power. And strong, like none I've ever encountered—save for the one we seek."

Marell stopped walking. He gazed out over the lake below where sails and whitecaps dotted the green-blue surface. "We know he is in this metropolis," he said, excitement in his voice. "Who else could it be? Has our quest finally ended?"

She did not reply. Marell had tracked their prey to this city. But he had grown too weak to project his astral spirit to continue their search. He now required all his strength just to stay alive in a series of quickly discarded hosts. Morrigan had feared that their prey might escape while she worked to find Marell a new host.

"Once I have adjusted to this new body," Marell said, "I will travel to this tower. I will know if it is our prey." A smile crept onto his face. "Oh, yes, I will know him. But for now, I am still too weak, even with your magicks."

She waited for a word of thanks or sign of gratitude but none came. They resumed walking. "There is something else," she said. "A newspaper reporter has begun a series on missing street urchins." She handed Marell the paper she carried, open to the front page.

He read the article. "He lists names."

"Yes. Of ones we've taken."

He twisted the paper in his fist. "We take them because they are unwanted. Invisible. This meddler makes them visible." He read the byline. "Harry Lyle."

"There's more." She handed him a business card.

He scowled at it. "Mr. Lyle again. Where did you get this?"

"From the pocket of our most recent acquisition. The boy who intruded on us last night."

"This Lyle is too close. We must remove him."

"Stryke and Stayne?"

"No. It must appear to be natural causes. Can you set a tracking spell for him? Something to mark him?"

"I have his name. And something he once held—this card. That is sufficient."

"Excellent. Have it in place before nightfall. Before he sleeps."

"Certainly. But mark him for what?"

Marell smiled. "I will send a Mara to him."

Morrigan shuddered. A terrible death. At least Stryke or Stayne would be quick.

"What a beautiful evening!" Marell exclaimed as they continued to stroll. "A wonderful day to be alive."

※

Will sat in lotus position on his circular bed. He gazed out of his windows, south past the lower downtown to where the dying sunset silvered the lake. The dance of light on the water helped focus his meditation as he prepared for

Dream.

He rarely started a ride this early, but he'd promised Case he'd find her brother. And his other three fingers were pointing to nothing. Harry Lyle, Winstone Zhang, and the police had discovered zilch on Fader's disappearance.

He had to rely on the Rider to find Fader tonight. And he wanted to give his alter ego as much time as possible in Dream.

Slowly, his meditation banished his anxiety. The calmness and clarity he needed for Dream settled on him like a familiar set of clothes. Calling into his mind the search construct he used for Doogles, he modified their design.

His last Ride had resulted in three dead Doogles. He'd decided to include logic not only for how Doogles searched but also what to avoid. Now, any Doogle encountering a Gray Boy would send Will a message along its leash. The Doogle would follow the boys if possible, but if pursued, it would break off and return to Will.

Next, he created and memorized three new sets of search data. The first was for Harry Lyle. Harry had met Fader. The Rider might pull additional information on Fader from Harry's subconscious. Something Harry hadn't included in his research files.

The other two data sets were for Fader and Case. Fader's included his photograph plus what Case had told him about her brother. His likes, his dislikes, his fascination with the Dream Rider.

For Case, he focused on his memories of their short time together. How she looked, her facial expressions, her mercurial moods. The sound of her voice, how she walked, how she smelled. The way she tilted her head, the curve of her neck...

He stopped. *Oh, crap. I've got it bad.*

Shaking his head, he returned to his meditation. He memorized the three new data structures until he was certain Nyx could pull them quickly from his subconscious.

Finally ready, he lay back on his bed and closed his eyes.

"He only comes out at night," he whispered in the dark. "He only comes out at night. He only..."

The doors to sleep swung open, and he stepped into Dream.

That evening, Case sat on a bench outside the change house at Cherry Beach. She was eating a hot dog, a gift from the vendor stationed here through the summer. The rain had stopped earlier, and now the dying sunset sparkled the waves of the lake. On most days, this place, one of her favorites in the city, would have lightened even her darkest mood.

But not this time.

She'd spent the day searching their regular haunts, looking for anyone who'd seen Fader. Or knew something about the disappearances. She checked with everyone on the street she could find. She'd even asked shop owners and vendors friendly to her and her brother.

No one knew anything, though several mentioned other kids they hadn't seen lately. A few recognized Tall Boy and Shorty from her description. No one had seen the red-haired woman.

Finishing her hot dog, she washed up in the change house. So tired. If she didn't sleep soon, she'd collapse. Time to find Rattle's crash site. And hope nobody was using it.

She walked east along the bike path that cut through the small park above the beach. Grass and sand gave way to trees as the path wound through thick groves of black willows, aspen, and birch.

Rattle was a street kid, older than her. He'd found a tiny hidden clearing along this shoreline. He'd let Case and Fader sleep there last summer. That set-up seemed sweet until she woke up one night with Rattle on top of her. She'd fought him hard, but he was bigger and stronger. He would've got what he wanted if Fader, awakened by her screams, hadn't bashed him with a piece of driftwood. Case added three kicks to the groin. They'd left Rattle lying on the sand moaning. She hadn't planned to return.

But she wasn't going back to the church basement. The street was saying Rattle had disappeared. She didn't wish that even on Rattle. But if it was true, then his secret crash site should be available—if she could find it again.

The light was dying when she spotted the concealed opening in the woods, almost invisible from the bike path. She squeezed her way through a maze of trees and dense undergrowth, emerging into the hidden clearing. Trees ran down to the water to her left and right, enclosing a tiny patch of beach and grass.

Rattle's dirty green sleeping bag lay on the grass beside a makeshift fire pit. A layer of sand and leaves covered the bag. Pop cans, beer bottles, and empty fast-food containers lay scattered. Nothing seemed recent.

Deeming the place safe, she shook off the sleeping bag and lay on it. With the sun down, the breeze off the waves brought a chill. She pulled her jacket over her for a blanket.

Not her jacket. Will's jacket. She smelled him on it.

Stop it, she told herself yet again. All day, although sick with worry about Fader, her thoughts had returned over and over to the strange guy in the strange tower. And now she was doing it again. She needed to sleep, not think about some weird rich guy. Weird, rich, *cute* guy...

Stop it!

But Will seemed nice. And funny. With genuine concern for Fader and helping her find him.

And he seemed to like her...

Stop it!

God, what would a guy with his money ever want with her? A street kid. A girl with nothing. All she had was Fader, and she'd let those creeps take him. She was useless. They would've taken her, too, if her Voice hadn't helped.

Which reminded her—her Voice had fallen silent. She hadn't heard it since it had helped her sneak into Will's tower last night.

Her Voice didn't always speak to her. It wasn't as if they held daily "S'up?" chats. But if she needed it, the Voice answered her call. And if she was in danger, the Voice warned her, as it had last night.

So where was it? She couldn't think of a greater need than she had right now. *Please, speak to me. Help me find Fader.*

Silence was her only reply.

Overhead, stars winked into life, pushing through the glare of the city. She closed her eyes, seeking sleep amidst the whirl of faces and fears in her head.

Fader. Will. Her Voice. The red-haired woman. Tall Boy and Shorty. Around and around they spun until sleep finally took her.

Mr. Stayne crept silently along the bike path winding through the woods. Night had fallen. A single crescent moon hung low over the lake, its points turned skywards as if waiting to catch a falling star. The sliver of a moon gave little light, even less so amongst the trees, but Stayne didn't need light. He listened. And sniffed.

"We've lost her," Mr. Stryke hissed from behind him.

"Quiet," Stayne snapped in a hoarse rasp over his shoulder.

They'd followed the girl from a distance all day, waiting for her to be alone and unobserved. They'd watched hidden behind a car in the beach's parking lot as she ate her hot dog. When she set out along this path after sunset, they'd followed again.

But the path twisted its way through thick groves of trees, and the girl soon disappeared ahead of them. When they had emerged from the woods onto a long stretch of road, the girl was gone.

They'd turned back then, searching the trees lining the path. They were now on their third circuit of the route.

"We should call the witch," Stryke said. "She can use her tracking spell."

Stayne stopped, so suddenly his partner bumped into him in the dim light. Stayne stared down at his smaller companion. "Call the witch? Tell her the girl escaped us? *Again?* Do you think that wise, old friend?"

Stryke's hands balled into fists. "No," he growled.

"We'll find her. She left the path before the road," Stayne said, for the third time. "She hides in these woods."

"You don't know that," Stryke replied, for the third time.

A breeze wafted past them through the trees. Stayne sniffed. He smiled. There.

Girl smell.

"Oh, but I *do*," he whispered. He touched his nose. Stryke smiled. Stayne resumed walking, sniffing the air, Stryke following. As Stayne walked, his knives slid into his hands. *Soon, sweet meat. Soon.*

Chapter 15

Street Fighting Woman

C ase was dreaming. Or, at least, she thought she was.

She stood on a city street lined with gleaming office towers. Some leaned at crazy angles. Some rose so tall they vanished into clouds sliding across a too blue sky. Instead of streetlights, statues of cats with flaming eyes lined sidewalks of green crystal. Beside them, Egyptian vases (correction, "canopic jars") took the place of garbage cans.

Between the crystal sidewalks ran an ebony road. No—not a road. She blinked. Red-sailed boats and gray swans now floated down a sluggish black river.

Part of her knew she lay asleep in the hidden grove at Cherry Beach, so this must be a dream. And yet, every sight shone clear and bright. Each smell wafted thick and rich. Every noise rang sharp and crisp. This dream felt more *real* than any she remembered, more real even than waking life.

A movement caught her eye. She stiffened as a creature loped around a corner of the nearest building, a tall white tower. She stepped back, then relaxed. It was a dog.

She blinked. Or not.

The creature was dog-shaped with white and black splotches like a Dalmatian. But the rest of its features were very non-doggish. Its eyes and ears were huge and round. It had large nostrils at the end of a flexible snout that twisted back and forth as it snuffled along the ground.

Its head snapped up, eyes locking on her. It sniffed again. A thin tail shot straight up—a tail so long it had to be twice the creature's length. The thing trotted towards her.

It looked so comical and enough like a weird friendly dog that she felt no danger. *Besides, I'm just dreaming. Right?*

Reaching her, the creature sniffed her leg. Its tail coiled into a spiral. Around its neck, a silver collar appeared. From it, a silver cord grew, suspended in the air like a leash held by an invisible dog-walker.

The cord disappeared around the corner of the white tower where the dog creature had appeared. Sitting down, the animal gazed up at her with an expression that, on a human, she'd call a satisfied grin.

Case considered the floating silver strand. She frowned at the strange beast. "Am I supposed to follow that?" she asked, feeling ridiculous talking to the thing.

To her surprise, it shook its head.

"O—kay. Should I wait here?"

A nod.

She considered the cord again. "Is that your leash? Are we waiting for your master?"

Two nods.

"Is your master nice?"

The creature nodded so fast, its big ears flopped back and forth with a slapping sound.

She laughed. "Okay, okay. I'll wait for your wonderful master."

The grin on the thing's face grew bigger. Its strange tail curled into an even tighter spiral.

"What's your name?" she said, not expecting a reply.

A silver tag popped into existence, dangling from the creature's collar. It had writing on it. She bent down closer.

"Hello," she read. "My name is—"

"Brian," came a voice.

"Shit," she cried, jumping back, startled.

A guy stood three paces away, one foot on a skateboard. He held the end of the silver leash in his hand. A guy in a hooded costume. A very familiar costume.

"Holy crap. You're that comic book guy!"

"Graphic novels."

"The Dream Rider. You're the Dream Rider."

The Rider gave a deep bow. "At your service." His voice was deep and husky.

She saw nothing but blackness inside his hood. "Why are you in my dream?"

"Will sent me."

"Will?"

"Will Dreycott." He sounded disappointed. "You met him today. Up there." He jabbed a thumb towards the white tower looming above them.

"Yeah, I know. I'm just surprised I'm dreaming about him. I mean, what does that say? Sure, he seems nice and kinda cute—"

The Rider stepped closer. "You think he's cute?"

"What? No!" She appraised her dream visitor, running her eyes over his slim, muscled frame. And his skin-tight costume that was...well, tight. Everywhere.

"I'd like to dream about you walking away from me," she muttered.

"What?"

"Nothing. What do you mean he *sent* you?"

"To find you. Will's...a friend of mine."

"This is the weirdest dream. Why find me?"

"To help you find Fader."

Case swallowed, suddenly guilty. Here she was fantasizing about muscle-ly guys, while her little brother was still missing. "You can't help me. I'm dreaming you. I'm making you up. I met Will, who does your comics—"

"Graphic novels."

"—and Fader loves your comics—"

"He has excellent taste."

"—and all I've been thinking of is finding Fader. That's why I'm dreaming about you helping me find him. Dreams are how we process what happens to us each day, right?"

"That's one theory."

"So that's why you're here. I'm just dreaming you."

"No, I found you. In Dream."

"Dream?"

"Where we are now." He waved his arms. "An entire land created from all the dreams being dreamed everywhere in the world. Dream is where you go when you, well, dream. Where you can meet and interact with other dreamers if you know how. If you read my stories, you'd know that."

"Yeah. Right."

"Didn't expect you to believe me. So, pretend I'm your subconscious, and you're having an incredibly detailed and coherent dream—"

"There. You see? I was just thinking that."

"Proving you're predictable."

"Now my subconscious is insulting me. What's that say about me? Okay. Whatever. It's just a dream. So, subconscious-me, how will you help me find Fader?"

"Actually, *you* will help *me*. Well, me and Brian."

She looked down at the dog creature, which was rubbing its head against her leg. "So what *is* Brian?"

"He's a Doogle."

"Doogle?"

"He's a dog who searches Dream for things I'm looking for."

"A dog...that searches." She smiled despite herself. "Cute. My mind is even weirder than I thought." She scratched Brian behind his ears. Brian responded by curling and uncurling his tail several times. "What's with the tail curling?"

"He's happy."

"He can't wag?"

"With those tails, wagging is whipping. Very painful."

"Weirder and weirder. Okay, I've conjured a fictional comic book dude from my subconscious to help me find my brother." She shrugged. "Why not? Maybe my subconscious can remember something I can't."

"Thank you. I love being humored."

"So how does this work?"

The Rider held out a crystal ball on his outstretched palm. Leaning closer, she saw a swirling cloud of numbers, letters, and pictures. She caught a flash of the photograph of her and Fader she'd given to Will.

"This data ball," the Rider said, "has everything you told Will about Fader." He held it out to Brian.

Brian sniffed at the ball, then shot out a long black tongue to suck it into his mouth. Silver lights flashed and danced in his huge black eyes.

"I gave that same data to three other Doogles and sent them to look for Fader." He raised his hand. Three more silver cords appeared around his wrist, stretching down the street. He ran his fingers across the cords. "But so far, none of them have found anything. I'm hoping you can give Brian more to work with. Concentrate on Fader—and on last night, when that woman and those two men attacked you."

She preferred to forget rather than remember last night. Still, maybe her subconscious was right. She might discover a clue to finding Fader. "Okay, I'll give it a shot."

Closing her eyes, she focused on that night in the church basement. Her Voice waking her. The golden light in the hall. Tall Boy and Shorty. The beautiful but frightening red-haired woman with the strange inner glow and stranger moving tattoos. Her nightmare escape from the church. Trapped on the street between Tall Boy and the woman. Trapped, trapped, trapped...

"Case!"

Someone was shaking her. She opened her eyes. The Rider gripped her arms, his hooded face before her.

The scene had changed. Night had fallen. Flickering flames from the cat statues now lit the street. The tall white towers were gone. In their place, black churches with crumbling domes loomed like a canopy of shadows. Triangular fins cut the surface of the black river, long shapes undulating beneath them.

"Get back," the Rider yelled. He jumped forward, his eyes on something behind her.

She turned to look. Down the darkened street, a black ball twice her height careened toward them, bouncing off church fronts and cat statues. As it neared, she saw it wasn't a single object, but a seething mass of smaller ones, each a spinning jumble of spikes crackling with electricity. A high-pitched screech like metal scraping on metal tore at her ears.

"Nyx!" the Rider shouted over the squealing. "Shield and sword! Now!"

A crystal sphere popped into each of his hands. One ball morphed into a round shield, the other a sword. Both glowed silver in the darkness. Standing in front of her, the Rider raised the shield. The spinning mass gave one final bounce and hurtled down at them.

Desperate for a weapon of her own, she spun around, searching the ground. There. The Rider's skateboard. Grabbing it by one end with both hands, she stepped up beside him.

"No! Stay behind me," he yelled.

Screw that. As the black cloud descended, she swung the skateboard with all her strength.

The shock of the impact shivered down the board into her arms. The cloud exploded in a shower of sparks, scattering the creatures in all directions. Ozone stung her nostrils. Several of the things, each the size of a basketball, lay stunned and twitching on the sidewalk. She stomped on them. They disappeared with a squeal and puff of smoke.

The rest reformed into smaller clumps, bobbing back and forth several paces away. Raising the board again, she advanced on them. "What? Still want a piece of me? Well, c'mon! Hit me with your best shot."

The things retreated before her. When she continued to advance, each clump broke apart into individual spiny black balls. The closest ones quivered for a second, then vanished with a loud crack and more smoke. The rest of the things followed, filling the night air with a cacophony of screeches and squeals. Lowering the skateboard, she turned around.

The Rider stood leaning on his crystal sword. "Can I have my skateboard back now?"

Dropping the board, she kicked it to him. "Sorry, did I mess up your hero moment?"

He tossed the sword and shield into the air. They vanished with a pop. "Yeah, kinda."

She shrugged. "Well, I'm used to guys trying to impress me with their big swords. I usually end up having to do it myself, if you know what I mean."

"An image I will save for later. Anyway, nice work."

"What the freak were those things?"

"Emojis."

"You're kidding, right?"

"My term. Short for emotional djinn. Or genies, if you prefer. Think of them as a life form that exists only in Dream, feeding off the emotions of dreamers.

These were *fear* emojis."

She thought about that. "I brought them, didn't I? When I remembered last night."

The Rider smiled. "Will said you were smart. Yeah. And you sent them away. You defeated your fears by facing them. Literally. Plus swatting and stomping on them."

"Ooh, subconscious, are you going all metaphor on me? So, are there other kinds of emojis?"

"Sure. Love—soft, warm, golden. They take different shapes for each dreamer. Depression—black holes that suck you inside them. Grief—gray, cold, clouds that envelope you. And, uh, lust—you get them a lot—pink, spongy, throbby, and wet. They come in two shapes."

"I can guess. What, no hate?"

"Weaker versions of fear emojis. Hate comes from fear. Fear's the emotion you have to look out for in Dream. Fear rules here if you let it."

"My mind is *so* weird. Hey, what's happening?"

The sky brightened. The churches faded. Above them, the office towers shimmered back into existence. Sails and swans floated again on the black river.

"You've controlled your fears, so we're back to normal."

"You call this normal?"

"For this dream, anyway." He snapped his fingers, and Brian trotted to his side. "Now, let's find your brother. Hold out your hand."

"Why?" she asked but extended her hand. Brian gave her palm a wet lick. She wiped her hand on her jeans. "Yuck."

"I asked you to remember the night Fader was taken. Brian just picked up those memories from you. Now let's hope Fader is dreaming. And that your memories are enough to find him." He kicked his skateboard into the air. When it landed, the board was twice its previous size. The Rider put one foot on it. "Get on behind me."

"What?"

"Two ways to do this. I send Brian out. If he finds Fader, he shoots me a message along his leash. But then we have to follow his leash through Dream, during which you or Fader might wake up. The faster way is a Dream Ride."

"What's a Dream Ride?"

He grinned. "Hop on and find out."

She sighed. "Fine. Sure. Why not? It's only a dream." She stepped onto the board behind him.

"Put your arms around me."

"You wish."

He shrugged. "Or fall on your ass. We won't be going slow."

Glaring at the back of his head, she wrapped her arms around his waist, clasping her hands in front of him. She tried not to notice how firm his stomach was or how his bum rubbed against her. "Weirdest. Dream. Ever," she muttered.

Brian stood quivering as if ready to explode. "Okay, Bry-guy," the Rider said. "Find Fader."

The Doogle leaped down the street, pulling the leash taut. The skateboard shot forward, propelling the Rider and Case with it.

Chapter 16

Dreams So Real

D ream scenes flashed by faster and faster. Despite her best intentions, Case tightened her grip around the Rider to keep from falling off. It let her move with him as he rode the board, too, although she didn't mind an excuse to hold him tighter.

If I'm having a dream like this, I need to get laid soon.

The white towers gave way to suburban streets lined with tiny, too perfect houses. Moments later, they rode a twisting path through rolling parkland where stunted trees walked on gnarled root legs. Next, they sped along an undulating boardwalk beside a beach of silver sand. Far out on a purple lake, water shot into the air like eruptions from a volcano.

"Why does it keep changing?" she shouted into the Rider's ear.

"We're riding through other people's dreams. People living nearby. Those are always the strongest."

"I'm in other people's dreams?"

"Because you're with me. That's my power. To walk in their dreams, and to control those dreams. Sort of."

She started to ask another question, then stopped. This wasn't real. She was dreaming. This was all her subconscious—her apparently very screwed-up subconscious.

The boardwalk became pavement that dipped into a tunnel under a street. When they emerged, day had become night. They hurtled now through dark alleys snaking between crumbling tenements. Feral red eyes peered at them from broken windows.

The buildings loomed over the alleys, blocking out sickly moonlight from above. Soon the only light came from Brian's glowing leash. A leash that fell slack as she leaned with the Rider into another corner.

They emerged into an explosion of color and sound. The Rider dragged a foot, stopping the board. They stepped off.

Ahead, Brian sat in a carnival midway. On either side, game booths stretched into the misty distance. Crowds of people filled the space between. Some played games, some strolled. Others danced with each other, oblivious to who they jostled. Some wore formal eveningwear, others pajamas, others nothing at all. Still others resembled refugees from an animal-themed Halloween party, until she realized those weren't costumes.

Behind the booths, a Ferris wheel rose into the darkness. It had no cars. Its passengers clung to metal bars as it rose higher and higher. As she watched, a woman fell screaming to an unseen fate below.

Beside it, a packed rollercoaster roared down an impossibly steep incline then up another. It disappeared into a red cloud at the top. When the cars emerged, the seats were empty. Shivering, she switched her attention to the game booths.

And wished she hadn't. At the nearest game, people threw puppies at giant spider webs. Every time a puppy stuck, a dark shape scuttled from the shadows toward it. She quickly turned away. "Where the freak are we?"

"In someone's dream. Or nightmare," the Rider replied.

"Whose?"

"I'm guessing his." He pointed.

The midway was suddenly empty. Almost. Ten paces away, Brian sat curling and uncurling his long tail, a satisfied grin on his face. Beside the Doogle stood a boy.

"Fader!" Case cried. They ran to each other, and Case pulled him into a hug.

"I knew you'd find me," Fader whispered. "I knew it."

I'm just dreaming this. She pushed the thought away. She didn't care. Right then, in that moment, she only wanted to hold her brother and believe it was truly him.

Fader let go of her and stepped back. "You got away! You're safe."

She nodded, unable to speak, guilty again over leaving him behind.

Fader's smile faded. "I'm dreaming you, aren't I? You haven't really found me, have you?"

"I...I don't know. Ask this guy."

Fader frowned. "What guy?"

She glanced behind her. The Rider stood holding his board, watching their reunion and smiling. "What do you mean 'what guy?' That guy. Your fave superhero."

"He can't see me, Case," the Rider said. "Dreamers can't see me unless I let them."

"So let him!"

Fader frowned at her. "Case, who are you—?" He stopped, staring over her shoulder, wide-eyed and open-mouthed. "No way! Where did you come from?"

The Rider walked up to him. "Hi, Fader. I hear you're a fan."

"Omigod omigod omigod," Fader said. He did a fist bump with the Rider, then jumped as a now visible Brian licked his hand. "Oh wow! A Doogle, too?" Fader beamed a huge grin at Case that almost broke her heart. "This is the coolest dream *ever*."

But that's all it is, she thought. *Just a dream. My dream.*

"Did you save Case?" Fader asked the Rider.

The Rider shook his cowled head. "Nah. She saved herself."

But I didn't save my brother. "Fader, I'm sorry. I couldn't wake you up. In the church. I couldn't carry you..." Her words ran down, choked off by guilt.

Fader hugged her. "That's okay. I'm just glad you got away."

Best kid ever, she thought, hugging him back.

"How'd you meet the Rider?" Fader asked.

"After I...escaped..." *Left you behind*. "...I ended up in the Dream Rider tower. Met that Will Dreycott guy—"

"You met *him*, too? You're staying with him? Oh, man. You're having *all* the fun!"

"Well, no. I'm not *staying*—"

"Fader," the Rider interrupted, "I need to ask you some questions before you wake up."

Fader grinned. "I know how this works. I've read *every* issue. You're trying to find me."

The Rider smiled. "That's the plan. So you *are* a prisoner. Are you okay?"

"Yeah, I guess. Just scared."

"I'd be scared, too. Do you know where you are?"

Fader shook his head. "They keep me and another kid locked in a room. The windows are boarded. I can't see outside." He looked at Case. "The other kid. It's Slip."

Case swore. Slip was one of their friends on the street. "Anyone else we know?"

Fader rhymed off names. "And I snuck out once."

He started to explain, but the Rider stopped him then waved his hand. A white rectangle appeared, floating in the air, Case's height and twice again in width. The Dream Rider symbol appeared followed by the words "A Dream Rider Production."

"Huh?" Fader said.

"We're going to watch a movie," the Rider said. "Complete with smells. Just look at the screen and concentrate on what happened."

Fader grinned. "Awesome!"

As Fader described his brief escape, images danced across the magical screen. Case shivered when the red-haired woman appeared in his room.

She held her breath as her brother followed the woman and the strangely silent Link and Tumble to the room with the skeletal man-boy. But her fear turned to horror at the man-boy's apparent transfer into the body of Rattle.

The man-boy and the woman called each other by their names—Marell and Morrigan. Marell seemed in charge, but Morrigan remained the one Case feared most. A glowing golden bird flew from Morrigan, striking Fader. The screen faded to black.

"Did that really happen?" she asked Fader.

Fader nodded, looking frightened himself. She glanced around the deserted midway, half expecting another mob of fear emojis to appear. Nothing. Her brother controlled his fears better than she did.

Stop it! she thought. This was a dream. *Her* dream, not Fader's. He wasn't here. He was out there, in the real world. Kidnapped by creeps and waiting for her to rescue him. And she was sleeping. She should be awake and trying to find him. Except...

She remembered sneaking into the Ex—the Canadian National Exhibition, Toronto's annual fair—when Fader was eight. They'd had a great day. Free food samples, free shows, even played some games. But then she'd lost him in the crowded midway. Only for a minute, but he said he still had nightmares about it.

Was *this* that nightmare? *His* nightmare? Was he really here? He seemed so solid, so real, so...

Transparent?

Fader looked...fuzzy. Color was draining from his face, his clothes. She saw through him now to the strange carnival scene behind.

Fader was fading.

"Fader!" she cried.

"Case!" he called. "Find me!" Then he was gone.

She spun to face the Rider. "What happened to him?"

The Rider sighed. "Wherever he is, he just woke up. We can't talk to him anymore until he sleeps again. But that memory he shared told us a lot."

"Like what?"

"That place looked like an abandoned hospital. Last night, I tracked four of the missing kids in Dream to a building with a sign starting with an 'H.' I didn't make the connection until now. This is great. Will's people can search for hospitals—"

Fighting back tears, she shoved him hard. "Stop it! This doesn't tell us *anything*! This is just a dream. My dream, not Fader's. He wasn't here. You're not here. None of this is real."

"Case—"

"Shut up! I shouldn't be sleeping. I should be awake. Awake and looking for my brother." She let the anger come, let it push her tears and fears away.

Case!

"I said shut up," she snapped at the Rider.

"Uh, that wasn't me."

Case! The word was so loud the carnival shapes around them trembled.

"Who is that?" the Rider asked, turning around, searching for the source of the voice.

Suddenly, she understood. "That's my Voice."

"Your lips weren't moving."

"No, I mean it's a voice I hear. Sometimes."

The Rider spun to face her. "Sometimes? When?"

She swallowed. "When I'm in—"

Danger! her Voice called.

"Case, you have to wake up," the Rider said. "Now! Wake yourself up."

As she willed herself awake, the dream scene began to fade, and with it, the Rider. Despite her belief he wasn't real, she wanted him to be. She needed him to be. She needed to know she wasn't alone in this. "What should I do?" she cried.

He was only a murky shadow now. "Get safe," he called, his voice faint. "Go back to Will. You can trust him, Case. He...*we*...can help you find Fader."

The scene vanished.

Case opened her eyes, fighting to orient herself.

Stars overhead. The sound of waves slapping sand.

Right. Rattle's crash site on the beach. Probably why Rattle had been in her weird dream...

Get up!

She remembered. Her Voice had returned. It always did when she was in—

Oh, shit. When she was in danger.

She leaped up, awake and aware. Aware she wasn't alone. For above the noise of the waves came another sound. The sound of something moving through the trees toward her.

Run! her Voice screamed.

But she didn't. She stood frozen in fear as Tall Boy and Shorty emerged from the cover of the woods.

Run!

Where? Trees and water surrounded her.

No answer came. With growing terror, she realized her mysterious voice wouldn't save her this time. She couldn't get past the men, and they'd catch her before she reached the trees. Even if she did, the undergrowth was dense and high. She wouldn't make it three strides in before Shorty dropped her with a slingshot or Tall Boy with a knife. She was trapped.

Unless...

She slipped off her sneakers.

The two men drew closer, their lips squirming into smiles like writhing maggots. Moonlight glinted off the blades Tall Boy held in each hand, but he made no move to throw them. He grinned at his companion. Beside him, Shorty raised his slingshot.

Case dove to her left as something sang past her right ear. Rolling, she came up running and headed straight for the trees, counting off seconds in her head as she ran.

One, two...

She stopped hard, an eyeblink before another shot from Shorty thunked into a tree in front of her. Turning in one motion, she sprinted again. But not for the trees.

For the water.

One, two...

She rolled, still moving forward. Another shot plunked into the water ahead of her. When she regained her feet, she noticed a silver blade protruding from the sand.

The lake got deep close to shore in most places along here. She hoped this was one of those places.

One, two...

She dove and rolled again, but to her right this time. Something whizzed by her again, but she didn't care. With a final burst of speed, she reached the water. Before she hit the first incoming wave, she took a deep breath and dove.

Cold. So cold. She'd forgotten how cold this lake was, even this far into summer. Something stung her left shoulder. Fighting an urge to open her mouth to cry out, she pulled herself deeper and deeper, ignoring the cold, ignoring the pain. Darkness surrounded her.

She touched bottom. Wriggling out of her baggy jeans, she kept swimming. She crawled along the bottom, farther and farther, until her lungs burned. Clawing to the surface, she gasped in air as quietly as she could. Treading water, she looked around trying to get her bearings.

There.

The hidden clearing shone in the moonlight, its white sand bright against dark trees behind and darker water in front. Two black shadows stood on the sand, one short, one tall. Their heads moved in unison from side to side, scanning the water.

Scanning for her. Which meant they hadn't seen her.

She'd surfaced forty meters from shore and twenty meters east. Turning east, she took another deep breath and dove again.

Chapter 17

Rat Men

Harry Lyle was dreaming. A gut-churning sweat-drenched horror of a dream. A nightmare, one from which he desperately tried to wake.

Something was hunting him. He didn't know what it was. He didn't want to know. He did know, however, with the certainty that dreams bring, that it hunted him.

Hunted him through the dark. Hunted him through narrow alleys and twisting backstreets of a city that was a sick parody of his own. The streets curled back on themselves. No matter which turn he chose, he'd emerge once again into the same bizarre square where he now stood.

The square was thirty paces a side. Windowless, gray-bricked walls enclosed it, towering to a night sky above. And in the middle sat a perfect recreation of his bedroom, including his bed.

And on that bed lay...himself.

Dead or dying, he wasn't sure. Once, he thought he saw his body twitch, but he never got near enough to be sure. Not after his first encounter, when he'd approached close enough to recognize himself.

And to see the look on his own face.

Harry never wanted to see that look again. More than that, he never wanted to meet the reason for that look. And the more Harry ran, the more he was certain the reason was gaining on him. Behind him in the alley he'd just escaped, something shuffled closer.

He broke into a run again.

Keeping as far as possible from the bed and its too familiar occupant, he started around the square. He'd take the next exit out of the square. He'd keep running. Keep ahead of the thing behind him.

He stopped, his terror rising. The square had changed.

There was no next exit.

He spun around, searching all four walls enclosing this space. In each visit to this square before, each wall had held an entrance to a dark alley. Now the only opening was the domed arch of the narrow lane he'd just left.

In that archway, the outline of something huge and black appeared, its features hidden in the gloom. Terror seized Harry. Without waiting to see what emerged, he ran to the bed and its prone figure. Maybe if he shook himself, there on the bed. Maybe if he woke himself there, he'd wake for real. Wake and escape this nightmare.

He ran, the shuffling sound close behind.

❧

When Case left Dream, Will reached for the jewel at his neck to wake himself. If Case was in danger, he needed to help her. He wasn't sure how. He didn't even know where she was. But the first step was to wake up.

But before he could touch the jewel, Brian nipped his leg. He looked down to see a data ball at his feet, still dripping with Doogle spit. Will recognized it as his data construct for Harry Lyle. The Doogle must have picked up news of Harry from Dream.

"What's this, boy?" Picking up the ball, he tapped it with a finger. Harry's face appeared, but twisted into such a look of horror that Will almost flung the ball away.

Harry was in trouble. In Dream. But Case was in danger in the real world. What should he do?

Brian nipped him again, clear on what choice to make. The Doogle was right. He didn't know where Case was or how to help her in the real world. The world where he could never go.

But Harry needed his help here. In Dream. *Here, I rule.*

He touched Brian's collar, and the silver leash reappeared. "Okay, take me to Harry."

❧

Harry Lyle opened his eyes. He was awake! He'd escaped the thing in his nightmare. He was safe at home, lying in his own bed.

His sigh of relief became an unintended sob. He'd never been so terrified in his life, either dreaming or awake.

Enough. It had just been a bad dream. He should get up, have a scotch to calm his nerves, and go back to bed. He'd laugh about this in the morning. Yeah, he should get up.

He should get up. Get up. GET UP!

He couldn't move.

He couldn't move at all. He knew he was awake. He recognized his room, recognized the sensation of being awake, really awake. But he couldn't move a muscle, except for his eyes.

He fought down a rising panic. *Get a grip. You know what this is.*

Doctors called it sleep paralysis. He'd researched it for an article once. A person partially wakes up but can't move.

Okay, this is weird, but that's all it is. Could happen to anyone.

Most doctors, he remembered, believed disrupted REM sleep caused the paralysis. Well, he'd certainly disrupted his REM sleep, forcing himself to wake from that nightmare.

It could last from a few seconds to a few minutes. *Already been more than a few seconds*, he thought, fighting the panic again.

Stay calm, dammit! What else could he remember? Doctors described it as being caught between sleeping and waking. Was that it? Was he still in his nightmare?

He remembered something else from his research. Dreamers experiencing terrifying visions, feeling a presence in the room.

Was that a sound? Something beside the bed? *Dammit, get up! Move!*

He focused again on making his muscles obey him. *Move. Move. MOVE!*

He moved. A wave of relief washed over him—then died, replaced by horror. He hadn't moved.

The *bed* had.

Something brushed his arm. Something pressed on his chest—light at first, a mere touch. But the pressure grew until he fought to draw a breath. His vision blurred. He couldn't see across the room.

No. It wasn't his vision. An image took shape before him. Above the pressure. On top of him.

Something was sitting on his chest.

In Dream, Brian the Doogle ran. And Will followed, holding tight to the silver leash, riding his board, and fighting to not wipe out. He'd never seen a Doogle run like this. Brian took every corner at full speed. On straight stretches, the creature seemed to find fresh reserves and ran even faster.

The Dreamscape had changed from the strange carnival where he and Case had found Fader. Now he rode through dark twisting alleys that curved back on themselves but somehow never crossed another. They reminded him of the route he'd followed last night ending in his encounter with the Gray Boys.

A brightness grew ahead. Seeing it, Brian put on a final spurt. A second later, they shot through an archway into a cobblestoned square. Looming, blank-faced, gray-bricked walls enclosed the space on every side.

Brian stopped, head down, long tail pointing at the scene before them. Will stepped off his board.

In the middle of the square sat a bedroom. Bed, lamps on side tables, a dresser, an armchair. A window hanging in mid-air, as if attached to an invisible wall. Through the window, a suburban backyard shone in bright sunshine.

A man lay on the bed, too far away to see his face, but Will guessed his identity.

"Harry?" he said, looking at Brian.

The Doogle straightened its tail in confirmation.

Will nodded. "Now, we just have to get by *them*."

Surrounding the bed, facing outwards, stood a circle of Gray Boys. Or Hollow Boys, as that red-haired woman, Morrigan, called them according to Fader. Whatever their name, they stood between him and Harry. If his hunch was right, each represented a kid snatched off the street. He counted twenty boys. How many kids had Morrigan and Marell taken?

"Stay here, boy," Will told Brian. The design changes he'd made to the Doogles should prevent Brian from attacking these things, but he wasn't taking any chances.

As he strolled towards the Hollow Boys, he searched Dream for what he needed. "So, guys, how ya doin'?"

As one, the entire ring of boys turned to him, their eyes locking on his. "Stay away. Stay back," they intoned together, in flat, dead voices.

"Now, is that friendly? Aren't we best buds now? You know, after you killed my Doogles, tried to kill me. Major bonding experience, I thought." He drew closer, still rummaging around in the dreams of nearby sleepers.

There. Yes. He could use that.

"Stay away. Stay back," the boys said in one voice again.

"Yeah, your villainous banter? Needs work," he said, focusing on the sleeper he'd found. Selecting elements from that person's dream, he tied silver cords to each in his mind.

Attached to Doogles, the cords served as leashes. But he could attach them to anything in Dream. He'd find what he needed in the dream of some sleeper. Then he'd mentally attach a cord to that thing and pull it into his current Dreamscape.

"Stay away. Do not approach," the Hollow Boys repeated, a hint of menace coloring their words for the first time.

Will ignored them. Behind the Boys, on the bed, the air above Harry shimmered. A shape formed.

"Holy shit," Will whispered, staring at the thing on Harry's chest.

It was a rat. A giant black rat. As large as a man, with red eyes and yellow incisors. But with human arms and hands. Hands that now gripped Harry's throat.

The thing tightened its grip. Harry spasmed, his entire body shuddering. A puff of white vapor escaped his mouth. The rat-thing brought its snout to Harry's lips, sucking in that vapor.

Will broke into a run. The Hollow Boys moved to form a wall of gray-clothed, gray-skinned bodies in front of Harry. Reaching into Dream, Will tugged on the silver cord, pulling what he'd found into this scene.

A white marble staircase with a red carpet appeared before him, rising above and past the Hollow Boys. Men and women descended the steps, dressed for a royal ball. The prince's ball from Cinderella, he guessed. The staircase came from the dream of a little girl whose mother had read that to her at bedtime.

Nice imagination, kid. Good solid construction. He rushed up the stairs past startled party guests and over the Hollow Boys. "Nyx! Sword. Now!"

He reached the top. The staircase ended. He leaped, just as his sword appeared in his hand.

At the sound of his voice, the rat-thing's head snapped up. Will struck the creature feet first, kicking hard. The thing screeched, a sound like being stabbed in both eardrums with ice picks. The beast toppled sideways off Harry and onto the cobblestones of the square.

Will hit those stones and rolled. He bounced to his feet, his blade raised before him—a defensive move that saved his dream life. The rat lunged at him as soon as he landed. Huge incisors glanced off Will's blade, just missing his throat but catching his cloak, pulling him off balance. Ripping off his cloak, he flung it at the beast.

The rat's momentum took it past Will. It spun to face him. But that spin whipped his cloak over the beast's face, blinding it for a breath.

A breath was all Will needed.

He closed on the thing as it dislodged the cloak with a vicious shake of its huge head. As it poised to leap at him, he plunged his blade into its throat.

Black ichor spurted in gouts from the wound. Drops hit his sword hand, burning him. The rat-thing quivered. With a sighing exhalation of rancid breath, it fell to the stones, dead.

Will ran to where Harry lay on the bed, expecting to find himself and Harry in the middle of a tightening circle of Hollow Boys. He had more cords prepared to pull Harry and himself away from this Dream location and the Boys.

To his surprise, the Boys were backing away. And for once, an emotion played over their normally blank faces. He couldn't place it until an approaching squeal cut the night.

Fear emojis.

The Hollow Boys were afraid.

But of what? He'd killed the rat-thing. And the Boys obviously weren't afraid of *him*. Then what—?

A hiss made him turn.

Behind him, the rat-thing melted, dissolving into a steaming pile of rodent parts. Above the dead beast, wisps of steam rose. The wisps darkened, solidifying into a writhing black tendril, a tendril that became a red-eyed fanged snake.

Time to go, Will thought, suddenly afraid. But why? He'd fought worse things than snakes before. But his fear grew as this snake grew. The thing rose taller and taller, until it swayed three stories above him.

Yep, definitely time to go. Take Harry and run. He tried to move his feet. He tried to move anything.

Frozen to the spot, he could only stare as the snake's head lowered to hover an arm's length from his face. A forked tongue flicked from its slit of a mouth.

A voice, male and cruel, rasped in his head. *You have grown powerful. To kill a Mara.*

Will glanced at the puddle that had been the rat-thing. A Mara?

Brave, but foolish. To face me here. But thank you, fool. After all my searching, I have finally found you.

Will swallowed. Now for a clever quip—followed by an equally clever escape. But he remained powerless to move, let alone escape. He tried to call Nyx, but no sound would pass his lips.

The snake drew closer. Its mouth opened to reveal long white fangs.

One bite. One taste, said the voice, the words slithering through Will's head and down his spine. *One bite, one taste—and you're mine.*

Nyx! Will screamed in his head. He shouldn't have to voice her name. The thought should bring her. Shouldn't it? *Nyx! Get me out of here! Wake me up!*

Something touched his mind. No, not something. *Someone*. The touch of another mind. A touch like a warm hand grasping his own and gently tugging.

The snake shot towards him.

Time slowed.

As the snake closed on him, it grew hazy. So did the scene in the square. The Hollow Boys were now gray smudges in the background.

Time sped up again. The snake's jaws snapped shut.

On nothing.

He screamed. And woke up.

Gasping, Will sat straight up in bed. *His* bed. His huge round bed in his office tower. He was home. He was safe. Safe from Hollow Boys and giant rat-Mara-things. And snakes. He ran his hands over his body just to be sure. *Nope. Didn't get eaten.*

He flopped back onto the covers. What had just happened? And what was happening in Dream? For the second night in a row, something in Dream had kicked his butt.

Then he remembered. Case was in danger. Harry Lyle, too.

"Your female friend is quite safe," a voice said from nearby.

"Aaagghhh!" Will cried out. He tried to leap into a defensive crouch but got tangled in the covers and fell back. He peered up from where he lay.

At the end of the bed, clad in a long maroon robe, stood the figure of an old Asian man. Or maybe not that old. The figure exuded an aura of youth and vitality that belied his wrinkled face and long white hair and beard.

The man smiled. "My name is Yeshe. And I say again, the young lady is safe. She waits with me downstairs." The man's figure had a translucent quality to it, edged by a shimmering silver aura.

"Waits with you? But you're here."

Yeshe smiled again. And disappeared.

"Or...not," Will said. He looked around his bedroom, but he was alone.

Hallie's computerized voice sounded from the room speaker. "Call for Mr. Dreycott from Ms. Archambeault."

"Answer."

Adi's voice replaced Hallie's. "William, you need to come down to reception." She sounded strained. "You have...visitors."

"Case and an old guy in a dark red robe?"

Pause. "Yes," she said, "although the gentleman is wearing jeans and a Grateful Dead t-shirt. How did you know?"

"Long story. Long weird story—again. Take them to the main boardroom, please. I'll be right down. Oh, and Adi?"

"Yes?"

"Call Harry Lyle. Make sure he's okay."

"In the middle of the night? Again? What's wrong?"

He rubbed his face and sighed. "Let's just say I had a bad dream. See you in a minute."

Grabbing his jeans from the floor, he pulled them on. The belt brushed against his right hand, and pain shot up his arm. He cried out.

"Lights on," he called.

As the lights in his room came up, he stared at three red blotches on the back of his hand. They resembled burn blisters he'd had once when he'd been scalded. But what could burn him while sleeping?

Then he remembered. Stabbing the rat-thing. Hot black blood splashing his sword hand.

He stared at his hand. A burn. From Dream.

Something was very wrong—in *both* of his worlds.

Act 2

You've Haunted Me All My Life

Chapter 18

Glass Ceiling

When Will entered the main boardroom on the second floor, few lights showed in the neighboring towers. Not surprising at four AM. Inside, two security guards flanked the door. Adi sat at the head of the long maple table that dominated the room. Arms folded, face stern, she nodded at him, then turned back to their two visitors.

At the opposite end, as far from Adi as possible, Case slumped in a chair, head back, eyes closed. She looked exhausted. Her hair was wet, and she wore different clothes. Different but familiar—a July Talk t-shirt and baggy jeans.

When he entered, her head came up. Their eyes locked. Something twitched at the corner of her mouth. A smile? Whatever it was, it died as her head dropped back against the chair.

Halfway between Case and Adi, his back to the windows, facing Will from across the table, stood the old man who had...

Had what?

Had *appeared* to Will? In a vision? In his dream? Whatever had happened, this was the same person. Torn jeans and a faded Grateful Dead t-shirt replaced maroon robes, but he was unmistakable. Long, wispy, white hair and beard. Sun-browned face, lined like crumpled paper. And bright eyes twinkling with a light belying his apparent age. He smiled and bowed to Will, hands clasped before him.

Will nodded back, then walked to where Case sat. She stood, running a hand through wet hair. Hooking her thumbs in the top of her jeans, she stared at him, as if searching his face for something.

"Uh, hi," he said.

"Hi."

"Are those my clothes?" *Right! That's the first thing you say to her. Idiot.*

Looking down at what she wore, Case shrugged. "*She* got them." She glared down the table at Adi.

"Well, that was nice of Adi—"

"No. She didn't want me dripping on your precious leather."

"She was soaking wet," Adi snapped. "And half-naked."

"Why?" he asked Case, storing an image of a wet half-naked Case for consideration later.

"Went for a swim."

"In your clothes."

She folded her arms. "I crashed on Cherry Beach. Tall Boy and Shorty showed. I left."

"By jumping in the lake."

"Gee, you're quick."

He bit back his own retort. "Well, I'm glad you're safe." Leaning closer, he dropped his voice to a whisper. "And I'm glad you took the Rider's advice and came back here."

Case's eyes widened as if trying to match the O-shape of her mouth. "How did you know that?"

He shook his head, nodding toward the guards. "Later." At least he'd have her attention the next time they talked. He walked over to the old man. "You are Mr. Yeshe?"

The man smiled. "Yeshe will do, young master."

Will held out his hand. "I'm Will Dreycott."

Ignoring Will's hand, Yeshe bowed again. "I know. And I am honored. However, before further conversation..." He looked around, taking in Case, Adi, and the guards. "...it would be best if our audience was smaller."

Will turned to the guards. "Thanks, guys. You can leave us now."

Both guards looked at Adi.

"Seriously?" Will said.

Adi sighed and nodded. The men left the room, shooting both Yeshe and Case hard stares.

"They realize I'm the guy who pays them, right?" Will said.

Yeshe raised an eyebrow, his eyes running from Case to Adi.

"No," Will said. "They stay. Adi's my closest advisor, and Case is in the middle of this. Whatever *this* is."

Yeshe smiled. *And are they both aware you are the legendary Dream Rider?*

Will jumped, startled. Yeshe hadn't spoken, yet the man's words sounded in his mind. He wasn't sure which was more shocking—that Yeshe was telepathic or that he knew Will's greatest secret. *So how do I answer you? Can you hear me?*

Yes. I cannot read your mind, but I can hear any thoughts you direct to me.

Could this night get any weirder? *Sure. Why not? Okay, so Adi knows. Case doesn't—and I'd like to keep it that way. But she needs to hear what you have to say if it involves her brother.*

It does. Then I will guard your secret from your girlfriend.

She's not my girlfriend. She's just...oh, crap, I have no idea what she is...what we are...oh, forget it.

Yeshe smiled again.

"William, what is going on?" Adi said. "You appear to be having a staring contest."

Yeshe spoke before Will could reply. "My humblest apologies, Ms. Archambeault. I am here to answer what questions I can concerning recent events. However..."

A loud snoring interrupted him. Will turned. Case lay slumped forward in her chair, her head on the table, arm for a pillow, her mouth open and slack.

"Oh, that's attractive," Adi muttered.

She still looks cute to me, he thought. *Oh yeah, I have it bad.*

"However," Yeshe continued, smiling at the sleeping Case, "perhaps we should delay my story. The young lady is exhausted from her adventures these past two nights..."

Will and Adi exchanged glances. How much did Yeshe know?

"...and I myself am of the habit of sleeping during daylight hours," Yeshe finished.

"Vampire?" Will offered.

The smile flickered on Yeshe's face. "A routine arising from my quest."

"Quest?"

"A quest that has brought me to your city. And to you, young master."

Will rubbed his face with both hands. "Okay, we'll do this later. Case needs the sleep, and I could use some Zs myself."

"William..." Adi began.

"No," he said. "We do this my way. Please have our two guests escorted to the hotel floor."

I do not require a room, young master. Yeshe's voice sounded again in Will's head.

"Please stop calling me that," Will said, turning back to Yeshe. "And I thought you wanted to sleep... Oh."

Yeshe now sat cross-legged on the floor, his eyes closed. He sat in lotus position—hands palm up on his knees, thumbs touching forefingers, other fingers extended.

"Yeshe?" No response came. Will sighed. "Let's leave him here and get Case a room."

Adi appeared ready to argue again, but then shook her head and stood. "Very well. But I'm leaving a guard on this room. And on hers, too. Wake your girlfriend."

"She's not my—oh, forget it." Walking to Case, he nudged her shoulder. She woke with a start, her hand flashing out, catching his wrist and twisting.

"Ow! Okay, ow!"

She released his wrist. "Sorry." Rubbing her eyes, she looked around, glared at Adi, considered the sleeping Yeshe, then shrugged. She peered at Will. "S'up?"

"C'mon, I'm taking you to bed."

She stood, yawning. "In your dreams."

"No, I mean...oh, never mind. Just follow me." He started toward where Adi waited grim-faced by the doors.

Case grabbed his arm. "Hey! Wait a minute."

"What?"

Shooting Adi a look, she turned her back to the older woman. "When you came in," she whispered, "you told me—"

"Yes, I did," he whispered back, cutting her off before she said something he didn't want Adi hearing. "And I'll explain in the morning."

She narrowed her eyes at him, but didn't say anything more. They walked past Adi into the hall and toward the elevators.

Adi followed. "Explain what?"

"Nothing," they both replied.

Adi sighed and punched the up button. "I hope you know what you're doing."

"I do." *Not really*, he thought. Inside the elevator, he scanned his hand and pressed the button for the guest floor. The doors closed.

"I called Mr. Lyle, as you asked," Adi said. "No answer."

"Maybe he shut off his phone after I woke him last night." But he remembered his dream—Harry lying on the bed, that rat-thing on his chest. "Keep trying. If you don't get an answer, send someone over."

Adi frowned, but nodded. They both fell silent.

He stole a look at Case, now slumped against a wall, eyes closed. Adi was right. What *did* he know about her? But then her face took on that softness he'd seen as she'd slept on his couch.

And he knew. No warnings from Adi or his own doubts would make any difference. He felt a connection to this girl, and he needed to know if she felt it too.

Case awoke, rested and recharged. Stretching out on the bed, she thrilled at the soft coolness of the sheets on her naked skin.

Wait a minute.

She sat up. Where the freak was she? She looked around.

It appeared to be a hotel room, based on movies she'd seen as a kid. The bed was huge. She could stretch out in any direction, arms over her head, and not hang over at either end. She ran her hand over the sheets. Smooth, shiny. Silk?

Whatever. How did she get here? A clock on the bedside table showed 1:05 PM in red digits. In the afternoon? She'd never slept that late. Still groggy from sleep, she slid to the side of the huge bed. She swung her feet over the edge. They didn't even reach the floor. Hopping down, she grinned as she wriggled her toes in the thick brown carpet. She began a tour.

In an adjoining room, a couch and two armchairs flanked a low glass table scattered with Dream Rider comics. A giant TV screen hung on the wall, between posters of the Rider. A small kitchen sat to the right, complete with stove, fridge, and sink.

To the left, sunlight peeked from behind thick drapes. She pulled them open.

And jumped back.

Behind the drapes, the windows ran from floor to ceiling. A cityscape fell away beneath her feet. She shivered. At first sight, her stomach had tumbled as if she were falling, falling all the way to the street below.

Her fascination battled her fear. She'd never seen the city streets that were her home from up high. Fascination won. She pressed her forehead against the glass and looked straight down. It took a moment, but she recognized the stretch of King Street in front of the Dream Rider tower where Will lived.

Will. She remembered then. Will showing her to this room last night. Undressing. Falling into that huge bed. She must've been asleep as soon as she'd hit those sheets.

She looked around the room. This was Will's building. This was his home.

She shook her head. Home. Not a dirty sleeping bag on a sidewalk. Or the floor of a church basement.

Or a beach. She shivered, remembering more of last night. Her narrow escape from Tall Boy and Shorty. And before that—meeting the Dream Rider, searching for Fader...

And finding him. Finding her brother. Holding him again.

No! That had been a dream. Just a dream.

But it had seemed so *real*.

She remembered something else. The room with the big table and the old man with the long white beard and the lady who hated her. Something Will had said to her there...

I'm glad you took the Rider's advice...

She sat on the couch. How could he have known she met the Rider? Met him in a dream? *Her* dream? Did that mean...? Was the Rider...?

Was the Dream Rider *real?*

If so, then everything in her dream had been real. Which meant...

She swallowed. Which meant Fader was alive. A prisoner of some creeps, yeah—but alive. Her brother was still alive.

She had to talk to Will. Finding the bathroom, she peed then checked out the huge walk-in shower. She told herself she needed to wake up, to get clean. But really, she couldn't resist trying it.

She washed, relishing the smell of perfumed soap and apple-scented shampoo. She let the hot water pulse over her long after she'd rinsed, trying to wash away the horror of these past days.

Getting out finally, she slipped into a thick terry-towel robe hanging on the wall, letting it dry her. So this was how the rich lived. She could get used to it. And Will seemed genuinely nice. She didn't think nice guys existed. And he seemed to like her. *It could happen*, she thought with a grin.

Still grinning, she found her clothes—correction, Will's clothes—where she'd tossed them last night. Dressed, she headed for the door.

And stopped.

Walking to the window, she gazed down at the streets again. The streets where she was Hard Case. Where she lived by stealing and hustling, running and hiding.

She took in the room again. The thick carpets. Big TV. Big bed. One room in an entire building. A building that was Will's home.

This was *his* world.

She stared at the streets below. And *that* was hers.

Turning from the window, she walked to the door. It could happen? Yeah, right. Who was she kidding? What would someone like Will ever want with someone like her?

Chapter 19

Escape Is at Hand

Their screams were helping. Morrigan's early morning anger was abating. She sat in the room where two nights before she'd assisted Marell in his transfer. Her lover sat beside her in his new and younger body. They occupied the twin high-backed chairs. Behind them hung the ancient portrait of the man and woman who bore a striking resemblance to them both. Well, not to Marell anymore. But his eyes were still the same. Dark—and dangerous.

Before them lay the Weave. The red-and-black woven rug bearing the triskelion design—three skeletal legs running widdershins around a circle. The same design that inscribed the medallion around her neck. This morning, she wore a dark olive blouse with tight beige slacks and stiletto heels. Marell again wore a black suit and a white shirt.

The drapes were drawn over the boarded windows, but torches burned in wall sconces, sending shadows writhing around the room. Writhing just as the two figures on the carpet writhed.

Mr. Stryke and Mr. Stayne.

They twisted and rolled. They screamed. They tore at their clothes, exposing their pale skin. On that skin, rune characters glowed as if on fire. From the perspective of her two blundering lackeys, she knew, their skin *was* on fire.

She lifted a hand. A rune script danced along her arm and shot at the two men on the floor. The symbols on their skin brightened again, and their screams grew shriller.

"Mercy, Mistress!" Stayne screamed.

"*Mercy?*" she snapped. "You let a mere street urchin make fools of you. Twice!" *And of me.*

"Morrigan, enough," Marell said, impatience in his voice. "We have much to discuss. And this exercise will increase neither the intelligence nor competence of these idiots."

Sighing, she flicked her hand. The glowing symbols on the two men dulled then disappeared. Stayne and Stryke collapsed sobbing onto the carpet.

"Now go," she said. "Fail me again, and I will not show such kindness."

"Yes, mistress," Stayne gasped. "Your mercy is boundless."

"Your beauty knows no—" Stryke whispered.

"Leave!" Morrigan cried. The two men began to stand. She glared at them. "Did I give you permission to rise?"

Stayne and Stryke exchanged glances. Dropping to their hands and knees again, they crawled from the room.

Marell chuckled. "Feeling better?"

She sniffed. "A little."

"And this girl? What became of her after she evaded those dolts?"

"My tracking spell—which those fools should have used—was fading last night. But I managed to trace her. She returned to that white tower."

To her surprise, Marell smiled. "Good."

"How so?"

"Last night, I sent a Mara after that reporter you marked for me."

Morrigan shuddered. Hunted by a Mara. "But how does this tie to the white tower and our search?"

Marell stared at the triskelion design on the Weave. "Someone killed the Mara."

Killed a Mara? She sat back in the chair, her eyes also running to the Weave. She fingered her medallion. "Our prey?"

"Who else?"

"How can you be sure?"

"I faced him. The Mara's death drew me to him."

"And?"

He hesitated. "He eluded me."

She drew in a breath. "He's grown more powerful."

Marell glared at her.

"To kill a Mara," she added, not voicing her true thought. Their prey had escaped Marell's astral spirit in Dream? How could that happen?

"More powerful, yes," Marell said. "I believed our work would end when we found him. But this may prove more difficult than we envisaged."

"You've found him?" she said, as the meaning of his words sank in.

"Your suspicion of the other night proved true. The mind that killed my Mara dwells in your white tower. I tracked its spirit there before my contact broke."

"But, my love, that is wonderful. Our search is over."

"There remains the problem of his capture. Something in that tower blocked my astral spirit from entering. I believe our prey has erected an astral shield."

Another surprise. *His powers have indeed grown.* But she kept that thought to herself, too. "Then we cannot compel him to leave the white tower's protection."

"No. We must remove him. Physically."

"That will be difficult. According to Stayne and Stryke, the building entrances are secured. And guarded around the clock."

"We have the mercenaries," Marell mused.

"A forced entry will trigger an alarm and attract the authorities."

"To be so close..." Marell's hands clenched into fists.

Morrigan rose and paced the room. The hospital beds from two nights ago had disappeared. What remained were the few items she insisted they carry on their pursuit—the portrait, the two chairs, the wall sconces.

And, of course, the Weave.

Completing her circuit of the room, she stood on the rug, drawing some of its power into her. "If we cannot compel him to leave, perhaps we could lure him out."

Marell's eyes narrowed. "How?"

"That reporter. He was investigating the children we've taken. He even talked to the young boy we took last night and his elusive sister. The boy had his card, remember? From your encounter in Dream, our prey must also know the reporter. And that girl has fled twice to the white tower where he hides."

"And from this you infer...?"

"Like the reporter, our prey is interested in the fate of these children."

Marell snorted. "Why?"

She shrugged. "Playing the hero again? Does it matter? Regardless of his reasons, these children could be bait, to lure him."

Marell stroked his chin with one finger. An old habit that jarred her seeing it in this new body. "Your logic holds. But lure him where? To the children? To here?" He shook his head. "No. He could send the police."

"My protections on this place would hold."

"Still too dangerous. But you've given me an idea."

"How so?"

"There are two ways to use bait. One is to lure your prey into a trap. But I wish to lure no one here."

"And the second use?"

Marell smiled, a cold thing, yet familiar and comforting to her. "To let the bait *be* the trap. The Greeks knew that."

Understanding came, and with it, a chill. "Which child?"

"You know."

"No! Not him."

"Which better? You said yourself his sister hides in the white tower."

"No. Use another boy."

Marell rose and pulled her to him. She was still unaccustomed to looking down at him in this new, shorter body. "Now, now, it must be done. Do not fret. Your little favorite will return unharmed."

She allowed herself to soften in his embrace, fighting her resentment. What choice did she have? If she refused, Marell would proceed without her. Better for her to prepare the boy for his role than Marell. At least her way was reversible.

"Very well," she said. "But I need time to ready the child. I must cast such a spell in layers."

Marell released her. "And I need a day to assemble the men and plan the operation. Tomorrow evening?"

She nodded, but her thoughts were of the boy Fader. *Oh, little one, these are not the plans I had for you.*

⁂

Early that morning, Fader awoke. He kept his eyes closed, wanting to hold onto the wonderful dream. Reunited with Case. Meeting the Dream Rider. The Dream Rider! His hero was real.

And his sister was safe. She'd escaped these people, just as he'd known she would. No one made Case do anything she didn't want to. He wished she'd saved him, too, but he knew now she'd tried. And she'd never stop looking until she found him, just as she had in his dream.

He never doubted he'd met Case and the Rider in Dream last night. They were looking for him. And they'd find him.

He opened his eyes. His joy vanished as he found himself once again in the small room with the barred windows. The same room, but different now.

The other boys who'd shared the room with him were gone. Slip and Rattle. Somehow, that man, Marell, now lived *in* Rattle. He didn't know where Slip was. Gone, too, were the mattresses. He lay on a hospital bed with raised metal bars.

He turned his head. Beside his bed stood the red-haired lady called Morrigan. Her eyes were closed, her bare arms extended over him. She whispered in a strange language. He gasped when he saw her. Her eyes snapped open. Green, beautiful eyes.

"How are you awake?" Sighing, she pointed an arm at him. The golden characters danced again on her skin.

He knew what would happen next. "No! Please! Let me go!"

"Sleep, little one," she cooed. "Later, we will walk. And we will talk."

The glowing symbols shot from her arm, striking him. Sleep took him once more. A dreamless sleep. No Case. No Dream Rider.

Fader woke to find Morrigan again beside him. But this time, her eyes were open, and she was smiling. She wore her long green cape. The sides of his bed were down.

"Come," she said. "Follow me."

What if he refused? But he wanted to leave his dark prison of a room. And, he realized, he wanted to be near Morrigan. She led him down to the first-floor lobby, walking with an easy grace. He trailed behind her like an obedient puppy. But as he followed, he memorized the hospital's layout against a hope to escape his room again.

Outside, he thrilled at the summer sun on his face and fresh air in his lungs. From the sun's position overhead, he guessed it was about noon. They descended crumbling steps flanked by two stone lions. He was surprised to discover that the hospital grounds were the size of a small park.

They crossed a driveway of broken asphalt and an overgrown lawn. A thin forest separated the lawn from the top of a cliff. Reaching the forest, they continued beside it. Between the trees, he saw water and whitecaps far below them. Was it the same lake he knew? How far was he from his familiar downtown streets? The surrounding trees were too thick for him to see any skyline.

They walked in silence. The wind blew strong off the water, lifting Morrigan's red hair and billowing her cape behind her like great green wings. To him, she seemed a fiery angel fallen to earth.

She wrinkled her nose, probably at the odor of dead fish the wind brought. He didn't mind. He was used to living around bad smells and was just happy to be outside again.

Morrigan turned into the woods, weaving through trees until she reached the lip of the bluffs. There she stood, still and silent, staring out over the water.

Fader hesitated. She hadn't checked if he'd followed her into the trees. Behind him, the long driveway that cut the grounds lay ten steps away. He knew it led to a road. He'd heard car horns and the air brakes of big trucks. If he could reach the road, he could flag down someone to help him.

Twenty steps away, Morrigan still stood motionless at the cliff edge, her back to him. He yearned to rush to her, to cling to her, to feel her fingers ruffling his hair, to hear her call him "little one."

No. This might be his only chance for freedom. He wanted to be free, right?

Part of him did. But he realized, with both horror and delight, that another part of him wanted to stay with Morrigan forever.

Stay? Or run?

An image of Case rose in his mind, and with it, his deep love for his big sister. He ran.

When he reached the driveway, his heart was pumping faster than his legs. When he was halfway to the end of the driveway, he knew he'd make it. When the gate came in sight, he snatched a glance behind. To his amazement, Morrigan still gazed out over the lake.

He was going to escape. He was going to be free. He was—

His legs stopped running.

They didn't stop because he wanted them to stop. They stopped because *they* wanted to stop—as if they now answered to another mind. Not his mind. Hers.

With his feet rooted to the spot, he twisted his upper body to look behind him. Morrigan walked toward him, not running, not hurrying, as if she was continuing her stroll. Unable to move a step, he could only wait.

When she reached him, she smiled. "Thank you, little one. I began to worry you wouldn't run. Then how would I know if my runes worked?" She ran her fingers down his cheek, a touch that both frightened and thrilled him. He shivered.

Pulling his face away from her hand, he shouted in his mind at his legs, ordering them to move, to listen to him. They didn't move. They didn't listen. Instead, they burned. Gasping in pain, he dropped to the asphalt driveway, clawing up his pant legs.

Those strange characters that had appeared on Morrigan now glowed golden and throbbing on his own skin. He screamed. At least, he tried to. He opened his mouth but could force no noise from it. The skin of his throat burned, and he knew without seeing them that the strange characters lay there too.

He looked up. "What are you doing to me?"

Morrigan still smiled at him, but it was a sadder smile. Kneeling beside him, she stroked his hair. "Keeping you safe, my special one."

Chapter 20

Follow the Yellow Brick Road

Opening her guest room door in Will's tower, Case stepped outside. And stopped. Whatever she'd expected, it wasn't this.

She appeared to be on a busy city promenade. Men and women in business clothes scurried by carrying briefcases. Others in casual wear strolled and chatted, coffee cups in hand. Sunshine lit the scene. Above, wispy clouds floated across a deep blue sky.

How...?

Looking again, she realized she stood in a broad indoor hallway. The "sky" was a huge video screen forming the ceiling of the entire corridor. Her side of the "street" had facades of upscale townhouses, complete with tiny flower gardens. Cafes and shops lined the far side, including a Starbucks opposite her.

"Seriously?" she muttered. When Will brought her here last night, she was so bagged none of this had registered.

"Miss?"

She jumped. One of Will's security guards stood beside her. He was big, burly, and—unfortunately—familiar.

"Um, hi," she said, recognizing the guard she'd kicked yesterday. What was his name?

"Mr. Dreycott is waiting for you, miss. I'm to take you to him." His face displayed how much this assignment thrilled him.

Not my biggest fan. Not that she blamed him. "Okay. Yeah. Great. But can I eat first?"

The guard stared at her unsmiling for a breath, then pointed to the shops. "You can eat in any of those. I'll wait here."

"Yeah. Right. Small problem. Kind of left my money in my other pants."

"You don't need money. Mr. Dreycott provides these apartments and services for his guests. Anyone with..." He considered her. "...business in the tower."

Of course he does. Nodding to the man, she started across the "street" for the Starbucks. She and Fader panhandled outside their stores whenever they could. Their patrons were flush and sometimes generous. She looked back at the guard. "You want anything?"

His eyebrows shot up. "Uh, sure. Venti. Bold. Black."

She nodded, hoping that would make sense to whoever took her order. Inside, she got an obscenely large coffee for the guard, plus a smaller coffee and blueberry muffin for herself. She devoured the muffin and ordered another. Finishing, she returned to the guard.

"Here you go." She handed him his coffee.

"Thanks," he said with a real smile. He nodded down the street, curling up the lid on his cup. "The elevators are this way."

She sipped her coffee—sweet with lots of cream—as they walked. "Your name's, uh, Burlington?"

"Close. Bevington."

"Right. Listen, Mr. Bevington, about yesterday..." she started. He grimaced but said nothing. She pushed on. "I mean, I'm really sorry, you know, for kicking you..." She left it at that, guessing he didn't need details. "I'm not great with authority figures."

He considered her, then shrugged. "That's okay. More embarrassing than anything. The guys won't let me forget it soon." He held out his hand. "And people just call me Bev."

She shook his hand. "So we're good?"

"Just don't try it again," he said with a grin. Stopping in front of an elevator door, he pushed the *up* button. "Anyway, Mr. Dreycott really likes you, so that's enough for me."

Will liked her? Well, she knew that, right? But *really* liked her? Maybe there *was* a chance...

She considered the street scene and the coffee in her hand. Yeah, right. Will had everything. She had nothing. It didn't matter what either of them wanted. Everything Guy and Nothing Girl? *So* not going to happen.

The elevator came. They got in. Bevington scanned his hand then pushed a button at the top labeled "Roof / Jungle." The doors closed on the fake street scene...and on her fantasy.

The elevator ride and its stomach-tumbling acceleration made Case regret that second muffin. To distract herself, she inspected the floor buttons, each of which had names instead of numbers. What was with that? The floor she'd just left read *Hotel*. She read a few of the others. *Musée d'Orsay. The Louvre. Tibet. Egypt.*

She grimaced at that last one. Egypt was where she'd met Will. She felt her face flushing as she remembered the canopic jar.

The car slowed, and she fought again to keep down her hasty breakfast. The doors opened. She blinked at the scene before her. "Are you freaking kidding me?"

Bevington chuckled. "Yeah, I had the same reaction the first time. Just follow the yellow brick road, and you'll come to a fountain. Mr. Dreycott's waiting for you there."

"Yellow brick road? Seriously?"

Bevington grinned. "Off you go, Dorothy."

The doors closed behind her as she stepped out. She looked around. She listened. She sniffed. Trees and rolling grassy hills. Birdsong and insect buzzes and squirrel chatter. The smell of roses and fresh cut grass. And overhead, blue sky and scudding white clouds. The real sky.

She was in a park. On the top of a skyscraper. She kicked the cobblestones with the toe of a borrowed sneaker. A park with a yellow brick road.

"Toto," she muttered, "we are *so* not in Kansas anymore." Shaking her head, she started along the path.

Will sat on a grassy rise overlooking a fountain that spouted and sparkled in the sunlight. A smaller replica of the one from the Tuileries in Paris, he believed. He had trouble keeping track of his reproductions.

The hill, high enough to give a view of the rambling park, was his favorite spot for mulling over problems. His current problem was how to tell Case about the Rider without revealing he *was* the Rider.

His phone beeped—a text from Bev saying Case was on her way. A minute later, she emerged from behind a grove of aspens, following the bricked path.

His heart did a skip. *Seriously, dude? Heart skipping again? This isn't a date.* Although, he could ask her out on a date. Well, *in* on a date. *Stop it! Focus on the problem. Gotta save Fader.*

Because if I save her brother, she'll really like me...

Stop it!

Case climbed the hill. He stood, trying not to stare at her. She stopped in front of him, thumbs hooked in the top of her jeans. Well, *his* jeans. "You are the weirdest person on the planet."

He nodded. "Nice to see you, too. And yeah, you're probably right."

"Sorry. Didn't mean... It's just..." She swung an arm at the expanse of the park. "It's just...*why?* Why do you have all this?"

"I like squirrels?"

"No! Not just this park. This whole building. All the weird freaking floors. Like, seriously, what gives?"

He swallowed. This was *not* the conversation he wanted to have. Not now. Not yet. Maybe never. What could he say? That he was *afraid* to go outside? That he was sick and didn't even know why?

That he was *broken*?

"I, uh, don't get out much." He looked down and then back at her. She stood with her arms folded, waiting. "Look, it's kind of personal? Could we discuss it later? When that Yeshe guy wakes up, he'll explain what's going on, and there's stuff I need to tell you first."

She shrugged and sat on the grass. "Sure. Fine. Whatever. Your life. None of my business, right?"

But I want it to be. "No, it's not that—"

"So what's this shit you have to tell me?" she said, cutting him off. "And why don't you start with how the freak you knew about my dream?"

Handled that well, didn't you, dumbass? Now she's pissed. He sighed and sat beside her. "Because the Dream Rider told me."

"The guy in your comics."

"Graphic novels."

"He told you."

"He's real, Case."

"Yeah, right."

"He *is*."

"Uh huh. Sure he is."

"Okay, then tell me how I know this." He described her dream from last night. Meeting the Rider. Finding Fader. Her Voice waking her.

As he talked, an expression grew on her face. It wasn't until he'd finished that he recognized the expression.

Fear.

She shook her head. "This can't be true."

"Coming from the girl who hears voices."

She glared at him but said nothing. They sat in silence. Finally, he spoke. "Look, I know it's hard to believe—"

"I believe you."

"Or not so hard." He frowned at her. "You do? Why? Because I'm not sure I would."

She shrugged. "Because, like you said, I can't explain how you knew all that shit unless you're telling me the truth. No matter how weird that truth is." She paused, and the softness returned to her face. "And I don't think you'd lie to me."

He didn't reply. He hadn't lied—but he knew he'd have to soon.

"So I really met Fader last night?" she asked. "He's alive? He's okay?"

"Yeah, he seems to be." He hadn't told her about the Hollow Boys, not wanting to worry her even more. He guessed that would be Fader's fate if he and Case didn't find her brother in time.

Looking away, she wiped at her eyes then turned back. "Then that's all that matters. Fader's safe. So, yeah, I believe you."

Tough outside, soft inside. Shit, girl, I like you.

"So," she asked, "how do you know this Rider dude?"

And now the lies begin. But what choice did he have? Only Adi knew the Rider was real, let alone that *he* was the Rider. Adi would be furious he'd told Case as much as he had. He had to keep his secret identity...well, secret. "He came to me in a dream once, just like he came to you."

That, at least, was true. Sort of. Kind of. The original idea for the Rider character *had* come to him in a dream, shortly after he'd returned from Peru. That dream vision, complete with costume, had spawned his early scribblings with the Rider in his comic form. It was only over the next several months he discovered the very real powers he had while dreaming.

As he'd developed those powers, he learned how Dream existed as a separate world. A world where he could do what he couldn't while awake. Go outside. Go *anywhere*. Do *anything*.

He could be *normal*. More than normal. He could be a superhero.

But only in his dreams.

"So why'd he pick you?" she asked, pulling him back to the moment.

Good question. Why *had* this power come to him? Was the universe trying to balance things out? Make up for the damage done to him on that mysterious jungle expedition? Or was it the other way around? Had whatever happened to him in Peru *caused* his strange abilities? Was his problem inseparable from his powers?

If you're listening, Powers That Be, you can keep the superhero stuff. I'd rather be able to walk in a real park.

But he couldn't tell Case any of that. "The Rider comes to lots of people in Dream," he said, which again was true. "He came to you, right?"

"Yeah, but you said he's your friend. And he seems to know you pretty well. He told me to come back here." She studied his face. "He said I could trust you."

He dropped his eyes. "You can. Trust me." *Yeah, trust me to lie to you.*

"Uh huh. So, you, him—friends. Spill."

"I use my private investigation team to help on his cases." Again, that much was true.

"Cases?"

"He helps people, like he's doing with you and Fader. Solves crimes that stump the cops. And when he solves them, I tell Harry Lyle, and Harry tells the cops. The crime gets solved, Harry gets a story, and the Rider stays unknown, except to me." Mentioning Harry Lyle reminded him to ask Adi if she'd contacted the reporter since last night's disturbing dream.

Case lay back on the grass, her arms behind her head. "Wow! He's like a superhero."

He grinned and stretched out beside her. "Yeah, he is."

"I met a superhero. A real superhero. He saves people. He has superpowers. He's brave. And all noble and stuff. And he is *so* freaking hot."

"Yeah, he—wait, what?"

"That tight costume? Oh, shit! I mean, right?"

"Uh..."

"It shows his muscle-ly stuff. And his guy bits."

"Guy bits?"

"And his butt. I mean, wow."

"His butt? You're wowing his butt?"

She shrugged. "It's wowable." She smiled, staring up at the sky. "Yeah. Totally."

He sat up, angry and not knowing why. "You know, he might look completely different in reality than how he does in Dream."

Her face fell. "Why?"

"Well, he can make himself appear however he wants in Dream. In real life, he might be short. And fat. He might be...old."

She glared at him. "Wayda go, buzz-kill."

"Bald. Big nose. Bad teeth."

She sat up. "Okay. I *get* it."

They both fell silent while he wondered why he'd enjoyed destroying her fantasy of the Rider. Why? Because he wanted her to be thinking about *him*, not the Rider.

"So you've never met him?" she asked. "The Rider? In real life?"

"Uh, no." *You can never meet yourself, right?* But he still hated himself for not telling her the whole truth. "So how long have you heard this voice?" he asked, changing the subject.

She looked at him. "*Look, it's kind of personal,*" she said, mimicking his earlier words.

"Guess I deserved that. Okay, how about explaining what happened after you woke up last night."

She shrugged. "Fine."

He listened as she described her escape from Tall Boy and Shorty. "Quick thinking," he said when she finished. "I'm not clear on one part, though."

"Which part?"

"Where you walk into my lobby half-naked and dripping wet. Could you go over that again? Slowly and with more visuals?"

She punched him in the arm. "No."

"Fine. The security cameras caught it. I'll replay it tonight when I'm alone."

"Perv." But she laughed, and that softness showed again in her face. The smile disappeared. The moment slipped away, and she was tough girl once more. "So when do we see this Yoshi guy?"

"Yeshe."

"Whatever. You really think he knows what's going on? Where Fader is?"

He checked his watch. Quarter past two. "Only one way to find out. Let's go wake him up and ask." He stood, offering her his hand. She ignored it, getting up herself.

"I am awake, my young friends," came a voice.

Case stared past him, eyes wide. He turned.

At the bottom of the hill stood Yeshe. He wore the same maroon robes as when he'd appeared to Will last night. Once again, his figure had a shimmering translucent quality.

"Uh, hi?" Will said.

"I have found the most wonderful place in your marvelous home," Yeshe said. "On a floor named 'Tibet.' Perhaps we could meet there, and I will tell my story."

"Found? You don't have access to that floor...oh, right. Security—not a problem for you."

Yeshe just smiled.

"Okay, Tibet it is."

"Thank you. I will ask Ms. Archambeault to escort me there."

Knowing what was about to happen, Will leaned closer to Case. "Watch this."

"Watch what? Oh, shit!" Yeshe's robed figure disappeared as if someone switched off a movie projector. She looked at Will.

"Yeah, it's a thing he does. Showed up like that last night in my bedroom when..." He stopped. He'd almost said "when I woke up from Dream." Keeping his secret was going to be harder than he'd thought. "...when you arrived in my lobby."

"But he was in the lobby with me. So, like...how?"

He shrugged. "Dunno. But he said he'd answer questions, so let's go ask some."

Case hugged herself. "All I want to know is what happened to Fader."

They walked along the yellow brick path, heading for the elevators. "What if he can't help?" she asked, her voice subdued. "What if he doesn't know where Fader is?"

"Then tonight, the Rider will meet you again in Dream. You'll track Fader like last night. And this time, the bad guys won't crash your crash site, so we can figure out where he is."

"We? You gonna show up in my dream, too?"

Oops. "Uh, no. I mean, after you wake up. We—you and me—can use what the Rider discovers to find Fader."

She shot him a look he ignored. At the elevator, he pushed the down button. The door opened immediately.

"Hey," she said, as they got in. "If the Rider is real, are your comics true, too?"

"Graphic novels. And no, I make up those stories."

"So no Cockroach King and giant bug army in our sewers?"

"Nope." He scanned his hand and pressed the button for "Tibet."

"Good to know. That creeped me out."

"Thank you."

"You are so weird."

You have no idea, he thought as the elevator doors closed on them.

Chapter 21

Ahead by a Century

On the Tibet floor, Will led Case along a hallway lined with towering Buddhist statuary. Some were originals from his parents' expeditions, others reproductions. He couldn't tell which. He hadn't visited this floor for a while.

They passed a massive Buddha, twice his height. It sat cross-legged, eyes closed, hands in the position Yeshe had adopted last night. "The temple should be down the next hall...I think."

Case gawked at the statues and artwork. "This is like a museum. Like that Egypt floor."

"Aw, that's sweet. You're sentimental."

"What?"

"The Egypt floor. You haven't forgotten how we met."

"Trying to," she muttered.

"I'm glad our first moments made such an impression."

"Dream on, lover boy."

Dream on. What he did best.

They turned left at the next hallway. Case stopped, staring at the panorama ahead. "Whoa."

He stopped beside her. "Yeah," he agreed, making a mental note to visit this level more often. "Whoa."

A two-story open space stretched the width of this level to the windows on either side. The floor was gray-black marble. Dark red columns marched before them, rising to a ceiling of red beams and gray-black plaster.

Ahead, the columns ended five paces from wide marble steps. The steps led to a raised dais in the center of which sat a tall wooden throne. On a backdrop behind the throne, an image of the Buddha towered to the ceiling, flanked by smaller images.

Adi sat on the lowest step. A row of red prayer mats lay before the steps, each depicting a Buddha in a different pose stitched in ochre thread. On one of these mats, facing the throne, his back to them, Yeshe sat in lotus position. "Good day, young master, young mistress," he called without turning as they approached.

"Good ears for an old guy," Case muttered.

Will was sure Yeshe knew of their presence long before he'd heard their footsteps.

Adi came over. "William, we need to talk." She eyed Case. "Alone."

Case folded her arms. "Nice to see you, too."

Adi ignored her. "It concerns Mr. Lyle."

"Adi, it's okay," Will said. "Case knows Harry. What about him?"

Adi hesitated. "We never got an answer to our phone calls. Or texts. Or emails. And he didn't show up at his office this morning."

A chill seized him as he remembered his dream encounter with Harry. "Did you send someone over?"

"Mr. Zhang went himself. He used his...skills to enter Mr. Lyle's apartment."

"Picked the lock, you mean. And?"

"No sign of a struggle or forced entry. Mr. Lyle was in bed. He wasn't breathing. Mr. Zhang called 911, then attempted to revive him while he waited for them." She hesitated. "He failed. As did the paramedic team." She met his eyes. "I'm sorry, William. Harry Lyle is dead."

Case swore. Will felt something slipping away inside, part of his belief in the world's inherent goodness. Dead? Had he actually seen Harry die last night in Dream?

"We'll set up a trust for his son, Dylan," Adi continued. "I'll reach out to his ex-wife, Carla to see—"

"How did he die?" Will interrupted, his voice barely a whisper.

Adi hesitated. "We won't know until the autopsy, but the paramedics thought it was asphyxiation. They found nothing blocking his airways, yet somehow, he couldn't breathe."

Images from his dream rose unbidden in his mind. The terror on Harry's face as he lay in bed. The rat thing sitting on his chest, its human hands around Harry's throat.

But that had been in Dream. It hadn't been real. It *couldn't* have been real.

He rubbed his hand where the hot blood from that thing had splashed him. He swallowed. Or maybe it could.

"A Mara."

Yeshe's voice. They turned to face him. He now sat on the top step of the dais in front of the golden wooden throne, facing them. "A Mara killed your friend."

Will walked up to Yeshe. The snake beast he'd faced last night in Dream had called the rat monster a Mara. "A Mara?"

"A beast of Dream that feeds on the spirits of Dreamers. Once a Mara finds its prey, it bites into their spirit, never letting go. The terror of that attack awakens the Dreamer."

"Which is good, right?" Will said. "You have a nightmare and wake up."

"No. The Dreamer cannot fully wake. They remain trapped between Dream and the waking world. And they have brought the Mara back with them. The few who have escaped describe lying awake, unable to move or call out, unable to breathe, as if *something* of great weight sat on their chest. But most victims report nothing—because they die, by asphyxiation."

Mr. Lyle was in bed...yet somehow, he couldn't breathe...

Will's face was grim. "I think it's time you told us your story."

Yeshe nodded. "Indeed, it is."

Yeshe smiled down at where Will and Case now sat cross-legged on prayer mats below him. Adi was again seated on a step to their left. Yeshe considered the huge room. "An accurate reconstruction of the debate hall at the Ganden Monastery in Tibet."

"You've seen it?" Will asked.

Yeshe's face became wistful. "Once, I was the Ganden Tripa there."

"Ganden Tripa?"

"The spiritual leader of the Gelug school of Tibetan Buddhism." He glanced back at the throne. "And holder of the Golden Throne, too. The reason I chose this location to tell you my tale."

"Thought the Dalai Lama was the leader," Case said.

Will raised an eyebrow.

She snorted. "What? Think I don't know stuff?"

"No. I mean, it's just..."

"Ever heard of libraries? I take..." She swallowed, then continued. "I take Fader at least twice a week. Try to give him an education. He was into learning about religions a while ago."

Yeshe smiled. "I am glad you included Buddhism in his studies. But no, even the Dalai Lama must bow to the Ganden Tripa when they meet."

"When were you this Trippy guy?" Will asked.

"The Ganden Tripa is elected for a seven-year term. One hundred and two of us have served in the role, beginning in the early fourteen hundreds. I was the eighty-second to hold the position."

"Wait a minute," Will said, calculating in his head. "That can't be right. That would mean—"

"That Yoshi here is way over a hundred years old," Case finished. Will raised an eyebrow. "Yeah, I do math, too," she said. "Twenty people after this guy, at seven years each—"

"Some, regrettably, died before their full term," Yeshe said.

Case shrugged. "Still, even at five years each, it's at least a century since you were the head honcho. And I'm guessing you didn't start in the cradle."

"Yeshe," Will asked, as doubt grew in him, "what are you saying? How old are you?"

The monk smiled. "One hundred and ninety-eight years."

Will caught the look Adi shot him. "Yeshe, that's...hard to believe."

Yeshe's voice sounded in his mind. *Given your own abilities and recent events, is my age so difficult a truth to accept?*

Okay, Will replied. *Tough to argue with that.*

"William?" Adi stood now, her phone in her hand. "Do you need anything?" she asked, which was Adi-speak for "Should I have security throw this nut job out?"

"No, let's hear his story."

Adi raised an eyebrow, but she put her phone away and sat again.

Yeshe smiled at them. "Thank you for your indulgence."

"Now, story please," Will said.

"First, you must learn who you face." Yeshe turned to Case. "The red-haired woman who took your brother—"

Case stiffened. "Morrigan?"

"She calls herself that. It may be her true name. I don't know. Perhaps no one does. Witches guard their true names well. She calls herself Morrigan the Bright."

"Witches? She's a witch?" Will glanced at Adi. She shook her head. Yeshe's story wasn't getting any easier to believe.

Yeshe nodded. "A powerful one, well versed in rune magic."

"Which is? I've been skipping my witch studies class," Will said.

"Magic using rune scripts. Spells written in characters from a runic alphabet. Those were alphabets used by peoples such as the Norsemen, before the spread of Latin."

"Norsemen? She's a Viking?" Case asked.

Yeshe smiled. "Her ancestors may well have been. She is of Manx origin, as is her magic."

"Manx?" Case said.

"Isle of Man," Will said. "Little place between England and Ireland. See? I know stuff, too." He turned to Yeshe. "You were explaining rune magic."

"The magic user writes a spell script in runes on a strip of paper or wood. They then burn the script to execute the spell, often speaking words to enhance its effect." Yeshe's face became grim. "Morrigan employs an unusual technique, one making her formidable, indeed."

"Her tattoos," Case whispered.

Will realized it must be tough for Case to remember that night—Fader disappearing, facing Morrigan and her weird henchmen, her own narrow escape.

Yeshe nodded. "Long ago, she magically tattooed a rune alphabet on herself. The runes are invisible until she needs them. They then appear, rearranging themselves on her skin to form any script she composes in her mind. And then—"

"She throws it at you," Case said. They looked at her. "I think she tried a spell on me the night they took Fader." She described Morrigan's attempt in the church basement. "I guess it didn't work."

Yeshe considered Case. "You were fortunate. Never have I known anyone to escape Morrigan. And you then evaded her two lackeys."

"Tall Boy and Shorty?" Case asked.

Yeshe smiled. "Is that what you call them? Their real names—or again, what they call themselves—are Mister Stayne and Mister Stryke. Your Tall Boy and Shorty, respectively. They are..." He hesitated. "Rather than straining your credulity further, for now, let's say they are long-time associates of the witch. Very long." He considered Case again. "And very dangerous. To escape them and Morrigan both..." He shook his head.

"But I *did* escape," Case said "So back to the problem—finding my brother. Do you know where he is?"

"No. I do not."

Case swore, slamming her fists on the floor. She jumped up. "Then I'm done wasting time listening to you. Fader's out there somewhere—"

Yeshe raised a hand. "But I know who took your brother and why. And I can help you find him—and the other missing boys."

Case glared at him. "So tell us something useful." She remained standing, arms folded.

"Yeah," Will agreed. "Yeshe, we already knew Morrigan took these kids."

"Morrigan is capturing the boys," Yeshe said. "But she herself has no need for them. They serve another's purpose."

"Who?" Will asked.

"His name is Marell," Yeshe said. *And, young master, you have met him.*

The last words sounded in Will's mind. *What do you mean?*

Last night, in Dream. Marell was the mind behind the snake demon you faced. He sent the Mara to kill your friend. It was from his grasp I pulled you. Had I not, your mind, your very will, would now be his.

Will suppressed a shiver, remembering. "Who is he? And why does he need these kids?"

"To answer those questions, I must explain how I first encountered both Marell and Morrigan." Yeshe raised an eyebrow to Case.

She shot Will a look. He shrugged. Shaking her head, she sat on the meditation mat again. "This better be good."

Yeshe smiled. "It will, at the very least, be unique." He regarded the three of them, then leaned forward, his hands on his knees. "My name is Yeshe Norbu, eighty-second Holder of the Golden Throne. My story begins at the Ganden Monastery in the year eighteen hundred and eighty-four. I had been Ganden Tripa there for two years..."

Chapter 22

Seven Years (or So) in Tibet

Seated, eyes closed in meditation, Yeshe felt a shadow fall across him. Felt it in the sudden coolness on his skin as his intruder blocked the afternoon sun warming his back.

"Master?" came a voice from behind him.

Yeshe suppressed the sigh that fought to escape his lips. That voice had become familiar in these past weeks. Too familiar. Opening his eyes, he unfolded himself from lotus position. He stood, turning to face his visitor.

The young man was taller than Yeshe, but lean and stooped, with sunken eyes above prominent cheekbones, a thrusting jaw, and protruding ears. He reminded Yeshe of a hunched gargoyle looming over him.

"Initiate Marell, to what do I owe this unscheduled visit to my personal garden?"

Marell gave a perfunctory bow, showing no sign of noticing Yeshe's gentle admonition. "I have questions, Master."

"It is right for a student to have questions," Yeshe replied. *But perhaps not so many as you.* Marell had arrived a month ago, and interruptions such as this had become part of Yeshe's day. Still, the young man was here to learn, and Yeshe was here to teach. "What are your questions?"

"They pertain again to the astral body."

Now Yeshe allowed himself a sigh. "When we first met, I stressed that the path to enlightenment does not lie in such studies." Indeed, when he had interviewed Marell as a possible new student, the man had shown interest in nothing else.

"And I took your advice to heart, Master. To develop the abilities you yourself hold over your astral body must not concern an initiate. I have abandoned such inquiries."

"I am pleased."

"But then, last night..." Marell hesitated.

Yeshe now noticed how pale the student was, and how he sweated, despite the coolness of the day and the light breeze. "Go on, please."

Marell took a deep breath. His words came in a rush, bursting out like birds escaping a cage. "I believe my astral spirit left my body."

Yeshe smiled. "I do not doubt your belief, but you likely were dreaming. To even sense your astral form within yourself takes years of practice. To achieve the control required to send it from your body is unheard of in one so young."

"Master, I believe you." Marell's hands were trembling. "That is what frightens me. I had no control. It just...happened."

Yeshe frowned. "Tell me."

Marell wrung his hands. "I was lying awake on my sleeping pallet. I could hear the other students talking. I could see the shadows in our bedroom lengthen with the setting sun. Then, suddenly..."

"Yes?"

"I was in the village."

The monks relied on the charity and alms of the village. But it was in the valley, a two-day journey from where the monastery perched on the mountain peak. For an initiate to project his astral body that distance was unthinkable. "Again, it was but a dream."

Marell shook his head hard. "No, Master. I was in the village. In the tavern. I saw those gathered there and heard their voices. I smelled the food, the tobacco smoke, the human bodies."

"Initiate, I am certain you did not. A lucid dream, perhaps, but no more."

"I wish you were right, Master. I wish I had not been there. I wish I had not seen what happened."

A chill settled on Yeshe that the sun's warmth could not dispel. "Tell me what you saw."

"A murder!" Marell cried.

Five days later, Yeshe sat on a mat in his garden facing Lobsang Chinpa. The younger monk had studied under Yeshe the past five years. Yeshe trusted Chinpa, for his honesty and his discretion. Both traits were required for the task Yeshe had assigned him.

Chinpa had just returned from the village, sent by Yeshe upon hearing Marell's story. Two days down, one day in town to make his inquiries, then two days back. Chinpa was now completing his report.

"You're certain of the date? And location?" Yeshe asked.

"Six nights ago, Master. At the Inn of the Middle Path."

Yeshe kept his face serene, hiding the turmoil inside him. The night and location of Marell's dream. Or was it a dream? "The village has not seen a murder in three generations."

"No, Master."

"What precipitated it?"

Chinpa hesitated. "No one knows, Master."

Yeshe frowned. "A man murders a neighbor in a tiny village, and no one knows why?"

"Master, I agree. It makes no sense, but each witness told the same story. The attack was unprovoked."

"Tell me."

"The two men, close friends, were eating together in the tavern. They were talking civilly with each other, even laughing." Chinpa opened his hands in a gesture of exasperation. "Then, without provocation, the killer grabbed his companion where he sat across the table..." He swallowed. "And drove his knife into his friend's chest."

"This blow killed his victim?"

Chinpa winced. "That blow...or one of the many that followed. By the time those present pulled him off, he'd stabbed his friend a dozen times."

Just as Marell had described. Yeshe focused on slowing his breathing, trying to restore his calm. "What reason did the killer give?"

"The killer has not spoken since. They've locked him in a storeroom. I questioned him myself..." Chinpa stopped, dropping his gaze.

"You received no answers, either?"

The monk looked up, and the fear on Chinpa's face startled Yeshe. "Master, I received no response at all. The man sat with open eyes, but showed no awareness of me. Or of anything. It was as if I addressed a corpse."

"No doubt a brain fever, prompting both the killing and his current state. In the meantime, do not speak of this."

Both men rose and bowed to each other. Turning to go, Chinpa hesitated.

"Brother Chinpa, have you more to say?"

Chinpa bowed his head. "Only to express my awe for the Ganden Tripa's astral abilities. Only a great master could travel so far, see so clearly." He looked up, his eyes wide. "Such power."

Yeshe considered this. When he'd sent Chinpa to the village, he told the monk to inquire about any recent violent incident. Never expecting Marell's story to be true, he'd not foreseen a need to explain how he came by such knowledge. But the young monk was providing him with that explanation. His astral studies and abilities were common knowledge among the monks.

He bowed to Chinpa in reply, saying nothing. A tiny lie, one of omission. He would atone for it later. For now, until he learned more, the other monks must not know of Marell's astral journey.

He watched as Chinpa left the garden.

Such power.

He suppressed a shiver. Such power, indeed. Power rivaling his own, and in one so young. Time to talk to Initiate Marell.

The next day, he and Marell walked in the temple's gardens, speaking in low voices. A stone bridge arching over a pond led them to an island of ornamental trees dotted with white blossoms. Yeshe sat on a stone bench, Marell beside him.

"Then we are agreed?" Yeshe asked.

"Yes, Master. And thank you again."

Yeshe had offered to tutor Marell in the disciplines of astral projection. In return, Marell would tell no one of his abilities. He would attempt no further astral journeys, although he insisted his visit to the village had not been by choice. Marell would also continue with the daily routine and studies of an initiate.

"For your path to enlightenment must not suffer due to these other studies," Yeshe said.

He had made the young monk his clerk. Marell would assist him in his duties as Ganden Tripa, deflecting questions about why he conferred special attention on an initiate. Yeshe did not want others to learn of Marell's astral studies with him.

"When do we begin, Master?"

"Today. I see no reason to delay." Far from it. The situation was urgent if Marell was experiencing uncontrolled astral journeys.

His unease returned. An astral journey to the site and time of a murder. Such a coincidence stretched credulity. But he could not see how Marell's visit might tie to the killing, beyond being an unfortunate witness.

"Thank you, Master! I am so grateful," Marell bowed several times.

"Thank me with diligent study."

"Will you begin by showing me how to take an astral journey?"

"No. You are not yet ready."

"Why not?" Marell asked, then added a belated, "Master."

Yeshe noted Marell's tightened jaw. "First, you must control your emotions."

Marell reddened, then bowed from where he sat. "Forgive me, Master. I only wish to learn."

"Then learn patience."

"Yes, Master," Marell replied, his head still bowed.

"Before you may safely journey, you must learn to see your silver cord."

"Silver cord?"

"During astral travel, your consciousness resides wholly in your astral body. As does your spirit, your true essence. The silver cord is a delicate thread connecting your astral form to your physical body."

"And if I cannot see my silver cord?"

"You risk becoming lost on the astral plane. Your consciousness may never find its way back to your body again."

Marell frowned. "And then?"

"You will wander this world as a disembodied spirit until you fade into nothingness. Your body will wither and die."

Marell bowed again. "Then I will be the patient student and learn from you, Master."

"Then I shall teach you," Yeshe said, chiding himself for his own excitement. If Marell's abilities were as powerful as he suspected, then the teacher might learn from the student.

For three months, Yeshe trained Marell in the ways of the astral plane. One night, Yeshe called his student to his quarters. "Walk with me, please."

They entered Yeshe's walled and private garden, where they would not be disturbed. Above, the moon was a fresh-born sliver hanging in a sky swarmed by stars. On a pebbled path between flower beds lay two sleeping pallets.

Marell turned to Yeshe, frowning.

Yeshe smiled. "Are you ready, Initiate Marell, to take your first true astral journey?"

Marell's eyes widened. His mouth opened and closed, making no noise. He nodded several times. "Yes, Master. Most ready." Tears streaked his cheeks. "More than ready."

"Yes, I believe you are."

Even with the most diligent study, he hadn't expected Marell to progress so quickly. But Marell had soon learned to project his astral body and to detect his silver cord. Yeshe had never encountered a student so attuned to the astral plane. He no longer doubted Marell had astral traveled to the village that night. Yeshe was as eager as Marell to test the student's abilities.

"Lay down, initiate, and we shall begin."

"Two pallets, Master? You will accompany me?"

"To ensure your safe return and to continue to guide my student." *And to continue to learn from my student, too*, he admitted to himself.

"Master, believe me..." Something flickered behind a brief smile. "...I would not take this journey without you."

They lay on their pallets. Closing his eyes, Yeshe began the meditation to reach the astral plane. From the soft chanting beside him, he knew Marell did the same.

His meditative state deepened. His breathing slowed. His heartbeat slowed.

He sensed his astral body. It hovered above him, a man-shape glowing in silver radiance, bright and beautiful against the night sky. A slender silver thread led from the shape to where he lay on the pallet.

To where he lay on the pallet.

He regarded himself lying below, arms folded, chest barely moving, so slow was his breathing. Beside him, in a similar posture, lay Marell.

He was in his astral body. And beside him hovered Marell's glowing astral form.

Master! I have done it! Marell's excited words sounded in his mind.

Yeshe sensed jubilation, but arrogance, too. Yet, had he not shown arrogance when he first attained this level? Marell was young. Arrogance could be taught away. *Yes, my student. You have. I am proud of you.*

Now can we travel?

Yes. I have selected a destination for us.

The village?

Yeshe thought it unwise to return to where Marell had witnessed a horrific crime. But he didn't tell Marell that. *Too distant for a first journey. Instead, we will travel to the shrine halfway down the valley.*

The shrine served as a way-station between the monastery and the village. The villagers kept it well stocked. Tonight, neither he nor Marell would need shelter or sustenance. The shrine provided a familiar destination, where he could test Marell's astral abilities. Far but not too far.

The shrine is perfect, Master, Marell replied, projecting satisfaction. And something else, something hidden underneath, something that disappeared before Yeshe could identify it.

Yeshe hesitated, taken by a sudden disquiet.

Master?

Now he sensed only excitement emanating from Marell. He dismissed his unease.

Follow me, Initiate. His astral body rose over the monastery wall. Marell's own glowing form followed.

Yeshe could have reached the shrine instantly, by willing his astral form there. But this was Marell's first self-controlled trip. They descended the mountain flying invisible above the land but still making an actual journey from monastery to shrine much as they would in physical form.

Marell's experiments with astral travel further delayed them. Weaving between snow-covered trees. Skimming the surface of icy streams. Skirting the misty bottoms of clouds.

At last, they hovered above the small pagoda of the shrine. Yeshe sensed a gloating exultation in Marell. *Calm yourself. You have not gained a power, merely learned to see a path that always existed.*

Yes, Master.

I have tests for you. First, let us see how you manage physical barriers. He pointed his astral arm to the shrine. *Pass through its walls. Once inside, pass to the upper floor and exit through its roof. Then return here.*

Without acknowledging the command, Marell flew to the shrine's carved wooden doors. He floated forward, hesitated, then sank into the doors as if they were the surface of a vertical pool. He disappeared inside.

Yeshe allowed himself a disembodied smile. He had taught the young man well. He waited.

And waited.

As he estimated the progress of time by the stars, his concern grew. When an hour had passed and Marell had still not returned, Yeshe descended to the shrine. Inside, the tiny structure was empty. Returning outside, he spread his senses wide, but detected no astral presence nearby.

He had to return to the monastery. Marell's astral spirit was lost. But he could locate Marell by following the man's silver cord from his sleeping body.

Focusing on his own cord, he reappeared above where he and Marell lay in his private garden. He floated closer, searching for Marell's silver cord.

No!

If he'd had a physical mouth, Yeshe's scream would have awakened the monastery.

A knife, buried to its hilt, protruded from Marell's chest. Blood soaked his robes, staining the maroon cloth a deeper red that shone black in the starlight.

How had this happened? Who could have done this?

A figure slid from the shadows. Yeshe experienced another shock. It was a woman in a long cloak. She was tall, with flowing red hair. In her hand, she held another knife.

She approached Yeshe's body. Kneeling beside it, she pulled his robe open to expose his chest. She raised the knife.

Panicked, Yeshe dove towards his physical form. He had to reinstill his astral spirit and wake immediately. This woman had killed Marell. Yeshe did not understand why, and in that moment didn't care. He had to defend himself before she killed him, too. Entering his mind, he reached for the spark to reunite his spirit with his body.

And encountered another presence.

Hello, Master.

What? Who are—? Yeshe cried in his head. Then came recognition. *Marell?*

The same.

Confusion fought with his fear of his present danger. Fear won. *A woman is here!*

Yes, Marell said.

She has killed you!

My body, yes.

She will kill me!

No.

Yes! She is poised to strike.

This body is in no danger, Marell replied. *Here. See for yourself.*

An image appeared to Yeshe. The red-haired woman now smiled down at Yeshe's sleeping form, empty-handed.

I do not understand, Yeshe said. *What happened? How are you here, inside my—?*

Marell struck.

To Yeshe, the attack was like a metal rod slamming into his head. He had never known such pain. His focus wavered. An invisible force thrust him upward, outward, away...

Away from his body.

His body.

He floated again in his astral form, looking at his physical body lying below.

Marell's mind touched him. *Goodbye, old man.*

Marell, he cried. *What is happening?*

He sensed the mental equivalent of a shrug. *My body was diseased, dying. I needed a new one. I've taken yours.*

Yeshe's mind reeled. *That is impossible.*

Yet here we are. I mastered this technique long ago. I used it most recently on that stupid peasant in the village.

You! Then you... you *murdered that man.*

Another shrug. *I needed to create this situation. My power is great but I could not have taken over one as strong as you unless your astral spirit was absent.*

Why me?

You are a person of power. I like power. And you have tuned this body and mind to the astral plane. Plus, you have access to secret teachings on the astral way. With those learnings, my abilities will grow even stronger.

Marell, I forbid—

Now, Marell continued, ignoring him, *there remains but one task.*

As Yeshe watched in horror, his eyes—*his* eyes in *his* body—opened.

The red-haired woman took a half step back. "Marell?" Her voice was deep and musical.

Yeshe watched himself turn and smile up at her. "It is I, indeed, Morrigan, my love."

Upon hearing those words, the face of the woman called Morrigan transformed. Yeshe had seen that look before, on the faces of young monks. The look of devotion. "Now?" she said.

"Now," said Marell with Yeshe's mouth. "Sever the link."

Morrigan raised her hands overhead. Her cloak fell back, revealing milk-white arms. On those arms, strange golden symbols glowed as if on fire.

She chanted in a tongue Yeshe did not recognize. The symbols spun and whirled in a matching rhythm, realigning on her skin. Her chanting stopped. The dance of the symbols stopped. She lowered her arms over Yeshe's body.

The symbols flew from her skin to Yeshe's bare chest, flaming brighter. His body convulsed as if in pain.

Yeshe's astral form, floating above this scene, convulsed as well. He did not understand how, but his silver cord was unraveling from where it attached inside his body. With each passing second, the connection between his astral and physical forms grew weaker.

If that link disappeared, if the last thread of his cord slipped its tie, no trace of his spirit would remain in his body. He could never return there. His spirit would wander as a disembodied wraith until he dissolved into nothingness.

He convulsed again. Only a few slender threads of his cord remained attached. A desperate plan came to him. His cord floated before him. He seized it in his astral hands.

And twisted. Twisted and pulled with all his spiritual strength. Tugged and tore at it with the full power of his will, commanding it to come apart.

Just as the last thread was about to slip its connection inside his body, the cord outside his body broke. Thrown skyward, his astral form tumbled through the night sky high above the monastery. Regaining control, he focused his astral senses on his garden, now far below him.

"Marell?" Morrigan cried.

Yeshe watched his own eyes open and his body stand. Marell-as-Yeshe raised his arms before him, smiling down at his new body.

"Marell?" Morrigan cried again. "Is it you?"

Marell-as-Yeshe took her in his arms and into a long deep kiss. He released her. She threw back her head and laughed. "Yes! Oh, yes. It *is* you!"

"It is I. The transfer worked," Marell said. Yeshe's spirit chilled in hearing another speak with his voice.

"The monk? Is he gone?" she asked.

Marell didn't answer. He looked around. He looked up.

Yeshe sensed Marell searching for him. He stayed hidden and quiet, praying Marell would not sense the part of Yeshe still inside his stolen body. When he'd broken his silver cord, a small piece had remained attached inside his physical form. As long as that bit of him lived there, he might one day restore his astral spirit to his body.

Finally, Marell nodded. "He is gone." He stared down at his own corpse. "We will bury that and say Initiate Marell left in the night, realizing a monk's life was not for him."

Morrigan kissed him again. "Well, that last part is true. How will you explain a woman in your quarters?"

Marell shrugged Yeshe's shoulders. "I am the Ganden Tripa. I will do as I please."

Over the following days, Marell acted in Yeshe's name as the Ganden Tripa. As Yeshe watched, his shame grew. Marell presented Morrigan as a visiting *Bhik-shuni*, a female monk, from the West. To account for her dress, he told the monks that Buddhist customs were different there. She stayed in his quarters.

Worse, Marell ignored the *Vinaya*, the rules governing the monastery's daily routines. He no longer led the *Tara Puja*, the morning prayer. Nor did he partake in any teachings of the dharma with students in the debate hall.

Instead, Marell spent his waking hours in the library. He studied obscure sutras, the teachings of the Buddha. He poured over arcane treatises in the *Ab-hidharma*, scholastic interpretations of the sutras. Always his research focused on the astral plane, on how he might increase his powers.

And always too, Yeshe hovered nearby, his mind quiet, his presence undetected. Waiting. Waiting for Marell to grow over-confident. Waiting for him to test his growing powers once accustomed to his new body.

My body. Stolen from me.

One night, as Marell lay on his sleeping pallet, Yeshe's patience was rewarded. Hovering invisible above, he watched Marell enter the meditative state required for astral projection. Sensing Marell's spirit preparing to leave his body, Yeshe quieted his thoughts.

Marell's astral body rose from his sleeping form, connected still by its silver cord. It hung glowing in the darkened room for a breath, then sped through the window and down the mountain.

Off to torment another poor soul, no doubt, Yeshe thought. Once he could no longer sense Marell's presence nearby, he struck.

Diving into his own mind, he seized the remnant of his own silver cord still attached there. Binding it once again to his astral spirit, he pulled his full essence back into his body.

But Marell's powers had grown. Detecting Yeshe's presence, Marell's spirit flew back to his hijacked body.

And the battle began.

A witness to the scene would have observed nothing. Perhaps a twitch or tremor in Yeshe's limbs. But inside, two titanic wills fought over a single body, fought for their very existence. For many minutes, the outcome hovered on a knife-edge. But in any battle, the general who best knows the battlefield prevails.

And this battlefield was the body Yeshe had occupied for over six decades. That body recognized its true spirit. His body and spirit united, unraveling Marell's silver cord where it connected to that body. Yeshe then expelled Marell's invading spirit, like a cat spitting up a hairball.

And there it should have ended.

As Yeshe told his tale, the afternoon sun had dipped lower, its rays creeping along the floor to where Will, Case, and Adi listened. Yeshe now sat lit from the side, his profile split into light and dark.

Will wondered which of his many questions to ask first. "But it didn't end. Marell and Morrigan are here. Now. Today."

Adi snorted. "So he says."

"Morrigan's here," Case snapped, glaring at Adi. "She took my brother."

"They're both here, Adi. I *know* they are," Will said, hoping Adi would realize he spoke from Dream Rider knowledge. Adi's eyes widened. She gave a little nod.

He looked at Yeshe. "What happened next?"

The monk hesitated, as if considering his answer. "Expelled from my body, his own dead, Marell's spirit had no connection to the physical plane. Without a host, his spirit would soon slip from this physical plane, never to return."

"Which obviously didn't happen," Case said. "So how?"

"With Morrigan's help once more," Yeshe said, his face grim. "Around her neck that night, she wore a gold medallion, one with a triskelion design."

"Try-whatee-what?" Will asked.

"Triskelion. Three legs inscribed within a circle. Skeletal legs. Equally spaced and radiating from the center, running widdershins."

"Widdershins?" Case asked.

"Counter-clockwise," Yeshe said. "Did she wear it the night you encountered her?"

Case nodded, hugging herself.

Yeshe sighed. "As I feared. A powerful amulet, endowed with her magicks. She uses it as a repository."

"For what?" Will asked.

"For Marell's astral body. It can provide him a haven for a time if some poor soul's body is not available. They used it that night I expelled him. Marell's spirit flew to Morrigan. She took him into the amulet and fled the monastery."

Yeshe paused. "They fled. And I followed." He regarded the room, the reconstruction of a place that must hold so many memories for him. "Turning my back on my duties. And on my life. I left the monastery and pursued them."

"Why?" Case asked. "You'd won. They'd split. Why leave a cushy life to chase after a couple of creeps?"

Yeshe considered Case. "Because he had killed before. Perhaps many times. And I knew he would kill again. Perhaps many times. He needed a new body and would soon expel another poor soul's astral spirit into the void. So I pursued them. Across the world and across the years. To here. To now." Leaning back against the replica of the Golden Throne, symbol of a life abandoned, Yeshe closed his eyes. He looked exhausted. He looked ancient.

"But why here? Why now?" Will asked.

"Because," Yeshe said, his eyes still closed, "Marell is searching for someone. Someone with astral powers of their own. And I believe that here, in this city, he has finally found that person." Yeshe opened his eyes. "Someone you all know."

A fear grew inside Will, as great as when he tried to step outside. "Who?" he asked, knowing the answer. "Who has he found?"

Yeshe stared hard at Will, then around at the others. "The Dream Rider."

Chapter 23

The Ties That Bind

O f all the creepy things Fader had faced since waking in the strange hospital, this was the creepiest.

It was late afternoon, and he was having tea with Morrigan.

He liked the buns (called scones, she said), especially smothered in thick cream and strawberry jam. And hot tea was a new treat for him, one he could learn to like. Morrigan let him add as much sugar as he wanted. Case never let him do that to his rare coffee.

All of this would have been fine by itself...if not for their other "guests."

Fader and Morrigan sat at opposite ends of the table, Morrigan nearest the door. Between them, three on either side, sat six Hollow Boys.

He recognized Link and Tumble again, but not the others. He'd seen more Hollow Boys around, mopping floors or carrying boxes. Or standing like statues outside rooms with closed doors. Standing guard, he guessed. When he tried to open those doors, the Hollow Boy would stop him.

Here, each boy stared across the table at the boy opposite. But Fader didn't think they were looking at each other. He didn't think they looked at anything. They remained motionless unless Morrigan ate or drank. Then, they copied her every action. At the same time and together, like puppets tied to her.

She raised her cup. They raised theirs. She took a sip. They took a sip. She set her cup down, and a chorus of tiny clicks filled the room as six china cups met six china saucers.

He shivered. Creepiest thing *ever*.

Morrigan smiled down the table at him. "Isn't this nice?"

Six Hollow Boys pivoted their heads to stare at Fader. Six mouths writhed in horrible copies of Morrigan's smile.

Those smiles did it. The fear he'd been hiding overwhelmed him. The words escaped his mouth before he could think. "Am I going to be like them?" he blurted.

The Hollow Boys turned to Morrigan. She studied him with narrowed eyes, drumming the tablecloth with her fingers. Her expression softened. Raising her hands, she flicked her fingers at the Hollow Boys. Their eyes closed, and their chins slumped to their chests. "No, my little one. You will not become like my Hollow Boys."

Encouraged, he pressed on. "Why are they hollow?" He didn't ask why she *called* them the Hollow Boys. He knew why. They *were* hollow. The boys who used to live inside these bodies were gone. Or were lost in some dark forgotten place.

She sipped her tea. "Do you understand what you saw that first night? In that room before my Boys caught you?"

He shivered, remembering. "You helped the Master..." He hesitated, trying to find the right word. "You helped him *move* to another body. From one boy to another." She had explained he must never call Marell by name, but always as "the Master."

She smiled at him. He felt his face flush. He loved to make her smile.

"Yes," she said. "Once, the Master could take over anyone he chose. Stay as long as he wished. But then he...lost something. Since that day, he may remain in a new body for only a short time. He soon uses it up. When he leaves the body..." She regarded the Hollow Boys and shrugged.

"Are they...alive?"

"Yes, but broken. Fortunately, they are susceptible to suggestions, when reinforced by my magicks."

He remembered the symbols she'd drawn on Rattle that first night. These boys must wear those invisible marks. *That* was how she controlled them. He swallowed. He wore those marks now, too.

Around the table, the Hollow Boys sat slumped and silent. *He soon uses up each body.*

"He'll use me up, too, won't he?" he whispered.

Her eyes narrowed. "No."

"But that's why you take these boys. Why you took me—"

"No!" She slammed down both fists, tipping her cup.

He jumped. He slid down in his chair, afraid. Anger changed Morrigan. She remained beautiful, but it became a dark and dangerous beauty.

She righted the tipped cup, a pout replacing her anger. "Now look what you made me do." Dabbing up spilled tea with a napkin, she studied him from under long lashes. "No, little one. The Master will not use you. I will not allow that."

Although still afraid her anger would return, he had to ask one last question. "Why do you like me?" he whispered.

Her eyes widened. She tilted her head, considering him while the Hollow Boys sat like slowly breathing mannequins. "Perhaps you remind me of some-one..." She shook her head, as if to dislodge that thought. "I don't know."

He swallowed. "I like you, too."

Her brows arched. She opened her mouth, but then closed it again. Her eyes glistened.

"Are you *making* me like you?" he asked, voicing another fear. "With your magic?"

She smiled. "No, little one. I am not." She hesitated. "You like me?"

He nodded. "And I don't know why either." That was a lie. He knew why. She reminded him of someone, too. Or rather, of what it was like to have someone.

To have a mother.

They stared at each other, the Hollow Boys unconscious witnesses to their declarations. She picked up the napkin again but this time to dab her eyes, not spilled tea. She raised her arms, and the strange golden symbols appeared.

She was putting him to sleep. He started to protest, then noticed that symbols now glowed from his wrists to his elbows. First his legs, now his arms? "No!" he cried.

"Sleep, little one," she whispered.

The room grew dim, and he slipped lower in his chair as Morrigan rose from hers.

Morrigan stood beside where Fader slept, slumped in his chair. She touched his hair, then ran a long green-painted fingernail down his cheek. She let out a sigh.

Why do you like me?

Why indeed? Frustrated maternal instincts? The Hollow Boys were sad broken things. Pitiful substitutes for the child she'd always wanted. The child Marell had never given her.

Perhaps you remind me of someone...

Her words. She pushed that memory away. No, something more was at work. Something about this boy.

Something special.

Perhaps it was how he slipped beneath her attention. Out of sight, he often disappeared from her mind. She'd see a Hollow Boy guarding a room and have no memory of who the prisoner was. She'd unlock the door, find him there, and only then remember him.

Even in her presence, he could evade her notice. Like when he'd tried to escape earlier as they strolled the grounds. She'd told him she hoped he would run, to test her spells. But that had been a lie.

In truth, as she gazed out over the lake, she'd forgotten he was there. He would have escaped if the rune scripts hadn't worked.

She frowned. The rune scripts. Another mystery this boy presented.

Her and Marell's plan demanded a complex spell. One she needed to set down in layers on the child, each layer tested before she added the next. But each time she went to trace the next script on his skin, she found the prior one almost gone, as if it were fading.

Fading.

Fader. His name. A nickname he said his sister gave him. Interesting.

And his sister—yet another mystery. The failed spell that should have killed her the night they snatched her brother. The girl's uncanny ability to escape Stryke and Stayne. Escape not just once, but twice. Some family trait the girl shared with her brother?

She considered Fader sleeping in the chair. She could detect no magicks on the child, nor had she sensed any on his irksome sister. This boy held a mystery, one she would keep to herself until she could solve it. That was why she protected him. Why she would ensure Marell would never use him. Never make him an empty shell like the others.

No. That was a lie. She would protect him for another reason, too.

She truly liked the child. Perhaps something even more.

Another secret she could never share with Marell. He would kill the boy for that reason alone. He tolerated her pitiful "family" of Hollow Boys. But he would never permit her to hold such feelings for a real person. She clenched her fists, surprised at the resentment that realization brought.

She woke the Hollow Boys with a flick of a hand. Link carried Fader back to his bed in his now private room. There she laid the spell's final layer on him, after restoring the earlier scripts, which were again fading away.

Bending down, she kissed his forehead. The spell was ready. It now remained only to test it. Leaving Fader sleeping and his door open, she went to tell Marell.

⚜

Fader awoke, fresh and rested for the first time since his capture. He blinked and sat up in bed.

Something was different.

From the sunlight sneaking through the boarded windows, it was late afternoon. He looked around, but the room was as he remembered it, empty except for him and the bed. And a single wooden chair.

He often woke to find Morrigan sitting in that chair, watching him. He liked that, something he imagined a mother would do. He barely remembered his own mother. Someone had told him she'd left when he was four. Who'd said that? Oh, yeah. Case. His sister. Right. He'd never known their father. Case said she couldn't remember him. That didn't bother him. He never thought much about having a father.

But he'd always wanted to have a mother again.

Wait, something *was* different in the room. The door stood open. Not closed. Not locked.

He frowned. Locked? Why would he think that? Who would lock it? He wasn't a *prisoner* here.

Something else was different. He wore pajamas. Soft, cuddly, powder blue. And covered with smiling puppies (okay, *that* was embarrassing). But they felt wonderful. He couldn't remember the last time he'd worn pajamas.

He also couldn't remember changing into them, thrilling to their softness against his skin as he fell asleep. Maybe Morrigan had changed him. He hoped she had. Mothers did things like that.

Someone had laid out his clothes on the foot of the bed. Morrigan again, he guessed. Getting up, he started dressing, then stopped. These weren't his old clothes. These were *new* clothes. New jeans, new underwear, new socks. And a new t-shirt with one of his fave superheroes on it. Not the Dream Rider, but still...*new!*

And new sneakers!

Changing, he slipped on the sneakers last. Oh! My! God! They felt awesome. Cushy and squishy and huggy to his feet, like having a foot massage with every step.

He stopped. When had he ever had a foot massage? Had Morrigan given him one? No. It had been...

Case. Right, Case. She was...his sister. Right.

He frowned. Weird. He'd almost forgotten her.

Dressed, he walked into the hall, heading for the room where he'd spied on Morrigan and Marell his first night here. A room where he knew Morrigan waited. She wanted him to do something.

She was sitting in one of the high-backed chairs when he arrived, her eyes on the doorway as if expecting him. The man called Marell sat in Rattle's body in the chair beside her. Torches burned on the walls, washing the room in a flickering battle of light and shadow.

She smiled at him. "Hello, little one."

He shivered with happiness. He loved it when she called him that. "Hello, ma'am."

"Come. Stand here." She indicated the carpet with the strange skeleton legs design.

Avoiding Marell's cold eyes and cruel smile, he stepped onto the carpet. A sudden tingle like an electrical shock raced up his legs and into his chest.

Then it was gone. He blinked, facing them both, but keeping his eyes only on Morrigan. He hesitated, forgetting why he was here. "Did you want me to do something?"

She smiled at him. "Yes. To come to this room when you awoke. Which you have done. And right on time, too. I am proud of you."

His heart jumped. He'd made Morrigan proud of him.

She turned to Marell, her face now serious. "Well?"

Marell's cold stare made Fader wish he could run back to his little room. Back to bed. Back to sleep. Marell nodded. "I'm convinced. He's ready."

"When?"

"We'll send him today. The mercenaries will move tonight. You will lead them."

"I will take Stayne and Stryke as well."

"Just bring back our prey."

"And?"

Marell considered her with narrowed eyes. "*And?*" he repeated, making that single word sound dangerous.

Morrigan hesitated, and Fader realized she was *afraid* of Marell. "Your promise?"

Marell waved a hand as if batting away a fly. He considered Fader. "You can bring your little plaything back."

"And the girl?"

Marell shrugged. "Do we care?"

"She has escaped us twice, fleeing to where our prey hides both times. I wish to discover what she knows."

"Bring her, too, then."

Morrigan shone her wonderful smile on Fader again. "Little one, would you like to see your sister again?"

The question confused him. He thought hard. "Do I have a sister?"

Marell frowned. "Morrigan, will that not be a problem?"

"Part of the spell," she replied. "He will remember her when he sees her." She turned to Fader again. "Yes, you have a sister. And we are sending you to her."

That worried him. "Will I come back here after? Will I see you again?"

Marell snorted at that, but Morrigan's smile grew. "Yes, little one. You and your sister will both return here."

Relieved, Fader nodded. "Then, yes, I'd like to see my sister again."

Marell rose. "Enough. Prepare him. We'll send him as soon as you have him ready." He left the room without looking back.

Fader followed Morrigan from the room. As they returned to his bedroom, he sorted through jumbled memories. He gazed up at Morrigan where she walked beside him, his flame-haired angel-mother-protector. "Do I really have a sister?"

"Yes. You do." She smiled, but this smile held some of the cruelness of the Master's. "At least, for now."

Chapter 24

Lie Lie Lie

A t Yeshe's words, Will felt a chill that the late afternoon sun creeping across the Tibet floor could not chase away. Marell, a cold-blooded murderer with frightening powers, was hunting the Dream Rider. Hunting *him*.

The words of the snake thing (Marell, he now knew) last night in Dream returned to him.

After all my searching, I have finally found you.

He hadn't understood those words at the time. He'd been more concerned with not becoming a snake snack. Now, they made sense—a frightening, gut-clenching sense.

Adi's voice pulled him back to the moment. *"Someone you all know?"* she said, repeating Yeshe's words. "Would you care to explain, William, how *every-one* happens to know about the Rider? Including a stranger off the streets?"

"Hey, Yoda here seems okay—" Case said.

"I meant *you*."

Case frowned at Will. "Wait...*she* knows about the Rider, too?"

"Of course, I know!" Adi snapped.

"Okay, okay," Will said, raising his hands. "Time out. Let me explain."

"Very well," Adi said, glaring at Case. "Explain."

He turned to Case. "Can I tell about your dream last night?"

Case pursed her lips, then leaned over to whisper in his ear. "Okay, but not about my Voice."

He nodded, trying to ignore her closeness, her smell, her hair brushing his cheek, her breath on his ear. Trying—and failing.

"What did she whisper to you?" Adi asked.

"None of your business," Case snapped.

"It is most certainly—"

"WILL YOU TWO PLEASE STOP?" Will shouted. Both stared at him, eyes wide. "Bigger things to worry about, don't you think?" he said. "Your brother kidnapped?" he said to Case. He turned to Adi. "Marell hunting the Rider?"

Looking contrite, they both nodded, but not without shooting each other a final glare.

"Okay, so yes," he said, "Case knows about the Rider." Adi's eyebrows shot up. "And that I am a *friend* of his," he added, hating himself for continuing to lie to Case.

Adi looked relieved and gave him a little nod.

He went on. "They met in Dream last night. I'll tell you what the Rider told me. Case can fill in anything I leave out." He gave Adi a summary of their dream encounter with Fader.

"An abandoned hospital?" Adi said when he finished. "I'll get Mr. Zhang and his team working on that right away. There can't be many options. It would need to be within a short drive of downtown." She reached for her phone.

He held up a hand. "I asked his team to start looking this morning, after I... talked to the Rider." He'd almost said, "after I woke up." Thinking of the Rider as a separate person from himself was harder than he expected. Secret identities were a *pain*. "There's more." He turned to Case. "You haven't heard this part yet, either."

He related the Rider's attempt to rescue Harry Lyle. And his battle with the Hollow Boys and the Mara. He finished with the arrival of Snake Marell and the Rider's rescue by Yeshe. *Which I never thanked you for*, he said in his mind to Yeshe. *So, uh, thanks*. Yeshe responded with the slightest head bow.

"Holy crap," Case said.

"Horrible," Adi said. "Just horrible. Poor Mr. Lyle. But why kill him?"

"His series on disappearing street kids, I'm guessing," Will replied. "Harry must have been getting too close." He turned to Yeshe. "But too close to what? *Why* does Marell need these kids? What *is* his problem? How can the Rider solve it?"

"I can only give a theory. Ten years ago, Marell began switching bodies more often. At first, I assumed he was trying to hide himself from me." Yeshe shook his head. "Which was foolish of me. Whatever body he wears, I can detect his astral spirit. I know its..." He paused, as if searching for the best word. "Its *taste*. From when it occupied this very body. I still have that taste inside me." His disgust showed on his face. "All his hosts carry it."

"So why swap bods more often?" Case asked.

"I believe he must. Marell's power to *take over* a body is greater than when I first faced him. However, I believe his ability to *remain* in each host is diminishing."

"Why?" Will asked.

Yeshe hesitated. "I do not know, young master. But each body now soon rejects him, forcing him to find another victim."

"How soon?" Case asked. Will knew she was thinking of Fader.

"His current tenancy in a body appears to last at most a week."

"And dropping?" she asked.

"Yes."

She jumped up. "Meaning it might be only a few days now. They snatched Fader two nights ago. This Marell creep could be taking him over right now."

Will walked to her. "Fader was fine last night, right? And Fader said Marell transferred to a new kid just the night before. Plus, he saw another boy in his room."

"Slip. So what? Fader might still be next. It could still happen tonight."

"How old is your brother?" Yeshe asked.

"Twelve. Why?" she snapped.

"And Slip, the other captured boy?"

"Fifteen. Maybe sixteen. So what?"

"Another recent observation. Each of Marell's hosts is younger than the one before. Again, I do not know why. But Marell will use the older boy before your brother. He will not move to a host any younger than he needs to."

"Which means Fader's safe," Will said, looking at Case.

"Yeah, I guess." Her shoulders slumped. "But for how long?"

"Until we rescue him," Will replied.

"We?"

"Uh, well, the Rider. In Dream. The Rider'll find Fader before Marell can hurt him. With your help. And Yeshe's, too." He tried to sound more confident than he felt, remembering Snake Marell from last night. He turned to Yeshe. "Right?"

Eyes closed, Yeshe sat once again in lotus position before the Golden Throne. He looked pale and shrunken and old as if the telling of his tale had used him up. Will wondered how much help Yeshe could provide.

"I will aid you against Marell," Yeshe whispered. "For over a century, that has been my quest. But remember my warning, young master. Marell searches for the Dream Rider. For the Rider to hasten that encounter before he is prepared..." His voice trailed off.

"Would be bad, I'm guessing," Will said. "But you haven't explained *why* Marell is chasing the Rider."

"I will meet the Rider tonight in Dream. There the lessons will begin..." Yeshe's chin dipped to his chest. He began snoring.

Case shook her head. "So this is how we save Fader? Old tired dude who can't stay awake? Awesome."

Adi got up. "We'll find your brother. I'll meet with Mr. Zhang to see what he's discovered on this mysterious hospital."

Case's eyebrows shot up, no doubt at support from Adi. Will figured Adi's attitude changed once she realized Marell was real and after Will himself.

"Thanks," she said.

Adi nodded. "By the way, I googled 'Yeshe Norbu' while he was talking. A Ganden Tripa by that name served from eighteen eighty-two to eighty-four, one of the few not to serve a full term."

"Matches Yeshe's story," Will said. "Then he's telling the truth."

Adi snorted. "Or he knows how to google." Her phone beeped. She checked it.

"Zhang?" Will asked.

She shook her head. "Maintenance is checking the ventilation system. Three people in accounting fell asleep at their desks today."

"They're accountants," Will said. "Boredom is a professional hazard."

Giving him one of her looks, Adi left. Will's phone chirped with a text message. He read it. A new flower had arrived, again from Peru. His pulse quickened. Could this be the one?

Case stood staring at him, arms crossed. He couldn't run off and leave her alone after what Yeshe had explained about the danger facing Fader.

And he had real feelings for this girl. Ones that were growing stronger. He didn't want to leave things between them the way they were after their talk in the park. The flower's arrival was like a sign. He decided. "I need to tell you something."

She shrugged. "So spill."

"Actually, I have to show you. In the Jungle."

"The not-in-Kansas-anymore floor?"

"Uh..."

"Yellow brick road."

"Right. Yes. There."

"Okay. So let's go. Off to see the Wizard."

They walked to the elevator as he tried to decide which of his secrets to share with this strange girl who'd captured his heart.

Inside the elevator, he scanned his hand and pressed the button for "Roof / Jungle."

"Who you gonna be?" she asked.

"Huh?" he said, startled. Had she figured out he was the Rider?

"Well, I've got dibs on Dorothy. And this Morrigan has Wicked Witch Bitch totally locked. So that leaves Tin Man, Scarecrow, or Cowardly Lion."

"Can't I be Toto?"

"Nope. Got him right here." She cuddled an imaginary dog.

He thought about his life, his affliction. Never being able to step outside. The fear that seized him if he tried. He leaned his head back against the elevator wall. "Cowardly Lion."

He felt her eyes on him, but she said nothing. They rode the rest of the way in silence.

Chapter 25

Jungleland

On the roof, Case followed Will along another yellow-bricked path winding through the park. Between trees, she caught glimpses of the greenhouse he called the Jungle, their destination.

She tried to ignore her guilt. She should be saving Fader, not enjoying being alone with Will again.

But she *was* enjoying it. She shook her head. Just that morning, she'd convinced herself this could never work. Him, her. Them. Now she wondered again what it would be like. What *they* would be like. Together.

Because she liked him. *Really* liked him. And logic didn't matter then, did it?

As they walked, Will talked. And she listened.

She wasn't used to someone opening up, sharing their past, their secrets. Kids on the street never shared. And you never asked. Never asked how they got there, what they were running from. Never asked if they ever had a home. Because whatever had happened in that home was why they were on the streets.

But now Will, this guy she'd only met two nights ago, was confiding in her. Telling her about the darkest time of his life. It made her uneasy. And she didn't know why. Because she couldn't handle this much honesty? Or was it something else?

They reached the Jungle as he finished his story. Mysterious expedition in Peru. Disappearance of his parents and everyone involved. Except him. His loss of memory.

Total weirdness. Weirdness about *himself* he was sharing with her. What did that mean?

A corkboard hung beside the doors to the greenhouse. He pointed at one of the yellowed newspaper clippings hanging there behind a pane of glass. "That's them," he said quietly.

She leaned closer. Faded pictures of a white man and an Asian woman, smiling and confident, both attractive in their own way, gazed back at her. She studied Will, who waited expressionless behind her, then the images again. "Can't decide which one you look like."

"Yeah, I never could either."

Most of the articles made his parents sound like thieves and smugglers. Will had been nine. She remembered how it felt discovering bad things about a parent at that age. She'd been eight.

He stared out over the park behind them. She considered him from the corner of her eye. The two of them, so different, such worlds apart, yet they shared this. Both orphans before they'd seen their tenth birthdays.

She nodded at the greenhouse. "So what's this place?"

"C'mon, I'll show you."

Inside, the heavy cloying scent of flowers hit her like a physical force. Worse, the heat and humidity inside would have made the muggiest summer day feel like a polar chill. In seconds, sweat pasted her thin cotton t-shirt to her. Will glanced at her, then looked quickly away.

"I catch you checking out these puppies again," she growled, "I'm gonna smack you."

"Yes, ma'am." He grinned. "Puppies? So...which one is Toto?"

She punched him on the arm. Hard.

"Ow!" he said, but kept grinning.

"You are *so* dead," she muttered, but she had to fight not to smile back. And he kept his eyes above her neck.

They passed row after row of wooden tables, each covered with flowering plants. She'd never seen so many colors and shapes. Will stopped outside a smaller greenhouse within the larger one. A sign labeled "Isolation" hung over its door.

"What's in here?" she asked.

He paused, hand on the door. "One day, an answer, I hope." He looked at her. "Maybe even today."

She followed him into a sealed room like the airlocks in space movies. The air here was cool and dry. The door clicked closed behind them. A soft hissing began. Warm dry air blew at them from all sides from nozzles lining the walls.

Raising his arms, Will turned around. She did the same. After a minute, her damp clothes had dried, and the thick smell of flowers that had clung to them was gone.

The jets died. A click sounded. An inner door swung open. She followed Will into a small room.

In the middle sat a single table. On it, in a ceramic pot, a plant rose tall and spindly, with fern-like leaves and tiny blue flowers.

"Hmm," he said. "Not an orchid."

"Is that good or bad?"

"Different."

"What's this about?" she asked, still confused.

"The scent of a flower." He described his search for the source of his sole memory from the doomed expedition.

She watched him as he spoke, seeing him as if for the first time. As he told his story, Will transformed in her eyes. Transformed from the wisecracking weirdo in the strange tower home into someone who shared her broken childhood. Someone strong enough to keep searching for answers to a mystery that had shattered his life.

She had never tried to do that.

"You're not giving up, are you?" she said when he finished.

He shook his head. "It's all I have."

All I have. He owned a skyscraper filled with more stuff than she'd ever imagined. And yet all he cared about was this search, this hope.

"Here goes," he said. Moving to the table, he leaned over the largest cluster of flowers on the plant. He breathed in. He straightened.

She read it in his face.

He walked back to her, and it hurt to see how forced his smile was. He gave an exaggerated shrug. "Oh, well. Maybe next time."

"Right," she said, a little too quickly. "Next time."

"Yeah. Sure." He shot the plant a final look, his smile disappearing. "Let's get out of here."

They left the Jungle, walking in silence. Will didn't talk, and she didn't know what to say. From her own life, she knew words couldn't stop that kind of pain. She saw pain on the streets every day and had learned to ignore it. But, she realized to her surprise, she wanted to stop *his* pain.

They reached the hill where she'd found him earlier. He climbed to the top and sat. She joined him. "Fave spot?"

He nodded, not looking at her. "I need to tell you something else. About me."

"Will, you don't need to tell me anymore." His sharing personal secrets with her made her uncomfortable. And she still didn't know why. *Liar*, she thought. *You know why.*

"No, I *do* need to. Earlier today, right here in this spot, you asked me *why*. Why I have all this. This park. This whole building. 'All the weird freaking floors,' as you put it."

She winced. "Sorry. I can be a little...blunt."

He laughed. "Really? Gee, I hadn't noticed." He laughed again. And kept laughing.

"Stop it!" She punched his arm again, but smiled, enjoying the sound. She caught herself. *What's with that, girl?*

"Sorry." His smile ran away. "Okay, here's what I should've told you this morning." He looked at her, and the pain in his eyes made her hurt. "Only I was too afraid."

"Afraid?"

He dropped his eyes. "Afraid of what you'd think of me."

She swallowed. He cared what she thought of him?

He explained what happened whenever he tried to go outside. How it had started after he'd been found in the jungle. How it forced him to live his life inside this building, never leaving his strange high-rise home. How therapy, hypnotism, and drugs had never helped.

"I can never go outside. Into the real world," he said quietly, looking at the sky above them. "So I've brought the world to me. This tower is my pretend world."

He hadn't looked at her the whole time he'd been speaking. She realized, with a sudden ache for him, that he was ashamed. "You're not, you know," she said.

He turned to her.

"You're not the Cowardly Lion. You're not *afraid* to go outside. You just *can't*. It's like..." She stopped, searching for the right words. "It's like you picked up a bug in that jungle."

"You mean I'm diseased?" he said, but she caught the twitch of a smile before he hid it again.

"Hey, this is me being nice. Don't make it hard, or I won't do it again."

He grinned. "Point taken."

"You're no coward, Home Boy," she said softly. "I think you're brave. Brave to keep trying. Brave to tell me."

He didn't answer, just nodded. She pretended not to notice him wipe his eyes.

"Will, why *did* you tell me?" she asked, even though she knew. "About your parents, the flower, your..." She almost said "problem," but stopped herself. "About why you live like this."

"I wanted to be honest with you." He hesitated, then turned to her. "Because I like you, Case. I like you a lot."

So there it was. Out in the open.

But wasn't this what she'd hoped for? Didn't she like him, too?

Yeah, she did. She definitely did. She knew it from how much she thought about him, despite worrying about Fader. She knew it from how she felt whenever they were together.

And he was kind and gentle, funny and fun. Cute and sexy too, in a gangly, lost puppy dog sort of way (what was it with puppies today?). He found her attractive, too, from the way she'd catch him checking her out.

And she knew it wasn't just about sex with him. He treated her like an equal. A friend. He *listened* to her. Really listened, then considered and respected whatever she said. Crap, how many guys did that? How many *people* did that?

And he had a good heart. On the street, she'd learned to read people, and she saw the goodness in him. He'd proven it, too. She'd broken into his home, crash-landing into his life with her crazy story. Yet he'd done everything he could since then to help find Fader. He'd trusted her.

He *trusted* her. She wasn't used to that, not one bit. He trusted her so much he'd opened up to her, telling her his whole story, including parts he was ashamed to tell.

And *that* was the problem. The reason for her discomfort when he'd shared his past, his secrets, his fears with her.

Because now she had to share *her* past, *her* secrets, *her* fears. And that would make her vulnerable. That would give him power. Power over her.

Power to hurt her.

You never let that happen on the streets. You never gave someone power over you. Because they'd use it. Maybe not right away. But some day, some night, when you were most vulnerable, they'd use it. Use it to get what they wanted. Use it to hurt you.

She'd sworn she'd never give anyone that power. The streets had taught her that.

Liar. The streets hadn't taught her.

Her mother had.

Will was looking at her, all lost puppy dog again, waiting. So what would it be? Secrets and fears?

No. She wasn't like Will. She didn't have his kind of courage—the courage to share something that...intimate.

But there were other kinds of intimacy.

She turned to him. "I like you, too. A lot." It was true. Even if she couldn't tell him her secrets and fears, at least she wasn't lying about that. She leaned in closer, tilting her head.

His eyes widened, then he smiled. He leaned in to meet her.

And they kissed.

They kissed, and it was wonderful. Warm and soft and exciting and tender, and she wanted it to go on forever. She moved closer. He wrapped his arms around her. She held him tight against her, and the kiss did go on and on and on and felt so right.

Finally, she broke it off, or maybe he did. She didn't know. She didn't care.

They sat there, holding each other, not speaking, until he leaned back to stare at her, his face serious. "Case, there's something else you need to know about me."

She shook her head. The more Will shared, the more he'd expect her to share her own secrets. "No. Not now."

"But it's important—"

"So's this." She kissed him again, hard, and he responded. When it ended, she stroked his cheek.

"Um..." he said.

"So...?"

"So? You mean...?"

"Yeah. Very much," she said, surprised at how much she meant it.

He stood and offered his hand. This time, she let him help her up. They walked along the yellow brick road, an arm around each other's waists.

They took the stairs to his apartment. All the way to his bedroom, she kept telling herself that not sharing her own past, her own pain, her own fears, wasn't the same as lying to him.

Chapter 26

You and Me

Case lay in the huge round bed in Will's bedroom, watching him sleep. Late afternoon sun streamed through the west windows. She felt amazing. She felt miserable.

The sex had been the amazing part. He was a much better lover than she expected for someone his age. He'd even asked her what she liked. And *didn't* like. She'd never had a guy do that. After, they'd cuddled, and he'd fallen asleep.

Cue the miserable part. Had she really used sex to avoid opening up to him the way he had to her? Had her mother screwed her up that much?

She sat up, burying her face in her hands. It was as if she'd lied to him twice. First by not sharing her own secrets, and then by avoiding the issue by kissing him.

Which had led them here.

Which made what they'd shared here seem like a lie, too.

But it wasn't. She'd been honest with him in that. She'd *never* felt like this about a guy before. So why couldn't she tell him about her own secrets and past?

Because her mother had broken something inside her. Will thought *he* was broken, but *she* was, too. So broken she couldn't even bring herself to talk about it with someone she...

Someone she...what?

Loved? Is that what this was? If it *was* love, would she ever *tell* him she loved him? She loved Fader with all her heart, but she'd never been able to tell him. The words always caught in her throat.

Because she'd loved someone else once with all her heart. Her mother. Loved her more than the world. Trusted her. Believed she'd always be there for her, for Fader.

Fader.

More guilt. She should be searching for him. Not being here, doing this. Not being...*happy*. And she *was* happy with Will.

Stop it. She had to find Fader. Getting out of bed, she picked up her scattered clothes from the floor and started dressing.

"I thought the *guy* is supposed to sneak out after without saying goodbye."

She jumped. Will leaned on one elbow, half under the covers, all hair tousled and grinning and adorable. She pulled her t-shirt on and zipped her jeans, stalling. "Uh, yeah. I'm going to look for Adi."

He raised his eyebrows. "Okay, *now* you have me worried. Do your plans involve a blunt instrument?"

She forced a smile. "No. Just want to ask if they found that hospital," she said. That was at least true. "You know, the reason I'm here. To find Fader."

Will's smile melted away. He sat up. "Yeah. No. Right. I get that. I just thought..." His voice trailed off.

I can't do this! She slipped on her sneakers. "I gotta go."

"Case, wait. Please. I still need to tell you something about me." Slipping on his boxers, he swung his legs over the edge of the bed and started to stand.

"No!" she yelled, stepping back. "No more! No more secrets. No more...sharing."

He sat back, looking as if she'd hit him. She felt she had. "What did I...?" He stopped. "Wasn't I...? Didn't you...?"

Why was she doing this? "No, it's not that. It was great. You were great. I just can't..." What could she tell him? *The truth would be good, girl.* But she couldn't. She couldn't make herself that vulnerable. She couldn't *trust.* Not just Will. She couldn't trust *anyone.*

"Case, what's wrong?" he said, his eyes pleading.

Stop asking me! she wanted to scream. In desperation, she threw up her hands, waving them around the room. "It's this!"

"This?"

"This whole place. Your money. Your life. Everything."

"But I explained why I live here," he said, confusion on his face. "I thought—"

"*You* live here. What about me? Where do I fit in?" she said, plunging on, grasping for a reason to give him. Anything. Anything but the truth.

"I hadn't thought that far ahead. I mean, we just..."

"Well, think about it. Where would I live? Here?"

"Yeah. Sure. That is, you can if you want."

"Oh? So you'd 'keep' me?"

"That's not what I meant. I mean you wouldn't have to live on the streets."

"Because that'd be embarrassing, wouldn't it? To tell your friends?"

His jaw clenched and unclenched. "I don't have friends."

What was she doing? She wanted to run to him and hug him. But she didn't. Instead, she hurt him more. "So buy some."

Will paled.

The words had come out before she could stop herself. Now it was too late.

She kept going, kept making it worse. "You have the money, right? So much money. It's...it's *obscene*."

The word hung in the air, like a physical object. Like a wall between them, growing more solid with each passing second of silence.

"You think I'm obscene?" he said finally, the hurt plain on his face.

What had she done? Why was she doing this? "No. No. I didn't mean—"

"That's what you said."

"Your money," she said, holding herself back from running to him. "Your money. Not you."

He said nothing. And she'd said too much. She'd said stupid hurtful things.

"Will," she said, her voice softer, "you have everything. I have nothing. Everything Boy and Nothing Girl. It would never work." She told herself it was true. That it was better this way.

He stared at her, unspeaking, pain in every line on his face. She couldn't do this. She couldn't hurt him. She started to say she was sorry, to explain. To tell him she was broken, too.

But before she could speak, a computerized female voice from an overhead speaker interrupted. "Mr. Dreycott, I have a call from Ms. Archambeault."

"Answer, Hallie," Will whispered.

"My apologies. Your voice volume was insufficient for me to—"

"ANSWER!" he snapped. Case jumped at the anger and hurt in that single word.

Adi's voice came over the speaker. "William, where are you?"

"In my bedroom."

"Where's Case?"

He looked at her, then away. "Here," he replied, his voice a flat dead thing.

Pause. "Oh," Adi said.

"Adi, what do you want?" He sounded so tired.

Another pause. "You both need to come to reception."

"Why?"

"There's...been a development."

"Adi, what *is* it?"

"There's a boy here," Adi replied. "He's asking for Case..."

Case's heart did a somersault in her chest.

Adi continued. "He says his name is Fader."

Turning her back on Will, Case ran from the bedroom, heading for the elevators.

The elevator ride down to the lobby was the longest trip Case had ever taken. Even her stomach tumbling with the drop didn't bother her. She just wanted the trip to be faster. She just wanted to see her brother.

Fader was here! Alive and safe.

She caught herself. Safe? She didn't know that. What if he was hurt? Adi had said only that he asked for her. Asked for his big sister. The big sister who should have saved him. That's what big sisters did.

But she hadn't saved him. He'd done that. Saved himself while she fooled around with her boyfriend.

Ex-boyfriend, she corrected herself. Definitely "ex" now after the horrible, hurtful things she'd said. Shortest relationship *ever*. Even for her.

She shook her head. No time for that now. Fader was back, and he'd need her.

The elevator finally slowed. After what seemed a lifespan, the doors opened, and she burst into the secure reception area.

And there he was.

Fader sat on a white leather couch opposite the reception desk, Adi and Bevington on either side of him. Adi was talking. Fader stared straight ahead. He wore different clothes, but he appeared unhurt. A bottle of water sat on the table before him untouched. Case ran toward him, and Fader turned to her.

Later, when she looked back on this scene, she'd remember what she ignored at that time. How expressionless his face was. How, when he met her eyes, he showed no sign of recognition.

No sign he knew his sister. For a heartbeat, two heartbeats.

Then he broke into a huge smile. Jumping up from the couch, he ran to meet her. And in that moment, she pushed away what she'd seen. She forgot it all as she hugged him to her, telling herself over and over she'd never leave him behind again.

"Case," Fader said, "I can't breathe."

Letting him go, she stepped back, wiping her eyes. "Sorry, bro. I thought I might never..." She gave him another quick hug. "I'm just happy you're safe." She studied him more closely. He was cleaner than she'd ever seen him, and his clothes were brand-new. "Are you okay? They didn't hurt you?"

"I'm fine."

"How'd you find me? How'd you know to come here?"

Adi came to stand behind Fader. "He said you told him."

"Me?"

"In our dream," Fader said. "When we met the Dream Rider. You said you went to his tower."

Adi's eyes widened at that. As Bevington joined them, Adi gave Case an almost imperceptible shake of her head.

Yeah, I get it. Don't talk about the Rider. She flicked Fader's new t-shirt with a finger. "Nice threads. Where'd you get these?"

Fader considered his clothes as if just realizing he wore them. "From her."

Case fought back a sudden fear. A fear from her memories of the red-haired woman the night Fader had disappeared. The woman Yeshe called a witch. "Her? Morrigan?"

Fader nodded.

"Fader, what happened to you?" she asked softly, almost too afraid to ask, but knowing she had to. "Where did they take you? How did you get away?"

He tilted his head, as if listening to something, then he rubbed his eyes and yawned. "Case, I'm really tired. All the time I was there, I was so scared I didn't sleep much. Can I crash somewhere? I'll tell you everything after."

"Can I take him to my room?" Case asked Adi. "He needs to sleep."

Adi raised one eyebrow, probably at her "my room" reference, Case guessed. Well, after how she'd treated Will, it wouldn't be her room much longer. That would make Adi happy.

To her surprise, Adi nodded. "Certainly. We'll send up food, too." But then Adi turned to Fader. "Before you go, Fader, do you know where they were keeping you?"

"He said he'll tell us after," Case snapped.

Adi ignored her. "Fader, I understand you're tired—"

"Which part of 'after' did you not get?" Case said, stepping between Fader and Adi.

Bevington moved forward, but Adi raised a hand. She faced Case. "Your brother's escape might prompt these people to relocate. We have a small window to alert the police to where they were holding Fader. A small window to save the other boys who weren't lucky enough to escape as he did."

Case bit back a retort. She couldn't let other kids stay in danger just because Fader was safe. She looked at him. "*Do* you know where you were, bro? *Can* you help?"

Again, he tilted his head, not answering right away. "It was still dark when I snuck out. I was scared and running as fast as I could. I'm not sure I'd remember the way back."

"Perhaps this will help," Adi said. Pulling her tablet from under her arm, she held it out. The screen showed an aerial shot of a long three-story brick building. Behind it, an expanse of lawn ran up to a ribbon of trees lining a cliff that dropped off to water far below.

Adi continued. "Mr. Zhang's team followed up on that hospital lead from your... *meeting* last night," she said, eyeing Case. Case understood she was hiding any reference to the Dream Rider from the others in the lobby. "They identified one candidate hospital within the assumed range of downtown. An abandoned psychiatric facility, closed five years ago. This is a satellite shot of the location. Do you recognize this building?"

Fader's eyes widened. Another head tilt. Another pause. He shook his head. Shook it hard. "No. It didn't look like that."

Adi frowned. "You're sure?"

"Yes. I'm sure."

"Well, can you tell us how it *did* look?" Adi asked.

"Hey," Case said, "he answered your question. Now he needs to sleep."

Adi ignored Case. "Fader, if you can tell us anything—"

"Adi!"

Case turned. Will walked toward them from the elevators. His hair was a tangled mess, and he wore the same clothes from before they—

She pushed that thought away, along with the wave of guilt and confusion that swept over her. *Not important*, she told herself. Fader was back. Her brother was safe. That was all that mattered.

Except it wasn't. And she knew it.

"Adi," Will said, "the kid's exhausted. Let him sleep."

Adi sighed. "Very well. We'll keep searching for other hospitals. Fader, I am so glad you're safe. We'll chat more when you're rested." She looked at Will. "I'll wait in your studio. We need to talk." Shooting Case a glare, she headed for the elevators.

Case felt Will's eyes on her, but she didn't meet his gaze.

Will held out his hand to Fader, smiling. "Hi. I'm Will."

Fader shook hands but said nothing. An awkward silence fell.

"Hey," Case said, "Will's the guy you told me about. The one who does the Dream Rider comics." *And the guy I just slept with and then treated like crap.* "You were right. He lives here."

"I hear you're a fan, Fader," Will said.

Fader blinked at Will, still saying nothing.

"Bro, you okay?" Case asked.

Fader looked at her. "I met the Dream Rider."

"Yeah," Will said so only they could hear. "That really happened. In Dream. That's how we knew to look for a hospital. You were a big help."

Fader's eyes went wide. "That's *not* the hospital. I told you that."

"Yeah. No. We get it," Will said, flashing Case a look. "No problem. Not the place. We'll cross it off the list."

Fader appeared to relax. He let out a big breath and even managed a timid smile.

Case was getting more worried. This wasn't like Fader. He'd shown no sign of excitement over meeting Will. Worse, he still seemed afraid of something. But, she reminded herself, she didn't know what he'd been through these past three days. It must have been traumatic. He'd need time to get over it.

"Case will show you where you can catch some Zs," Will said. "We'll talk after. I'll even show you the next Dream Rider issue I'm working on."

Fader just nodded. "Can we go now?" he asked Case.

She turned to Will. Shit, she couldn't even meet his eyes. "Uh, can you take us up? The elevators don't recognize me. I can go down to reception, but nowhere else."

Will stared at her, expressionless. "Better idea. Follow me." He led them to the reception desk, a glass rectangle on a single support post, slanted towards the seated receptionist. The receptionist, a short blonde wearing a crisp white blazer with the DR logo, beamed up at Will.

"Josie," he said, "I'd like to add my friends to the building security list."

Josie touched something on the desk surface, then tipped the desktop so it slanted towards them. A keyboard image appeared.

Will tapped on the keyboard, spelling out "Case" then "Fader." An image of a hand appeared below each name. He moved aside. "Okay, put your hands there and wait for the green light." They did that. A list of options appeared above their names. Will selected "Full Building Access" for them both, then placed his own hand over a flashing "Authorization" sign.

He tipped the desk back. "There. Now you both can go anywhere in the tower. Just don't blow up anything, okay?" He grinned at Fader.

"What?" Fader said, looking scared.

"That was a joke," Will said. "Unless you're thinking of blowing up stuff. In which case—don't."

Fader just stared at Will, expressionless. Case bit her lip. What was wrong with him? "Thanks. We gotta go. He needs sleep." Putting her arm around Fader, she guided him to the elevators.

"Case," Will called.

She turned, keeping Fader between her and Will like a shield.

"What?" she said, ashamed at how harsh she sounded.

Will swallowed. "I want to make this work."

"This?" She knew what he meant.

He pointed to her, then himself. "You and me. Us."

She couldn't deal with this now. Maybe not ever. Pushing away the shame of how she was treating him, she shook her head. "I'm sorry, Will. I don't think it can." She took Fader's hand and walked to the elevator. She pressed the button, keeping her back to Will and trying hard not to sob.

"Why are you crying?" Fader asked.

"Just happy to see you," she said. "Now shut up."

Chapter 27

Sick Muse

Hurt and confused, Will stormed into his studio. Adi sat on the black leather couch, tapping on her tablet. Snatching a Dream Rider coffee mug from his desk, he flung it at the bookcases. It exploded, scattering shards across the floor. He felt better for about five seconds.

Adi considered the ceramic carnage. "Very mature." Sighing, she laid her tablet on the couch. "Well, you have my attention."

"You should come with manuals."

"Excuse me?"

"Women! Nothing you do makes sense."

"I beg your pardon, but *everything* I do makes sense."

"Not you. *Case!*"

"Ah. I see." She fought back a smile, which made him angrier. "What happened?"

"We just had sex—"

"Oh, god, William! Must you share that with me?"

"And then we had this *huge* fight—"

"Yes, by all means. *Do* continue." She sighed. "A fight over what?"

"I don't know! That's my point. I mean, we had just...you know. And I thought she... But instead, she... Arghh!" He slumped down on the couch beside her. "Manuals. Definitely."

Adi hesitated. "You won't want to hear this—"

"Then don't tell me."

"—but I warned you that girl was trouble. She is only interested—"

"I think I love her, Adi."

There. He'd said it. At least to Adi. He should've told Case. But couldn't she tell? Didn't she know? No. She couldn't. If she knew he loved her, then she wouldn't have done what she did, said what she'd said. Would she?

Adi closed her eyes. "Oh, god, William, no. You just met her."

He clenched his fists. "Don't start."

"Why on earth would you say such a thing?"

"What? *Why?* Why am I in love with her? Seriously? Why does *anyone* fall in love?" He stood, raising his arms and dropping them in exasperation. "I don't know *why* I feel the way I do about her. I just do. She's...she's..." He smiled despite himself, thinking of Case. "She's smart and tough and brave—"

"Rude and abrasive and violent."

"That's just the front she puts up. She has to. She lives on the streets. Inside, she's kind and caring and warm."

Adi raised an eyebrow. "Warm?"

"Okay, yeah. That's pushing it. But she loves her brother and would do anything to protect him."

Adi snorted. "Oh, yes. That's why she ran away when he was captured. Why she was tumbling with you while he was missing."

"That's not fair, Adi. Case almost died last night looking for him."

"So she says."

"Are you saying she's lying?"

Adi rose to face him. "I think she'd say anything to get at your money."

"Yeah? Well, you're wrong. That's what we fought about. She said I had too much money. That it was...obscene." He swallowed, remembering how much it had hurt to hear Case say that.

Adi hesitated, looking unsure for a second. Then she shook her head. "I find that hard to believe. This girl is a vagrant. She lives by begging and stealing. Worse, she spent six months in juvenile detention. She then removed her brother illegally from his foster home and—"

He held up his hands. "Whoa. Wait. You *investigated* Case?"

She straightened her suit jacket. "I had Mr. Zhang look into her, yes."

"*What?* What gives you the right?"

"Oh, god, William, grow up. Do you think I'd let some stray get this close to you, to us, without checking into her?"

"Without asking me? Without telling me?"

"Who do you think runs this building? Runs your company? I do a thousand things every day without consulting you. To protect your interests. To protect *you*!"

"You're not my mother, Adi!"

"I *know* who I am," she shouted back. He'd never seen Adi so angry. "And who I am *not*. *I* didn't drag a child along on a dangerous expedition that almost killed him, that left him broken and—" She stopped as he stiffened. Her hand went up to cover her mouth. She dropped it again, reaching for him. "Oh, William. I'm sorry. I didn't mean that."

He backed away. "Get out."

"William, please—"

"GET! OUT!"

She took a step back. Her mouth opened, closed. Her lips quivered. She gave a short nod and walked to the doorway to his studio. Stopping, she looked back. "I should never have said those things. Please forgive me. Everything I do is for you. To protect you."

He turned away, not answering. After a few seconds, he heard her heels on the track, heading towards the elevators.

Slumping down on the couch, he buried his face in his hands. Images swirled through his head. His mom. His dad. Case. Adi. People he cared for.

People who disappeared. People who hurt him. People who betrayed him.

And some crazy guy with astral powers who wanted to kill him.

Sliding into his tall chair at his design desk, he called up the most recent scenes of the next issue he'd been working on. After reviewing them, he made a few changes, then started sketching the following frames.

He threw himself into his work. He added a battle scene, then another, and another. Monsters appeared. Monsters died. It was the bloodiest issue he'd ever done.

It felt good.

He worked through his normal dinnertime. At some point, his dinner arrived. Grilled cheese sandwich, a mountain of fries with gravy, and a chocolate milkshake. His favorite comfort food. Adi was trying to make up.

Well, he wasn't ready to make up. Ignoring the meal, he kept working, trying to lose himself in his art, lose his memories of today.

But he didn't want to lose all the memories, did he? Some he wanted to keep forever—the thrill of Case's skin against his, the taste of her kiss, the smell of her hair.

He shook his head, trying to drive those thoughts from his mind. No. Those memories meant nothing. It could never work. She'd said that. Never.

He returned to his work. About nine o'clock, he sensed a tingle at the base of his skull, followed by a now familiar voice in his mind.

Young master, Yeshe said.

Yeah? What? he snapped back.

A pause. *You are upset.* Will caught a visual flash of a sad smile.

Sorry. Bad afternoon. Well, a great afternoon—then not so great. Why are you...calling?

Two reasons. First, have your people located the hospital where Marell is hiding?

He began to form the thoughts to explain Fader's arrival and inability to identify the hospital. But Case's face and voice and smell flavored every memory of that exchange, so he pushed it away. *No*, he replied. *A dead-end so far. Unfortunate.*

Will sensed disappointment in the monk's mind. *You mentioned two reasons. I promised to meet you tonight in Dream. To prepare you to face Marell.*

Marell. The other problem in his life. A problem that should make a broken heart unimportant—except it didn't.

Right, he answered. *Yeah, sure. How...?*

It would be best if I am physically present with you. We will enter Dream together. Else, we would waste time locating each other there. And time is not a luxury we possess.

Okay. I'll tell security to bring you up here. About midnight?

He felt the psychic equivalent of a nod, then the contact faded. Turning back to his artwork, he sighed. For the first time ever, he was not looking forward to Dream.

Chapter 28

Satellite Mind

J ust before midnight and Yeshe's expected arrival, Will shut down his design
table. Sliding off the chair, he rubbed his face. Tired. So tired.

And hungry. Sitting on the couch, he took a bite of the grilled cheese
sandwich. Cold, hard. And the fries were a soggy mess. He forced himself
to eat half the sandwich, washing it down with warm milkshake. He'd just
finished when Yeshe appeared in the doorway. The monk still wore the jeans
and Grateful Dead t-shirt outfit. He was barefoot.

Yeshe bowed. "Are you ready for your lesson?"

"Yes. No. Not really." The last thing he wanted was school. But what choice
did he have? "What are we going to do, Yeshe? What's your plan?"

Yeshe sat beside him. His face became grave, a jarring contrast to his normal
kind smile. "Together, young master, you and I must stop Marell. No one else
can do this. I have grown too weak with age to face both Marell and Morrigan.
But together, you and I, we stand a chance."

"A *chance*?"

Yeshe smiled. "These lessons will increase that chance greatly."

"Wonderful. Why not hand him over to the cops? If they find him with
kidnapped kids, he'll go to jail."

"Do not assume your local constabulary could capture him. Or hold him
confined once captured. He has evaded the law around the world for over a
century. Even in his weakened state, he remains powerful. And he has Morrigan. Her magicks alone could defeat your police, and his spirit could flee to her
amulet at any time. Then our hunt would begin again."

"But if the police can't defeat him, how can we?"

"We must expel Marell's astral spirit from his current body. And, once expelled, prevent him from taking over another or escaping to Morrigan's amulet."

"But if we do that, won't his spirit...die?"

"It will fade from this plane of existence, yes."

A chill seized him as he realized what Yeshe proposed. "Meaning we'll kill
him. Yeshe, that's murder. I'm not sure I can do that."

A sad smile flickered on the monk's face. "I would have grave concerns if that did *not* disturb you." His smile disappeared, leaving only the sadness. "But Marell has killed scores of people over the past century. Or left them as empty husks, like the Hollow Boys. If we do not stop him, he will continue to kill. More will die. Many more."

"Yeah, I get that, but still..." His words trailed off as he struggled with what Yeshe was asking.

"Remember, too, Marell is now hunting *you*. If we do not destroy him, he *will* destroy you."

Then it would be self-defense. But they'd still be killing Marell. "Why is he even after the Rider? What does he want from me?" He was avoiding the real question. Could he *kill* another person, no matter how evil they were?

Yeshe hesitated. "I believe he plans to take *you* over, to gain the astral power you have in Dream. Perhaps he thinks your power could heal him, allowing him to remain in a body as long as he wishes."

"Remain in *my* body, you mean."

"And since you are attuned to the astral plane, his powers will grow with you as his host. He will become even more dangerous."

Will slumped back on the couch. "This gets better and better. How'd he learn about the Rider, anyway? How'd he find me?" He sat up, looking at Yeshe. "Wait a minute. How did *you* find me?"

"Marell found you in Dream, as did I. I have chased Marell for over a hundred and thirty years, following his astral spirit when I detect him. In the beginning, I searched for his spirit in the waking world, but now he rarely takes astral journeys. He is too weak and fears not being able to return to his host body."

"So now you search for him in Dream?"

Yeshe nodded. "One night, two years ago, I sensed him in Dream. As I followed him, I realized he himself followed someone. He escaped me that night. But whenever I have detected him in Dream since, I have also detected that other presence. The person he hunts." He looked at Will. "You."

Will didn't reply. Ever since he'd discovered Dream, he'd considered it his personal realm, one he ruled. But unknown to him, for two years in that realm, he'd been the unsuspecting prey of a crazed killer.

He felt numb. This wasn't happening to him. Except it was. "How would we—and I'm not saying I'm agreeing—but if I did, how would we..." He let his words trail off, not able to complete the thought.

"We cannot trap his astral spirit in Dream. He could escape by waking up. So, we must face him in the *waking* world."

"The waking world? You mean the real one? As in outside this building? Sorry, dude, but your plan has a major hole in it."

"I know of your challenges, young master. I mean that our astral spirits must face his own. In the real world."

"Hole number two. I can't project my astral spirit."

Yeshe smiled, like a teacher with a favorite student. "Bringing us full circle. *That* will be the focus of your lessons. I will teach you astral projection. Once mastered, your spirit will be able to journey into the world."

"Into the world? You mean..." Was he hearing right? "You mean, I'll be able to go...*outside?*"

"Yes. Only your physical body is trapped here. An astral spirit may roam anywhere in this world."

Anywhere in this world. Could he finally escape this tower that was both his home and prison? Could he finally be *free?*

Standing up, he started pacing the studio. For eight years, he'd considered himself broken, trapped here by his own weakness. He'd thought his weakness was the price he'd paid for his powers in Dream. But Yeshe was saying those powers could give him both worlds—Dream and the real world. He could have it all.

He stopped pacing. No. Not all. Not Case. He couldn't have her.

Yeshe came to stand beside him. "So, young master, will you let me teach you?"

Anywhere in this world.

Maybe he wouldn't have to kill Marell. Maybe they'd find another way. For now, he needed Yeshe to teach him, to learn to defend himself, didn't he?

He nodded, telling himself he was doing the right thing. "Yeah. I'm ready. Let's do this."

The monk gave a huge smile of relief. "I am pleased." He patted Will on the shoulder. "Yes, very pleased. You will be an apt student, I am sure."

"Great. So what's your 'wax on, wax off' plan, Mr. Miyagi?"

Yeshe frowned.

"I mean, how are you going to teach me to astral project?"

"Ah! You already know how to."

"What?"

"When you enter Dream, you project your astral spirit into that realm. We will therefore begin in Dream, building on your skills as the Rider. I will lead you to where Dream connects to the waking world. From that place, it is a small step to project into the waking world."

"You mean I'll astral project into the real world *from* Dream?"

"The mental trance I use for an astral journey resembles the one you use to enter Dream. Eventually, you will learn to project while awake. But for our urgent problem of defeating Marell, Dream is our quickest route."

"When do we start?"

"Now, if you are willing. Enter Dream in your normal way. I will join you."

"Okay, let's rock." With Yeshe following, Will climbed the stairs to his bedroom.

And stopped.

A tangle of sheets still covered the big round bed. From that afternoon. From when he and Case had been there. From when they had...

No. There was no "they." No him and her. Just him. Just her. Separate.

"Is there a problem?" Yeshe asked.

"No," Will said. The quilted comforter lay on the floor. Grabbing it, he threw it over the bed, hiding the sheets but not the memories. "No problem at all."

Stripping down to his boxers, he settled into a lotus position on the bed. Yeshe assumed the same pose on the floor and closed his eyes. Will took a deep breath and slowly exhaled. Closing his eyes, he began his meditation for entering Dream.

Most nights, it took only five minutes for the calmness to settle on him. Tonight, his mind refused to empty. Memories of Case swirled through his head. Case kissing him. Case beside him in this bed. Case walking out on him after, turning her back on him. Those memories battled with fantasies of traveling the world in his astral body. Seeing the real Musée d'Orsay, the real Egypt, the real Tibet. But even then, in each imagined scene, Case was there, her warm real body walking beside his astral one.

Finally, the calmness came. He lay on his back and called for the room lights to dim. Closing his eyes, he chanted his mantra in the dark. "He only comes out at night, he only comes out at night, he only..."

"...comes out at night," he said.

"A restriction we will soon remove." Yeshe's voice.

Will opened his eyes. As usual, he lay on the Bed of Awakening in the House of Four Doors. And, as usual, he wore the costume of the Rider.

But *usual* ended there.

He found neither Brian nor any other Doogle waiting for him. Instead, hands folded before him and wearing his red robes, Yeshe stood beside one of the doors.

Will blinked. Correction—Yeshe stood beside the *only* door.

Tonight, the House resembled the dark bricked square where he'd encountered the Mara. And Marell. He shivered at those memories. Fastening his hooded cloak around his neck, he walked over. "Can't say I like what you've done with the place."

Yeshe raised an eyebrow. "I have done nothing. This room manifests your subconscious, applying the visual metaphors you use in Dream."

"Meaning the House is reflecting my thoughts and..." His words trailed off. *And fears, meaning Marell.* "And only one door? Am I telling myself I'm running out of options?"

Yeshe smiled. "Perhaps a more positive view—that you have now chosen which path to follow."

Or I only have one path left. To kill Marell, whether or not I want to. But he didn't voice that fear. "So where do we start?"

"You must learn to track a dream element back to the person who is dreaming it. Back to the doorway where they themselves entered Dream. Learn to step through that doorway, and your astral spirit will enter the waking world."

Will again imagined his astral form strolling the streets alongside Case. "Okay, so let's roll."

"There is more. You will enter the waking world *in the place where the dreamer is sleeping.*"

"We can find people in the real world by tracking them back from their dreams? Cool." He considered that. "Oh wow. We can find where Marell is. And the missing kids." He stopped. "Oh wait. That means we'd have to face Marell or the Hollow Boys in Dream. Not high on my list."

"Nor on mine. But we can locate the hospital more safely. If you again find the young Fader in Dream, we can track *his* dream back to where he is a prisoner." Yeshe turned towards the single door in the House.

"Oops. Forgot to tell you. Fader escaped from that place. He showed up here about dinnertime, asking for Case."

The monk spun around. "What did you say?"

"Uh...Fader escaped. He's here."

Rushing forward, Yeshe grabbed Will, his eyes wide. "Young master, you must wake up. We are in danger. It is a trap!"

Chapter 29

Gold, Guns, Girls

C ase lay on the bed in her room in Will's tower, wide awake and still dressed. Beside her in the dark lay Fader, also in his street clothes, but now fast asleep and snoring softly.

That familiar sound should have been comforting. It should have been the lullaby sending her to sleep. Her brother was back. They were together again.

But to her growing horror, she was finding little comfort in Fader's return. Something was wrong with him. She didn't know what, but she knew her brother. And Fader wasn't acting like Fader.

She reminded herself she had no idea what Marell and Morrigan had done to him. Was that all this was? He'd been living a nightmare and needed time to recover? Yes, that *must* be it. She had to be patient and understanding. She'd help him. Help him heal. Help him become Fader again. The real Fader. *Her* Fader.

Still trying to convince herself, she rolled over on her side. Slowing her breathing and relaxing her body, she tried again to fall asleep. Instead, her thoughts ran back to Will. His face, his smile, his touch, his kisses. Everything they'd done together in his bed.

And everything she'd said to him after.

She lay there, hearing her words, seeing Will's face, over and over again.

At some point, sleep took her.

She was awake again. Something had woken her. But what?

The bed had moved. There. It moved again.

Fader.

She wanted to call out to him. But her earlier fear returned, and she stopped herself. She stayed silent. She didn't open her eyes. She didn't move. Instead, she focused on keeping her breathing slow and sleep-like.

The bed moved again. Beside her, she felt him sitting up.

Watching her.

She continued to feign sleep. Seconds passed.

Fader broke the silence. "Case? Are you awake?" Low and quiet. It was Fader's voice. But it wasn't. Not really. In the dark, with no other distractions, she heard the difference now. She heard the deadness in his voice. In that moment, she accepted what she'd refused to believe before.

Something was terribly wrong with her brother.

Seconds passed. Still she pretended to sleep. The bed moved again. Fader was getting up. More silence followed. She imagined him standing there, staring at her. She tried not to shiver.

Finally, she heard him move away. A moment later, the door to their room opened and closed.

Her heart pounding, she slipped quietly out of bed. The clock beside her glared a quarter past midnight in red numbers. She crept to the door. Easing it open a crack, she listened to the slap of his bare feet in the hallway getting farther and farther away. The sound stopped. Opening the door, she peeked down the hall.

The corridor was dark, its simulated street scene empty except for Fader's small figure about fifty steps away facing the wall. Raising an arm, he poked at something with a finger. She realized he was at the elevators. Will had given Fader access to the entire tower. He might be heading anywhere.

A ding sounded. Fader stepped forward, disappearing into an elevator.

She jumped into the hallway and ran. The elevator closed before she reached it, but she was in time to see the "Down" button wink from lit to unlit.

Down? Why was he going down? The floors below this level contained only meeting rooms. The museum floors that would fascinate the Fader she knew were above this level. She watched the number on the elevator's display tick lower until it stopped on "G."

Ground floor? The lobby? Why the lobby? It held nothing except the reception desk, the waiting area, and...

And the exit to the street.

Was Fader trying to leave?

Panic seized her. She'd sworn nothing would separate them again. She jabbed the down button, hitting it again and again. After an eternity, an elevator arrived. She jumped in, slapping her hand on the security scanner, then punching the lobby button over and over until the doors slid shut.

The elevator descended with agonizing slowness. Slumping against the wall, she tried to calm herself. She had no plan. But she would not lose her brother again.

On the ground floor, Fader approached the receptionist's desk. A single light over the desk formed a tiny island of brightness. Beyond the locked security doors and glass walls enclosing the reception, the gloom deepened in the building's public lobby. The lobby was accessible from outside even at night but was lit only by lights from the street.

He moved forward, still fighting his internal battle. The battle he'd fought since reuniting with his sister.

He'd tried to tell her the moment he saw her. To warn her. But every time he tried to say the words, something strangled them in his throat. Something inside him. Something that wasn't supposed to be there.

But it was there now, forcing his feet to move. To walk towards the security doors.

He fought the command as hard as he could. But the more he fought, the more his arms and legs burned. Clawing up one sleeve, he stared at the strange symbols glowing hot on his skin.

The pain won. Exhausted, he surrendered. The burning eased. His feet moved forward again.

Reaching the glass wall, he placed his palm on the scanner beside the doors. A light flashed green, and an audible click sounded, loud and sharp in the silence of the night.

Ahead in the darkened lobby, spectral shapes slid from the shadows. The shapes resolved into figures as they moved toward him and the now unlocked reception doors.

The elevator opened on the ground floor, and Case burst into the hall. Ahead, a dim glow came from reception. Was she in time? Had Fader left the building? Why would he do that? Her heart pounding in her chest, she dashed down the hall.

She turned the corner.

Time slowed as her mind struggled to grasp the scene before her. And, as understanding came, to confront the horror of it.

A smiling Morrigan strode towards her, flanked by Stayne and Stryke, black clad and goggled as always. Behind them came four lean, muscled men in black combat gear carrying automatic rifles.

But more frightening still was Fader. He walked beside Morrigan, his hand in hers. His face beaming, he gazed up at the witch with unquestioning adoration. "Hey Case!" he called, grinning. "Look who I brought!"

Chapter 30

Combat Baby

C ase backed away, shaking her head. "No. No, no, no."

Morrigan kept walking towards her, her stiletto heels clicking on the marble floor. She smiled with narrowed eyes. "Ah, my dear. I had so hoped we'd meet again." Like their first meeting, she was all in green. Tight slacks and a low-cut, silk blouse, cape thrown back over her shoulders. Behind her, Stayne and Stryke grinned like ghoulish Cheshire Cats. Stryke pulled a slingshot from his long coat. Gleaming blades slid into Stayne's gloved hands.

Run!

Her Voice had returned. Too little, too late.

Nowhere to run, she shot back, but she kept retreating from the advancing figures.

The elevators.

Maybe. The one she'd taken might still be on this level. But then she looked at Fader, holding Morrigan's hand, oblivious to the monsters around him. She'd left him behind once. She'd never do that again.

Run!

Piss off, Case replied. She stopped retreating.

She sprang at Morrigan. The witch's eyes flew wide open. The runes appeared on her face as she raised her left arm. Beside her, Stryke pulled back on his slingshot as Stayne jumped forward.

They were all too late.

Stryke gave a cry of rage as his shot whizzed past Case's ear. Stayne was still a stride away when she slammed into Morrigan. She hit the witch in the midriff with her right shoulder. Morrigan flew off her feet, crashing into the armed men at her back. They all collapsed in a heap, Case on top of Morrigan.

Case pushed herself up to her knees, straddling the witch. The beauty of Morrigan's face vanished beneath a contortion of hate as she clawed at Case. Knocking her hands away, Case slammed a fist into the woman's mouth. Morrigan cried out, raising her hands against another blow.

A blow Case never landed. Something smashed into the back of her head.

Pain exploded in her skull. Lights flashed behind her eyes, then everything dimmed. Morrigan's snarling face, her lip cut and bleeding, rushed closer as Case collapsed on top of her.

Screaming with fury, Morrigan pawed at the limp form pinning her to the floor. "Get her off! Get her off!"

A mercenary pulled the girl from her. Stayne and Stryke helped her to her feet. Shoving them away, she stood over the intolerable guttersnipe lying unconscious before her. *Attack me, will you?* Trembling with rage, the copper taste of her own blood in her mouth, she began chanting. The runes tingled, swirling over her skin as she pondered the most painful spell. She would burn this brat alive. She would flay the skin from her. She would...she would...

Something tugged at her sleeve. The child Fader stared up at her with his beautiful brown eyes. "Please, my lady. Please don't hurt her."

"She struck me, child," she snapped, but she had to force the emotion. Something softened in her whenever she saw him.

"Mistress," Mr. Stayne rasped from beside her, "you promised us the girl."

She whirled on the man, striking him with the back of a fist, happy to release her anger. Crying out, he stumbled and fell to the floor.

"Morrigan the Bright does not make promises to dogs." Her voice was low and dangerous. "Especially, ones that allow trash to lay hands on me..." She spun on Stryke, who cowered back. "...and ones that miss...*again.*"

Rubbing his jaw, Stayne glared up at her but then lowered his eyes. "Yes, Mistress."

"Yes, Mistress," mumbled Stryke.

Her anger now cooled, she remembered why she wished to bring this girl back with them. Her magicks had failed on this waif on their first meeting, a failure she'd kept from Marell. She must learn how the girl had managed that. These two idiots could assist with that...questioning.

She motioned to the nearest mercenary. "Bind and gag her. Put her on that couch out of sight from the lobby."

Pulling two plastic zip cuffs from a pocket, the man bent over Case's still form.

Morrigan called up a healing spell, touching a finger to her swollen lip.

Fader tried to get closer to the wretched girl. "Is she alright?"

Morrigan stopped him with a hand on his shoulder. "Of course. She's...resting."

"Why are you tying her up?"

Morrigan smiled down on him. "So she won't run away again. Remember how she ran away when we first met?"

Fader frowned.

"Ah, no. You were sleeping, weren't you? Well, she did. Ran away and left you alone. Abandoned her own brother, you poor dear." She ruffled his hair. "We can't have her doing that again, can we?"

Fader considered his sister, now lying bound on the sofa, then looked back at Morrigan. He shook his head.

She smiled at him. "She'll sleep there, safe and cozy, while we go upstairs. Once we finish our business here, she'll return with us so you two can be together again. Won't that be nice?"

Fader nodded.

Morrigan turned to the mercenaries. "Enough delays. You know the target?" The men nodded. Glaring at Stayne and Stryke, she lowered her voice so the boy wouldn't hear. "As for you, if you wish to have your little plaything, do not fail me again."

"Yes, Mistress," they replied in unison, bowing their heads. Smiles twitched on their lips as they stole a glance to where Case lay helpless.

And now to find their prey. Closing her eyes, she sent her magical senses climbing up through the building, searching each floor, higher and higher. As she neared the top, she began to despair. Had they erred? Was their prey not here? One more floor...

There. On the highest level.

She allowed herself a smile. *Finally, Marell, my love, you will be whole again.*

An alarm wailed inside the building. Their presence was known. A stun spell tingled down her arm. As she led the way to the elevators, a car arrived. The doors opened. Two uniformed men jumped out, guns raised. She threw the spell. Both men stiffened, then collapsed and lay still.

Morrigan stepped over them and into the elevator, followed by her gang. She gestured to Fader. "Child, if you would, please?"

Fader placed his palm on the security scanner. The floor lights flashed green.

Morrigan pressed the button for the penthouse. As the car accelerated upward, she felt a tug on her sleeve.

Fader gazed up at her with those lovely eyes. "When we take my sister back, we'll stay together, right? Her and me?"

She stroked the boy's hair. "Yes, little one." She touched her lip again where the girl had struck her. "For as long as you both shall live."

In the House of Four Doors in Dream, Will pulled himself free of Yeshe. "What are you talking about? What danger?"

The monk's eyes cast around the House as if for unseen threats. "No one escapes Marell and Morrigan. They have *sent* the boy here."

"Case escaped. I escaped. And Fader would never put Case in danger. Besides, this building's as safe as a bank vault. Nobody could ever—"

Will broke off as Nyx's face appeared, hovering in her mist above the Bed of Awakening. "Your subconscious—that would be *me*—detects alarms sounding in your building. Ms. Archambeault is trying to contact you. She is coming to your room."

"What's happening?" Will asked, a cold lump growing in his belly.

"It seems we are under attack," she replied, then disappeared with a pop.

"Please, young master," Yeshe said, his voice quavering, "we must awaken."

Will hesitated, then touched the jewel at his neck.

And woke up.

Yeshe struggled to his feet from the floor beside Will's bed. "We are in danger. We must flee this building before they find us."

Will rolled out of bed. Grabbing his t-shirt, he pulled it on. "I'm not going anywhere. I *can't* leave. And nobody could get past the security in this place." He slipped into his jeans. "C'mon. Adi's on her way. She'll know what's happening."

He scooted down the stairs to his design studio. The lights came up as he entered. Yeshe descended slowly after him, his eyes darting around the empty room.

The floor was silent. But from somewhere below came the faint whine of a siren. It didn't sound like an ambulance or fire engine or police car. It didn't sound as if it came from the streets. It sounded as if it came from inside the tower, rising from the floors beneath them.

Did his building have an alarm? Did it sound like that? Maybe Adi was right. Maybe he should get more involved in things around here.

Yeshe opened his mouth to speak, but Will put up a hand to silence him as he strained to listen. The siren faded away. He let out a breath he hadn't realized he'd been holding as an eerie quiet settled on the floor. A quiet broken by the single, sharp ding of a bell.

"What was that?" Yeshe cried in a hoarse whisper.

"It's just the elevator. That'll be Adi. She's coming up, remember? She'll tell us what's going on and..." His voice trailed off as footsteps sounded on the running track.

Many footsteps.

He swallowed. Okay, so Adi had somebody with her. Maybe there *had* been a break-in. Sure, that was it. Adi was in over-protective pseudo-mother mode, bringing security guards to stay on his floor.

Except, from the number of footsteps, it sounded like she'd brought a small army.

His design studio stood open to the track as did all the rooms on this level. The area outside his studio brightened as motion detection lights clicked on, pacing the approaching footsteps.

He walked toward the track.

"No!" Yeshe cried. "Stay back."

Will ignored him. It had to be Adi. Or some of his own people. No outsider had security clearance for this floor. Except for Case now and...

He stopped. A chill ran down his spine.

And Fader.

They have sent the boy here.

Yeshe's words came back to him as the approaching figures rounded the corner of his studio.

It wasn't Adi.

The intruders numbered a half dozen or more. He didn't count them right away because at first, he couldn't pull his eyes from the woman leading the invasion.

This, he knew, was Morrigan the Bright.

She was tall, even more so in the stilettos she wore. Flaming red hair flowed in waves like a crimson sea to her waist. A green cape hung from her neck. Her clothes were green as well, and tight, highlighting her figure.

She stopped just inside the studio. "Good evening. I hope we aren't intruding." She laughed. "No, that's a lie. I love that we're intruding."

Her voice was rhythmic, melodic, enchanting. She was the most beautiful woman he'd ever seen. But then he looked into her eyes. Green as emeralds. And just as cold.

Those eyes broke her spell. He stepped back, taking in her companions. Two pale thin men flanked Morrigan, one short, one tall. They wore black suits and shirts, with black bowlers and gloves. And black goggles. Stayne and Stryke, he guessed, fighting a shiver as he remembered Case's stories. Four men in black combat gear and carrying automatic rifles stood behind Morrigan.

A smaller figure completed the group. Beside Morrigan stood Fader, his hand in hers. Magic had to be at work there. Fader's presence raised another fear. Where was Case? When he'd last seen her, she'd been taking Fader to their room.

Pushing that fear away, he looked at Morrigan. "A cape? Seriously?" he said, trying to sound flippant.

Fader tugged on Morrigan's hand, pointing at Will. "He writes the Dream Rider. That's my favorite comic."

"Fascinating," Morrigan replied, her tone implying she found that news anything but.

Will knew he had no chance. But still he stepped forward, his fists clenched. "You're not taking me without a fight."

Huge grins appeared on both Stayne and Stryke, revealing rows of pointed yellow teeth. Behind them, the soldiers chuckled.

But Morrigan just frowned as she considered him. "Now, why would I take you anywhere?"

Bad news. If they weren't taking him away, then whatever Morrigan planned for him would happen here. As if to confirm that fear, golden runes glowed on her face, then flowed down the bare skin of her left arm. He realized she was casting a spell, but before he could move, she flung out her hand. The runes flew through the air, striking him in the chest. His arms pinned themselves to his sides as if bound by an invisible rope.

Morrigan smiled. "Excuse me, child. You are in my way." She lifted her hand. He rose off the carpet. With a flick of her fingers, she threw him across the room to slam into the bookcases. He crashed to the floor, books pelting down on him.

Stunned but free of her grip, he pushed himself up on one elbow. In her way? What did she mean? His vision swimming before him, he looked up, expecting to see Morrigan closing in to finish the job.

Instead, she walked toward Yeshe, humming to herself. The fear that had etched the monk's face was gone. His features were calm as he drew himself up tall.

Morrigan stopped before him. "So many years we have chased you, monk. Now you will finally return what you stole from Marell." She smiled. "After we rip it from you."

Chapter 31

The Price You Pay

Will struggled to his feet as understanding battled pain in his throbbing head. He stared at Yeshe. "You? They're after *you*, not me?"

Ignoring Will, Morrigan motioned to one soldier. "Bind the monk. You'll carry him from here. And you..." she said, pointing to another soldier, "will carry the girl we left downstairs."

Girl? That had to be Case. They had Case, too? No, no, no.

A soldier pulled Yeshe's arms back, binding his hands with zip ties. Yeshe bowed his head. "Forgive me, young master."

"You said *you* were chasing *them*," Will cried. "You lied to me. You lied to all of us. Why?"

Yeshe looked at Will, his eyes pleading. "After running for so long, I thought I had found someone who could save me. I thought your powers could save us all."

Morrigan frowned at Will. "Now why would the old fool think *you* have powers?"

Yeshe paled. "Lady Morrigan, I misspoke. I am old and weak. I was mistaken. The boy has no powers."

In the distance, the faint ding of the elevator sounded again. Hope returned. Was that Adi with security guards?

Will glanced around the room. No one else seemed to have noticed it. All were focused on Yeshe and Morrigan. Except Stayne, who was nowhere to be seen. His hopes sank. Stayne's absence explained the ding. The man had left the floor on some mission for Morrigan.

Will's mind raced. Morrigan and her thugs would take Yeshe and Fader to where the missing boys were. They'd take Case, too.

Case. In the hands of these people.

"No," he said. "Yeshe's lying again. I have powers." If Morrigan took him, too, he could tell Adi in Dream where to send the police. He could save the missing boys. He could save Fader.

He could save Case.

Morrigan looked him over and laughed. "You? What powers could a child have?"

"Astral powers. In Dream," he said, trying to sound more confident than he felt. "More than this Marell guy has. I killed his Mara, that rat thing. Escaped his big snake, too. Yeah, I kicked his butt."

Morrigan regarded him, one eyebrow raised as if considering him anew. "Well, well. We thought the monk had killed the Mara but wondered how. His powers have waned, and killing a Mara seemed beyond him."

"No, young master," Yeshe pleaded. "Do not do this."

Fader was staring at Will wide-eyed, understanding dawning. "You're the Dream Rider!" he whispered.

"We're wasting time, ma'am," one soldier growled.

Morrigan pointed to Yeshe. "Take him."

The soldier who had bound Yeshe lifted the helpless monk over his shoulder in a fireman's carry.

Stryke eyed Will. "What of this one?"

"He killed a Mara. What do you think?" Morrigan motioned to Will. "The boy, too."

Two soldiers started towards Will, zip ties in hand. The other two mercenaries stood talking, one carrying Yeshe over a shoulder, the other smoking a cigarette, his rifle slung. Stryke was poking Yeshe in the ribs and grinning as he squirmed. Morrigan was smiling down at Fader, stroking his hair.

Several things happened in a few seconds.

The head of the soldier with the cigarette snapped up. His eyes widened. Dropping his smoke, he grabbed for his rifle. An ear-splitting crack shattered the silence. The man's head jerked back. He slumped to the ground.

The two soldiers approaching Will spun to face the running track, blocking it from Will's view. They reached for their rifles. Two more cracks rang out. The backs of their heads exploded. The men crumpled to the carpet. And he had a view of the track.

Adi stood at the studio entrance, barefoot, dressed in sweats, a rifle to her shoulder. In one short, smooth movement, she swung the gun to cover the remaining invaders. Morrigan, Fader, Stryke, and the surviving soldier stood unmoving near the center of the studio.

Adi? With a gun?

Morrigan remained motionless, eyes wide and fixed on Adi. Fader peeked from behind her cape. The last mercenary, with Yeshe still over his shoulder, reached for his rifle. Stryke's hand stabbed inside his coat.

"I just shot three men in the head from across the room," Adi said, her voice calm. "*Do* reconsider."

Both Stryke and the soldier froze. Stryke looked at Morrigan. She shook her head. She smiled at Adi, eyes narrowed. "And you are...?"

"The one with the gun. Now shut up," Adi replied. Morrigan's nostrils flared, but Adi ignored her. "You," she said to the soldier, "place your weapon on the floor."

The man complied.

"You," she said to Stryke, "lie on his gun."

Stryke hesitated.

"Or you can fall on it after I shoot you. I'm indifferent on those options."

Muttering under his breath, Stryke lay on the rifle.

Adi nodded to the soldier. "Now lay that man you're carrying on top of short-and-gruesome there."

The mercenary lowered a silent Yeshe onto the prone Stryke.

"Now lie down. On your stomach, facing away from me, hands behind your neck. And keep them there."

The soldier did so. Adi took a step into the studio.

Morrigan smiled. Her skin glowed. Rune characters appeared on her face.

"Adi," Will cried. "She's doing a spell."

Adi aimed her rifle at Morrigan. "Lose the tats, Red, or I *will* shoot you."

Morrigan's eyes shot daggers at Will. Turning to Adi, she sniffed. "I don't believe you."

"You don't know me, dear," Adi said, her voice level.

Will stared at Adi. She'd been in his life as long as he remembered, and he was thinking the same thing.

Morrigan snorted. "You'd shoot an unarmed woman?"

Adi smiled. "You won't be unarmed when the police find your body."

Morrigan's eyes went wide. She considered Adi, then gave a small nod. "Well, well. I believe you would." The runes and glow faded from her face.

"Wise," Adi said. "Now lie on that soldier. The one who isn't dead yet."

Morrigan straightened, eyes wide, nostrils flaring. "You go too far. Morrigan the Bright lies down before no one."

Adi twitched the rifle at her. "Dwell on the positive, dear. You get to be on top."

Morrigan opened her mouth, but only choking sounds escaped. Her fingers bent claw-like. She stamped her foot and let out an inarticulate snarl. She drew in a breath. Straightening, she swirled her cape around her and stalked to the prone soldier, her chin high. Fader followed. She began to kneel beside the man.

Adi lowered her gun. Her shoulders relaxed. She was two paces inside the studio now, her attention on Morrigan, her back to the track.

Behind Adi, a tall, dark-clad figure appeared, something glinting in his hand.

"Behind you!" Will cried.

Too late.

Stayne covered the space between him and Adi in one long stride. His arm circled her throat, wrenching her head back. His knife flashed forward, stabbing hard into her side.

Adi stiffened. Her mouth flew open. The rifle slipped from her hands. A wet gurgling cry escaped her lips.

Stayne, his face a rictus of rapture, stabbed her again. Adi spasmed. He released her, and she collapsed in a twisted heap.

"No!" Will screamed. He ran forward, but before he reached her crumpled body, pain exploded in the back of his skull. He stumbled. His last memory was of the carpet rushing to meet him.

Morrigan was on her feet before the Mara-killing boy hit the floor. Beside her, Stryke lowered his slingshot. He smiled up at her.

The fool expected praise. "I am pleased," she said in her iciest tone, "you can still hit *something.*"

Stryke's smile collapsed. He lowered his head. "Yes, Mistress."

The mercenary—the last one alive, she realized—was standing again. She pointed to Yeshe's bound form, lying at his feet where Stryke had pushed him. "Pick him up," she snapped.

Stayne stood over the woman's body. As she approached, the man raised his knife and ran a gray tongue along its blade, licking off the blood.

Disgusting creature. But useful. If not for her knife-wielding ghoul, tonight's entire enterprise would have failed.

Blood, dark and red, soaked the cream-colored carpet where the woman lay. Her lips moved, but no sound emerged as she stared up at Morrigan.

Strong, this one. Still clinging to life. But not for long. Even now, the light faded from the woman's eyes. A begrudging admiration rose in Morrigan. She turned to Stayne, lifting a questioning eyebrow.

He grinned. "I heard the elevator, Mistress, and went to investigate."

"You did well."

His grin widened, and he shot a sneer at Stryke. Bending low over the dying woman, he brought his blade to her throat.

"No," Morrigan said. "Leave her."

Stayne straightened, frowning. "Mistress?"

She considered the woman at her feet. "She was brave and fierce, strong and arrogant." *Much like myself.* "I grant her these last moments." She waved at where the Mara-killing boy lay unconscious. "Bring him," she said to Stayne.

She led her reduced squad down the long hallway toward the elevators. Fader walked to her left. To her right, the lights of the city flickered uncaring outside the tall windows. Behind her, the surviving soldier carried Yeshe. Stayne and Stryke followed, the boy hanging unconscious in Stayne's arms.

The mercenaries' deaths were of no concern. She had the monk. Plus an unexpected bonus if this boy truly had astral powers.

They neared the end of the running track where it curled around the wall to the elevator bank. And, she reminded herself, she now had that bothersome girl in hand, too. She smiled to herself. Yes, a successful night. Marell would be pleased.

A sharp crack shattered her thoughts. She spun to see Stayne sinking to his knees, his mouth wide in surprise, a neat hole in his forehead. He collapsed sideways, dumping the boy onto the floor. Shrieking, Stryke leaped for his fallen comrade. Morrigan looked back down the hall.

In a pool of light spilling from the room they'd just left, a figure lay on the track, sighting along a rifle. The woman she'd left for dead.

A second shot came, shattering the window at the end of the hallway. The soldier carrying Yeshe sprinted to the corner and ducked out of the line of fire. Morrigan did the same, pulling Fader with her.

Another shot cracked. Oblivious to the shooting, Stryke bent over the fallen Mr. Stayne. With a strength belying his size, he lifted the larger man in both arms. He stumbled toward where the others waited. Another shot. Stryke's bowler flew off his head, but he reached the safety of the wall.

Morrigan peeked out. The boy who had killed a Mara—if he could be believed—lay ten paces away. He stirred. Alarms sounded again, in the building and in the streets below.

She had only the boy's word for his supposed powers. The child might have merely repeated Yeshe's own story, hoping to delay her until help arrived. She had what they came for—the monk himself.

"We're leaving," she said, striding to the elevators, pulling Fader along. She pressed the down button. The doors opened. Inside, she pointed to the security panel. Fader placed his hand, and the lights flashed green. The car descended.

Consciousness crawled back into Will's mind like a castaway clawing for the shore. One by one, his senses returned. He lay on a hard surface. Where? He listened. Silence. He opened his eyes. Darkness. He moved his head.

Agony. He almost blacked out. It subsided, and he tried again. A wall lay to one side of him, windows to the other. He blinked. He was on the running track.

Why was he here? What had happened? Something…something…

Something bad.

He remembered.

Adi. Stayne. The glint of a knife. Adi's face. Adi lying on the carpet. Lying so still.

The fear those memories brought gave him strength. Strength to shove the pain away, to move, to push himself to his hands and knees. He looked back down the hall, toward his studio where it all had happened.

A figure lay unmoving just outside the room. Adi.

"No," he croaked. "No, no, no." He fought his way to his feet. He took a step towards the figure. His knees buckled, and he fell back down. He got back up, stumbling forward again.

He didn't know how many more times he fell. How many times he fought off the pain to get back up, before he collapsed beside Adi's still form.

A trail of blood led from the studio. She lay face down, head to one side, eyes closed, rifle cradled in her arms. He checked her neck for a pulse. Her skin felt so cold. There. A faint pulse? His hands trembled too much to be sure.

"Hallie," he croaked, his voice refusing to cooperate. His mouth—so dry. He swallowed. He tried again. "Hallie!" he called, this time louder.

Nothing. Then, a welcome voice.

"Yes, Mr. Dreycott?" Hallie replied, her voice echoing along the track.

"Call 9-1-1. Adi's been stabbed. She's bleeding. My floor."

"Calling now, sir," came the immediate response.

"Hurry. Tell them to hurry. I think…I think she's dying."

Oh god. Oh god. Oh god. He waited. And waited. "Hallie!"

"I've placed the call, sir. They're on their way. My medical protocol routines recommend applying pressure to the wound to slow the bleeding."

Yes. He knew that. Why hadn't he done that? He'd done everything wrong. He should have called Hallie right away.

He tried to find her wound. So much blood. It soaked Adi's sweatshirt. Where was the wound? He struggled to remember Stayne's attack—from behind, the blade in his right hand.

It should be on her lower right abdomen, towards the back. Lifting her blood-soaked shirt, he found it—gaping, gushing, and horrible. With shaking hands, he pulled off his shirt, wadded it up, and pressed it onto the wound.

Adi's eyes flickered open.

"Adi! You're alive!" He was sobbing. "I'm sorry. This was my fault. I should have listened to you."

Her lips moved, but he couldn't hear. Keeping pressure on the bleeding, he leaned forward, putting his ear near her mouth.

"Must..." she whispered, "...tell you..."

"Not now. Save your strength. Help's coming."

"Important..." she muttered. Her eyes closed.

"Adi?"

She didn't answer.

"Adi!"

No response. Hunched beside her, his hand pressing on her wound and soaked with her blood, he waited alone for help to come.

Act 3

As the World Falls Down

Chapter 32

Helpless

W ill stood in his studio watching a scene in a hospital room, displayed stark and cold on his wall screen. Amidst a jumble of snaking tubes and flickering monitors, Adi lay in bed, unconscious and unmoving.

She looked fragile. She looked small. He'd never thought of Adi as either before. For the past eight years, she'd been the largest thing in his life. Indomitable, unstoppable. Always *here*. Always here for *him*.

Now she wasn't here. Her injuries were beyond what could be treated in the Tower's own medical facility. She was in Toronto General. She was there. And he was here, in his tower prison, unable even to be with her.

He'd tried. Tried to go outside. Tried to be with her. He'd followed the ambulance in his limo. But only two blocks from his tower, he'd had to tell his driver to turn around. He couldn't make it to the hospital. Couldn't be with the woman who'd raised him for the last eight years. Who'd just saved his life. Who was now...

Dying?

Maybe.

Maybe not.

The surgeon who'd operated on Adi couldn't tell him. What was her name? Jin? Speaking to the camera, she gave yet another update. He searched her face for signs of what she wasn't telling him.

"I'm sorry, Mr. Dreycott," Jin said, "but Ms. Archambeault's condition is unchanged."

Winstone Zhang stood beside Will, implacable and silent. Zhang had installed the camera in Adi's room. Being the hospital's leading donor bought Will that much. If he couldn't be at Adi's side, at least he could be this close.

"You told me that an hour ago," Will said.

"Yes, I did." Jin looked exhausted. He reminded himself she'd saved Adi's life—or at least given her a chance. "And as I said then, it's still too early to say. The stab wounds were deep. One lacerated her liver, causing massive bleeding into her abdominal cavity. The other perforated her diaphragm, puncturing and collapsing her right lung. But she was lucky. Both missed the inferior vena cava, or she wouldn't have survived."

Lucky? Doctors had strange ideas about luck.

"We repaired her liver and diaphragm. And inserted a tube in her chest, which will remain until her lung heals."

"That's good, right?"

She hesitated. A bad sign. "There's a risk of more internal bleeding and infection. The next forty-eight hours will tell." Her face softened. "I'm sorry, Mr. Dreycott. I know it's hard. But she's receiving the best care available, and we'll monitor her around the clock. All you can do is wait."

No, I can do more than wait. But he nodded. "I understand. Do you have my cell?"

"Yes."

"Please call me if..." He stopped. *If what? If she dies?* "...if anything changes. I'll leave the camera on and mute the audio link, if that's okay."

"Of course," Jin said.

Tapping his phone, he muted the connection. He took one last look at Adi, then turned to Winstone Zhang. Will didn't know his head of security well. As in not at all. Adi always dealt with Zhang. Adi, he began to realize, always did everything.

Zhang was maybe five foot eight, but solid, with easy fluid movements, like a cat on the prowl. He was the former head of the Hong Kong police force and an old friend of Adi's. She'd convinced Zhang to come here when he left the force. How had Adi known a cop from half way around the world? Again, he realized how little he knew about her.

Zhang stood beside a tarp covering part of the studio carpet and running track, thrown there by somebody to cover the blood. The gunmen's blood. Adi's blood. The pool of it where she'd fallen when stabbed. The trail of it where she'd crawled out to the track. To save him.

And what had *he* done? Nothing.

Zhang cleared his throat. "Sir, I've left a man outside Ms. Archambeault's room. And I've checked Jin's background. She is one of the best—"

"Where *were* you, Mr. Zhang?" Will interrupted. "Where were your people?"

Zhang straightened as if hit. His jaw clenched, and his eyes narrowed, but he said nothing.

"Huh? Where were you?" Will's voice rose as he gave vent to his anger and fear. "Where were you when an armed gang invaded my home? When they stabbed Adi and abducted my friends?" Correction. Not all friends. Yeshe was no friend. Yeshe had lied to him. But Fader. And Case... Case, god. Where was Case?

Zhang took a deep breath. "I was home, sir, asleep," he replied, his voice level. "My men were in the control room. When they saw intruders in reception, they triggered the building alarm and went to intercept." He frowned. "They were...overpowered. They are unclear as to how."

Morrigan, he thought remembering how she'd tossed him aside. "But how did these people get into the building?"

Zhang hesitated. "Sir, someone *inside* this building opened the reception doors."

"What? Who?"

"If I may?" Pulling out his phone, Zhang tapped its screen. Adi's hospital room disappeared from the wall display. Zhang paged through menus until he reached "Security Cameras." Selecting "Reception" and "12:30 AM," he hit play.

At the bottom of the screen, a small figure appeared. A sick feeling rose in Will's stomach. Fader walked slowly to the lobby door and pressed his palm to the security scanner. The door swung open. Shapes moved forward from the shadows. The figure leading the group resolved into the tall form of Morrigan. Will felt as if someone had punched him in the gut.

Fader had let them in, using the building access Will had given him. He'd trusted Fader—just as he'd trusted Yeshe. All this was his fault. Adi lay dying in hospital, and Case was a prisoner because of him.

Zhang's voice was low, almost gentle. "The boy also provided this group with elevator access to your floor, sir."

"His name is Fader," Will whispered. Why had Fader done it? But he knew. Morrigan and her magic. Case's brother had seemed mesmerized by the red-haired woman last night.

"I'm afraid there's more, sir."

Will watched the screen. "Oh, god, no," he whispered as Case appeared.

His fear mixed with pride as she tackled Morrigan, even landing a blow. But that turned to horror when a soldier slammed his rifle down on Case's head. The soldiers left her bound and unconscious on the couch in reception.

Zhang paused the playback.

Will swallowed. "Do you know what happened to her?"

"Only this." Staying with the reception camera archive, Zhang selected "1:30 AM." *After Stayne stabbed Adi*, Will thought. *After Morrigan left.* Zhang hit play.

Morrigan reappeared in reception, Fader at her side. Yeshe, his hands bound, trailed Morrigan like a whipped dog, pulled along by a cord around his neck. The one surviving soldier lifted a still unconscious Case from the couch and slung her over his shoulder. Stryke, struggling to carry the body of the much taller Stayne, completed the group. *Stayne dead? At last some good news. Had Adi done that? Made him pay for what he did to her?*

Fader opened the door to the outer lobby. The raiding party and their captives disappeared through the door and beyond the range of the cameras. Zhang stopped the video. The display returned to Adi, lying unmoving in her hospital bed.

"The police have no leads," Zhang said. "My men canvassed for witnesses on the street not five minutes after this video was taken. We found several people, but no one remembered seeing anything."

Will suspected Morrigan's magic in that. "We have to find Case. And Fader, too."

Zhang raised an eyebrow. "The boy aided these people."

Will shook his head. "Someone was controlling him. I can't explain it right now." *Without you thinking I'm nuts.* "You need to trust me. We have to find them *both*."

Zhang frowned, but nodded. "Understood, sir. Unfortunately, our only lead came from the boy."

Will groaned. "The abandoned hospital."

"And if the boy's being controlled, I doubt his information is reliable."

Will remembered finding Fader in Dream. He was certain the kid he'd met that night was the true manifestation of Fader's astral spirit. A normal and uncontrolled Fader, so happy to see his sister and excited to meet his hero. So unlike the Fader who'd appeared in Will's lobby.

That meant Morrigan's control of Fader had started *after* that Dream encounter. Which meant Fader's story during Dream of being a prisoner in a hospital was true.

"What if the hospital lead was real?" he said.

"But if someone's controlling the boy—"

"Someone was—when he showed up here. But not when he gave us that lead. I think he told the truth about being in a hospital."

Zhang frowned again. "When we checked possible locations, one stood out. But Ms. Archambeault said the boy denied it was the place."

"Yeah, I was there. Fader didn't just deny it. He totally freaked, like he was afraid we wouldn't believe him."

Zhang smiled. "Afraid we wouldn't believe it's *not* the place—"

"Because it *is* the place."

"You believe his denial while being controlled constitutes proof?"

"Yeah." Will sighed. "Look, Mr. Zhang, I'm asking you to take a lot on faith. I mean, somebody controlling Fader remotely, how I know the hospital lead's real..."

Zhang held up a hand. "Sir, I've known for some time that you can somehow..." He frowned, then continued. "...access unusual information sources."

Will hesitated. Had Adi told Zhang about the Rider? "Why do you say that?"

Zhang smiled. "Several times, you've directed my team to gather information on unsolved crimes. In each case, the leads you provided were not publicly available. Nor, I believe, even known to the police."

"Uh, yeah. It's kind of hard to explain."

"You don't need to. I raise this only to explain my easy acceptance of your advice. I'm proud to work for you, Mr. Dreycott. I know how many times you've helped people, without recognition for your role."

"Thanks," Will said, feeling even worse for how he'd treated Zhang earlier. "Should we contact the cops? Have them send a SWAT team? Or whatever they'd do?"

"I doubt they'd do that, sir."

"But, like you said, they follow my tips all the time. Why wouldn't—? Oh, right. Crap. Harry."

Zhang nodded. "All past tips came from Mr. Lyle. The police aren't aware of your involvement in those cases. Unlike me, sir, they will require evidence. And a search warrant. That means convincing a judge that people are being held prisoner at this hospital."

Will slumped on his couch, burying his face in his hands. All his money, all his resources, yet with each passing moment, he felt more and more helpless. He realized how isolated he'd become. How dependent he was on everyone around him. Adi, Harry, Zhang.

Zhang cleared his throat. "There is another option, sir."

Will looked up. "Yes?"

Zhang hesitated. "It's not exactly legal."

"Mr. Zhang—"

"In fact, it's extremely *illegal*—"

"Please. Just tell me."

Zhang sat beside him, lowering his voice. "I can assemble a SWAT team. My people are trained and former police. We'd hit the hospital, subdue any hostiles, safeguard the prisoners, then call the police. We'd leave before they arrived."

"Your *own* SWAT team...?" Will's voice trailed off. That meant *he*—seventeen-year-old Will Dreycott—had *his* own SWAT team. He considered Zhang. How had Adi known this guy? What sort of people was she hiring? And why?

Screw it. Only one thing mattered.

"Nothing would tie back to you, sir."

"I don't care about that. I only want to save Case. And Fader. And any other kids who're there." He nodded, mostly to convince himself. "Okay. Yeah, let's do it. How soon could you...do it?"

Zhang checked his watch. "It's just before nine AM now. I'll assemble the team this morning. Plan the assault this afternoon. Dry run tonight. We'll be in place at the location and ready to move by two AM."

"Okay. Yeah. Great." He rubbed his face. Tired. So tired.

"Sir, you've been through a lot. You need to sleep."

"Yeah, sure." No, he wouldn't sleep. Not during the day. He needed to sleep that night. To walk in Dream, the only place he wasn't helpless. This hospital might not be the place, so in Dream, he'd search for Case and Fader. And Yeshe, too. His fists clenched, remembering the monk's betrayal. Besides, he admitted to himself, he had to see Case again, to know she was safe.

"I'll update you this evening, sir." Zhang hesitated. "One last thing. I don't want to trouble you, but you'll hear, regardless."

No more. I can't take any more. "What?"

"People are asking for direction in Ms. Archambeault's absence."

"Who? Why?"

"Pretty well everyone. Ms. Archambeault is CEO of your company and was..." Zhang stopped. "...*is* very hands on. Many people, in both your firm and this building, feel rather lost."

Tell me about it. "I'm sorry. Adi handles the business part. I just..." *Just what? Just do nothing.* "I'm sorry. I can't help."

"The Board is looking for a solution—"

"Great. Works for me."

Zhang hesitated. "They will need to talk to you."

"Okay. Sure. Anything else?"

Zhang frowned, but then shook his head. "No, sir." He turned to leave.

Will could almost feel Adi's presence in the room, arms folded, foot tapping, glaring at him. He sighed, glancing at her image on the screen. *Yeah, okay.* "Mr. Zhang?"

Zhang stopped at the edge of the track. "Sir?"

"I'm...I'm sorry. For how I spoke to you earlier. For blaming you for what happened." He swallowed. "Looks like this was all my fault."

Zhang raised a hand. "No need to apologize. I've made mistakes myself." He looked at where Adi lay on the hospital bed. "And I understand how you feel. She's important to me as well, sir."

"Please stop calling me 'sir,' Mr. Zhang. Will is fine."

"Ok, Will. But only if you'll stop calling me 'Mr. Zhang.'"

"Winstone?"

Zhang smiled. "Stone." He nodded at Adi. "That's what Archie calls me." He left the room.

As Zhang's—Stone's—footsteps faded away, Will turned to the view of Adi. *"Archie?"*

He remembered the Adi he'd seen last night. Adi the dead shot, showing no emotion after killing three men. He remembered, too, her words as he'd reached her side. Something she had to tell him. Something important.

He was starting to think Adi had a *lot* to tell him. He clenched his fists. And she'd have the chance. Because she was going to live. "Because you *have* to," he whispered.

Hallie's crisp, computer voice sounded from the room speaker, pulling his thoughts away from Adi. "Sir, the Board of Directors wish to see you."

"Why do they...? Oh, right," he said, remembering Stone's comment. "Um...okay. When?"

"Now, sir, if convenient."

Suddenly, sleeping seemed like the best idea ever. "Not so much. Tell them I've been up all night and need to grab some Zs. I'll see them later."

"I will communicate that, sir."

He shrugged. The old guys had probably decided how to manage things until Adi came back and wanted to tell him. Not that he'd understand. Or care. Adi handled that stuff. Whatever. It wasn't important.

Or maybe it was, because Hallie's voice sounded again. "Sir, Mr. Kinland says it is urgent they see you as soon as possible."

He sighed. He didn't know who "Mr. Kinland" was, but he might as well get this over with. "Okay, okay. I'll be down. Just let me change."

"I will inform them, sir."

"Uh, Hallie?"

"Sir?"

"Where are they?"

"In the boardroom, sir."

"Right. The Board is in the boardroom. I knew that."

Hallie clicked off. He headed to his bedroom, grabbed a quick shower, then stood in his closet, trying to decide what to wear. He guessed his normal rock band t-shirt and torn blue jeans stretched "business casual" past the limit. Suit and tie? Probably best, but *so* not him. Adi would know, but...yeah, that.

He settled for a black denim shirt with a collar (no tie), khaki pants, and black high-tops. Taking another look at Adi on the screen, he left the studio. He rode the elevator down, thoughts of her and Case whirling through his head.

He walked to the boardroom, feeling like he was back in the public school he'd attended before the ill-fated expedition. Silly, but that's how he felt.

Like he was back in school—and had been called to the principal's office.

Chapter 33

Miss You

Awareness returned to Case the same way she approached someone on the streets. Slowly, warily, and ready to run. And the more her awareness returned, the more she wished it *would* run away and leave her unconscious again, blind to her situation.

Because her situation wasn't good. Her head was several sizes too large. Worse, something was going "woosh woosh woosh" over and over, far too close and far too loud. She took a while to recognize the sound as her own blood pounding in her aching skull. No other sounds came to her, but her nostrils burned with the acrid smell of dust and mold. Where was she?

She wondered if opening her eyes was a good idea. She opened them. Bad idea. Blinding light. Sharp pain behind her now stinging eyes. She closed them again.

What had happened? She coaxed her sluggish brain to think, to remember. At first, her only reward was a haze of pain and confusion. Then a memory came.

Will. What they'd done together. And then what she'd said to him, how she'd treated him.

Another memory returned, and with it, fear. Not about Will. About someone else.

Fader.

It rushed back then with sickening clarity. Her concern over her brother's behavior. Following him down to the reception. Attacking Morrigan. And her last memory—her fist smashing into the witch's lipsticked mouth. Then darkness.

But even through lingering clouds of pain, she remembered her fear for Fader. Morrigan had done something to him. Her brother was...wrong. She had to find him, to save him from that woman. And what about Will? The witch and her goons had invaded his building. They must have been after Will. She had to know if he was safe.

"So move, dumbass," she muttered to herself. This was going to hurt. She tried to sit up.

Nope. She'd been wrong. Moving wouldn't hurt. Because she couldn't. Panic seized her. Was she paralyzed? Had the hit to her head damaged her brain or spinal cord? She tried moving again, her arms first, then her legs.

Good news. She wasn't paralyzed.

Bad news. She was tied down.

Forcing her eyes open, she blinked away tears until her vision adjusted to the fluorescent lights. Her head wasn't restrained. With a struggle, she raised it just enough to see her circumstances.

She lay on her back, arms at her sides, on a dirty mattress in a hospital bed. Both sides of the bed were up. Leather cuffs encircled her wrists and ankles. Thick straps ran across her knees, hips, and chest. She still wore her t-shirt and jeans from last night.

Her bed sat against a wall to her right, bare except for gray-green flaking paint and patches of mold. At the opposite end of the room, ten paces away, a boarded window faced her. She guessed the door was behind and to her left.

A stainless-steel cart stood beside the bed, bearing a silver tray. On the tray, atop a stained white cloth, lay several instruments with short gleaming blades. Scalpels.

She shivered, then remembered what Fader had told her and the Rider in Dream. This must be the hospital where he'd been held. Where he was probably still being held. She had to get free.

She twisted her arms. She twisted her legs. She pulled and pushed. Again and again, until finally, she collapsed back against the mattress. She could barely move any of her limbs or raise any part of herself off the bed, except her head. Squeezing her hands as small as she could, she tried to wriggle free of the leather cuffs. No luck.

A metallic click to her left froze her in her struggles. A squeal of rusty hinges and a soft thud followed.

Someone had opened the door.

She lay still, her eyes closed, breathing slowed, feigning sleep. The floor creaked as her intruder approached, humming. The footsteps stopped. So did the humming.

"Cut the act, dearie," gurgled a too familiar voice. "I know you're awake."

She opened her eyes. Mr. Stryke's face hovered above her. She'd never seen either him or Stayne this close—and would've preferred to keep it that way.

His eyes remained hidden behind the cups of his dark glasses. In those black lenses, she glimpsed her own frightened face. He wore makeup, caked from sweat. The makeup had flaked off in spots, exposing skin even paler than she'd imagined.

He smiled at her, revealing yellow-brown teeth. Pointed teeth.

And then his smell hit her. A sour sharp stench, like earthworms and wet mud. Like something once buried dark and deep, now dug up.

Seeing the pale little horror recalled a memory from the previous night. Of regaining consciousness briefly. Of being carried slung over someone's shoulder.

But she remembered seeing something else before blackness took her again. A sobbing Stryke, cradling a much larger body in his arms. Stayne. A dead Stayne, a hole in his forehead.

At last, good news. Fighting the panic creeping up her spine, she forced words out. "All alone, little man? Where's your buddy? Mr. Tall-and-Creepy? Oh, yeah. He's *dead*."

She hid her fear behind a brave face. But as Stryke stepped closer, it occurred to her that provoking him in her current situation wasn't the smartest plan. She waited for him to scream at her, to strike her. She waited for his anger.

Instead, he smiled. And started humming again. She didn't recognize the tune. From his throat, it was melancholy and discordant and frightening.

Bending down, he cranked her bed up. Slowly, slowly, humming all the time, until she sat bolt upright, still strapped down.

He straightened, staring at her, still smiling, still humming. After a few breaths, the smile slid off his face. His humming stopped. Case swallowed, trying to think of something smartass to say.

Stryke's black-gloved hand flashed out. His fingers wrapped around her throat. She gasped, choking as his grip tightened. She couldn't breathe. Blood pounded in her head. She couldn't breathe, she couldn't breathe. His hand tightened even more. Lights danced before her eyes.

Leaning forward, he hissed into her left ear. "You...made...me...*miss!*"

He let go.

She threw her head back against the bed, gasping for breath. As air filled her lungs again, she fought her rising panic. She was going to die. This little monster would choke her to death, and she couldn't raise a hand to stop him.

She expected him to grab her again, but he smiled and stepped back. Strolling to the far end of the room, he stopped. Turning to face her, he tilted his head, considering her. He shuffled to his left until he lined up with where she lay propped up in the bed.

His lips writhed into another smile. "Yes, dearie, you made me miss. Several times you made me miss." He reached inside his black coat, and she knew what would be in his hand even before it appeared.

His slingshot.

He slipped something into the pouch of the weapon. Raising the slingshot in his left hand, he drew the sling back, sighting along his arm at her. "Let's see how you do *now*."

❧

Morrigan strode along the hospital corridor towards the Weave room where Marell waited. Caught in morning sunbeams, dust motes danced in her wake as if celebrating her triumphant return.

Her diminished squad followed. First came the remaining mercenary leading the precious Yeshe. The monk walked head down, hands bound. She glanced back at the soldier. What was his name again? Karmalov? She shrugged. No matter. Only one task remained for him, after which his name would be meaningless.

Behind the soldier and Yeshe, Link the Hollow Boy carried Stayne's body draped in his arms. Mr. Stryke was not with them. Having exchanged his burden of Stayne for that horrid girl, the little man was now securing her in a room, where he would no doubt use the waif for target practice. That made her smile, remembering how that ragamuffin had attacked her. She frowned, trying to recall telling Stryke she needed the girl kept alive for questioning.

And hadn't she made someone else a promise about the girl? Who could that have been?

She felt a tug on her cape. The boy Fader stared up from where he walked beside her. Of course. Why had she forgotten him? Her fondness for the child still amazed her, as did his ability to slip from memory, even in her company.

"Where did that man take my sister?" he asked.

Again that cursed girl. But she smiled. "Why, to her new room." Which was true.

"So she'll stay here with me?"

Morrigan hesitated. Once she'd learned how the girl had resisted her magicks that first night, she could envision no further use for her. She'd have to tell the boy sometime. Or would she? "Well, that depends. She might run away again. Like she did when we first found you."

Fader seemed to consider that. "But I can see her later?"

She smiled. "Certainly. If she's still...with us."

They reached the Weave room. She reached for the doorknob, but then remembered Marell's dislike for unannounced intrusions. Swallowing a sudden resentment, she knocked.

"Enter!" came a hoarse cry. Pushing the door open, she stepped inside, the others following.

Black curtains still covered the windows. Torches flickered in the wall sconces, giving life to squirming shadows. Marell huddled in the nearest wing chair under their ancient portrait. The Weave lay before the two chairs. Marell's feet rested on the rug, soaking in what power it could provide his failing body.

And failing it was. She'd seen him not six hours ago, when he had still appeared to be the sixteen-year-old boy he had last taken over. Thinner, paler, yes. But still young and vibrant.

Now he was a shriveled shadow of before. Rheumy eyes peered from sunken sockets above hollow cheeks. Cracked lips pulled back from decaying gums and teeth. Only patches of wispy hair remained on a liver-spotted scalp. Skin like dried parchment stretched too tight over the skull beneath. His body seemed lost in the folds of clothes now much too large.

She tried to hide her shock, but something must have shown on her face.

"Yes," he rasped. "My time in this vessel runs out. Faster than the last. Tell me, did you find—" His words cut off as she stepped aside, revealing Yeshe. The sight of the monk seemed to fill Marell like wind billowing a sail. Gripping the arms of the chair with claw-like hands, he pushed himself to standing.

An impatient wave brought her to his side. Leaning on her arm, he took two shaking steps to stand before Yeshe. He raised a skeletal hand to poke Yeshe's chest with a finger, as if to prove the man was real.

Marell smiled. "*Master*," he said, his tone mocking. "How wonderful to meet again after so many years." His hand crawled like a spider up Yeshe's chest until it wrapped around the monk's throat. "So *many* years!"

Yeshe's eyes bulged and a gurgling sound escaped his lips as Marell's grip tightened. Morrigan touched Marell's arm. "My love, we need him *alive* if we wish to recover what he stole."

Marell scowled but released his grip. Yeshe dropped to his knees beside the Weave, gasping in wheezy breaths. Morrigan led Marell back to his chair, then took the one beside him. As she placed her feet on the Weave, her triskelion medallion grew warm between her breasts.

"When?" Marell said.

"Tonight," she replied. She smiled at where Yeshe knelt. "Preparing our old friend—and your next host..." She glanced at Karmalov. "...will take time, but we will be ready by then."

Marell shook his head. She heard vertebrae cracking. "Too long. This body..." He left the thought unfinished.

Touching her medallion, she summoned the spell she had used so many times. As the medallion grew warmer, she laid her other hand on Marell's withered wrist. Rune characters flowed down her arm and onto his.

Marell straightened, seeming to expand where he sat. He sucked in a deep breath. "Yes. Better."

She waited for a word of thanks that never came.

Marell glared down at Yeshe. "Tonight, monk, I take back what you stole from me. I will tear it from you."

"I stole nothing," Yeshe said, his voice calm. "What you lost was your own doing." The monk tried to struggle to his feet.

Karmalov pushed him back to his knees. "Enough of this crap," the soldier said. "You said this job was foolproof. In and out with no trouble. I lost three good men last night. Three friends."

"My condolences," Morrigan replied. "On the positive side, fewer parties remain to share your considerable fee."

Karmalov's eyes narrowed. "I get their shares, too?"

"How strong of you to move past your loss so quickly. Grieving can be so draining," she replied, as another rune script flowed down her arm. "Yes, you will receive everything we planned for your team."

Karmalov considered that, then nodded. "Then we're good. When do I get paid?"

"Why, right now." She raised her arm. The stun spell struck Karmalov in the chest. His mouth and eyes flew open. His head snapped back. His entire body stiffened, then crumpled to the floor.

Marell wrinkled his nose. "I hope you didn't damage him."

She bit back a retort. "He meets with your approval?"

Marell shrugged. "He'll do to start. Soon I will have my pick of whoever I wish."

She smiled, pushing away her resentment. She would have her own harem of lovers. And grown men again, not these teenage boys.

She signaled to Link who still held Stayne's body. Stepping past Yeshe and the unconscious Karmalov, the boy placed Stayne's corpse on the Weave.

Marell regarded Stayne, raising an eyebrow to her. Shrugging, she turned to Link. "Bring two beds to this room. Place each of these men..." She pointed to Karmalov and Yeshe. "...on a bed and strap them down. Remain here to guard them."

Without a word, Link left the room. Morrigan smiled at Yeshe where he knelt. "Normally, monk, I would *draw* the necessary scripts on your skin. But Marell and I feel we must repay you for the many years of our lives wasted in your pursuit. So instead..." Reaching down, she stroked Yeshe's cheek. "I will *carve* them into you."

Yeshe's face was pale, but when he looked at her, his gaze was unwavering. "Yes, many years. Years where I kept the world safe from this monster."

"Ah, old master. Now I see," Marell replied from where he huddled in the chair. "All these years, I thought you a coward, afraid to face me again. But now I learn you fled us in the noble cause of humanity." He winked at Morrigan.

To her surprise, Yeshe smiled. "Mock me. I deserve it. I *am* a coward. But never a fool. I knew facing you both again was too great a risk. So, I ran. Around the world, I ran. And as I ran...I *searched*."

She tensed, fearing where this was going.

Marell's face darkened. "Searched for what, old fool?"

"A power," Yeshe replied. "One great enough to destroy you."

Marell laughed, a gurgling choking sound in his fading body. "Such great success you have met in your search, you decrepit fossil. You kneel before me, my prisoner."

Our prisoner, Morrigan thought, with a twinge of anger. *Her* prisoner.

Yeshe smiled. "Great success, indeed. A power I sought. A power I found. One you have faced...and failed to defeat."

Marell forced himself up in the chair. "What lies are you spouting?"

"No lies. Ask the witch. She had him in her grasp tonight. And lost him."

Marell spun to face her. "Morrigan? What of this?"

Damn the monk! "He is just a boy—"

"Who killed a Mara," Yeshe interrupted. "And then escaped you, oh *great* Marell."

"Shut up, fool!" Marell snapped. "Morrigan?"

She should have stunned Yeshe along with the soldier. Too late now. *You shall pay in pain for this, Yeshe.* With a shrug to feign indifference, she told of her encounter with the boy in the white tower. "We have only the monk's word for this boy's powers," she finished. "He showed none to me. I swatted him aside like a fly."

Marell slumped back into the chair. "Yet someone killed the Mara. And we both doubted this weakling kneeling before me could manage that."

She gave another shrug. "It matters not. If it was this boy, he ran from you," she said, careful not to say *escaped*. "He is no threat. Tonight, we will restore you to your full power. No one will stand before us then. And certainly, no mere child."

"My full power," Marell said, as if savoring the words. "Yes. Once I am restored, no one will challenge me."

Challenge us, she thought with another flush of anger.

Bowing his head, Yeshe fell silent.

Finally defeated, monk? she thought. *No more words to vex me?*

"Tonight!" Marell rasped, nodding to himself.

"Yes. Tonight," she replied, swallowing her resentment. She settled back into the chair, resting her feet on Stayne's corpse where it lay on the Weave. The power in the rug flowed into her, restoring her strength, refilling the medallion.

She closed her eyes, congratulating herself on everything she'd accomplished, her anger ebbing. Yeshe captured. That intolerable girl, too. And tonight, Marell would become whole once again. Then, they could at last put their plan in motion.

Yes, all was well. All was good.

Still...

Still, she couldn't help thinking she'd forgotten something. Or some*one*.

Chapter 34

Hit Me with Your Best Shot

F ader wandered the halls of the hospital, searching for...

He shook his head, trying to clear the fog from his mind. What was he searching for?

He'd used his fading ability to slip away while Morrigan talked to the shriveled thing in the chair. Something had made him leave. Something important. A memory.

A memory he no longer remembered.

His mind still had strings attached, tugging at him with a will not his own. And his memories remained a jigsaw puzzle scattered on the floor in a hidden room in his head.

But he was figuring things out.

The first thing he'd figured out was that Morrigan had used him. Used him to break into the Dream Rider tower. To capture that old man. People had been hurt, killed even. Because of him. And now Case was a prisoner. Just like him.

Yeah, that too. He still felt a strange affection for Morrigan, but now he remembered he was a prisoner. He stared at his arms. If he concentrated, the way he did when fading, he saw the symbols drawn there. On his legs and chest, too.

He knew those marks let her control him. They'd faded since she'd drawn them, but they were still there. As long as they were, she could make him do things he didn't want to. If only the marks would fade faster.

He stopped, grinning.

Fade.

He held up his forearms. As the strange characters came into focus, he tried to think about them the same way he thought of himself when he faded. As if they weren't really there.

Nothing happened. The strange symbols remained distinct, unchanged.

Disappointment almost gave way to defeat. But then he got angry. He was tired of being scared. Being used. Being a prisoner.

New plan. He focused on fading *himself*. But *just* himself, taking only the parts that were *Fader* to wherever he went when he faded. Leaving the non-Fader parts behind.

He felt himself fade. Counting ten breaths, he brought himself back. He inspected his arms. His heart pounding, he checked his chest and his legs, too.

The marks were gone.

He'd known even before he checked for the marks. The strings on his mind had vanished. The fog on his memories had lifted, and as it did, one memory came back to him cold and clear.

The memory of Mr. Stryke carrying off an unconscious Case.

And with it, he remembered why he'd slipped out of the Weave room. Somewhere in this creepy hospital, his sister was in danger.

Fighting his fear, he ran down the hall, trying doors as he went.

Mr. Stryke didn't miss Case this time.

His first shot hit her. Hit her in the fleshy part of her chest, above her right breast, below the collarbone. Hit her hard.

She screamed, more from shock than pain at first. But the pain came. She screamed again, throwing her head back, clenching her fists, gasping in air as waves of agony crashed down on her.

She'd been shot, her body attacked, violated. Her right arm was numb, and her shoulder throbbed. Had the missile gone into her? Through her? Was she bleeding? Blinking away tears, she peered down to where he'd struck her.

No blood showed on her t-shirt, but a gleam of metal caught her eye. A round steel ball, two fingers wide, lay in her lap against the leather strap over her hips. A ball bearing.

At the end of the room, Stryke danced and giggled. She started trembling. Those things would shatter bones. Major damage if they struck an organ. And if he hit her in the head?

Panic threatened to seize her, but she fought back hard. Fought back against herself.

She was Hard Case. She'd survived on the streets for all these years, protecting herself and her brother. She'd faced so many creeps, she'd lost count.

Grinning an idiot's smile, Stryke aimed another shot at her.

She swallowed. Except all those times, she hadn't been tied down and helpless.

Helpless? Maybe not. This time, it came not as words but as a feeling. A command to her body, to her muscles.

Her Voice.

Stryke fired. Not resisting, she let her body respond to her Voice's command. The shot struck her high in the chest again, this time on her left side. But her muscles had bunched as tightly as they could, right in that spot, just before it hit. She cried out again, but as the pain faded, she could still feel her shoulder and move her left arm. It had been like tightening her stomach to take a punch.

But how long would that work? The damage to her would build. The pain, too. Soon, she'd be in too much pain to react to her Voice. And what if he tried a head shot?

Yeah, she thought. *What if he did?*

No way! her Voice said. *That's too dangerous.*

Danger's already here. And he'll do it eventually. I'd rather he tries while I can still react.

She smiled. Smiled despite the pain. Smiled at the small ray of hope glimmering through the haze of agony.

Stryke, still grinning, pulled another ball bearing from his pocket.

"Still not much of a shot, are you?" she called.

His grin disappeared. He glared the length of the room at her. "I hit you, didn't I? Twice I shot. Twice I hit you."

"Oh, yeah. *So* impressive. Hit me in the body. Hit me where I can't move. Easy shots. Afraid to go for my head, aren't you? Cuz I can move my head. So, you'd...*miss*."

Stryke made a gurgling, choking sound. "I wouldn't m-m-miss!" He took a deep breath, then smiled. "The head shot will come, dearie. But not yet. The head shot will kill you. And before you die, I want your pain." His smile disappeared. His mouth twitched. "*Much* pain."

He *was* going to kill her. She *was* going to die. Panic tried to seize her again.

No! Stick with the plan. "Is that what you're telling yourself? Truth is, you *need* me in pain, so the head shot will be *easy*. Without the pain, I'd dodge. And you'd *miss. Again*."

"I WOULDN'T MISS!" Stryke screamed.

"How many times so far, Shorty? Let's see... Four that night in the church. At least five at the beach. Another last night. Woo hoo! Big ten spot in the *miss* department."

"Shut up!"

"Missy miss miss, missy miss," she taunted. "Shit, they shouldn't call you *Mister* Stryke. You should be *Miss* Stryke."

That did it. A wordless wail escaped Stryke's lips. Face contorted in rage, his arm flashed up as his hand pulled back the sling in a single smooth motion.

Oh, shit. What had she done? But her Voice spoke. Not in words, but again in messages to her muscles. And again, she let her body respond to those phantom commands.

Her head snapped to the right an eyeblink before the missile slammed into the mattress, ticking her ear as it passed. *Shit, that was close.* "And Miss Stryke hits eleven!" she called, as her aching head protested the quick movement.

Stamping in fury, Stryke screamed. He fired again. She dodged.

"A dozen for Little Missy Miss-Miss!"

Another shot. Another miss.

"Lucky thirteen! How high can he go, folks?"

Twenty was the answer—after which Stryke flung his slingshot down. It bounced, then skittered to the wall. His eyes went wide. He cried out, leaping after it. Falling to his knees, he picked it up as if it were a bird with a broken wing. Cradling it in one hand, he inspected it with his other. "I'm sorry, I'm sorry, I'm sorry," he whispered.

He tugged the sling back a few times, sighting at an imaginary target. Apparently satisfied his precious weapon was undamaged, he rose again. He turned his goggled eyes toward her.

Case readied herself for another shot. How long could she keep this up?

But Stryke didn't take another shot. He didn't even raise his arm. Instead, he walked slowly down the room to stand beside her. His jaw muscles clenched and unclenched. Sweat streaked his face, tracing pale tracks in his makeup.

Producing another ball bearing, he loaded it into the sling. "Enough," he croaked. He shoved the slingshot against her left temple, forcing her head over. She tried to twist away but couldn't.

"Think I'll miss now?" he hissed. He pulled the sling back.

She was going to die.

Listen! said her Voice.

She heard it then. A squeal of hinges, followed by the thud of the door slamming into the wall.

"Stop!" hissed a voice.

Snarling, Stryke lowered his slingshot and spun to face the intruder. He blocked her view of her unseen savior as footsteps approached.

"No!" cried Stryke. "That's not fair!"

"Fair? I would hardly call this scenario *fair*," said the voice.

Wait. She knew that voice. But, no... It wasn't possible.

"Is it fair," the voice continued, "to kill her without letting *me* play, too?"

Stryke moved aside, and another figure loomed over her. Taller than Stryke but dressed the same.

"No!" she screamed. "You're dead!"

Mr. Stayne leered a pointy-toothed smile at her. Unlike Stryke, he wore no makeup. This close, his skin was almost translucent. Except in one spot. In the middle of his forehead above his black goggles, a red-rimmed bullet hole stared at her.

Stayne reached out a long-fingered hand to the wheeled table beside her bed. Selecting a scalpel from the tray, he held it up, letting the light catch the surface of the blade. Then, ever so slowly, he moved it toward her left eye.

"Now," he said, "it's *my* turn."

Chapter 35

Surprise, Surprise

C ase raged against the straps pinning her to the bed. But all she could do was push her head to the right, trying to escape Stayne's advancing blade. "No! You're *dead*. I saw you *dead*!"

"Yes, dearie. He's dead," Stryke said from the foot of her bed. The little man smiled. "And so am I."

Stayne chuckled. "We've been dead for years, sweet meat. But thanks to the witch, we...continue." His smile faded. "Which is more than you'll be doing." His left hand flashed out, seizing her jaw in a vise-like grip, holding her head still. In his other hand, the scalpel's point drew closer and closer to her eye.

She fought with all her strength to free herself from his grip, but his gloved fingers were as unyielding as steel. The scalpel descended as she watched hypnotized. She would die, sliced to death by this ghoul. Her Voice couldn't save her now. Nothing could.

"Get away from her!"

Stayne's hand jumped at the sound, flicking the scalpel even closer to her eye. Releasing her with a snarl, he spun away from the bed, letting Case see her latest visitor. Not that she needed it. She knew that voice as well as her own.

Fader stood at the door. His mouth was set in a hard line, his brow furrowed, his eyes narrowed, his hands clenched at his sides. She'd never seen her brother look so fierce.

Stayne and Stryke laughed.

"Look, my friend," Stayne said to Stryke, "Another toy. Now we can both play."

Despite her own danger, Case found a new fear. "Run, Fader! Run!"

But Fader didn't budge. "I *said*...get away from her."

Stayne reached Fader in one stride. With his free hand, he seized her brother by the throat. Stayne raised Fader to eye level as easily as if he lifted an empty hand. His other hand flashed forward, and the scalpel hovered under Fader's chin. Fader kicked and wriggled, clawing at Stayne's grip.

Stryke hopped from one foot to the other, wringing his hands. "No, no, no.

This one's the Mistress's favorite. Under her protection, it is. Worth our lives to harm it."

Stayne chuckled. "Then she should take better care of her things."

"Should she now?" came a familiar voice from the doorway.

Stayne's eyes went so wide that Case thought the parchment skin of his face would rip open. Gently, he set Fader down and backed away. "Mistress, forgive me."

Morrigan stepped into the room. Case's heart fell. The witch had come to watch, bringing her enslaved brother to see her suffer.

Morrigan walked to Fader and ruffled his hair. Bending down, she examined his throat. Making a "tsk-tsk" sound, she touched a finger to his neck. Fader's skin glowed. He rubbed his throat, then smiled and nodded to her. She smiled back and straightened, one hand on his shoulder.

Stayne bowed and bobbed before her. "Mistress, my apologies. I didn't know."

Morrigan's smile faded. "You knew."

Golden runes flew from her arm to strike the tall man. Hurtling the length of the room, Stayne smashed into the end wall and crumpled to the floor. The runes covered him now, crawling over his skin like a nest of golden spiders. Angry, hungry spiders. He screamed and writhed, twisted and twitched as the runes swarmed over him.

Beside her, Stryke fell to his knees. "Mistress, I *told* him not to harm the boy. I *told* him."

"Yes. I heard. And for that, I will spare you your companion's reward."

Morrigan's gaze moved from Stryke to Case. Their eyes met, and Case felt again the terrible chill that hid behind Morrigan's beauty. Case fought back a shiver. She'd attacked Morrigan last night. Struck the witch. Whatever Morrigan planned for her, she knew it would be even worse than being left to Stryke and Stayne.

No. She wouldn't let Morrigan see her afraid. Hard Case took over. She returned the woman's gaze, unblinking.

The witch's lip curled as she considered Case. Her jaw clenched and un-clenched as if she fought an internal struggle.

Fader touched her hand. "Remember what I told you."

Morrigan sighed, but nodded. Turning to Stryke, she flicked a hand at Case. "Release her."

Wait. What?

She wasn't the only one surprised by Morrigan's words. Standing now, Stryke looked from Case to Morrigan. He repeated the action, open-mouthed disbe-lief on his face. "No! You promised her to us."

Morrigan rolled her eyes. "Really?" Runes danced down her arm again.

Stryke glanced at Stayne still screaming in the corner. His shoulders slumped. Glowering at Morrigan, he shuffled to the bed and fumbled at Case's straps. "You promised," he whispered.

"Yes, old friend, I promised," Morrigan replied, her voice now gentle. She waved at Stayne. The runes disappeared. The man collapsed, sobbing. "And I regret I must now break it." She sighed, considering Case. "I had questions for this one and would have enjoyed your help in that. However, I have learned this intolerable girl may be of use. We must keep her...intact."

So...good news, bad news. She wouldn't die horribly today. But discovering that Morrigan had plans for her didn't fill her with warm fuzzies. And what about Fader? He was safe, yes, but still entranced by Morrigan, unaware of the monster she was.

As if to prove her point, Fader touched Morrigan's hand. "Thank you."

She ruffled his hair again. "You are welcome, little one. And thank you for what you told me about your sister."

What? *Oh Fader, what have you done?*

Stryke undid the last strap. He lowered the side of the bed, glaring at Case. She pushed him away, only to have both her shoulders respond with screaming pain where he'd hit her. She didn't try standing. Her legs were numb, so she dangled them over the edge, waiting for circulation to return.

"You will stay in this room, girl," Morrigan said. "A Hollow Boy will remain outside. He will bring you meals and take you to the water closet when you need." She fixed Case with a cold stare. "Try to escape, and I will return you to these two." Waving at Stryke and a now standing Stayne, she motioned them out.

The two men filed past Morrigan, heads bowed, glowering hate at Case.

Morrigan smiled at Fader. "I'll leave you with your *dear* sister. Alert me if she tries to abandon you again." Firing Case a glare that made Stayne and Stryke's departing looks seem warm, she swept from the room.

Fader walked toward Case grinning, his arms raised for a hug.

But his face fell when she stepped back from him. "Stay away from me, Fader."

<hr />

Will assumed a Board of Directors would be large. When he pushed open the tall oak doors to the boardroom, he expected every chair to be filled. Instead, he found only three people facing him from the opposite side of the long boardroom table, their backs to the windows.

He'd also expected a bunch of old guys. Instead, he found two men and a woman. One man qualified as "old," at least in his books. But the other two appeared late thirties, around Adi's age. They wore dark suits, and both men wore ties, making him regret his wardrobe decision.

All three stood when he entered, which threw him for a moment. The principal in school had never stood when Will came to his office. But then it was *his* company, right?

The older man, positioned in the middle of the three, smiled. "Mr. Dreycott, thank you for coming." He motioned to the chair opposite him.

Will took the indicated seat. The man sat again, the other two following his lead.

From his position in the center and how the others deferred to him, Will guessed this guy was in charge. The principal. He had a triangular face, with a pointed chin and thin lips. Short-cropped gray hair sat high above a wide forehead. A manila folder lay closed before him. He leaned back in his chair, pale gray eyes locked on Will. "I am Lawrence Kinland, Chair of the Board of Directors. This is Kat McClay and Ted Osborne, also members of the Board."

"Nice to meet you," Will said. McClay and Osborne, unsmiling, gave small nods. His feeling of being in the principal's office grew.

"Mr. Dreycott—" Kinland began.

"Will. Call me Will."

Kinland smiled. "Will, then. We, of course, know who *you* are. But I suspect you have no idea who *we* are." He paused, considering Will. "Or what we do on your behalf."

Will swallowed. "Well, Adi...I mean Ms. Archambeault...she handles, you know..." His voice trailed off. Adi handled everything. But he guessed these people knew that.

Kinland shook his head. McClay and Osborne joined him as if on cue. "Poor Adrienne. Horrible. Horrible. I understand her condition is...uncertain?" He eyed Will.

"Yes...no... I mean, Doctor Jin... Her surgeon... She says the next forty-eight hours will tell whether—" He stopped. "They'll tell," he finished, leaving it at that.

Kinland nodded. "Adrienne is a fighter. We know that from our own dealings with her. I'm sure she'll pull through. However, we have a corporate empire to run—on your behalf, of course." His principal's gaze returned to pierce Will. "Which means, we must make a decision."

Will sank lower in his chair under that scrutiny. Catching himself, he straightened again. "Uh, okay. What decision?" And why did they need to talk to him?

"Adrienne is the CEO of your company. With her incapacitated, your company is rudderless. It needs a captain. We must fill the CEO role. On an interim basis only, of course."

"Okay, so pick a replacement. I mean, you're the Board, right?"

McClay and Osborne shifted in their chairs, both looking at Kinland. Kinland hesitated. "Will, we are an *advisory* Board of Directors. Do you understand what that means?"

"Nope. Didn't know that'd be on the exam."

Kinland gave a thin smile. "Yours is a private company. Its shares are not publicly traded, and you are the majority shareholder. You do not legally require a Board."

"Then why do I have one? What do you guys do?"

"We..." Kinland indicated McClay and Osborne. "...and the other Board members represent shareholders in your firm. But still a minority share in total. Adrienne formed the Board to advise her on running this huge empire. Our holdings—and our corporate experience and industry knowledge—bring us a position on your Board."

"So, you give her advice—"

"Yes," Kinland said, smiling.

"—which she can ignore."

Kinland smile slipped a little, but he chuckled. "Well put. And she often does."

Will frowned. "You said 'and the other members.' You're not the entire Board?"

More chair shifting. "The full Board," Kinland said, "comprises seven individuals. Due to schedule conflicts, they could not join us. However, they are aware we are meeting. We...*represent* the Board in this matter."

Whatever. Will shrugged. "Sorry, Larry—"

"Lawrence."

"—but again, why can't you just pick a replacement for Adi?" Will said, then added. "You know, until she's better."

"An excellent idea, and one we wished to propose ourselves."

"Great!" Will began to stand.

"However, therein lies the problem."

He sat again. "Problem?"

Kinland leaned forward. "Although the Board may *recommend* a new CEO, that person must be appointed."

Will shrugged. "Then get with the appointing."

"*Legally* appointed. By *you*."

"But I'm not of legal age yet—"

"—*or* your legal representative."

Will understood. "Adi."

"Yes. Adrienne may act as your legal agent only because, after your parents disappeared..."

Will stiffened. He hadn't expected his parents to come up.

"...the court appointed her your guardian until you come of age. This gives her Power of Attorney in your affairs, including your business affairs."

He'd known that. Kind of. Sort of. Maybe.

"We are, therefore, at an impasse, unless..." Removing a thick document from the folder, Kinland pushed it across the table. "Will, that document assigns your Power of Attorney to this Board. Temporarily, of course, until Adrienne can resume her role here. Which, we hope, will be soon."

Will began reading the document. His eyes glazed over by the second page. He flipped to the end. There were twenty-seven pages. "Well, it certainly is...long."

"And comprehensive, I assure you. It is..." Kinland frowned, as if searching for the best word. "It is *modeled* on the same agreement under which Adrienne operates on your behalf."

So that was a good thing, right? Adi had never done anything bad to him, and this was the same document. Not that Adi would ever do anything bad to him, document or not. Why was he thinking about bad things happening to him? This was just boring business stuff. He had real problems to solve. Finding Case. Finding Fader. Stopping two crazed super-villains. "Okay. Where do I sign?"

Kinland smiled. McClay and Osborne sat back. An air of tension he hadn't noticed left the room. Kinland slid a gold pen across the table. "On the last page, Will, if you would."

He picked up the pen. As his hand hovered above the signature line, he hesitated. But then images of Case as a prisoner filled his head. Yeah, bigger problems to solve.

He signed the document.

In the locked hospital room, Case stood using the bed for support as feeling returned to her legs. Unfortunately, feeling was also returning to where Stryke had hit her. She clenched her teeth against the pain, tears welling in her eyes.

Fader huddled on the floor by the closed door, his knees pulled to his chest. He'd retreated there after she'd refused to hug him. And she wanted so much to hug him.

So why didn't she? Because she was afraid. And ashamed. Afraid of her own brother and ashamed of being so. But she knew what she'd seen in Will's tower and again just now.

Morrigan had a hold on Fader.

"What's wrong, Case? I just saved you."

"*You* are wrong, bro."

It hurt to see him flinch at her words. "I am not!"

"Well, you sure were last night. You brought Morrigan and her creepazoids into Will's building. Stryke called you her favorite, and you still seem to be her little pet. She left you here to guard me."

Getting up, he walked toward her. She stepped back, and he stopped. He took a deep breath. "Okay. You're right. She made me...wrong. But I'm not anymore."

"Sorry. Need more than that."

"She wrote these marks on me..." he began.

She listened as he told about the spell Morrigan had used on him. And how he'd made the marks on his skin fade.

"So, no marks, no spell?" she asked as he finished.

"Yeah, seems to work that way."

She considered that. Morrigan was powerful, but she wasn't invincible. The night they'd met, her spell had failed on Case. And if Fader had freed himself, they might find other ways to defeat her magic. "And now you're...you?" She wanted to believe him so much.

"Yes! I pretend when I'm around her, so she doesn't put the marks back." He shook his head. "I can't believe what I did. I mean, I meet Will, the Dream Rider guy, and I don't even tell him how *awesome* the Rider is."

"That's your big concern? You didn't give your hero props?" Relief washed over her like warm summer rain. She fought back a sob. "Yeah, you're you again. Bring it in, bro." She opened her arms.

Fader ran to her, and they hugged each other. "Thanks for saving me," she said, finally breaking it off.

He shrugged. "That's what family does, right? We protect each other."

Yeah, family should protect each other. But her mother hadn't protected them. And she herself hadn't kept Fader safe. Instead, he'd had to rescue her. And they were still prisoners.

She pushed thoughts of their mother away as she remembered Morrigan's words. "Wait a minute. The witch bitch said you told her something about *me*. About how I could help her and Marell. What did she mean?"

Fader kicked the floor. He shoved his hands in his pockets. "I told her Will's your boyfriend."

"What? Will? He is not."

"Yeah, right. I saw you together. In the lobby of his building."

"Will is *so* not my boyfriend," she said, trying to ignore the sudden ache in her heart.

"He so *is*."

"Is not." He wasn't, was he? No. Not anymore. Not after how she'd treated him. Her thoughts ran back to their afternoon together. In the rooftop park. In his bedroom. Had that only been yesterday?

"I saw how he looked at you," Fader said. "And heard what he said to you. And you were crying after. Maybe you don't like him—and if you don't, you're stupid. He's the Dream Rider guy! And he lives in that wicked tower. And —"

"Focus, dude. He's not my boyfriend."

"Doesn't matter what you think. Even if you don't like him, he likes *you*. Likes you a *lot*."

She swallowed. Yes, Will did. She knew that. And she liked him. Also a *lot*. Maybe more than liked. And she'd pushed him away. She wiped at her eyes.

"See?"

"Shut up. Why do they care about Will? Wait! Is he okay? Is he here?"

"No, they didn't get him." Fader hopped up onto the bed and sat there kicking his legs. "They were after that Yeshe guy."

"Wait...what? Yeshe?"

"He stole something from Marell. That's why Marell has to keep switching bodies."

She sat beside him. "Bro, you'd better tell me everything that's happened since I got bonked on the head."

Fader told her of the invasion of Will's penthouse. Of how it had all been about getting Yeshe. And of how Adi, stabbed by Stayne, had still saved Will from Morrigan by shooting Stayne.

She sat stunned as Fader finished. Adi shooting people? She'd seriously underestimated her. But stabbed? "Adi? Is she...?"

Fader's face fell. "I don't know."

The nightmare continued. Adi wasn't her biggest fan, but the woman protected Will like a mother lion defending her cub. That made her one of the good guys. And look where that got her.

"But Will's okay?"

He grinned. "He is *so* your boyfriend. Yeah, he was fine, I think."

"Good," she said, fighting back the huge sigh of relief wanting to escape her. And the silly grin trying to own her face. A thought snapped her back to reality. "Stayne was dead. Now he's not. Because of Morrigan, he said."

"Magic, I guess."

"Yeah, but *how*? Did she do something to Stayne when they came back here?"

His brow furrowed. "She laid him on this rug in the Weave room where that Marell guy is."

So Marell was here, too. That figured. "Weave room?"

"That's what she calls it. There's this red and black rug with three skeleton legs. Like that locket she wears."

The locket that Yeshe said was part of her power—if she could believe anything Yeshe had told them. But there had to be a link if this rug had the same design. She filed that away. "That's it? Just put him on the rug? Did she do anything else?"

"Don't know. I slipped away to search for you. Found you here with Stryke shooting at you."

"He didn't see you?"

"Fading Boy, remember? I knew I couldn't help you alone, so I ran to get Morrigan."

"Oh, right. Because we're such BFFs. Dude, she gave me to Stryke to start with. Why would she save me?"

"I explained that. Because I told her Will likes you."

"Why would she care about that?"

"Because of the Dream Rider."

"But she and Marell aren't after the Rider, whoever he is. You said they were after Yeshe."

"They were. And now they have him. But now they want the Rider, too. Which means Will. And now they have someone he cares about. You."

"But why Will? Because he knows the Rider?"

Fader bit his lip. "You believe the Rider's real, don't you?"

She remembered how Will had known about her Voice after the Rider learned of it in their dream encounter. "Yeah. I do."

"Well, so do Marell and Morrigan. And Marell's afraid of him. The Rider killed something called a Mara. Then he escaped Marell."

"Yeah, Will told us—me, Adi, and Yeshe—about the Rider doing that in Dream."

"Well, there's something your boyfriend *didn't* tell you."

"He's not my...oh, forget it. What didn't he tell me?"

Fader hesitated. "You'll either really like this—or not so much."

"Fader! Spit it out."

"Will didn't tell you that—" He took a deep breath. "*He's the Dream Rider.*"

Chapter 36

Into Your Arms

Leaving his design table, Will walked from his studio to the windows of the running track. Far below, people and cars scurried ant-like in the streets. Streets where he could never go. Above the skyline to the west, the sunset began to pink the clouds. Evening approached. Finally.

Waiting for night to come when he could enter Dream, he'd spent the afternoon working on the next Dream Rider issue. He was almost finished. Just the final battle to do.

It was a great issue. Maybe his best. But now, as his mind retreated from the pretend world where he ruled, his thoughts returned to the real world.

The world where he'd screwed everything up.

Back in his studio, he checked the display on the wall for the millionth time. Adi still lay in her hospital bed, unconscious and maybe dying—because of having to save *him*. In a chair beside the bed, a younger woman with buzz-cut brown hair now sat holding Adi's hand. Laura Vasquez, Adi's on-again, off-again girlfriend. Another person in pain because of him.

And because *he* had given Fader the run of this tower, Case was a prisoner somewhere, kidnapped by crazies. Crazies who'd invaded his home only because *he* had trusted Yeshe.

His earlier meeting with the Board had reinforced how unimportant he was. Shit, he wasn't even important to Marell and Morrigan. They'd been after Yeshe all along, not him.

He stared at Adi lying unmoving on her bed. *All you can do is wait.* Jin's words.

No. He could do more than wait. He couldn't help Adi, but he had to do something.

And he would—in *his* world, in the world where he wasn't useless. He'd search for Case in Dream tonight. He had to know she was safe. And Case was smart. By now, he bet she'd figured out if Morrigan was holding her at that hospital.

But what then?

He slumped onto the couch. Even if he found Case and Fader, how could

he face Morrigan and Marell? He rubbed his shoulder, still sore from where
Morrigan had tossed him against this very wall. Tossed him with a flick of her
hand.

Tossed him with magic. How could he fight magic?

A chill seized him. How would Zhang and his team fight magic? They might
walk into something even a SWAT unit couldn't handle. More people might be
hurt. Or worse. Because of him. Again.

As if reading his mind, Hallie's voice sounded over the speaker. "Call from
Winstone Zhang, Mr. Dreycott."

Crap. What should he tell Stone? "Answer."

Stone's face appeared on the screen, replacing the view of Adi. He was
dressed completely in black, with his face blackened as well. A pair of what Will
guessed were night vision goggles sat on his forehead. Behind him, other men,
similarly clad, moved among stacks of crates and boxes. Beyond, the scene
faded to shadow.

"Will," Stone said, "I wanted to update you on that project you green-light-
ed."

The raid. Well, maybe they weren't ready. "Thanks. So?"

"Team assembled, plan complete. About to execute a dry run using an
abandoned factory in the docklands. Similar layout to the target location."

Shit. Now what? "When...?"

"If this goes well, we'll be in place at the target at oh-two-hundred hours. I
want to move before it's light."

Two AM. He thought again of Morrigan and her power.

Stone continued. "Once we're in position, I'll call you to confirm before—"

"Stone, I want you to hold off."

Stone's face betrayed no emotion, but a heartbeat passed before he spoke.
"Sir?"

"I'm getting information tonight confirming the location and what you'll be
up against. But I won't have that before two AM."

"I understand. I assume this information will come from those special
sources of yours? The ones you can't explain?"

"Yeah. Those," Will said, glad Stone hadn't pressed him to proceed with the
raid or for clearer reasons for delaying. "Could you do this tomorrow night
instead?"

Stone nodded. "Should I plan for that?"

"Yes, please," Will said, relieved.

"All right. I'll brief the team, rework the plan, and await your call."

"Okay. Yeah, good. And sorry about this."

Stone shrugged. "You're the boss." His face disappeared. The screen once more displayed Adi and her hospital room.

You're the boss.

Yeah, right. He didn't feel like the boss of anything. He felt like a kid. A kid who couldn't go outside, who screwed up everything in his life, who endangered people he loved...

Loved? Well, Adi for sure, like a mother. But Case? Was he in love with her? Even after what she'd said to him?

He swallowed. If it wasn't love, it was the closest thing he'd ever known.

And like Adi, he'd put Case in danger. With no idea how to fix that. Had he made the right decision to call Stone off? What if the raid had worked? What if delaying it put Case into even greater danger? He buried his face in his hands, feeling even more helpless and uncertain.

He needed answers, and he knew who had them.

Yeshe.

First, he'd find Case. Make sure she was safe. Find out where she was.

His hands clenched into fists. Then Yeshe.

Jumping up, he ran upstairs to begin his preparations for that night's Dream trip.

Will awoke. But in Dream.

Tonight, the House of Four Doors resembled his tower's reception space. Four flat translucent walls, beyond which lay only swirling mists. A door in each wall. The Bed of Awakening was a white leather couch. At the end of the Bed sat Brian.

Standing, Will patted the Doogle. Brian curled and uncurled his tail in return greeting.

"Okay, Bry. Let's find Case. Nyx!"

Nyx's face appeared, long purple hair floating in the swirling mist behind her. Her violet eyes were hooded, her lips drawn in a tight line. Raising a long-nailed finger, she wagged it at him. "No," she said before he could speak.

"Uh..."

"No, I'm not giving you the data ball for your girlfriend yet. Or for that naughty monk."

"She's not my girlfriend."

"I'm your subconscious. She's your girlfriend."

"Is everyone's subconscious as big a pain as mine?"

"Yes, but other people don't have conversations with theirs, so they can ignore it."

"You say that like it's a bad thing. I need to find Case."

"And so you shall, oh Great Master. But you need to find someone else before that."

"I'll find Yeshe later. First, I have to know Case is safe."

"Not Yeshe."

"Who?"

"You know who."

His stomach tightened. "No. I can't. Please, Nyx."

Nyx's features softened behind a sad smile. "You have to, Will. You know that," she said, but her voice was gentle.

Tears formed in his eyes, so he pulled his hood up to hide them from Nyx. "It was my fault. Everything was my fault."

"All the more reason, kid."

He took a deep breath. "Yeah. Yeah, okay. You're right."

She chuckled. "Your subconscious is *always* right. People would be happier if they understood that. Need help with the search?"

"No. I can find her."

Nyx gave a nod and then vanished with a pop. Brian whined and nuzzled him, seeming to sense his creator's unease.

Will rubbed him behind his ears. "Ok, Bry-guy. You heard the lady. Let's find Adi."

He found her in a hospital. But not her hospital room, whose every feature had burned into his memory so deeply he could draw it if needed. And not lying in a bed dressed in a blue hospital gown.

Adi stood in a hallway, staring through a glass partition. She wore khaki pants tucked into hiking boots, a worn leather jacket, and a brown hat with a floppy brim, buttoned up on one side. He'd never seen her dressed like that.

Still keeping himself hidden from her awareness, he approached, following her gaze. Through the partition, two rows of bassinets filled a maternity ward. In each lay a baby. Adi stared at one, her cheeks wet.

He tried reading the name on that bassinet but the letters blurred as they sometimes did in Dream. Ashamed of spying on what must be a personal and private memory, he stepped forward into her dream.

She turned as he appeared. A broad smile creased her face. "William! How nice of you to come." She looked around, frowning. "Although, I can't remember how I got here." She seemed to notice his Dream Rider costume for the first time. "Oh, I'm dreaming."

The maternity ward had disappeared. They now stood in Adi's hospital room, staring at where she lay in bed, her eyes closed. Monitors beeped and pulsed around her. Beside her, Laura sat holding her hand.

Adi peered at the sleeping figure. "Is that me?"

Words caught in his throat. He just nodded.

"How odd. But Laura came." She smiled.

"Adi, I'm sorry. It's all my fault." The words came then, bursting from him as he told of last night, of how she came to be in that bed.

She nodded slowly. "Yes, I remember now." Reaching up, she stroked his cheek. "Stop blaming yourself. I should never have trusted that monk. I focused too much on your girlfriend." She shrugged. "It was my fault, too."

"But, Adi, I screwed up so bad."

"So *badly*," she corrected him. "Welcome to life." She sighed. "I'm sorry, William, for what I said when we last met."

"Me, too. I was afraid that would be the last—" He stopped.

She frowned. "What? The last time we'd talk?" She stared at herself in the bed. "Am I dying?"

Again, he couldn't speak.

She watched his face. "That close, eh? Well, don't give up on me yet. I'm tougher than I look."

"I'm realizing that. Last night, you said you needed to tell me something."

She raised an eyebrow. "Did I? Yes, I would have said that, given the circumstances. But, no. Not now. Not here. Tell me what's going on instead."

Knowing better than to argue, he explained about the SWAT team and his own plan to locate Case and Yeshe in Dream.

Adi nodded. "You can trust Mr. Zhang. Completely and in all things. He is..." She paused, and a smile twitched at a corner of her mouth. "He is a man of honor." She turned from where her other self lay in bed. "I agree about finding Case. Her information may help Mr. Zhang. Not that it would matter what I said—you'd go after her regardless. But as for Yeshe..." She shook her head. "He's a liar. The monk used you. He used us all."

"He has answers."

"How can you be sure?"

"He has to. He certainly knows more than we do. I can't save Case and Fader without knowing what Marell and Morrigan are after. And what their weaknesses are, assuming they have any."

"Everyone has weaknesses. How do you know Yeshe won't lie to you again?"

"I don't. But I have to try."

"He's dangerous, William. He has powers. Powers you don't. Ones that have let him evade dangerous enemies for over a century—if that wasn't another lie."

"Powers he promised to teach me."

Adi snorted. "Promises from a liar."

"He's still our best shot at— Adi? What's wrong?"

Adi—the Adi who stood beside him—was fading. She grabbed onto the bed to steady herself. "I don't know. I feel... Everything is so confusing..." She looked at him. "I am proud of you, William."

"I love you, Adi," he called out.

Too late. She was gone. He stared at where Adi lay unconscious in bed as Laura kept vigil. He didn't know what her sudden departure meant. Had something changed in her condition? Or had her unconscious mind simply moved out of the dream state?

Awake, he could do nothing for Adi. *All you can do is wait*, Jin had said. If her condition changed, Hallie would call and Nyx would wake him. Asleep, in Dream, he could at least deal with his other problems.

Beside him, Brian whined. He patted the Doogle. "Yeah, you're right. Let's find Case."

⸙

Case was dreaming. Her first clue had been the white-faced scarecrow in the cornfield. A scarecrow wearing a black suit, black hat, and black goggles. And holding a slingshot. Her second had been the witch flying across a storm-clouded sky on a broomstick. A witch with long red hair wearing a green dress. Her final clue had been the yellow-brick road on which she stood. A road running through fields of too-red poppies toward a distant city of green crystal spires—and a single, tall, white tower.

The Dream Rider riding his skateboard along that road towards her, a Doogle by his side, had clinched it.

Seeing him, she remembered why she'd wanted to dream tonight. As the Rider approached, she waited, arms crossed, her foot tapping an angry rhythm.

He stopped a few paces away and gave the Doogle a pat. "Good work, Bry. Okay, off you go. You know what to do."

Brian curled and uncurled his long strange tail, then sped off down the yellow-brick road in the direction of the city of spires.

The Rider walked up to her. "I found you."

"Freaking obvious," she said, her anger growing.

He hesitated. "Are you okay? I mean, in the real world?"

"You mean, aside from the 'prisoners of nut jobs' thing? Yeah, I'm awesome."

"Prisoners? Plural?"

"Fader."

"He's okay, too?"

She just nodded, her foot still tapping.

"Will told me Fader was helping Morrigan," the Rider said.

"Oh, *Will* told you, did he? Yeah, well, Fader's fine now."

"Long story?"

"Rune magic, Fader controlled. Runes gone, Fader back."

"Short story. Do you know where they're holding you?"

She couldn't hold back any longer. "Were you *ever* going to tell me?"

"Tell you...?"

"That you're the Dream Rider!" she yelled, throwing her arms up.

He looked down at his costume. "To quote you, freaking obvious."

"No! Not *you*! I mean...*you*. The *Will* you! Will Dreycott. *You* are Will!"

He stared at her, not moving, not answering.

"You are, aren't you?" she said, no longer so sure. "You're Will. I mean, Will is the Dream Rider, isn't he? Aren't you? Oh, for shit's sake, answer me!"

For an answer, he pulled back the hood of his costume. She stared back at him, fighting back tears. Why did she feel like crying? She never cried. Damn him.

"Hi," he said.

"Hi," she answered. He reached for her, and she let him take her in his arms. They stood there just holding each other, for how long she didn't know.

"Oh, god," he whispered into her hair. "This feels so good. After we fought, after what you said, I didn't think we'd ever—"

Breaking off the hug, she punched him hard in the shoulder.

"Ow!" he said, rubbing his shoulder. "Okay, I seriously need to read your manual. Sex, fight, hug, punch. Are you mad at me or not?"

"I'm mad!"

"Why?"

"Because you never *told* me! Even after we...you know, in your bedroom. And you still didn't tell me."

"I *tried* to."

"No, you *didn't*."

"Yes, I *did*. In the bedroom. After...you know. But you totally freaked—"

"Totally did not."

"Sorry, but you totally did. *No more secrets*, you said. *No more sharing*. Remember?"

She folded her arms and looked away. She shifted from one foot to the other. Damn him again.

"Remember?"

"Maybe. Kind of." She sighed. "Okay, yeah, I remember." She considered him. "That was the secret you wanted to tell me?"

He nodded.

She kicked at a yellow brick. "Big secret."

"My biggest."

And he trusted her with it. She felt even worse about how she'd treated him. All because she'd been afraid to share her own secrets.

"And it's my last one," he said. "Now I've told you everything about me. My parents, why I live in my tower, who I really am."

She sat in a patch of poppies beside the road, hugging her knees to her chest. "Now it's my turn, right?"

He sat beside her. "Case, you don't have to tell me anything."

"Yes, I do. I want to."

"Why the change of heart?" he asked, searching her face.

Change of heart. Her heart *had* changed. Or maybe she was finally listening to it. She met his eyes, and he held her gaze. "Because I like you. A lot."

He swallowed. "Then what you said in my bedroom. About us..."

She sighed. "You mean, Everything Boy and Nothing Girl?"

"Yeah...and my money being obscene."

"Will, I'm sorry. I was just trying to stop—"

"The sharing."

"Yeah, the sharing. You'd shared so much with me, but I wasn't ready to do the same. I'm not used to talking about my life. Not something you do on the street. So I was a bitch." She looked at him. "Will, I hurt you. You didn't deserve that. I'm sorry."

His voice was low when he spoke. "But did you *mean* what you said? About us? How it could never work?"

"No. Maybe. I don't know." She shook her head. "Look, you and me, we're as different as different gets. Could we ever make it work? Probably not."

"Um, are you dumping me again?"

She smiled. "Nope. I'm saying I'd like to try."

"To dump me?"

"To make it work, dumbass."

He reached out and took her hand. "Me, too."

They kissed, a soft touch of their lips. Brief, tentative, like they were starting all over again. Which they kind of were. She sat back, her smile disappearing. "So now what? We're still prisoners, Fader and me. And I so want to stop Witch Bitch and her boy toy from doing whatever they're trying to do. What *are* they trying to do, anyway?"

"No idea, but it won't be good. Yeah, those are the problems. First one first. Do you know where you are?"

"Fader says it's the hospital in those pictures Adi showed him. Morrigan was in his head then and made him deny it."

"I *knew* it. That's what I told Stone. Now I can confirm the location."

"Told who?"

He explained about the planned raid on the hospital tomorrow evening. "If it works, you'll both be free, and Morrigan and Marell will be captured. All problems solved."

"Seriously?"

"Well, I'm worried about Morrigan's magic—"

"No, I mean, seriously, you have your own SWAT team?"

"Oh. Apparently yeah. I should pay more attention to stuff."

"You are the weirdest person on the planet."

"Possibly true," he said.

"I'm not sure guns will stop Morrigan."

"Adi got the drop on her."

"Adi. Shit. I didn't even ask. Fader told me what happened. Is she okay?"

He dropped his head. "Touch and go."

"I'm sorry. But she'll make it. Your den mommy's quite the badass."

"At least she got Stayne."

"Yeah, about that..." She told him of Stayne's resurrection.

He groaned. "This just keeps getting worse. Magic. Body swapping. Psycho ghouls that won't stay dead." He lay back among the poppies, staring up at a far too blue sky. "Case, I don't know what to do. If I send Stone's team in, they could be killed. If I don't, you and Fader..." He stopped.

"Could be killed. Yeah, I get that."

"It keeps coming back to stopping Morrigan and Marell."

"Got any ideas?"

"No, but I'm guessing who does."

She jerked a thumb towards the emerald spires of the distant city. "The Wizard?"

"Somebody like that."

"Yeshe. The guy who lied straight-faced to us."

"Well, the Wizard lied to Dorothy at first, too," he said.

"Before sending her to get captured by the wicked witch. So yeah, Yeshe's right on track."

"A witch she defeated. Look, we need to learn more about Morrigan and Marell. Who else has answers?"

"No one, I guess. You can find him in Dream? The way you found me and Fader?"

"I'm already trying." He touched his wrist, and a glowing silver cord appeared. "I sent Brian to search for Yeshe, but so far..." Running his fingers over the cord, he shook his head. "Nothing."

"So?"

He shrugged. "We wait. Give Brian a bit more time."

I'd like to try to make it work. That's what she'd said. She turned to him. "While we're waiting for Brian...do you want to hear a story?"

He looked at her. "Only if you're ready to tell me."

"Yeah. I think I am."

"Then I want to hear it."

Chapter 37

A Big Hurt

In Dream, in a field of red poppies, beside a yellow-brick road, Will sat beside Case. He'd willed his Dream Rider costume away, choosing instead a Billy Eilish t-shirt, black jeans, and high-tops. He felt he should be himself, the one she knew best. She was about to share something intimate. More intimate to her than what they'd shared in his bedroom. That made this important not only to her, but also to *them*—to the relationship they'd begun.

She sat cross-legged, twirling a red poppy between her fingers, gazing out across the field of flowers. "I hate my mother."

Too many recent conversations involved parents, in his opinion. But he said nothing.

"Didn't always," she continued. "Once, she was my whole world. I barely remember our dad. They were young when I came along. I was a surprise. They never married. I don't think it was ever great between them, but he hung around. Then she got pregnant with Fader."

"Jeez, protection much?"

She shrugged. "Maybe she thought it'd bring them closer. They'd been students together. She'd just got her Ph.D. in physics—yeah, thought that'd surprise you—and she was teaching at U of T. Maybe she hoped they'd settle down, have a real family life."

"I'm guessing that didn't work out."

"Good guess. Another kid was one too many, apparently. He cut out before Fader was born. We never heard from him again. She never talked about him after that. I don't even know his name. Mom kept her last name and gave that to us." She looked away, wiping at her eyes.

He pretended not to notice. "Things got bad after he left?"

"No. Things were great." A small smile grew. "It must've been hard for her. Single mom, not great pay. But I don't remember going without. We had a tiny apartment, clothes, food on the table, presents on birthdays and Christmas. And we loved each other. At least, Fader and me, we loved her. Thought she loved us, too." She ripped petals off the poppy she held.

When she didn't go on, he asked, "What happened?"

She shrugged. "She left us. I was eight, Fader four."

He blinked. "Left? As in abandoned you?"

"Left us with her parents. They lived in the west end. We used to stay with them a lot, with Mom being a single parent."

"But why'd she leave?"

Another shrug. "She wouldn't tell anyone. Not even where she was going. Said it was confidential, some big secret. Just said she was leaving on a trip, and she'd be back in three months."

"Only...?"

"Only she never came back."

"Oh." More silence followed. "You ever hear from her? Learn what happened?"

She tore off another petal. "Nope. Not a word. Our grandparents tried to find her." She shrugged. "No luck."

"She never talked about the trip?"

"Only that, when she came home, we'd be able to buy a house with a big yard. Get new clothes. We could both have bikes." She ripped the last petal from the poppy. "She said lots of things. All lies."

Will frowned. "Sounds like she expected to come into major money."

Case snorted. "Where? How? She was a university professor. She made it all up, so we wouldn't ask questions. It was one big lie. She wanted to run away. Leave Fader and me behind. She knew her parents would look after us. She wanted her own life." She threw the poppy away. "One without us."

Or something happened to her. But he didn't say that. "So how was life with your grandparents?"

"Short and sweet. They were kind, took good care of us. Fader and I loved them both. Everything was peachy." She pulled up another poppy.

"Until...?"

She tossed the poppy away. "Until they were out for their anniversary one night. We were home with a babysitter. Some drunk t-boned Gramps. Killed them both." She wiped at her eyes.

"Shit."

She chuckled, but the sound carried only bitterness. "A word describing our lives since then. Nobody could locate either of our parents. Or any other relatives—or at least none that wanted us. So we became wards of the province. Social Services found us a foster home. Then another. And another. We weren't exactly model kids." She shrugged. "Well, *I* wasn't. Fader was always a good kid. But at least they kept us together at first."

"Until you got sent to juvie," he said. She frowned. "You told me the first night we met," he explained. "How you took Fader from his foster home after you got out, and you've been on the streets since."

"I remember." She shook her head. "Seems so long ago. That night. Meeting you."

"Three days."

"Seriously? Feels like forever."

"I have that effect on people."

"I'm glad."

"Glad I affect people that way?"

"No, Home Boy. Glad I broke into your weird tower. Glad we met."

"You are?"

Her smile became a small thing, oddly timid for her. She nodded.

He had trouble speaking for a second. "Thanks, Case. For trusting me. For sharing. And you're not, you know."

"Not what?"

"You're not a Nothing Girl."

She swallowed, then leaned forward, tilting her head.

He kissed her, a kiss that went on and on and was as wonderful as their first kiss in the real world. She broke it off finally and sat back, stroking his cheek with a finger. "You give good Dream, Mr. Rider."

He grinned. "Takes two."

She smiled, then looked serious again. "How's Brian doing on his Yeshe search?"

He knew she'd changed the subject to break off her story about their mother. But he also knew better than to push her for more, grateful she'd shared as much as she had.

He touched his wrist, then ran his fingers over the glowing silver cord that appeared there. Nothing. Not even a tingle. "Still no luck." He tugged on Brian's leash. "I'm calling him back."

"Giving up?"

"Nope. We just need to give him more help. Nyx!"

Nyx's face popped into existence before them, hovering inside her cloud of mist.

Beside him, Case jumped. "What the freak?"

"I'll explain later. Nyx, I need my memory data on Yeshe again. What I gave to Brian."

Nyx's violet eyes settled on Case. "Ooh! It's your girlfriend."

"She's not my—"

"We had that discussion. You lost." Nyx looked Case up and down.

Case crossed her arms, glaring at Nyx. "See anything you like, bitch?"

Nyx laughed, a rich warm sound. He tried to remember hearing Nyx laugh before. Her long purple hair swirled as she spun back to Will. "Feisty! I *like* her."

"Explain *now*," Case said to Will.

"Uh, this is Nyx. She's—"

"I'm his subconscious," Nyx interrupted. "Girl, we need to talk. The things I could tell you about your boyfriend."

"He's not my boyfriend."

"Now don't *you* start," Nyx said.

Case turned to Will. "Your subconscious?"

He sighed. "When I'm the Rider, I need information on what I'm searching for in Dream. Before I enter Dream, I memorize whatever I need. I've taught myself a meditation routine. Kind of self-hypnosis. As I meditate, I tag the information in my memory with a keyword or phrase. Then, when I'm in Dream, I recall it by saying the key word."

"Which he does by waking me up," Nyx said, "usually from my own lovely dream."

"Nyx then pulls that information from my subconscious memories."

"I'm quite indispensable, you see. And very under-appreciated."

"I do the same for things I might need but don't want to carry around."

"Like that shield and sword you used when I first met you as the Rider," Case said.

"Ooh, you're quick," Nyx said. "But if I recall, he never used them because you saved yourself."

"Thanks for reminding me," he said. "Now, Yeshe's data, please."

A glowing data ball popped onto his outstretched palm. "Thanks, Nyx. You can go now."

"You see how he treats me?" Nyx said to Case. Holding up an imaginary phone to her face, she mouthed "Call me" to Case. She disappeared with a pop just as Brian trotted up to them along the yellow-brick road.

Case looked at him, shaking her head. "Weirdest. Person. Ever."

"You should see it from my side." He offered the data ball to Brian. "Ok, Bry, let's start this search again." The Doogle sniffed then wrapped a long tongue around it and pulled it into its mouth. Lights danced in its black eyes.

"Now," he said to Case, "think hard about your encounters with Yeshe. Keep those thoughts in your mind."

She closed her eyes. "Okay. Thinking."

"Hold out your hand."

Brian gave her palm a long slow lick. She wiped her hand on her jeans. "Yuck. So now Brian has both our memories of Yeshe? Now what?"

He kicked his skateboard from the grass onto the yellow-brick road, then took Brian's silver leash and held out his other hand to Case. "Now, we're off to see the Wizard."

But Case didn't take his hand. Instead, she stared over his shoulder. "Will?" He turned.

The Emerald City was gone. The yellow-brick road was gone. The endless fields of poppies were gone. Instead, across a deep valley, a full moon shone down on white-crowned mountains spearing a sudden night sky. Snowflakes, dark in the dim light, fell thick and fast. A chill wind rose from the valley, whipping snow into his face, wet and cold. Beside him, Brian whined.

"Did you do this?" Case asked.

"Nope. You? Were you thinking about a place like this?"

"No. But we're in Dream. Doesn't it change all the time?"

"Yeah, but we're in *your* dream. If neither of us changed it..."

"Someone else did," she finished.

"Someone with powers in Dream," he said, not liking what that implied. Marell had such powers.

From behind them came a voice. "Someone with powers, yes. But not who you fear."

They spun around.

As they did, the scene changed again. They now stood inside a Buddhist temple. A very familiar one. The same temple Will had recreated in his tower home.

Lines of red columns stretched ahead, rising from a gray-black marble floor to a red-beamed, gray-black plaster ceiling. Past where the columns ended, wide marble steps led to a raised dais. A wooden throne, painted gold, sat in the center of the dais before images of the Buddha.

And on the throne sat Yeshe, dressed in his maroon robes. "Young master, young mistress. I thought it best to save you the time and trouble of finding me."

Chapter 38

Save the Planet

At the sight of Yeshe, memories swarmed Will like angry hornets, each with a sting. The tower invasion. Adi's stabbing. Case's capture. And with each memory, his guilt. Guilt for causing it all. Because he'd trusted the man who appeared before them now.

"Please, my friends, join me," Yeshe called from where he sat on the throne.

"We are *not* your friends!" Will yelled back.

"But I am yours," Yeshe replied.

"No! You aren't!" Will cried.

"If you would only let me—" Yeshe began.

"You lied to us. You hurt Adi. She might...she might..." His words died, and with them, the worst of his anger. He dropped his head, his shoulders slumping. Beside him, Case squeezed his arm while Brian whined.

"Please," Yeshe said, his voice suddenly close.

Will looked up. They now stood at the bottom step before the golden throne. Yeshe gazed down at them. "You have a right to anger, but anger solves nothing. You came for answers. Good—you need to understand. For the situation is dire, and our time is short."

"You lied to us," Will said again, his fists clenched.

"Yes, young master, I lied. Now, if you allow it, I will tell you the truth. And why I chose not to when we first met. Please, be seated."

Will looked at Case, who shrugged as she settled onto one of two prayer mats that had not been there a second before. Still fighting his anger, he sat on the other. Brian lay between them, head on his paws.

Yeshe folded his legs under him on the throne. He considered the temple. "Forgive me for relocating us here, but it has been many years. It seemed appropriate to end my tale where it began."

"Not what you need to talk about," Will said, his anger growing again.

Yeshe smiled a sad smile. "The story I told of my encounter with Marell and Morrigan in Tibet was true—except in two respects."

"Like how *you* fled, not them?" Will interrupted. "Like how they've been chasing you, not the other way around?"

"Yes. That was my first lie."

"Kind of obvious after Morrigan came for you last night. Why'd you lie?"

"I feared you would refuse me shelter. And I had nowhere left to hide."

"Oh," Will said, less sure of his anger. "And your second lie?"

"My second untruth relates to *why* I fled. Why they have hunted me all these years."

"Morrigan said you stole something from Marell," Will said.

Yeshe smiled. "A creative interpretation of the facts. In truth, Marell left something behind."

"Explain," Will said.

"On the night Marell seized my body, I survived by severing my own silver cord. My astral spirit escaped and hid. They believed me dead, my spirit having faded without a physical host."

Will nodded, remembering Yeshe's story. "But some of your cord stayed in your body."

"Yes. A small piece, undetected by Marell. But that piece allowed my spirit to remain connected to the physical plane. Allowed me to reclaim my body when the time was right."

"You getting to the lie yet?"

"I said I expelled Marell's spirit by untying his cord's connection to my body. But during our battle, I had no time for that. Instead, I *broke* his silver cord as I had broken my own. A small change in the telling of my tale, but huge in its effect."

Case frowned. "You mean...some of Marell's cord stayed inside you?"

"Yes. Where it remains. I have carried that piece of my enemy these many years. Without it, he could never be whole." Yeshe gazed past them, his eyes distant. "And with it, I could never be free."

Will wondered how it must feel to carry part of someone inside you, someone as evil as Marell. His anger faded further. "Is that why he can't stay in bodies he takes over? Why he needs the street kids?"

Yeshe nodded. "Incomplete, his astral spirit lacks the strength to merge fully with a physical body—and to sustain it. Anyone he invades begins to wither and die, soon forcing him to find a new victim, again and again. He discovered that shortly after I expelled him from my body."

"He came back, didn't he?" Case said. "For his missing piece."

"Yes. Returning to the monastery, they attacked me again. I fought them off, but I knew they would never stop until they overcame me. Even incomplete, Marell was strong, and Morrigan's magic was great. Eventually, they would win. So I fled the monastery. Fled the only life I'd known..." The monk's words trailed off as he looked around the debating hall. "I have traveled the world since that night, living in hiding. But they were always close behind."

"How? How could they find you?" Will asked.

"Marell can sense the part of him I carry. The closer he is, the stronger the pull. Morrigan, too. She has carried Marell's spirit in her amulet and can detect what I carry with her magicks."

"Even across an ocean?" Case asked.

"Marell also tracked me in Dream, so I slept when I expected Marell was awake."

Will nodded, remembering Yeshe's habit of sleeping during the day.

"But always they found me. Or a Mara did, sent by Marell to search for me. And whenever Marell found me in Dream, he could track me to where my body lay sleeping in the physical world."

"You were going to teach me that last night. Before Morrigan crashed the party."

"I shall teach you now, if you will trust me again."

Will didn't respond. Could he trust Yeshe after the monk's betrayal?

"Why do his hosts have to be younger each time?" Case asked.

"Without the missing piece, his astral spirit weakened over the years. Younger bodies provide the greater vitality needed to hold his diminished spirit."

"After you fled," Case said, "couldn't you have untied the piece of Marell's cord inside you and—I don't know—toss it away?"

"I did not know where the piece might go once free of me. Would it leave this plane? Or fly to Marell? I could not risk him retrieving it." Yeshe sighed. "But now I am their prisoner. Soon, perhaps even today, Morrigan will pull the remnant from me. Marell will become whole. And humanity will never be safe again."

"That sounds...a bit much," Will said, looking for another lie, still not willing to trust Yeshe. "Humanity never safe again?"

"Consider Marell's powers, young master. Once restored, he will not target an old monk. He chose me in Tibet only to access my astral knowledge and the monastery's texts. No, Marell will target the most powerful—leaders of countries, armies, corporate empires. Their power will become his. His astral spirit, once complete, could roam the globe. He is that strong. No one will be safe. And Marell could also track his targets through Dream, entering their minds as they sleep." He eyed Will. "As he almost captured *you* the night you killed the Mara."

Will fought back a shiver, only now realizing the real danger he'd faced that night.

Yeshe continued. "Worse, once restored, Marell could live in his new body for the rest of its life. When his host ages or loses their position of power, he would move to a younger host of equal or greater power." He looked at them both. "He will become *immortal.*"

"So," Case said, "he'll be able to take over the most powerful people on the planet...and never die."

"He'll rule the world," Will said, as the impact of Yeshe's words sank in. "Forever."

Will sat on the prayer rug, a cold fear growing in his gut. Until tonight, the danger had seemed restricted to a small circle. The missing street kids, Case, Fader, Harry Lyle, Adi, himself. That had been bad enough.

But now, the entire world was at risk.

"Now you know the true story," Yeshe said. "You see what was at stake. What is *still* at stake." He regarded Will. "Now I must ask you, young master. Will you trust me again? Will you help me defeat Marell? Will you join my fight?"

"In the fight already, dude," Will said. But part of him wanted to walk away from this. Everything he'd been through since last night, from his defeat by Morrigan to Adi's fate to the Board meeting, had shown him the truth.

He was just a kid.

"There's something else," Case said. "Fader says they know you're the Dream Rider. That you told Morrigan."

"Yeah. I did."

"Why?"

"I wanted her to take me back to Marell, so..." He dropped his eyes. "So I could find you."

"Oh," she said quietly. Reaching out, she squeezed his hand.

"But it didn't work. Morrigan left me behind. They aren't interested in me."

Case bit her lip. "Uh, yeah. About that..."

With a sinking heart, he listened as she related how Marell and Morrigan planned to use Case as a pawn to get to him.

"But why do they want *me?*"

"Your astral powers are great, young master. You killed a Mara and escaped Marell."

"I was lucky with the Mara. And *you* pulled me from Dream, or Marell would've had me."

"Regardless, he believes you are a threat to him, the last that remains."

"Then they *are* after me," Will said quietly. "And worse, now they have Case."

Rising from the throne, Yeshe descended the steps. "All the more reasons to learn how to defeat them. Our time runs short. I ask again. Will you let me teach you? Will you trust me?"

Will looked at Case. Saving the world should've been reason enough to say yes. But he had another reason, a more personal one. Case was a prisoner now. Fader, too. And Yeshe was their only hope.

He stood. "Yeah. I'll trust you."

"Me, too," Case said, joining Will.

Yeshe let out a great sigh. "Then hope remains." Without waiting to see if they followed, he strode towards the exit from the hall. "Come. We begin your lesson—a lesson we must complete *tonight*."

Will turned to Brian. "You can sit this one out, Bry. Looks like we have a guide." The Doogle curled his tail. And disappeared with a "pop." Will kicked his skateboard, and it disappeared, too.

As Will and Case hurried to catch Yeshe, the hall shimmered. With each step they took, the scene grew less distinct. Details blurred, flowing into each other, until only a swirling, multi-colored mist remained.

The mist hid the surface beneath their feet, but they now walked on something soft. Something that shifted with every step. The mist cleared.

They stood on a beach under a night sky. Will shivered at a sudden chill breeze. Behind him came the sounds of waves washing sand. A grove of trees surrounded them, running to the water's edge on both sides. Four trees grew apart from the grove, closer to where he, Case, and Yeshe stood on the sand.

He blinked. The four trees had moved closer, only steps away. Their trunks were blacker than the other trees. And taller. He looked up.

And jumped back. Beside him, Case groaned.

Not four trees. Four legs. Two people. Two people who loomed impossibly tall. Two horribly familiar people.

Stryke and Stayne.

"No, no, no," Case whispered. The screech of fear emojis sounded in the distance.

A grinning Stayne reached for them with a giant black-gloved hand. Yeshe touched Case's shoulder. The scene shimmered again. The two giant ghouls disappeared, as did the beach and the sound of approaching emojis.

The three of them now stood in Will's bedroom at the foot of his round bed. In the bed, another Will and another Case lay in each other's arms under the tousled covers.

Case spun to face Yeshe. "What the freak is going on?"

"Given your previous dream," Yeshe replied, "I thought we should begin with one more pleasant."

"*My* dream?"

"Will and I can walk in the dreams of others, young mistress. Tonight, you will share yours with us."

Will frowned at her. "Stayne and Stryke on a beach?"

She hugged herself. "The night they almost caught me, after I first met you as the Rider. Guess they're on my mind, now I'm their prisoner."

Will nodded at the bed where the other Will and Case lay. "So that's on your mind now?"

"Shaddup." She turned to Yeshe. "Why *my* dreams? Why not Will's?"

"Tonight, the young master must learn to track a dream back to its dreamer. Back to the doorway where that dreamer entered Dream. Step through that doorway, and the young master's astral spirit can travel anywhere in the waking world."

Case looked at Will.

"I'll be able to astral project, like Yeshe and Marell." *Anywhere in the waking world. I'll be able to go outside.*

"Thought that took years of study," she said.

"It does," replied the monk.

"So how can Home Boy learn it in one night?"

"I'm special," Will said, earning him a punch.

"The young master is indeed special. His manipulation of Dream *is* astral projection. When he walks in Dream, he projects his astral form into this realm. I need only teach him to find the doorways between Dream and the real world."

"But when he steps through a doorway, won't he...wake up?"

"No, his physical body will remain asleep, as with any astral traveler. But his astral body will leave Dream...and enter the waking world."

The waking world. Despite the dangers Will faced, he couldn't help but thrill at the possibilities. He could spend a day with Case outside. Well, sort of.

"Equally important," Yeshe continued, "he will emerge where the dreamer lies sleeping. He can find you, young mistress, via your dreams. Or your brother." He paused. "Or Marell—which will be crucial if our foe regains his full strength and takes over a person of power. Will must be able to find Marell in his new host, whoever and wherever he is in the world."

Find Marell. Reality came crashing down on him again. "Yeah? Then what? Say Marell takes over the American president. What can I do? Call up the CIA or FBI? 'Hey, guys. You don't know me. I'm a seventeen-year-old kid in another country who never leaves home. But golly gee, wackiest thing just happened. You know your boss? Well, he's now a centuries old evil body snatcher with a witch BFF. Hello? Hello?' Yeah, right. That will go *so* well."

"You are correct, young master. No one will believe you. No one will help you." The sadness on the monk's face frightened Will more than any of Yeshe's words that night. "You must face Marell yourself. Alone."

Chapter 39

The River

W ill stayed silent, trying not to show his fear in front of Case. He'd been right. Yeshe had the answers he needed. But they weren't the answers he wanted to hear.

You must face Marell yourself. Alone.

Alone. Against two crazed super villains.

Case moved closer to him. "You're *not* alone in this. I'm in the fight, too." As she spoke, the Case on the bed threw an arm over the Will sleeping beside her, pulling him closer.

Will tried to speak, but his throat tightened. He just nodded.

"Small flaw in your plan of Will and Marell going toe-to-toe, though," she said. "Will doesn't get out much."

"The young master's *astral* body must confront Marell, not his physical form."

Will remembered facing Marell the snake beast the night Harry Lyle died. Facing him—and freezing. "You forgetting? I didn't do so well when I met him in Dream."

"You will not defeat Marell in Dream."

"Gee, thanks for the vote of confidence."

"You misunderstand. If Marell were losing to you in Dream, he would escape by simply waking. No, young master, you must face his astral form in the waking world. To fight him as I fought him years ago—your spirit against his. And expel him from whatever host he inhabits."

"Won't Marell just take over someone else?" Case asked.

"Yeah, I don't see an end to this," Will said.

"Once you expel his astral spirit from its host, you must hold it," Yeshe said. "Prevent him from taking over another person."

"Hold it? As in forever?" Will asked, even more afraid.

"No. Without a physical body, his spirit will soon weaken and lose its connection to the physical plane. You need only restrain it long enough for that to occur."

"Exactly how long is 'long enough'?" Will asked.

"And what about Morrigan?" Case asked. "She'll be wherever Marell is. You said he can run to her amulet."

"Will must prevent that. Or destroy the amulet."

"Yeshe," Will said. "This isn't much of a plan. At least not one that can, you know, *work*."

Yeshe sat on Will's round bed in the dream scene. The Will and Case in the bed continued to snuggle, oblivious to their audience. For an eyeblink, the monk seemed to age a century, becoming the ancient creature he truly was. "I do not have every answer. All I know is that only *you*, young master, can defeat Marell. That is why I sought you out when I first sensed your powers in Dream. You are our last hope."

But how much of a hope? "Great. No pressure. Thanks, I feel better now."

"Hey!" Case said. "Part of this, too, remember? Although, not sure what Prisoner Girl can do."

"You underestimate yourself, young mistress. Never have I known anyone to withstand Morrigan's magic. And you escaped Stayne and Stryke not once, but twice."

"Yeah, about them," Case said. "Stayne was dead—then back to life, complete with the bullet hole. He said Morrigan's magic lets them *continue*. What gives?"

"Morrigan recruited them in London," Yeshe said. "In 1894, if I recall. She and Marell had tracked me there. Stayne and Stryke were supplying cadavers to medical schools. And to less savory research facilities."

"Grave robbers?" Case asked.

"Undertakers," Yeshe replied. "A reliable source of fresh corpses. Although they didn't hesitate to rob graves—or kill—if supply ran short."

"But 1894?" she said.

"They have died many times, but as you saw, the witch can somehow revivify them. They are reanimated corpses."

"Wonderful. Now we have zombies, too," Will muttered.

"Morrigan's spells sustain them. Without her magicks, they would truly die."

"Without her magicks..." Case muttered.

"You got something?" Will asked.

"Maybe." She related Fader's story of Morrigan laying Stayne's corpse on the rug.

Yeshe frowned. "It is possible she stores a portion of her magicks in such a device. I do not know how. I do not understand her magic—only its power."

"Think you can get at this rug?" Will asked. "If we can weaken Morrigan, I might have a chance against Marell."

Case bit her lip. "We'll try. Me and Fader. But we're still prisoners. And the

Hollow Boys are everywhere."

Will suppressed a shudder, recalling his encounters with the strange boys. Empty shells with a soul-sucking darkness inside.

Yeshe stood again. "To stand any chance, the young master must learn to track a dreamer. And tonight. Our time runs short, so please..." He motioned to Case and Will in bed. "...consider your lovely lady friend lying before us."

"I like your teaching style," Will said.

Case smiled then frowned. "Wait. If I'm dreaming I'm here with you two, how can *that* be my dream?"

"The dreaming mind is a whirl of thoughts and emotions, memories and desires," Yeshe replied. "One dream melts into another and back again. This dream, where you stand with us, is under my direction. That dream—" He nodded at the bed. "—is from another part of your mind."

"Busted," Will said. She punched him again.

"Young master, please."

Will focused on the Case lying in bed beside his other self. "What am I looking for?"

"The connection between the dream and the dreamer. The young mistress's silver cord."

Will nodded. Seeing cords was easy. He used them in Dream all the time. He stared at the sleeping Case until a glowing silver ribbon floated up from her, winding off into the misty distance. "Okay, I see it."

Case looked around the bedroom. "I don't."

"You will not," Yeshe replied. "Only the young master. And myself."

"Now what?" Will said.

Yeshe smiled. "Now we follow."

And follow they did. Will tracked Case's cord from the bedroom scene to a meadow. A cartoon meadow like one drawn by a child with crayons. White squiggles of clouds dotted a turquoise sky. Red balls of flowers with lime-green stems sprouted from scribbled yellow grass. Cartoon bunnies in purple waistcoats hopped among brightly colored Easter eggs.

He raised an eyebrow at Case.

"I was five," she said, with a serious pout. "Asked my mom for a bunny for Easter. Didn't get it."

"Five? And you're still dreaming about it?"

She glared at him. "I like bunnies."

"Looks like," he said, filing that away.

Yeshe pointed to where Case's cord disappeared into a dark forest. "We should continue."

"Still want my bunny," she muttered.

They walked towards the trees, the meadow scene fading. Two steps into the forest, the trees became beige walls of a small apartment. Worn couch and mismatched armchairs. Porcelain lamp with a torn shade on a single table. Klimt prints on the walls.

And a Christmas tree, branches draped and drooping with ornaments and lights. On a threadbare rug, among an explosion of wrapping paper and opened presents, sat Case. She looked maybe eight years old. A younger Fader sat beside her. A young pretty Black woman sat on the couch, her feet tucked beneath her, smiling at them. She resembled an older, darker, short-haired version of Case.

"Your mom?" Will asked.

"Last Christmas together. Before she left." She wiped at her eyes, then turned away. "C'mon. Places to go. Baddies to beat."

Places to go. Places that came—and went, the way they do in dreams. Case's dreams...

Case in a jail cell, surrounded by jeering girls. Her fists raised, facing a much larger girl. Case's left fist flashing out, connecting. The other girl staggering back, falling...

Case and a bare-chested boy. Lying on a sleeping bag in a darkened room. Smiling, moving closer. A kiss...

Her and a younger Fader, moonlit. Slipping from a second-story window in a suburban home. Dropping onto a dew-covered lawn, disappearing into the shadows...

A different boy. A different room. A different kiss...

Shoplifting in the market with Fader. Panhandling outside a coffee shop. Running down an alley, pursued by blurry figures in the distance...

Another boy. Another room. Another kiss...

"Jeez," Will said, "how many guys—? Ow!"

"Shaddup."

He rubbed his arm. "Just asking."

"Threatened?"

"A little."

A smile flickered on her face and then was gone.

The last dream morphed into a downtown street at night, resembling Yonge Street where it ran down to the ferry docks and the lake, but empty of people and cars. No streetlamps lined this avenue, yet the scene was brightly lit.

Will stopped. "Hey, what's happening?"

Case frowned, looking around. "I don't see anything."

"What do you see, young master?" Yeshe asked.

Case's silver cord still floated in the air, extending ahead of them. But other cords had appeared, floating beside hers. Will took another step. More shining ribbons materialized. Another step. Still more cords became visible, floating down the street, disappearing into the distance.

"Silver cords," Will said. "Lots of them."

Yeshe smiled. "Good. Your Dream senses are strong."

"I'll take your word for it," Case said. "Why is Will seeing other cords? Am I having other dreams?"

"The cords are indeed other dreams, but not yours. Each cord represents a dreamer."

"But why are they going in the same direction?" Will asked. "I thought Case's cord would lead us to where she is in the real world." He waved at the glowing strands filling the air around them. "All these dreamers can't be in the same place. There must be hundreds of cords."

"Soon there will be thousands. Then millions," Yeshe replied.

"But—"

"Follow. All will become clear."

They followed. More cords appeared. Above and beside them, surrounding the three travelers. Soon, Will could barely see the street scene for the silver strands. He focused harder on Case's cord, afraid he'd lose it among the shimmering masses. Her cord grew brighter while the others dimmed.

With each step they took, the cords dropped further toward the pavement. Soon, every cord lay beneath their feet. Millions of cords, if he could believe Yeshe. He could no longer separate Case's cord from the glowing mass on which they now walked. The street had become a silver roadway, lighting their way.

Until the shining avenue ended at the banks of a river.

A dark river, but one shot through with shining, silver streaks. A river stretching wide before them, its far side lost in swirling mists. A river flowing with waves and swells, flowing swiftly from their left to their right.

He gazed over the water. Dark shapes leaped among the luminous waves. He thought he saw a long, scaled tail flipping above the surface, but it disappeared before he was sure.

Downstream, more silver roads emerged from the river on this bank at irregular intervals. Each disappeared into another part of Dream. Upstream, the same pattern repeated.

His gaze returned to the expanse of... What? Water? Cords? What was he seeing? It didn't matter. At that moment, all his thoughts were lost. Lost in the flashing flow of silver and black, the dance of luminous waves. Lost in the sparkle of spray lighting the night like clouds of frolicking fireflies.

"It's beautiful," he whispered.

Case's hand slipped into his. "Yes," she whispered. "It is."

"You see it, too?" he asked. She nodded, staring out over the flowing expanse of darkness and light.

"Welcome, young friends," Yeshe said, "to the River of Souls."

Chapter 40

Dead Disco, Dead Monk, Dead Rock 'n Roll

"The River of Souls?" Will asked, entranced by the shimmering flow rushing past them.

"It connects the waking world to Dream," Yeshe replied. "The spirit of every Dreamer—via their silver cord—travels the River each night. They emerge at some point..." He indicated the other silver roads leaving the flowing water upstream and downstream. "...and enter Dream. At that moment, their dreams begin."

"No one ever dreams of being *on* the River?" Case asked. "It's seems...familiar."

"It lies buried deep in the subconscious of every human being. A racial memory, if you will. Thus, our dream spirits find it each night. But never has a dreamer awoken with memory of it." Yeshe smiled. "Until now."

"We'll remember it?" Will said.

"Yes, and how to find it," Yeshe said, his face beaming with joy. "I had one goal for this night—to lead you here. And now that you can find the River, you must travel upstream to its source. There, you must track the young mistress's cord back to where she lies dreaming."

"Travel upstream?" Case said. "How?"

"Good question," Will said, looking at the swiftly flowing waters.

"A problem you must solve," Yeshe said. "Just as you developed a means to travel in Dream with your wheeled board, you must do the same for the River."

The silver road on which they stood continued into the River, dipping beneath the dark surface. Will moved to the water's edge. Away from the shore, the cords separated, becoming individual strands again as they sank below the water where they dimmed to the occasional sparkle. They remained visible enough, though, for Will to see they all bent upstream.

Upstream. Where all dreams began. Where all Dreamers dreamed. Where he had to go. But how?

"So we're done for tonight?" Case said. "Until Will figures out how to travel the River?"

"Maybe not," Will said, an idea forming. He'd walked on the silver cords when they formed the road leading here. Could he walk on them beneath the water, too? If the cords stayed near the surface, he could *walk* upstream.

One way to find out.

He stepped forward into the flow, aiming at the nearest bunch of cords. He sank up to his knees. The cords weren't supporting him.

Someone was calling. Calling something. His name? Cold. So cold. And wet. Just like a river. *Duh*. The water was numbing. He couldn't feel his legs. But his legs were moving anyway, taking a second step he hadn't asked them to take.

The water became deeper, the current stronger. The rushing water clawed at him, pushing, pulling. He lost his balance. He was falling. This did not concern him. It seemed right. It seemed fated. To fall into this beckoning flow, his dream spirit swept away, downstream to the River's end, to...

Strong hands pulled him back, dragged him from the water's welcoming embrace. He stumbled backwards, landing hard on the silver road, several steps from the River.

He looked up. Yeshe stared down at him. Case, too. She kicked him in the bum.

"Ow!"

"Dumbass," she said. "What were you trying to do? Walk on water?"

"Sort of." Standing, he explained his idea.

Yeshe shook his head. "In every metaphor of Dream I have encountered, the River is...a river. You will sink into it. The cords will not support you. They are but spirits."

"Then the River's really water?"

"Its perfect representation in Dream. An exact metaphor as you might say. Water is the essence of life in the physical world. Why would it not be so here?"

"Okay, if it's water, could I swim it? Swim upstream?"

"No. If your dream body touches the River, you begin to lose your memory of your current dream. Soon, you would forget your intent of traveling upstream. You would forget everything. The River would sweep your spirit body away, as it nearly did just now."

"Wouldn't I land on shore somewhere else in Dream?" He nodded downstream where other silver roads ran up from the flowing waters.

"Only the silver cords of Dreamers have the power to fight the River, to reach shore. And they do so unconsciously. You are not a cord. You are an astral body. You would not emerge. The River would carry you downstream."

"What's downstream?" Case asked.

"No one knows, young mistress. Some texts suggest this River is but one of many, all flowing to a great sea."

"Other rivers?" Will asked.

"Yes. From other Dream universes."

"Other *universes?*"

"Different realities from our own. No one knows for certain. I have encountered Dreamers who set out downstream to find that great sea, but never have I seen them again."

Will stared downstream. *Other universes. Other realities.* He shrugged. Questions for another time. He turned back. "Okay, back to traveling *up* the River. Walking, swimming—and skateboarding—all major fails as travel options."

He considered the weaving web of cords sparkling in the waves. "And how can I follow Case's cord through that mass? There are millions of them."

"Could a Doogle swim it, following my cord?" Case said.

"Not against that flow. It's too strong." He frowned. "I need new metaphors to handle the River. Which means, yeah, we're done for tonight. Tomorrow, when I'm awake, I'll figure out new constructs I can store in my subconscious—"

Yeshe screamed.

Will spun around.

Yeshe lay on the silver road, his body jerking, face contorted, eyes wide. Case ran to kneel beside him.

"What happened?" Will cried, joining her.

"I don't know!" she said, cradling the monk's head in her hands as he thrashed. "He screamed, then collapsed."

Yeshe's back arched. His mouth flew open. He screamed again, one long terrible cry of pain and fear and lost hope. The scream ended. He collapsed, his body limp. His eyes closed, and his head lolled to the side.

Will took the monk's hand in his. "Yeshe?"

Yeshe's eyes fluttered open. He looked around as if unsure where he was. His eyes fell on them. "Ah, my young friends. I have given you a fright."

"Yeshe, what's happening?" Will asked.

"Morrigan has begun the ceremony," Yeshe whispered. "To extract the piece of Marell's spirit from my body." The monk grabbed Will's arm and pulled him closer. "Marell will be restored, with his full power. You must find him, young master. You must defeat him."

Will pried Yeshe's hand free and laid it on the monk's chest. "Already working on it. Tomorrow night, I'll have a way to travel up the River. We'll track him down, and you'll show me—"

"I will not be there," Yeshe whispered.

"Wait, what? No, no." Will's memory of Marell as the giant snake returned. He couldn't face that alone. "You have to help me. I don't know what to do. You promised to help. You promised."

"A promise I meant to keep."

"Then keep it! You can't run away again."

"I am not running, young master," Yeshe said softly, "I am dying."

⁂

Will heard a sharp intake of breath from Case. "Yeshe," she said, "how can we help you?"

"You cannot. I have always known my fate. Once they recover Marell's missing piece, they will kill me. Marell cannot let me live. I defeated him once."

"Then do it again!" Will cried. "Fight him!"

"That was many years ago. I am old. So very old. I do not have the strength." He looked at Will. "Follow the River upstream. Find Marell. But beware the Gray Lands."

"Gray Lands?"

"The Maras..." Yeshe's words trailed off. He closed his eyes. The pain vanished from his face. His image shimmered, grew dim. And then it, too, vanished.

Case stared at her now empty hands. "Is he...dead?"

"I don't know."

"But he's gone—"

"Maybe he woke up." Will stood. "I have to wake up, too. If I send in the SWAT team now, we might still save him."

"But if he's already dead—"

"His astral spirit will stay nearby. If we move fast, if his body isn't too damaged, he can return to it."

"But—"

"Case, I have to go. I can't do this without Yeshe. You have to wake up. Find Fader. Get ready to move when the raid hits. With any luck, I'll see you soon, for real. Stay safe." He kissed her hard, and she returned it. Stepping back, he touched the jewel at his neck. And woke up.

⁂

Staring stern and stark from the display screen in Will's studio, Stone was doing his best to change Will's mind. "Will, daylight is not my preferred timing."

Stone still wore the black fatigues from last night, his face blackened, too. He appeared to be in the back of a large truck. The truck was moving, based on the jumpy image from Stone's phone. Will caught the occasional glimpse of the arm and shoulder of another black-clad man beside him.

Will tried to keep his voice calm. "I understand. But unless we move now, we might as well cancel the raid."

Stone pursed his lips, not replying. For a moment, Will feared he'd suggest doing just that. Cancel the raid. Cancel his only chance to save Yeshe. But then Stone nodded. "Okay, boss. Understood."

"How long?"

Stone checked his watch. "Thirty minutes. When we're in position, I'll call you for the go order."

"No. I trust you. Go as soon as you're ready. But turn on your video links. I'll follow from here."

"Roger that. Signing off."

Stone's face disappeared from the screen. The scene of Adi lying in her hospital bed reappeared. Laura still sat beside her, dressed as she was yesterday, clasping Adi's hand. Will opened the audio link. "Laura."

Startled, she looked up at the camera. Her screen would now show his face and the studio behind him. "Will." She glanced at Adi, then back at him. She shook her head. "No change."

"Have you been there all night? You need to rest. Why don't you go home?"

"They set up a cot for me. I wouldn't sleep any better at home. Worse, probably. Worrying if something happened." She stared at Adi. "The last time we talked, we fought."

"So did we."

She smiled a sad smile. "It's the fire in her. It's part of why I love her. But I keep going over that fight in my head. Over and over. I just want her to wake up, so I can tell her I'm sorry, tell her I want us to be together."

"I'm sure she knows." At least he'd been able to see Adi in Dream, to tell her he was sorry. He wished he could tell Laura that Adi knew she was there. "Call me if anything changes."

Laura nodded, her eyes on Adi. Will muted the connection, blanking Laura's view of his studio. He slumped onto his couch. Case and Fader prisoners. Adi's life still in danger. And now Yeshe dying?

If Yeshe died, then he—seventeen-year-old Will Dreycott—was truly alone. Alone and the only person left to defeat a murderous body snatcher soon to become immortal.

No. That wouldn't happen. The raid would work. Stone and his team would stop Morrigan and Marell. And free Case and Fader. And save Yeshe.

Because they had to.

Chapter 49

Chant of the Ever-Circling Skeletal Family

J ust after dawn, Morrigan the Bright stood naked on the Weave, her feet placed with precision within its triskelion pattern. She stood between two hospital beds. On each bed lay an unconscious man, stripped to the waist.

Runes covered not only her arms, but her entire body. Her face and neck. Her belly and back. Her breasts and buttocks. Her long legs. Front, back, and sides. All of her now carried the ancient symbols. The runes formed over a dozen scripts, each part of the three most complex spells she'd ever attempted.

On the bed to her right lay the body of Karmalov, the surviving mercenary. Karmalov's body, yes, but Karmalov no more. Morrigan had earlier transferred Marell's astral spirit into the soldier. Marell's recent vessel had once more not survived. The boy Rattle was gone. Her sad family of Hollow Boys would not grow today.

And if this worked, that family would never grow again.

To her left lay Yeshe Norbu, former Ganden Tripa of the Ganden Monastery, eighty-second Holder of the Golden Throne. On his naked chest, she'd drawn his true name in runes, for true names have power. She'd drawn his title, too, out of respect, for he had been a worthy adversary.

He had led them on a chase of many years. But those years, she'd realized in recent days, had been the happiest of her long strange existence. Through that time, she'd had purpose. She'd been with the man she loved. She'd known what she wanted from life.

Now...

Now their long quest—hers and Marell's—was over. With this spell, a new chapter in her life began. She didn't know what that chapter would bring. Worse, she didn't know what she *wanted* it to bring.

Once restored, Marell would have no need of her magicks. Not to aid him to find new bodies. Or transfer his spirit to those vessels. Or sustain him in those hosts. All that, he could do himself.

So where would she fit? She'd always believed, when this day came, nothing would change between them. Because she'd always believed Marell was with her because he loved her.

Now she was no longer sure. Just as she was no longer sure who Marell was. Or rather, who he had become.

One thing she did know—he was not the same man she had once loved.

She caught herself. Once?

When they met years ago, a thirst for knowledge had united them. For her, magical lore. For him, astral learnings. But Marell's quest changed. He craved power, not knowledge. Power over others. Had that always been his quest? Had she been blind all these years?

Her own search for magical knowledge had never been about power over others. She'd wanted power, yes, but only to defend herself, to avoid the fate of her mother, her coven...

She swallowed. Her brother.

She'd long ago gained that power. What remained to fill her life, now their quest had ended? Her Hollow Boys? Marell would no longer tolerate them when he and she departed here. He would refuse her the boy, Fader, too. Anger seized her at that thought, but so did a sudden realization.

She would fight to keep the boy.

With her new resolve, she turned again to the monk. Along with Yeshe's name and title, she'd drawn the necessary runes on the monk's pale skin. Drawn, not carved as she'd promised.

She'd planned to fulfill that promise. She'd held the ritual dagger over his chest, its obsidian blade glinting sharp and cruel in the flickering torch light.

But as she'd touched the blade to his flesh, poised to carve the first rune, she'd hesitated. A face rose unbidden in her mind. The face of the boy, Fader.

And his face wore the look she knew it would if he watched her do this thing. That imagined expression had made her lay down the blade.

What would Marell say of this surprising mercy? Nothing good. But he was not conscious to comment. After the transfer, he'd be too consumed with his renewal to notice what she'd done. Or not done.

Anger burned in her again. Of late, Marell was too consumed with himself to notice her. Failing, also, to acknowledge her accomplishments on his behalf. Or worse, belittling them.

She'd saved him time and time again. Found him new hosts. Transferred his spirit into each new boy. Sustained his failing bodies. Tracked Yeshe to this city, to the white tower. And now she'd delivered the monk, too. Success at last lay before them.

But instead of praise, Marell spoke only of her "failures." Letting that wretched girl escape. Letting her escape again. Leaving that boy who'd killed the Mara behind. And Marell held only contempt for her family of Hollow Boys. Worst, though, was his anger over her affection for the boy Fader.

She shrugged. His anger no longer mattered—she would keep the boy. She returned to the delicate task at hand.

To retrieve the lost fragment from within the monk, she needed to apply three spells in sequence. She touched her left hand to Yeshe's chest. The first script streamed down her arm, disappearing rune by rune into the old man. There, it took the form of a golden lioness. She followed her magical creature as, step by step, it stalked through the monk, hunting its prey.

Deeper and deeper, the lioness crept. Searching, searching...

There. So long sought for—and now within her grasp.

Marell's lost astral fragment.

To her magical sight, the missing piece clung like a throbbing gray stain on Yeshe's silver astral chest. *Like a tumor.* She pushed that image away. *Focus.*

The piece twitched, perhaps sensing danger. Closer and closer, her spell beast crept.

The cord fragment shot up, straining to escape from where it was tied. Thinner and thinner that connection stretched. Another second, and that bond would snap.

Marell believed the lost fragment would immediately fly to him once freed of Yeshe. But a belief, no matter how strong, was just a belief until proven. That the piece was about to leave the monk's body was clear. But where it would go then was unknown. It might even flee this plane, to be lost forever.

She spoke a word. The lioness sprang.

And caught the long-lost fragment in its magical jaws. Gently tugging it free of the monk's astral body, the lioness turned.

And leaped out of Yeshe.

Raising both hands before her, she threw the second spell. The lioness froze in its leap to hover before her, caught in a golden cage small enough to hold in her hands. In its jaws, the missing piece squirmed and writhed, trying to break free. If she lost control of the spell now...

With her normal sight, she noted Yeshe's chest continuing to rise and fall. *You're a tough old dog,* she thought, almost with affection. Not that it mattered. Marell would never let Yeshe live, even if the monk survived.

But she could spare the old man no more attention. Now came the most difficult step—reinserting the retrieved fragment into Marell's new body. In theory, once there, the piece would reunite with Marell's incomplete spirit, making his astral body whole again.

In theory.

Even to Marell's knowledge, the splitting of an astral body had never occurred. Therefore, no one had ever attempted such a reunion. Until now. Until this moment.

The missing fragment still thrashed in the lioness's jaws, trying to escape. She cupped her hands around the caged lioness and its captured piece. Slowly, she lowered the spell until it hovered above Marell-Karmalov's chest.

The fragment became still. She caught her breath. Did it sense its true astral body? Did it know it was "home?" Was this going to work?

She prepared her third spell, the most complex of the layers. This final spell would carry the lioness with the cord fragment into Marell's new host. Her bare skin tingled as the rune scripts flowed over her. Flowed from her legs and right arm. From her breasts and buttocks. Flowed to cover her left arm, ready to be cast.

She laid her left hand on Marell's bare chest. And prepared to say the magical words in her native Manx. The words to release the spell, to make Marell whole once more.

A horn screeched in her head, a magical alarm only she heard, but so loud and sudden, she almost lost control of the lioness spell.

Someone had entered the hospital.

She swore softly in Manx. Should she continue? No. These interlopers might interrupt her before she completed the transfer.

Leaving the lioness frozen above Marell, his missing piece thrashing in its jaws, she sent a mental command to Stayne and Stryke to secure their prisoners and to not engage with the intruders. That done, she left to greet their unknown visitors.

Will sat at his design desk, doing a final review of the next Dream Rider issue as he waited for Stone's signal. A beep brought his head up. The video display on his wall no longer showed Adi's hospital room. Instead, the screen now split into four views of the abandoned hospital. Views that were getting closer.

The SWAT team was on the move.

He walked to the big screen, clenching and unclenching his fists. This had to work.

The video was jumpy—feeds from body-mounted cameras worn by Stone's team. The four views represented separate teams, each poised to enter the hospital from a different side. He unmuted the display.

Silence. Then Stone's voice rasped over the speakers. "This is Alpha Leader. Team leaders, report."

"Bravo team ready," came another male voice.

"Charlie team ready."

"Delta team ready." A final voice, this one female.

Each team had stopped outside a door on their side of the building. Time seemed to stop, too. He held his breath, waiting for Stone to give the command.

Seconds passed. Had something gone wrong? Had Stone changed his mind? No, he wouldn't. He couldn't. This had to happen. He reached for his cell, to call Stone, to tell him—

He jumped as Stone's voice burst from the speakers again. "This is Alpha Leader. All teams—go!"

The raid began. The four scenes rushed towards him. And he could only watch—and hope.

Morrigan stepped from the Weave room into the hospital corridor. She'd thrown on a long, black silk robe. Her nakedness didn't bother her, but the hallway was chilly. And she *was* expecting guests.

The Weave room sat in the northwest corner on the third floor, at the intersection of two outer corridors. To her left, down the longer north corridor, sounds came from the stairwell. She closed the door behind her, killing the torch light spilling from the room and plunging her into murky shadow.

A second later, eight black-clad figures emerged from the stairwell. Each carried a gun like those Karmalov's team had used, barrels pointed down. She didn't know the kind or make. Weaponry bored her. Strange headgear covered their left eyes. Four of the group crossed to the hallway connecting to the south corridor and were lost from her sight.

The remaining four advanced toward where she waited, giving no indication they had seen her. Summoning the runes for a stun spell, she remained still, watching.

The intruders reached the first room in the corridor. Two positioned themselves on either side of the door, a third farther back in the hall. The fourth (the leader, she assumed) checked a display unit on his belt.

He shook his head. One man tried the door handle, found it unlocked, nodded to the leader who nodded back. In a flurry of motion, the team burst into the room, weapons ready, disappearing from her view.

Their obvious training worried her. These people were professionals.

The black-clad figures emerged again. They moved to the next door, where they repeated the previous scene. And again at the next room. The armed men continued working their way toward the Weave room. Toward where all her and Marell's plans for the past century sat poised on a knife-edge.

The four intruders emerged from the next-to-last room in the hallway. Only the Weave room remained.

Time to welcome her guests. She pushed open the door to the room. Torch light flooded the corridor, illuminating her in the doorway.

The men continued their stealthy approach.

She walked back into the room. Resuming her position on the Weave between the two beds holding Marell and Yeshe, she waited, stun spell ready.

A moment later, the men stormed into the room. Crouched and alert, weapons up, they scanned the room. Their gazes fell on her.

And kept moving.

Completing their scan, the men straightened, relaxing. The one she took for the leader pulled off his strange headgear. He touched something on his chest. "Delta leader, report."

She heard a crackling response from the man's headset, but not the words. He touched his chest again. "Alpha leader, this is Bravo leader. Finished sweep of third floor. No thermal readings. All rooms empty. Sorry, boss, but we've got nothing."

Another crackling reply.

"Roger that. Rendezvous at extraction point." He touched his chest again, then motioned to his team. They exited the room.

Their echoing footsteps in the hallway grew more distant. A door opened, and she knew they were descending the stairwell and would soon exit the building.

Relaxing finally, she allowed herself a momentary flush of pride. The alarm spell she'd placed around the hospital perimeter was a simple one. An invisible curtain that, once breached, notified her and triggered the cloaking spell.

The cloaking magicks were more complex. They imposed false images for the heat-detecting instruments Karmalov had warned such a team might carry. False visuals, too, for the rooms where humans resided. One for where the Hollow Boys and the last unused boy slept. One for Stayne and Stryke's shared room. Another for where Fader and his dreadful sister lay restrained. Another for the Weave room itself. Finally, visuals of dusty floors with no footprints throughout.

The spell imposed a veil of silence in the occupied rooms, too. She imagined that wretched girl screaming her head off as these men burst into her room. The raiders would see and hear nothing. She smiled, imagining the girl's confusion. Confusion, then horror, as the men retreated, leaving her a prisoner still.

With the raid now over, she withdrew those spells. The men would not search the hospital again, and she couldn't spare the magical energy. Standing on the Weave, she moaned with pleasure as the rug drank in the power of the canceled spells. Extra power she needed to complete the transfer.

She turned to where Marell-Karmalov lay unconscious. Above him, the lioness spell hung frozen where she'd caged it. Behind shimmering golden bars, it crouched, the missing astral fragment in its jaws. It was ready. Ready to leap. To carry the fragment back into Marell's new body. To make him complete once more.

Wrapping her hands around the spell, she spoke the words to free the magical beast. The cage disappeared. The lioness leaped from her hands...

And into Marell.

Chapter 42

Youth Without Youth

Will leaned against his design table, needing its support as Stone reported in. A report redundant to what he'd seen on the SWAT team's body cams.

Stone's people had found nothing. They'd searched every floor. All they discovered was that the abandoned hospital was just that. Abandoned.

On the screen, Stone stood on the lawn behind the hospital. Past him, his men talked in groups. Early morning sunshine lit the scene, bright and cheery as if mocking Will's mood.

"Nobody's been inside for a couple of years," Stone said. "Dust everywhere. No signs of disturbance. Sorry, Will. Looks like a bogus lead."

Will rubbed his face. He didn't understand. The hospital's interior matched what Fader had shown him in Dream. Matched perfectly. This was the place. And yet it wasn't.

Had Marell and Morrigan fled, taking their prisoners with them? He could ask Case and Fader tonight in Dream. But they were all running out of time.

A sound pulled his attention back. Sirens. Stone shouted to his men. The sirens got louder.

"Stone! What's happening?"

"Weapons down!" Stone shouted. "Weapons DOWN! NOW!"

"Stone!"

"Police," Stone said. "I'm dropping this connection and wiping my phone. We used a private satellite link. Nothing's traceable back to you." Behind him, police cars were approaching fast, lights flashing, sirens getting louder and louder.

"Sorry, boss." Stone's connection went dead. The scene on the screen disappeared, replaced again by Adi's hospital room.

Will collapsed on the couch, burying his face in his hands. Yeshe a prisoner, dying. Adi hurt, maybe dying. Case and Fader still prisoners, still missing. The raid a bust. Stone's team arrested.

His worst fear had come true. He was the only person left to stop a crazed super villain.

And he didn't have the slightest clue what to do.

Morrigan backed away from where Marell-Karmalov lay, hands raised before her face. The web of a shielding spell hung between her fingers protecting her from the fire.

The astral fire now blazing within Marell.

She was in no danger but needed to dim the blaze to see what was happening. Her lioness had done its job well. It had carried Marell's long-lost astral fragment deep into the Marell-Karmalov body. And released it.

Marell had been right. Once free, the missing piece flew to his incomplete astral body like iron filings to a magnet. The reunion was immediate.

And explosive. On the astral plane, that is.

To her magical sight, Marell's restored astral body flamed like a miniature sun inside him. Brighter than she ever remembered. Even brighter than when they'd met. Brighter than when he'd first faced Yeshe years ago.

Had time dimmed her memory? She suspected another reason. Over the years, Marell had continued to gain knowledge of the astral planes. He'd trained himself, honing his astral skills. Simply put, years of study and practice had magnified his astral form.

Restored, Marell was stronger than ever before.

Still unconscious, Marell writhed on the bed. Inside him, his spirit flamed even brighter. Stepping back farther from the blaze, she bumped against the other bed where Yeshe lay. Turning, she was surprised to see his chest still rose and fell, weak but steady.

For now. Marell, now restored, would kill Yeshe. For fear of the monk's powers. For revenge.

For enjoyment.

And he would kill the old man slowly and painfully. Because he could. Because that was who he was.

A vision of Fader floated before her. She made a decision, one surprising her even as she acted on it. Laying a hand on Yeshe's forehead, she spoke in her mind to the monk, not knowing if he heard her.

Yeshe Norbu, once holder of the Golden Throne, you were a valiant and worthy foe. For that, you won my respect. For that, I grant you this mercy.

She summoned a spell, used many times over the years. She cast it into the monk. With her magical sight, she watched as a golden hand wrapped long fingers around Yeshe's still beating heart.

And squeezed. Gently, almost lovingly.

Yeshe's eyes flew open. He gasped in a breath. And another. His body spasmed. His back arched up from where he lay. He collapsed. A final breath escaped his cracked lips in one long sigh. His chest did not rise again.

The monk was dead.

She searched for Yeshe's astral spirit, which would flee his dead body. To no avail. Gone from this plane? She shrugged. If not yet gone, it soon would be, beginning its journey to the Realms of the Dead. Disconnected from a living body, no astral form could remain long on the physical plane.

Closing the old man's eyes, she brushed a long strand of white hair from his face, mystified by the wave of sadness washing over her.

"Morrigan!" It was Karmalov's voice, from behind her.

She turned. The mercenary stood on the far side of the bed where he'd lain. Karmalov's voice, yes, but not Karmalov.

Marell-Karmalov gazed down at his body, flexing his arms. A delicious thrill ran up her as the man's bare chest rippled in response. Yes, a fine choice for her lover's new host.

"Strong in body," Marell said, a huge smile on Karmalov's face. "But what of the spirit?" He closed his eyes. His expression went blank, and she knew he was projecting his restored astral body. What would he find? Seconds passed.

His eyes flew open. Throwing his head back, he laughed, long and loud. No matter who he occupied, she could always recognize his laugh. A sound of pleasure without joy, triumph without mercy. It was, she realized, a cold thing. "Marell? Are you...?"

"Complete," he whispered. "After all these years, I am whole once more."

She waited. For a word of praise, of thanks. A mention of her role in his victory. In *their* victory. But Marell only stood there, new hands raised before his new face as he clenched and unclenched his fingers.

He lowered his hands. "I must test my abilities."

"Test?" she said, chewing on her resentment.

"Yes. Bring me someone. Someone to inhabit."

"We have one street boy left. Insurance, had the monk's retrieval been delayed." Or had her spells failed. But she didn't say that.

"*One* boy? Only one?"

She shrugged. "If anything had gone wrong with the monk, Stayne and Stryke could have acquired more on short notice."

Marell moved around the bed to stare down at her from new eyes. She battled an urge to step back. She'd grown accustomed to looking down at him as his hosts grew younger and younger. Karmalov was a head taller than her. She felt intimidated by Marell's new body. And his restored powers.

Intimidated? No. Afraid. She'd never feared Marell before.

"That is not what I meant," he said. "There is another, is there not?"

She understood. "Not the child."

Marell's jaw muscles clenched. He stepped even closer. "You refuse me?" His breath was warm and sour in her face.

Drawing herself up to full height, she met his gaze with narrowed eyes. "*Not* the child."

A touch on her mind. So soft, so brief she wondered if she imagined it. Had he dared? Had he *probed* her? Her? Morrigan the Bright?

Instinct took over. Her skin tingled with the runes of a stun spell, their glow reflecting in Marell's face.

Marell's eyes widened. His lip curled. Her left arm prickled as she prepared to cast the spell. His eyes flicked to the symbols on her arm. He stepped back. "Fine. Keep your little plaything." Grabbing Karmalov's shirt from the bed, he pulled it on. "Bring me the other one. But I'll need more subjects. I must prepare. I must be ready."

The spell's tingle faded. Her anger did not. "Stayne and Stryke will collect more from the streets. I'll bring the other boy now." As she stalked to the door, a thought struck her. She smiled. *Yes, that would be fun.* She turned back. "Actually, I *do* have a second subject for you."

Marell raised one eyebrow, waiting.

"That is," she said, "if you're not fussy about gender."

Chapter 43

We Exist

Case sat beside Fader on the bed, staring at the door to their room. Staring in disbelief. She'd been scared when the black-clad figures burst in, guns raised. Scared—then overjoyed when she realized this was Will's SWAT team. These people were here to rescue them.

But her joy changed to confusion and then panic. Their rescuers scanned the room, showing no signs of seeing what was in front of them—her and Fader strapped to beds, Link standing guard beside them.

She'd screamed then. Fader, too. Screamed, shouted, yelled. But the SWAT team, showing no more signs of hearing them than they had of seeing them, had turned and left.

Left the room. Left the hospital. Left them here—prisoners still.

Link, their Hollow Boy guard, had unstrapped Fader. After Link left, locking them again in the room, Fader unstrapped her.

The police sirens had brought new hope. A hope that died with the shouted commands she heard through the boarded windows. The cops had come to arrest Will's team, not search the hospital.

"Why didn't they see or hear us?" Fader asked, hugging his knees to his chest.

"Morrigan's magic, I'll bet. It doesn't matter. Will's raid didn't work."

"Will's raid?"

She related her Dream journey with Will and Yeshe last night. She left out the parts where she'd shared her feelings of their mother with Will. Shared her feelings for Will, too.

"So that old guy's dead?" Fader said quietly, not looking at her.

"Yeshe? I don't know. He said he was dying. But that doesn't mean—"

"I killed him." Fader said, his lip quivering. "I helped them take him."

Oh, Fader. She pulled him close. "No, bro. Not you. Marell. Morrigan. That witch made you help her. It wasn't your fault." She hugged him tighter, trying to remember when she'd hugged her little brother as much as today. She realized she never had—she'd been too busy being Hard Case. Hugging him felt good. It felt right.

He sobbed into her shoulder. She held him until he pulled away. He wiped at his eyes. "Now what?"

Good question. Their side kept losing people. Adi, Yeshe, Will's SWAT team. Who did that leave?

Will, Fader, and her. That's who. Three kids against Marell, Morrigan, Stayne, Stryke, and an army of Hollow Boys. *Yeah, that'll work.*

She shook her head. So what? She and Fader had beat the odds for years on the streets. She wouldn't quit now. A memory from last night's dream returned. "That rug you told me about…"

"Yeah?"

"Yeshe thought it might link to Morrigan's power. So do I. If we destroy it, it could take her out of the picture."

Fader said nothing.

"What do you think?"

He shrugged. "Have to get to it first. We're locked up, remember?"

"But Morrigan lets you wander around, right? I bet you're only in here because she somehow knew the raid was coming. I'm guessing she'll let you out again soon."

He kicked the bed. "Maybe."

"So? Can you get at that rug?"

He shrugged again. "Probably."

"Great. Now we need a way to destroy it. Think it'd burn?"

Another shrug.

"This was a hospital," she said, thinking. "Might still be supplies around."

"Like what?"

"Isopropyl alcohol." Sometimes, street people would try to get drunk on the stuff, not knowing it was poison. They'd swipe it during a trip to Emerg—and then end up back in hospital. "They use it to sterilize things, but it can make stuff burn."

Fader hesitated. "I saw lots of different bottles in the Tea Room."

"Tea Room?"

"Where Morrigan has tea with the Hollow Boys."

"Weird. But when you get out, check that room. Maybe we'll get lucky. Remember what you're looking for?"

He shook his head.

She repeated the name along with her best guess at spelling. "If it ends with alcohol, grab it. It'll work."

He just nodded.

"But we still need matches. Or a lighter. They took mine." She remembered something else. "I've smelled smoke here. Is there a fire somewhere?"

"The Weave room has torches on the wall."

"Again, weird. But perfect. Okay, that's the plan. You get out. Find that alcohol stuff and come let me out. We'll sneak into that room, pour it on the rug, and toss a torch on it. Then we'll make a run for it." All while avoiding the Hollow Boys, Stayne, Stryke, Morrigan, Marell... Suddenly, it didn't sound like much of a plan.

Fader didn't answer. Was he thinking the same thing?

She frowned at him. "You okay?"

A shrug.

"Bro, what's wrong?"

"Case?"

"Yeah?"

"Do you think burning her rug will hurt her?"

"Morrigan? I sure freaking hope so. That's the idea—" She stopped as understanding hit her. A nausea grew in her gut, trying to crawl up her throat.

She knew that feeling. Fear. The same fear that had seized her two nights ago as she lay beside Fader in their room in Will's tower. The fear something was wrong with her little brother. Minutes later, Fader had led Morrigan and her twisted crew into the building. Which had led to here, to this moment.

"Fader," she said, fighting to keep her voice calm. "She's not a good person."

"She's not all bad," he said, his face pleading. "I know she's not."

"Look at what she and Marell have done to these kids. We *know* these kids. And now they're empty *things*. Adi's dying. Yeshe may be dead. We're prisoners. Marell is out to get Will. And that sick freak will rule the world if we let him."

"There's good in her, Case. I know it."

What could she say? Was this still Morrigan's magic? She didn't think so. This seemed genuine. Which made it even more frightening. Morrigan was a monster, a killer. Yet Fader had feelings for her. Real feelings.

She used her last argument. "She'll kill me."

His eyes went wide. "No! She promised."

"Remember Stryke's target practice? Stayne ready to play Carve-the-Case? She *gave* me to them. She stopped them only when she learned I could help them get to Will. Once they have Will—and probably kill him—they'll kill me, too."

Fader sat staring at the floor. "You don't understand. The way she treats me..." He hesitated then finished with a rush. "It's like having a mother again."

"Oh." She sat back, stunned. "Oh."

"Yeah. Oh."

"And yuck. I mean...*YUCK*!"

He sighed. "Yeah. I know. I'm weird." He looked at her, his eyes wet. "I miss her, Case. I miss Mom."

She swallowed. Their mother was too much a topic of conversations. "I miss her, too," she lied. Except she wasn't lying. Worse, she wanted to cry, too. She shoved away thoughts of their mother as savagely as if she was beating off an attacker. "But she left us, and she's not coming back. And Morrigan isn't her. So... who's it gonna be, bro? Me or Morrigan?"

He didn't hesitate. "You."

She had to push down a lump in her throat before she could talk. "Really? Cuz she could give you a pretty good life. She's all super-powered and stuff. I mean, what am I?"

He grinned. His old grin. "You're you. You're Case."

She punched him in the arm. "Damn straight."

He leaned against her. "I love you, Case."

She started to tell him to shut up. To say he was a pain. To ignore him, as she always did whenever he told her that.

No. Not this time. "I love you, too," she whispered.

He sat back, staring at her. "You've never told me that. I mean, I always knew. But you've never said it."

Her face burned. She did her best to glare at him. "And never will again if you make this big a deal of it."

"You always tell me I'm a pain."

"You *are* a pain."

He grinned. "I think your new boyfriend's changing you."

"Shut up."

"He's making you all mushy and squishy."

"Shut. Up."

"Better change your street name to *Soft* Case."

"Listen, you little—"

A key rattled in the lock. They both jumped up, eyes on the door. Was Morrigan letting Fader out? Would he get to search for the alcohol?

The door opened. Link the Hollow Boy entered, followed by Stayne and Stryke.

Why had the ghouls returned? Reason battled fear inside her. These freaks wouldn't hurt her. Morrigan needed her. She was safe for now.

Wasn't she?

"You," Stryke snapped. "Come with us. The Master wants you."

Fader? Marell wanted Fader? Had the transfer from Yeshe failed? Did Marell need a new body? No, not that.

She stepped forward, pushing Fader behind her. "You're not taking him anywhere, creep."

Stayne and Stryke looked at each other, their head movements synchronized, then back at her. Stayne smiled. "You're right, dearie." He stabbed his finger at her like a knife. "We're taking *you*."

Case's stomach tumbled. Her legs wanted to collapse under her. Marell wanted her? Why?

Fader stepped in front of her, his fists clenched, their roles now reversed. "Stay away from my sister."

Stayne's smile became a scowl. "We don't have time for this." He reached for Fader.

Stryke grabbed his arm. "We mustn't harm the boy. The witch will not forgive us again." He motioned to Link, standing silently behind them. "Secure the boy, but do not damage him."

Link walked forward.

Case's heart fell. Link was bigger than her by a bunch and much stronger. He had a rep as one of the toughest fighters on the streets.

Link stopped in front of Fader, who still stood defiantly defending her. Case waited for Link to grab Fader. But Link didn't reach for Fader. Or for her. Instead, he turned to face Stayne and Stryke. He slowly moved his head left, then right. He repeated the movement.

Link was shaking his head. The Hollow Boy was saying no.

From their open-mouthed expressions, Stryke and Stayne were as shocked as she was. Stayne's eyes narrowed, anger replacing surprise. "Step aside, boy."

Link did not step aside. Link did not move. Link remained motionless, blocking the way to Case and Fader.

No. Not completely motionless. The fingers on his right hand twitched. Short jerky movements, as if each action took a supreme effort of will. Once. Twice. Again. The fingers stopped. Case stared, stunned by what she'd seen.

"Enough," Stayne rasped. Knives slid into his hands.

She jumped in front of both Link and Fader. "Wait. Don't hurt him. I'll go with you."

"Case!" Fader cried.

"I'll be okay. They need me alive, right?" She hugged him, then added in a whisper, "Find the alcohol."

Fader looked scared, but he nodded.

She turned to Stayne and Stryke. "Okay, creeps. Let's rock."

Stayne opened the door for her, grinning his death's head grin and giving her a mock bow as she passed. The two ghouls marched her down the hall between them, a tight grip on her arms to prevent any break for freedom.

But as each step brought her closer to Marell, it wasn't escape occupying her mind. It was the strange behavior of the even stranger Hollow Boy, Link. Although it made no sense, Link had acted like her protector, not guard.

Impossible. He was just following Morrigan's orders to keep her and Fader safe. Fader, because of the witch's affection for him. Her, because she was a hostage against Will.

But her thoughts ran to Link's twitching fingers as he'd faced Stayne. A pattern, repeated. A signal. A signal meant for her.

How did she know that?

Because it was a signal from the streets. A signal every kid on her turf knew.

Little finger and index finger extended, pointed down.

Warning. Danger.

Somehow, somewhere in the broken creature that was Link the Hollow Boy, Link the Street Kid still lived. And he was talking to her.

Chapter 44

My Body is a Cage

W ill sat on his leather couch in his studio, head back, eyes closed. It was mid-morning, two hours after the failed raid. He had three problems he needed to solve before that night's Dream journey.

First, how to travel up the River of Souls. Second, how to follow a *specific* silver cord among the millions filling the River. And his biggest problem: how to face and defeat Marell and Morrigan. Without, you know, dying.

Yep, those were the problems. And, yep, he should be solving them. But he wasn't. He was feeling sorry for himself. Adi's life still in the balance. Yeshe dead or dying. Case and Fader prisoners, bait to capture the Rider. The failed raid. Stone and his team arrested.

What else could go wrong?

"May I come in?" The voice was male. And recently familiar.

Will opened his eyes and sat up. Lawrence Kinland stood staring at his design table, an amused expression on his face. Will tried to recall what showed there. Right. Scenes for the next Dream Rider issue.

He stood. "Looks like you're already in."

Kinland glanced up from the table. "Ah! You're awake."

Will walked over. "Wasn't asleep. Just working out a few problems...uh, on the next issue."

Kinland tapped the display with a manicured finger. "Your famous little comic."

"Graphic novel. That little comic, Larry—"

"Lawrence."

"—is the reason all this exists." He waved in what he hoped was an "all this" gesture. He didn't know why he needed to make that point. Wrong. He knew why. He was in the principal's office again, and he wanted credit for the one course where he had an A+.

Kinland smiled. "Yes, certainly. Mind you, the company—"

My company, Will thought.

"—now derives but a tiny portion of its revenues from the actual Dream Rider issues. Negligible in the bigger picture." He raised an eyebrow at Will's expression. "Ah, but perhaps you're not current on our financials."

Will swallowed. "Uh, well, Adi handles..." His voice trailed off. So much for his A+. He felt like he'd failed an exam because he'd been reading comic books instead of studying.

Graphic novels, dammit.

"Ah, yes. Adrienne would." Kinland glanced at the video screen showing Adi in her hospital bed. "Any change?"

Will just shook his head.

"Pity." Kinland's eyes returned to Will. "But I'm afraid neither poor Adrienne nor your comic prompted my visit. A serious issue has arisen. One we need to discuss."

Will sighed. He couldn't afford to waste time on this. "Lawrence, I signed those papers so you could run the business in Adi's absence. I didn't expect I'd have to tell you how to do stuff."

"Nor will we involve you going forward. I've taken steps to ensure we never need impose on your—" Kinland glanced at the design table. "—valuable time for us to *do stuff*." Walking to the couch, he sat. "I'm here to *give* direction, not ask for it."

Will sat at the far end, feeling again like he hadn't studied. "What do you mean?"

"I believe you know an employee by the name of Winstone Zhang."

A cold lump formed in his stomach.

"Early this morning, Mr. Zhang led an illegal armed assault on an abandoned medical facility." His eyes locked on Will.

Will tried speaking but his throat wouldn't cooperate.

"Thankfully," Kinland continued, "a passerby contacted police, who intervened before any damage occurred. Mr. Zhang and his team are in custody." His gaze remained fixed on Will's face. "I cannot imagine the goal of such a ridiculous exercise, but I believe *you* ordered it."

Will swallowed, still saying nothing.

"Zhang denied any connection to you. Or the company, thankfully. But given his last known communication was with you, coupled with your lack of denial, I will assume I am correct."

Will found his voice again. "How did you find out?"

"That's unimportant. What matters is I've protected this firm and its shareholders. Zhang and his operatives are no longer employees of this organization. We should have fired him after the security breach two nights ago." He stood, straightening his suit jacket. "And, given your involvement, as of now, you will have no access to any other person, service, or financial asset in this company, unless authorized by myself."

Will jumped up, facing him. "What?"

"The company will continue to clothe, feed, and house you here. You may still receive visitors and will retain the full run of this building and access to your driver."

"Oh, gee. Kind of you."

"The least we can do, given your disability."

Will winced at that. "You can't do this."

Kinland raised an eyebrow. "You transferred Power of Attorney for your affairs from Adrienne to myself. Remember?"

Will could almost hear Adi yelling at him: *You signed it without reading it?*

Kinland waited for a response. When none came, he walked to the running track, then stopped. "One last thing. I'm canceling production of your comic. Immediately."

"*What?*"

"We lose money with each issue. It's a drain on this organization."

"Are you nuts? It's the heart of this organization. It's what we are." *It's what I am.*

"Not anymore. I'm taking us in a new direction," Kinland replied, continuing along the track toward the elevators.

Will ran to the track. "You can't do this!"

"We just had that conversation, young man," Kinland called back. "You lost."

Will screamed a long stream of profanity at Kinland's retreating back.

"Language, my boy. Language." Kinland disappeared around the corner to the elevator bank.

Will stormed back into his studio. Grabbing a table lamp, he threw it as hard as he could against the wall. The shade flew off, the bulb popped, and the lamp exploded. Ceramic shards and broken glass rained down on the couch and rug.

Bent over with his hands on his knees, he stood there swearing, loud and long. Finally, he ran down. Straightening, he looked at the mess from the shattered lamp. Adi's voice sounded in his imagination: *Very mature.*

Calmer now, he swept aside pieces of lamp and bulb from the couch and sat. "Hallie!" he called, half expecting no answer.

Hallie's voice sounded from the speakers. "Yes, Mr. Dreycott?"

"Has anyone changed what you can do or request done on my behalf?"

"Yes. Lawrence Kinland approved changes at 9:17 AM today."

"Please list."

Hallie detailed the services he could no longer request without authorization by Kinland. It was a long list.

He cut her off. "Just tell me what you *can* do for me,"

Hallie listed the remaining services. It was a short list.

"So basically, I can order food, laundry service, and my limo."

"That is correct. Do you wish laundry or limousine service, sir?"

He actually laughed at that. "No. Thank you."

"Would you like to order lunch, sir?"

"Kind of lost my appetite."

"Are you ill, sir? Should I call your physician? That service remains on my list."

"Goodbye, Hallie."

"Goodbye, Mr. Dreycott."

He leaned back on the couch, ignoring stray lamp shards poking him. He was the only person left who could stop two super-powered villains from ruling the world.

And he'd just been grounded.

Stayne and Stryke marched Case to a room in the northwest corner of the floor. The two ghouls came to a halt before a closed door. The smell of smoke was stronger here. Stayne held Case from behind, looming over her, his fingers digging into her shoulders. Stryke, looking like he wished he could be somewhere else, gave the door a timid rap.

The answer was immediate. "Come," called Morrigan's voice.

Stryke opened the door, and Stayne pushed Case forward. She stumbled into the room.

Two high-backed armchairs stood to her left. Morrigan sat in one chair. The mercenary who had carried Case from Will's tower two nights ago occupied the other. The man sat slumped to one side, eyes closed—unconscious or asleep, she couldn't tell. Black velvet curtains covered the windows. Torches burning in wall sconces provided the only light, sending shadows dancing around the room.

But shadows weren't the only things dancing.

In front of Morrigan, a street kid spun and leaped. He was thin, a skeleton in too baggy clothes. Recognition jolted Case. His name was Jarrod, but everyone called him Slip. He was about her age and someone she trusted on the streets.

Slip did a pirouette, ending with his arms over his head. Dropping his hands to his hips, he laughed. The sound was odd and cold and not the way Slip laughed.

Morrigan gave a brief clap for the performance. "Well, my love?"

"Restored! Restored, indeed," Slip said.

Case shivered. That wasn't how Slip talked, either.

"Your transfer appeared immediate," Morrigan said.

The boy with Slip's face smiled. "Yes, and my control complete. I met no resistance. The child remains inside, but his spirit now dwells in the Gray Lands."

Gray Lands? Case's ears perked up. Yeshe had mentioned the Gray Lands last night in Dream. What had he said?

Follow the River upstream. Find Marell. But beware the Gray Lands.

Her brain raced, trying to force sense onto this scene. Yeshe had said something else. Something about Morrigan and a ceremony. A ceremony to extract Marell's lost fragment.

Marell will be whole again, with his full power. Yeshe's words.

Restored! Slip's words—but not Slip.

Marell. Marell the body swapper.

With a sinking feeling, she realized Marell now occupied Slip's body. Morrigan had done it. She'd restored Marell's missing piece from Yeshe.

Yeshe.

Tearing her eyes from Marell-Slip, she scanned the room. Two hospital beds stood to her right. The nearest was empty. The other held a familiar figure. A figure who lay very still.

With a snarl, she wrenched free of Stayne's grip and ran to where Yeshe lay. Behind her, Morrigan called, "Leave her."

Yeshe's face was peaceful, his eyes closed. She touched his hands where they lay folded on his breast. His skin was cold. His chest was still.

Yeshe was dead.

Drawing in a deep breath, she stifled the sob trying to escape her throat. The battle the monk had fought for so many years—the battle to protect the world—was over.

"You were a good man, Yeshe," she whispered.

"He did not suffer."

She turned. Beside her, Morrigan stared down at Yeshe's body. Stayne and Stryke had left the room.

"You killed him," Case said, her voice a flat, empty thing.

An emotion played on Morrigan's face that Case could not name. Morrigan opened her mouth as if to speak, then pressed her lips into a thin line. "He did not suffer," she repeated.

Case leaped at Morrigan.

Or tried to. She sent the command to her muscles. The command to attack the witch. But something pushed that aside.

No. Not some*thing*.

Some*one*. Someone in her mind.

Interesting, a voice said.

A voice in her head. But not her own voice. And not her Voice. A paralyzing fear seized her guts and twisted. She realized who it was.

Marell. Marell was taking her over.

She fought him. Fought against his control. Fought to push him from her mind. She commanded her body to move, to run. Run from this room, from this latest horror.

But her body didn't listen. Her body ignored her. Her body was no longer *hers.*

Marell was *inside* her. She wanted to throw up. She felt as if she'd been physically attacked. She felt violated. She felt...

Nothing.

One moment, she was screaming in her head, aware of the room, aware of Marell's growing control over her. The next moment, something pushed her away. From that room. From that moment. From herself.

She still saw the room, smelled the torches, heard voices. But her senses were muffled as if wrapped in layers of gauze.

Her emotions, too. She felt numb, as if drugged. She remembered, just seconds ago, feeling horrified. Violated. Furious. She *remembered* those feelings. But she no longer *felt* them. She no longer felt anything.

The sensation of being pushed away continued. She viewed the room now from a great distance, a distance growing with every second. Another scene formed before her eyes. She struggled to see it, to make her vision adjust.

A mist drifted across this scene, obscuring details, shrouding all in a dull grayness. Here and there, the mist parted for an eyeblink, and she glimpsed a barren, desolate landscape. The hospital room was fading, replaced by this gray place.

This gray place...

She understood. If she could still have experienced an emotion, it would have been terror.

Marell wasn't just taking her over. He was sending her away. The part of her that made her Case. She knew now what happened to the missing street kids. She knew what had made them the Hollow Boys. Marell had sent them away, too. And now he was sending her there as well.

He was sending her to the Gray Lands.

Chapter 45

Scary Monsters (and Super Creeps)

C aught between two worlds, Case fought as never before. With each second, the Gray Lands grew clearer in her vision while the hospital room where she was in the real world faded.

Real? What *was* real? As the Gray Lands solidified around her, she struggled to remember.

No. This gray nightmare wasn't real. She seized onto a single thought, the one thing she *knew*. Her body—*her* body—was in that hospital room. And she had to get it back before her connection to that room, that world, that body disappeared. Disappeared forever behind the gray mist that every second grew thicker around her.

Through that mist, Case watched as her body walked around the room. *Her* body, picking things up with *her* fingers, holding them up to *her* face.

"Interesting," her mouth said. Marell's word. She stopped walking. No. *He* stopped. He ran her hands over her body and chuckled with her throat. "This would take getting used to," he said through her lips, turning her head to Morrigan.

Morrigan raised an eyebrow. "For us both."

She heard herself chuckle again. "Do not worry, my pet," her mouth said. "I will not remain here. Merely a test. And another successful one. My control of this girl was immediate. And complete. She offered no resistance."

No resistance? In that moment, Case discovered her emotions had not completely died. Anger flared, hot and strong.

No resistance? Hard Case gave no resistance? The invisible force still pushed her away from her body and farther into the Gray Lands. She focused on that force. And pushed back. Hard. Hard Case hard.

The hazy hospital scene jumped, swinging up and then down. There, in that room, her body had stumbled. She'd *made* it stumble.

"Marell?" Morrigan said. It sounded to Case as if she called from down a long corridor.

Case saw her own hand flash up, silencing Morrigan. Something shoved her. Not her body, but her spirit, her spirit lost somewhere inside her mind. The pushing sensation grew. The hospital scene faded even more as the mists of the Gray Lands grew thicker.

Marell was pushing back. And he was winning.

Here! Look here!

Yes! Her Voice had returned. If she'd still controlled her body, she would've shouted with joy.

Where? she asked.

Here.

A vision formed, replacing both the fading hospital and ever-sharpening Gray Lands. The vision lasted only a second. But she'd seen enough.

She'd seen Fader, waiting in their room. Waiting for *her*. Counting on *her*. Counting on her to win.

Coming, bro, she thought. And pushed back with all she had.

The mist thinned. The hospital room appeared again. And the floor rushed towards her.

Her body had fallen. She'd made Marell fall.

Morrigan called something, but Marell didn't answer the witch. Instead, he answered her. *Child, you cannot win.*

Yeah? Watch me, asshole.

The final battle for her mind and body began.

How long that battle lasted, she couldn't tell. With the slimmest connection to her body and the real world, she lost any sense of time. Her struggle with Marell might have been a minute. Or an hour. Or a day. It seemed unending. It seemed an eternity.

Whatever the time span, it was a battle she was losing. With every push from Marell, the hospital room faded more and the swirling mists grew thicker. The Gray Lands grew closer. She kept fighting, but she knew it was hopeless. How could she fight an invisible opponent, an unseen force? She needed a target. She needed something to hit.

A memory of first meeting Will as the Rider came to her. Of how she'd fought the emojis. She'd won because she treated that like any other street rumble. Step up and swing. She remembered, too, Will's story of facing Marell as the snake thing in Dream. *That'll work. Just give me something to hit.* She focused on trying to visualize her foe.

The grayness before her solidified. Something was forming. Something big.

Black as night, the snake swayed above her in the mists, three stories high.

Maybe not the best idea, she thought, stepping back in her mind.

And now, girl, Marell whispered, *we end this.* The beast reared, poised to strike.

Case! Here! her Voice called. *Look here.*

An image filled her thoughts. Snow-capped mountains above. A rocky valley below. In that valley, a village of stone huts sat beside a meandering river. It resembled the Dreamscape last night when Yeshe had appeared. This was somewhere in Tibet.

A man and woman labored up the mountain slope carrying a rough litter. On that litter lay a young man, his legs twisted and deformed.

The view changed. The mountain peaks loomed closer now. Far below, the village was but a group of black specks. The couple stopped. They set the litter on a bare rocky ledge, open to the elements. Snow fell, whipped by a strong wind. With a last fearful look at the young man, the couple turned away and quickly began to descend. The man on the litter called after them. Case did not recognize the language, but she still knew what he called.

"Mother! Father!"

The couple did not turn. He screamed at them. Still they did not look back. The crippled man continued calling even after he lost sight of them in the gathering darkness.

The mountain scene faded from her sight. But the young man still screamed in her head. *No! No!*

She waited for the mist-shrouded Gray Lands to return. She waited to see the snake thing looming over her. Neither appeared. With a suddenness that struck like a physical blow, the hospital scene flooded her vision again. And her senses. Torch smoke burned her nostrils. Her hands brushed rough fabric. Something cold and metallic pressed against her back.

And a man's cries filled her ears. "No! No!"

She opened her eyes. She was back in the hospital room. And back in her body, sitting on the floor, leaning against the bed that held Yeshe. A woven rug lay under her. As she struggled to her feet, she also struggled to understand what had happened.

She'd won. She'd beaten Marell. But how?

Across the room, Morrigan stood over the soldier in the chair. The man sat bolt upright, staring wide-eyed at Case.

"Marell! Marell, what is wrong?" Morrigan asked.

It took Case a few seconds to understand that Marell, no longer in her body, now occupied this soldier. Off in the far corner, Slip stood stiff and silent as a statue. She remembered Marell's words. *His spirit now dwells in the Gray Lands.* Bile rose in her throat. Slip was a Hollow Boy. And she'd just escaped becoming a Hollow Girl.

Marell the soldier pushed Morrigan away. "Nothing is wrong," he rasped. "I loathed being inside a woman's body."

Morrigan straightened. From her frown, she believed Marell as much as Case did.

No, Marell had fled from her. In fear. But why?

He saw what you saw, her Voice said.

Great, she replied, remembering the vision. *But what did I see?* No answer came. Her Voice was gone. Again.

Marell the soldier rose. Their eyes met. She held his gaze, wanting nothing more than to turn away but refusing to submit, even in this. She waited.

Morrigan had less patience. "Marell, what is wrong?"

In a practiced motion, Marell's hand flashed to the holster the soldier still wore. Before Case could even flinch, he was pointing a pistol at her. His finger tightened on the trigger.

With a hiss of breath, Morrigan placed a hand on Marell's gun arm. "We need her alive."

Muscles played along Marell's jaw. Case held her breath, not daring to move, her eyes on Marell's. Seconds passed.

Marell lowered the gun, breaking eye contact. Returning the pistol to his holster, he sat again. He waved in Case's direction. "Remove her."

Morrigan looked at Marell, then at Case, shooting darts at her from under lidded eyes. She motioned Case toward the door. "Out!"

Works for me, Case thought. She moved forward, but her foot caught on something. She looked down.

The rug where she'd fallen. Thick and round. Red and black with the same design as Morrigan's amulet. Three bent skeletal legs inside a circle, arranged like hands on a clock, chasing each other counterclockwise. *Widdershins.*

"Now, girl!" Morrigan snapped.

She left the room, Morrigan following. They walked in silence until they reached the long hallway leading to her and Fader's room. Morrigan grabbed her arm and shoved her against the wall. Taller and stronger, the witch held her there. Morrigan glared down at Case, her face pressed close. The woman's breath was warm and sweet. Her face and words were not.

"What did you do to him, you little bitch?" She whispered the question as if afraid Marell might overhear.

Case swallowed, fighting a temptation to smile. Despite Marell's attack on her, she still feared Morrigan more. "I don't know. One second, he's controlling everything I do. The next..." She shrugged. "He lets me go. Like he said, I guess he couldn't handle having girl parts."

Morrigan's green eyes played over Case's face as if searching for a lie. Releasing her, the witch motioned down the hall with a vicious flick of one hand. "Move."

Case moved. Her back now to Morrigan, she allowed herself that smile, one that was part relief, part hope.

She'd beaten Marell, made him flee her body. How, she did not know. But if she could figure that out, it might help Will when he faced the creep himself. And Link's attempt to communicate was making her rethink the Hollow Boys.

And she'd found the rug. Now they just had to get to it. And then...

"Burn, baby, burn," she muttered.

"What did you say?" Morrigan snapped.

Case smiled again. "Nothing."

With the wretched girl locked up again, Morrigan returned to the Weave room. Marell, in Karmalov's body, stood beside where Yeshe lay, staring at the dead monk.

A finger of fear ran down her spine. She'd told the girl Yeshe hadn't suffered. Had Marell heard?

"Are you not well?" she asked, aiming to distract.

"What do you mean?" he snapped, looking up.

"Your reaction to the girl."

Turning away from Yeshe, Marell walked to his high-backed chair. "I told you. I disliked having a woman's body." He sat, waving a hand, dismissing the discussion. "Enough. We have plans to make."

She sat in the other chair. Something had happened, something neither he nor the waif would share. For now, it was enough her small mercy to Yeshe remained undiscovered. "Yes. Eliminating the boy who killed the Mara. This William Dreycott."

"Eliminate? In a way. He will be my new host."

That surprised her. "I thought you wished to kill him." *To remove a threat to you*, she thought, but knew better than to say that.

"The boy's too valuable. I saw that in the girl's memories. His mind is attuned to astral planes. Strongly attuned. And he has wealth and power. And youth."

She considered that. Karmalov had researched the white tower before their raid. The boy who lived there was wealthy indeed. When he came of age, he would rule one of the largest corporate empires in the world. She nodded.

"You concur?"

"Yes. An inspired choice. You will take him where he lives? Karmalov claimed he never leaves the tower." Although she'd never learned astral projection, she understood its workings well. Distance presented no problem to an adept of Marell's level. His astral body could travel across the city to the white tower in an eyeblink.

He looked away before answering. "I have tried."

She raised an eyebrow. "Tried?" She left the rest unstated. *Tried—and failed.*

"Just now. Someone—or some*thing*—in that tower still blocks me. I could approach the building but not enter it."

She frowned. "Still? Before, we had assumed the monk was the cause. But if you encountered the same force just now..." She glanced at where Yeshe lay dead.

He nodded. "Not the monk. Perhaps a residual astral shield he raised to protect himself while he hid there."

Then why hadn't Marell detected Yeshe's spirit in the shield? A spirit he knew so well? But she didn't ask that. "Is such a thing possible?"

"Possible, yes. I could create such a shield given time. But the monk? And to survive his death? I would not have expected it."

"Could the Dreycott boy?"

Marell hesitated. "Unlikely. He lacks the power, the knowledge."

She didn't like this. Too many unexplained events. The failure of her spells on the girl that first night. Her runes vanishing from Fader. Marell's reaction when he tried to occupy the girl. Now an unknown astral force protecting the white tower? "Not Yeshe. Nor magicks. Nor the boy. Then what?"

He shrugged Karmalov's shoulders. "Its cause is irrelevant. If I cannot take the Dreycott boy in his tower, then we must lure him from it."

She forgot the strange force in the white tower. A new fear awoke in her as she guessed his plan. "And the bait?"

Marell's face wrinkled as if tasting something sour. "That girl. The one he cares for. And her brother."

As she'd feared. "*Not* the boy," she said, her voice low and cold.

Marell smiled. "Your little pet will stay safe. I merely need to borrow him. I will offer an exchange. If this Dreycott boy meets me, I will promise to free the girl and her brother." He held up a hand as she began to protest. "I will release no one. Once he is away from that tower, he is mine."

"Then why do you need the boy and girl?"

"Before this Dreycott abandons the shelter of his tower, he will want proof we have them. I will show him your pet."

"Why not the girl?"

"I will claim she is nearby. That once he meets with me, I will produce her. I will say that if he does not appear or if anyone tries to capture me, then the girl dies."

"Where will you keep her?"

"Here."

She frowned. "You said you would take her to the meeting. Keep her nearby."

"I will tell the Dreycott boy that. I have no intention of bringing that girl with me."

Again, she wondered what had passed between Marell and the girl. "Where will you meet?"

"I will suggest a public place. To make him feel safe." He shrugged. "It doesn't matter. Just so long as I draw him from that tower."

"When?"

"Tomorrow."

Another surprise. "So soon?"

"I am restored. Whole again and more powerful than ever. Too many years I've waited. I will wait no more. I will send a Hollow Boy today to the white tower with my offer."

"And the boy Fader? You will keep him safe at this meeting?"

"You can do that yourself. I want you by my side when I meet the Dreycott boy."

Pride filled her, but then she cursed herself for still wanting him to need her.

"Besides, your two undead fools have failed too often of late," he added.

Her pride became simmering anger. *Her* fools. Stayne and Stryke's mistakes became hers. "And the girl?"

Marell turned to her. Over a century she'd known him. No matter what face he wore, she could always read his expressions. She knew this look well.

Hate. But, she realized with a shock, hate tinged with fear.

"The girl?" he said. "She stays here. Stayne and Stryke will finally get to play with her. Uninterrupted. Does this meet with your approval?"

She ignored the sarcasm in his tone. Fader safe under her own protection? His wretched sister finally dealt with? Did it meet with her approval? She nodded. "Very much so. Very much indeed."

Chapter 46

Dead Man Walking

J ust past three in the afternoon, Will sat back from his design table and rubbed his eyes. He'd been at this since Kinland had dropped his bomb-shells that morning.

Well, not quite. He'd spent an hour on the couch, feeling sorry for himself again. A video call from Dr. Jin with an update on Adi had pulled him from that mope. Nothing new. Still stable. No change. A non-update, really.

But the call had snapped him out of his funk. Staring at Adi on the screen, he wondered what she'd tell him. Aside from, *Why on earth, William, did you sign that document?*

But then she'd tell him to quit moping over his problems. *Do something about them*, she'd say. *They won't solve themselves.*

So he'd solved them.

First, how to travel up the River of Souls. He'd known *what* he wanted, but designing and learning to operate the thing had required a morning of research and most of the afternoon to draft it. Then he had to memorize everything, so he could pull it into Dream, complete and ready to use.

He'd considered simpler solutions. But this idea would work and work well. And it was way cool—meaning it would impress Case. This was probably the last chance he'd have to do that.

Next problem? How to follow one specific cord among billions in the River. More research. More design. More memorizing.

But he was now ready for tonight's Dream journey. Ready to follow Case's silver cord up the River back to where she'd entered Dream.

Ready. Yeah. Right.

Assuming his new creations worked. Assuming he and Case reached and survived the mysterious Gray Lands. And they found the door where Case had entered Dream. And he could open it. And step through it.

Yeah, assuming all that.

But if he *could* step through that door, he'd astral project into the waking world.

Assuming Yeshe hadn't lied. Again.

And even if that all worked, he'd then face his final problem. His real problem. How to defeat Marell. Alone.

Enough. Tonight, he *would* learn to astral project. He'd then spend every moment practising until he was ready for Marell. All he needed was *time*. Time before that battle. Time to perfect his new skills.

Hallie's voice interrupted his thoughts. "Mr. Dreycott, you have a visitor in reception."

He wasn't expecting anyone. He was *never* expecting anyone. "Who is it, Hallie?"

"He will not provide a name, and my facial recognition module returned no match."

"Describe him."

"Male. Caucasian. Based on physiology and apparel, I estimate he is mid-teens and in a lower social stratum. Possibly homeless."

A street kid? "What's he want?"

"He has a message. One he will deliver only to you."

What could a street kid want to tell him? Where the missing boys were? Where Case was? Excited, he jumped up. "Okay. I'll be down."

As he rode the elevator, he recalled the last time a street kid appeared in reception. That had been Fader.

And that had not ended well.

Will had no trouble identifying his visitor among the dozen people waiting in reception. The kid wore a sleeveless black hoodie over a white t-shirt and torn baggy jeans, all dirty. In a sea of suits, he looked like Will had felt meeting with the Board. Out of place. But even if street kids had filled reception, Will would've picked this kid out.

While other visitors sat on sofas and chairs, this kid remained standing. He stood with arms at his sides, staring ahead. He stood straight and still. Very straight. Very still. He didn't slouch. He didn't sway. His eyes never moved. His eyes seemed to register nothing. His eyes seemed dead.

A chill seized Will. He'd seen those dead eyes before. When he first searched for the missing boys in Dream. When he first encountered the Hollow Boys. When they killed three of his Doogles. Almost got him, too, pulling him into those dead bottomless eyes.

Bevington came over from where he'd been watching the kid. "He hasn't spoken since saying he has a message for you, sir," the guard whispered. "Won't answer questions. Won't respond at all."

"Thanks, Bev," Will said. He approached the boy. Standing before him, looking into those eyes, Will was sure. This was one of the missing street kids. This was a Hollow Boy. "Okay, let's have your message."

No response.

"My name is Will Dreycott. Do you have a message for me?"

The boy blinked. He scanned Will's face. "You are Will Dreycott." It was a statement, not a question, delivered in a monotone. The boy pulled a letter-sized white envelope from the pocket of his hoodie. He held it out.

Will hesitated. The boy remained dead still, waiting, hand extended. Will took the envelope, and the kid's hand dropped back to his side.

The envelope bore an actual seal in red wax—three skeletal legs running counterclockwise. The triskelion pattern described by Case and Yeshe. Tearing open the envelope, he unfolded a single sheet of heavy yellowed paper. It was a handwritten note. The handwriting was small, fine, and elaborate, each word finished with a looping flourish.

To Master William Dreycott of the White Tower

Dearest child,

I hope my letter finds you well. Recent events may cause you to doubt the sincerity in that wish. However, I assure you I have the most intense and personal interest in your continued health.

Although we have yet to encounter each other in the flesh, we have met, you and I. Three nights ago, in a place we both frequent, drawn together by the sudden death of a Mr. Lyle. Your unexpected departure that evening brought our conversation to a premature end. I write requesting an opportunity to pursue that discussion to its inevitable conclusion.

I find myself entertaining several houseguests. I mention this only because I understand that you hold one, a young female, in high regard. Her young brother, too, enjoys my hospitality. Both remain well—for the moment.

Due to a recent improvement in my health, I will soon relocate, forcing me to terminate abruptly the residency of my temporary tenants. Such terminations may prove painful for those involved. I propose we meet, so I may explain how you (and you alone) can

*ensure your friends continue their lives, untouched by sudden
terminations.*

*You need not reply. I will expect you at the time and place noted
below. Until then, I remain...*

Your humble servant, Marell

Any hope of defeating Marell died as he read the time and location of the
meeting. Trying to hide the trembling in his hands, he returned the letter to
the envelope. "What's your name?" he asked the Hollow Boy, his voice hoarse.
"Where do you live?"

"Have you read the letter?" the boy said.

"Yes, but—"

"Do you understand the letter?"

"Yes, but I need to know—"

The boy turned away. He walked to the exit door and stood there, waiting.
The door guard shot Bevington a look.

Bevington rejoined Will. "Boss?"

What could he do? Hold the kid here? Prevent him from returning?
Returning. Yes.

"Let him go," he whispered. "But do me a favor? Follow him. See where he
goes, then call me."

Bevington hesitated, a pained expression on his face.

"Shit. Kinland?"

"Sorry, sir. We're not supposed to take any orders from you."

Will sighed. "Yeah. No. It's okay, Bev." It was definitely not okay. With every
passing hour, he became more and more isolated. Now a chance to locate
Marell was literally walking out the door. He turned away, but Bevington
grabbed his arm.

"Screw Kinland," Bevington whispered. "I've never liked that asshole. Don't
care what he says, Mr. Dreycott. I still work for you."

Will swallowed. "Thanks, Bev. Thanks a lot. This is important, or I wouldn't
ask."

"I got it, boss." Bevington nodded to the guard. "Let him out."

The door opened. Exiting, the boy headed across the building's lobby toward
the west doors and York Street. He didn't look back. He didn't look left or
right. Will waited as Bevington gave the kid a head start and then followed.
The kid stepped outside onto the sidewalk filled with scurrying commuters. A
few seconds later, Bevington did the same. Just beyond, cars sped along York.

Will let out a breath. With any luck, the kid would lead them to where Marell and Morrigan held Case, Fader, and the other kids. If he could convince the cops to get a warrant—

A screech of tires shattered his thoughts. A woman screamed. His attention snapped back to the scene outside. Beyond the west doors, a crowd gathered on the sidewalk, craning to see something on the street.

His phone rang. It was Bevington. He could barely understand the man. "Oh my god, the kid... He just... I couldn't stop him. Jeezus, I couldn't stop him."

"Bev, what happened? Tell me what happened."

He heard the guard suck in a breath. When Bevington spoke again, his voice was calmer, but still held horror. "The kid stopped at the curb. He looked down the street. I figured he was waiting for a break in traffic. The light was green. The cars... God, they go so fast up York." Bevington took another breath. "Shit, Will. He just stepped in front of a car. The driver never had a chance to stop."

"The kid?" Will asked, knowing the answer.

"He's not moving. I think he's dead."

Will didn't reply. He couldn't. He felt like he was going to be sick. Seconds earlier, that boy had been standing before him, alive.

"That kid just killed himself, didn't he?" Bevington said. "Boss, what's going on?"

"Sorry, Bev," he said, forcing the words out. "Sorry I got you involved. I gotta go." He hung up. Ignoring the stares from people in reception, he walked back to the elevators. Once inside, he slumped against the wall as the car rose.

Marell had sent him two messages. The first had been the letter. The second, the death of the Hollow Boy. That second message said, "I control all around me. I kill without remorse. Obey me, or your friends will die as this boy died."

Pulling the letter from his pocket, he read again the time and place decreed by Marell for their meeting.

Tomorrow. At noon. So much for having the time to perfect his astral projection skills.

And the location?

Toronto had built its new city hall in the mid-sixties, if he remembered his history. Its design had been unique and remained so—two curving towers of different heights partially enclosing the round central council chamber, dubbed the "flying saucer."

In front lay Nathan Phillips Square, named after the mayor who'd started the project. It was a huge, uncovered, wide-open space, over twelve acres in size. That number had stuck in Will's head. When you can never go outside, large public places hold a fascination.

Tomorrow at noon, he, Will Dreycott, the boy who couldn't go outside, must face a deadly enemy in the biggest, busiest public square in the country.

&

Will slumped on his couch, still shaken by the Hollow Boy's death. Shaken, too, because the same fate awaited him. Tomorrow, Marell would kill him. Then, despite what his letter promised, Marell would kill Case. And Fader. And the missing street kids.

Then the madman would take over the world.

And he was the only person left to stop that madman. A seventeen-year-old kid who never left home. Who *couldn't* leave home.

But tomorrow, he'd have to.

He'd faced Marell in Dream. And lost. Now he must face him in the waking world. He couldn't even step outside without collapsing into a quivering pile of twitching limbs. How could he face Marell in so public a place?

Even if he got that far, what then? He would've just learned to astral project. Maybe. Even if he astral projected tonight, he'd face a fully restored Marell. A Marell with over a century of experience in astral travel.

He didn't have a chance. Marell had more skill and would be at his full power. And with Morrigan at his side, no doubt.

He was doomed. Skill and power—Marell bested him on both fronts.

Getting up, he paced his studio, too anxious to sit still any longer. He passed his design table, where the latest Dream Rider issue lay displayed. The issue that, thanks to Kinland, his legion of fans around the world would never see.

Yearning for happier times, he tapped on a favorite scene near the climax. The scene expanded.

It was night. In it, the Rider swooped down the aisle of a dark gothic church on his skateboard. Outside, fires on the streets flamed the stained-glass windows to life, giving light to the tableau inside. His crystal sword raised, the Rider stood poised to slash through a swarm of fanged bats blocking his way. In the background, a shrouded body lay on an altar. Behind the altar, a cloaked figure waited beside the body. Waited for the Rider.

As Marell waited for him.

Two coming battles. In the comic, the Dream Rider would win. In life, Will Dreycott would die. Then, with the death of its creator, the comic Rider would die, too.

But just as he'd created the comic, the comic had also created him. Created the Will Dreycott who was the real Dream Rider. The real Rider drew power in Dream from people's awareness of the comic character. The more the Rider appeared in their thoughts each night, the stronger he was in Dream.

Even without Marell, Kinland's killing of the Rider comic would kill the real Rider. As the comic character faded from people's minds, the real Rider would fade from Dream. The Rider would die.

Marell was just changing the timetable. Oh, and killing him in real life, too.

The comic Rider and the real Rider. They'd created each other. Born together, it was fitting they die together.

Kinland, without knowing it, was being prophetic. The Dream Rider would die. Marell would kill him. Because Marell had more skill and more power.

More skill. More power.

Even if he learned to astral project tonight, he'd never match Marell's skill. As for power...

He blinked. *As for power...*

Wait a minute.

An idea came to him. He examined the idea, turning it over in his mind, the way he did with a concept for an issue. He played with it, adding to it, fleshing it out, until the idea grew into a plan.

Skill and power.

Skill? No.

Power? Maybe.

Hopping up onto his stool, he paged through the issue. *I'm taking this company in a new direction.* Kinland's words. "Larry, I think you're right," he muttered. "Time for a new direction."

He read the issue, panel by panel, nodding to himself as he went. The setup still worked. And that great twist in the middle, too. Even the big final battle. It all worked.

Except for the ending. The final two-page spread.

He recast that last scene in his head, breaking it into panels. Yes, that would do it. He redrew those final frames, humming as he worked.

He'd told Kinland the truth. *This* was what he was. The comic was the one thing he did better than anyone else in the waking world. And in Dream, well, duh—he *was* the Dream Rider.

If anyone killed the Rider, it would be *him*.

Chapter 47

Meeting Across the River

In Dream, Case waited beside the River of Souls, its dark waters shot through with the silver cords of dreamers. Yeshe had been right. She'd remembered the River and had found it again with no trouble. Will would search for her tonight. He might as well find her where they needed to start their journey.

A journey that might be the last time they ever saw each other. Despite her victory against Marell, she had no illusions about defeating him and Morrigan.

"Smart." Will's voice.

She turned. He walked toward her, wearing his Dream Rider costume again, but with the hood pulled back. Brian trotted beside him.

"Smart?" she said.

"Starting at the River. Saves us time. Guessed you would, so I came right here."

"Thought you liked me for my bod, not my brain."

"Smart girls are hot."

"You get better and better, Home Boy." They kissed, then held each other for a long while.

He stepped back. "So, how was your day? Better than mine, I hope."

She thought of what Marell had done to her. No, she wouldn't start with that. "Your SWAT team dropped by. Didn't have a lot to say."

"Then it *was* the place. I knew it." He described watching the raid by video link. "What happened? Why couldn't they find you?"

"Oh, they found us." She told of the team bursting into their room. "Couldn't see or hear us. I'm guessing Morrigan."

"What about Yeshe? Is he okay?"

His shoulders slumped as she described being brought before Marell, seeing Yeshe's body, trying to attack Morrigan. She had to force herself to tell him the rest. Of Marell invading her.

When she finished, he hugged her. "Oh god, Case. I'm so sorry. It's all my fault. You getting captured. The screwed-up raid."

"Hey, I'm okay. Kicked his butt. Made him stop. Don't understand how, but that scene on the mountain had something to do with it."

"How so?"

"Marell got inside my head—literally. I think I got inside his, too. That scene felt like a memory. *His* memory. Something that happened to him in one of his bodies in the past."

Will stared into the mists rolling over the black waters of the River. "We'll never know. Yeshe might have, but now we've lost him, too."

She'd never seen Will so down. She'd never seen him down at all. Well, okay, when she'd dumped him. But this was different. He seemed more than dejected. He seemed defeated. "Hey, buck up. At least now you know where they're holding us."

"Which does us no good with Stone's team arrested."

"Well, here's something else. I found Morrigan's rug. The one we think has her mojo. If Fader and I can get to it and destroy it—"

"If. *If* you can get to it. *If* you can destroy it. *If* that has any effect on her. If, if, if. So what? Even if all that works, I still have to defeat the new and improved Marell. Yeah, that'll happen."

"I stopped him. Maybe you can use that memory I saw against him."

"When I face him, I'll have trouble remembering my name let alone anything else."

"What do you mean?"

"Let me tell you about *my* day."

She listened as he told of the Hollow Boy's delivery of the letter—and his later suicide. "That's horrible," she whispered.

"Marell's a monster. And I can't stop him."

"Yes, you can. We can. Together."

He chuckled but with no humor. "You haven't heard what the letter said." He told her.

The square in front of City Hall? At the height of lunch hour? The busiest and most wide-open place in Toronto? She tried to find something positive to say, but failed. "Oh."

"Yeah—*oh*." He shook his head. "I don't know how I can *meet* him, let alone *defeat* him. He'll kill you and Fader because I'm too scared to step outside."

"You're not scared. You're just..." She stopped.

"Broken? Sick?" He shrugged. "Whatever. It doesn't matter. If I don't show up, you all die. If I do show up, Marell will kill me—and *then* you all die. Either way, he wins, we lose." He picked up a stone from the shore and flung it into the River.

That did it. She stepped in front of him. "So that's it? You're giving up? I die. Fader dies. Witch bitch wins. Evil villain rules world. And you're okay with that? You won't even *try* to stop it? You'll just hide at home feeling sorry for yourself?" She poked him in the chest. "I never took you for a quitter, Home Boy."

The muscles along his jaw tightened. His eyes narrowed. His mouth twitched, but he didn't speak. Then his face softened. He raised an eyebrow. "*That* was your inspirational speech?"

She folded her arms, glaring at him. "Yeah. It was." Her glare faded, and she shrugged. "Sounded better in my head."

He grinned. "No, no. It was good. Physical confrontation. Right in my face. List of people important to me. The over-arching danger to humanity. Closing with a challenging insult." He nodded. "Yeah, well done. Could've used a soundtrack. Maybe the 'Rocky' theme."

"Want me to go again while you hum along?"

"Sure. But more intensity this time. You kind of phoned it in."

"Asshole." But she grinned, too.

His smile faded. He took a deep breath. "Seriously, thanks. Don't worry. I get it. I'm not quitting. I just didn't want to get your hopes up."

She laughed. "No danger there. You convinced me. It's hopeless. Marell will kick your butt."

"I liked your other speech better."

"C'mon. Night's a wasting. The plan's the same. Fader and me, we'll take out Morrigan's rug—and hopefully Morrigan with it. You learn to astral project from Dream, meet Marell—"

"And get my butt kicked."

"And kick Marell's butt. Which means getting up this river, to start. You got that figured out yet?"

Grinning that grin she loved, he called out. "Nyx, bring us our ride for tonight."

Nyx's disembodied voice sounded. "On its way, oh great master. Oh, and girl? You will *love* this."

The mists over the river seemed to solidify. Something moved towards them, looming out of the darkness above the water. Something big.

Her eyes widened as she realized what it was. "Holy shit."

"Cool, eh?"

"Total. Tad on the overkill, maybe."

"Figured this might be our last date. I wanted to impress."

Coming straight toward them, sails billowing, a three-masted ship carved the waves. The ship was black, as were its sails. Those sails bore the moon, shooting comets, and drifting clouds of the Rider's costume. The high prow carried a carved figurehead of a leaping Doogle. On its flag, the hooded head of the Rider sat above two crossed skateboards. The Jolly Roger. Well, the Jolly

Rider.

A pirate ship. She was going on a pirate ship.

She slipped her hand into his. Together they waited on the banks of the River of Souls as the ship drew closer. "Impression made," she whispered.

Grinning, the old Will once more, he pulled the hood up on his costume. "M'lady, prepare to board *The Dream Runner*."

The Dream Runner sailed up river, pushed by a downstream wind. The dark waters, filled with silver cords, glowed as bright as the full moon above. On the left bank, the lands of Dream slid past, shining and sparkling. The right bank remained lost in mist and shadow.

Case, Will, and Brian stood on the forecastle of the ship. Or the *fo'c'sle* as Will had called it when she'd wanted to ride on "the front part." He'd told her more ship terms, which she promptly forgot.

"When did you become Sailor Guy?" She clutched the wooden railing, steadying herself against the ship's riding of the swells. She wondered if you could throw up in Dream.

"This afternoon."

"Seriously?"

"Yep. Once I'd decided what I wanted, I researched sailing ships so I could design and pilot one. Then I memorized it so everything was in my subconscious. Meaning with Nyx."

They weren't alone. Everywhere, the crew of *The Dream Runner* was busy doing, she assumed, whatever it took to sail the ship. On the deck. In the rigging (she'd remembered *that* term). Pulling on ropes attached to wooden things that held the sails.

"Your crew's a little sketchy."

"As in not to be trusted?"

"As in a sketch."

The crew resembled naked department store mannequins. They had human body parts (well, not *all* the body parts), but no faces or features or clothes. Only a single digit scrawled in black on their chests and backs distinguished each one.

"Uh, yeah. I was in a rush. No time for details. But they know their roles and how to sail this thing. I just give the orders." He called to the nearest faceless sailor, the digit "1" on its chest. "Hey, Number One! More speed, please."

Number One turned a blank face to Will, gave a snappy salute, then ran down the deck, waving hand signals to other sailors. Moments later, more sails were lowered.

"You're lucky with the wind."

"Last night, the wind was from downstream. I gambled it would be again. Worst case, we'd tack upstream. It would just take longer."

"Could've used a motor boat."

He wrinkled his nose. "Hey, trying to keep Dream green. Besides, not as cool."

She considered the mass of silver cords lighting the dark water from below. "So we're following my cord? Back to where I'm dreaming in the creepy hospital?"

"That's the plan. Right now, all the cords are together, so we don't need to know which is yours. But I'm guessing they'll split off near these Gray Lands, coming ashore at different spots."

"So how will we find mine then?"

Grinning, he pointed to a sleek shape pacing the ship, swimming with grace and ease, its triangular fin cutting the surface. She glimpsed a flash of black-and-white mottled skin before it disappeared into the next wave.

"Is that a dolphin?" she asked.

"Porpoise. Well, a modified porpoise."

"It's colored like a Doogle."

"It's a search porpoise."

"So, it's a...?"

"A Poogle. Didn't go with dolphins cuz I have Doogles with a 'D.' So I chose these guys—"

"Don't say it."

"—on *porpoise*."

She groaned but was glad to see him joking again. "Does he have a name?"

"She. No gender bias in my hiring. Her name is Beta. Bee for short. And it's time for Bee to go to work."

He held out his hand. A crystal sphere appeared on his palm with a "pop." A data ball, she now knew. She caught flashes of her face in the swirling cloud. A data ball for her.

"Hey, Bee!" Will called.

As the Poogle swam closer, Will tossed the ball. Bee caught it in her mouth with an acrobatic leap. Lights sparkled along her skin. With a burst of speed, Bee shot forward.

Turning again to Number One, Will pointed at Bee. "Follow that Poogle!"

The Dream Runner sailed on, up the River of Souls, following Bee the Poogle.

At first, Case saw no need for Bee. The shining cords of dreamers continued to flow down the center of the River unabated.

But soon, strands branched off from the main flow to disappear into the darkness on the right of the ship. A short time after, Bee turned as well, following a single slender cord. The ship listed to the side as it followed the Poogle.

My cord, she thought. *My link between this dream and where I lie dreaming, a prisoner in the hospital.*

Soon, they'd reach the Gray Lands. She shivered, remembering her visit to that desolate place during her battle with Marell. A visit that had almost become permanent.

As if echoing her fears, Bee slowed. The silver cord continued ahead, but the Poogle began swimming in circles. The ship slid by the porpoise. Before them, gray hills loomed out of the mist and darkness.

"Oh, crap!" Will cried, spinning around. "Number One, stop the ship! Or turn it. Or something. Uh, land, ho!"

"I don't think this thing has brakes, Home Boy."

"Hard to port!" Will called, as the mannequin crew scrambled to drop the sails.

She grabbed onto the railing just in time. The ship listed hard, throwing her, Will, and Brian against the railing. The *Dream Runner* continued to list, threatening to toss her or the contents of her stomach overboard. Finally, the ship righted itself, and she could stand again.

They glided now in calm waters along the shores of the Gray Lands. Ahead, her silver cord ran out of the River and up onto the rocky beach, disappearing into the mist that clothed this land. A chill and foul-smelling breeze stirred the mist, and through the swirling grayness, she glimpsed what lay inland. The little she saw only reminded her of her earlier visit. She shivered.

"You okay?"

"Yeah," she lied.

"Hey, you're not alone this time. And if things get bad here, you can wake up."

She shook her head. "No. If I wake up, my cord will disappear, and we'd be right back at the beginning. So let's do this before that happens."

A mannequin sailor rowed her, Will, and Brian ashore in a wooden dinghy, then rowed back, leaving them alone.

On the shore, a fresh fear seized her. A fear that she had never defeated Marell. *That* had been the dream. *This* was reality. He had won and sent her to this awful place to dwell here forever.

She clenched her fists, angry with herself. *Stop it. Hard Case time. I won. I beat him. And we'll beat him again, too*. "Okay, let's rock." She started forward, trying to psych herself up.

Will grabbed her arm, looking ahead. "Wait."

The mist lay thick along the shore, but as she stared, dim shapes appeared. Human figures. Figures moving toward them. Figures as gray as the land itself.

The Hollow Boys had come.

⸙

"Nyx!" Will called. "Shield. Sword. Now!" Both objects popped into existence, one in each of his hands. He moved in front of Case.

The Hollow Boys continued to emerge from the mist. Case counted ten. They walked at a slow but unwavering pace, their movements eerily synchronized. Ten right feet took a step. Ten left feet followed.

They wore what any street kid might wear. Torn, poorly fitting, mismatched clothes. But those clothes were gray. Their hair was gray. Their faces were gray, except for black, black eyes. Their faces... She swallowed. She knew these boys. Some were her friends—Link, Tumble, Slip. Some not. She'd lived with them on the streets. Before they'd disappeared. Before Marell had made them into Hollow Boys.

A thought tickled her. Something had happened today. Something about Hollow Boys. She searched her memories, trying to remember... What? Whatever it had been, it hid behind the horror of seeing Yeshe lying dead. Of fighting Marell for her own body. It hid, refusing to emerge.

The ten boys stopped, spread in a semi-circle before them, blocking any escape in front and on both sides. Behind lay the River. They were trapped.

Will raised his sword, ready to attack. The Hollow Boys clenched their fists.

No. They weren't making fists. They were moving their fingers.

She remembered. She grabbed Will's arm. "Wait!"

Will looked at her, then back at the Boys. "What? Why?"

"Something happened today. Marell freaked me out so much, I forgot." She told him of how Link the Hollow Boy had protected her and Fader from Stayne and Stryke. How he'd sent Case a hand signal.

"Like they're doing now," she finished, nodding at the ten boys blocking their way. "They're saying we're in danger."

Will had kept his eyes on their visitors as she talked. "Yeah. In danger from *them*. Case, I've come up against these dudes three times now. First time, they killed three of my Doogles. Then they tried to stop me from saving Harry from the Mara. And today, one of them delivered Marell's message—and then killed himself. They almost killed Brian that first night, too, but I—"

Brian leaped from Will's side, charging straight for the Hollow Boys.

"Brian! Stop!" Will cried, starting forward.

Too late. Brian had already reached the nearest Boy.

"Don't hurt him," Will cried.

But the Hollow Boy didn't attack Brian. And Brian didn't attack him. The Doogle sat curling and uncurling his tail while the Hollow Boy patted him. Brian licked the Boy's hand, then trotted back. Reaching Will, he spat out a data ball. Relieved but confused, Will picked it up. It collapsed into a flow of words and pictures.

"What's that?" Case asked.

"Brian's memories," Will said, staring at the images. He nodded at the gray blank-faced boys arrayed before them. "And theirs, too. From when Brian first met these guys." He lowered his sword. "They didn't kill my Doogles. Or attack Brian."

"What happened?"

"That night, I sent the Doogles to track four missing street kids. But Marell had already taken those kids over. The Doogles didn't find the kids in Dream—they found Marell. Snake-beast Marell."

"Marell killed the Doogles," Case said, understanding.

"And nearly killed Brian. The Hollow Boys were just bringing the Doogles back to me."

The gray boys nodded in unison. Brian curled and uncurled his tail.

"And when you fought the Mara?"

"They weren't blocking me from reaching Harry. They were blocking me from reaching the *Mara*." He stared at the Hollow Boys. "You were protecting me, weren't you?"

More nods.

"Holy crap," he said.

A small spark of hope ignited inside Case. "Yeah. They're on *our* side."

Chapter 48

I Died So I Could Haunt You

C ase, Will, and the Hollow Boys trudged through the Gray Lands in silence. Brian kept bounding ahead, then waiting for them to catch up. They were following Case's silver cord, which had remained visible to her even after it left the River of Souls.

The Hollow Boys formed a protective circle around her and Will as they walked. Will warned her against staring into their eyes, telling how he'd almost fallen into their depths in his first encounter. The Hollow Boys were strange, but she found the Gray Lands even stranger.

Its silver-gray landscape resembled a sheet of aluminum foil a giant had crumpled and then tried, unsuccessfully, to flatten again. The ground sloped up and down, right and left, at odd angles. Each slope was perfectly flat, meeting the next at a sharp crease like the facets on a huge silver jewel. The surface was gritty, giving traction on the slopes, but climbing was still difficult.

The Lands lay under a black sky. Or a black something. No moon, no stars. Just a deep and infinite darkness above in every direction. The only light came from the ground itself, casting the travelers in an upwards glow, as if they held flashlights below their faces.

Ready to tell spooky stories around a campfire. She remembered doing that with her mom and Fader every Halloween. *Already in a spooky story*, she thought, pushing memories of her mother away again.

Distracted, she didn't notice the end of the slope she climbed. She stumbled as she crested the rise, her foot coming down hard on the far side. The ground collapsed under her with a musical tinkling, like glass shattering on stone. She fell, rolling forward. Picking herself up, she looked back.

Will stood beside where she'd stumbled, staring down. He motioned to her.

She walked over. "No, it's okay. I'm fine. Thanks for ask—" She stopped.

In the previously unmarked surface, a jagged hole now gaped. If "hole" was even the correct term. It was as if the silver surface had crumbled in this spot, revealing what lay beneath. And what lay beneath was blackness. The same blackness, she knew with sudden insight, that lay above them.

Will tapped with his shoe at a sharp gray protrusion at the hole's edge. It broke with a chiming sound and disappeared into the black. It didn't *fall* into the hole. Rather, the blackness seemed to absorb it at the surface, as if the hole was not a hole, but a black pool. Peering at its edges, she saw no depth to the gray ground.

She shivered. They stood on a surface so thin it almost did not exist and yet was all that separated them from that blackness. A blackness of bottomless depth, she knew with the same flash of insight. A depth she could join if she stared a little longer, a little deeper, if she leaned forward, let herself fall, into the blackness, into the depths...

A voice pulled her back, broke the spell. A familiar voice.

"Gazing into the Nothing, like staring into the sun, is unwise, my young friends."

She shook herself, back in the moment again. Next to her, Will was rubbing his eyes. She guessed the call of the blackness had snared him, too.

Beside them, dressed in his maroon robes, stood a smiling Yeshe.

⁂

"Yeshe!" Will yelled. Leaping forward, he threw his arms around their rescuer. Or tried to. His arms passed through Yeshe, and then so did he. Will looked back at Case. She looked at him—*through* Yeshe.

She blinked. Yeshe was translucent. And glowing. He radiated a silver light as if he burned with an inner fire. He also hovered just above the gray surface.

"Yeshe," she said, "great to see you and all, but I don't understand. I saw your body. Morrigan said you were dead."

Yeshe's smile remained but tinged now with sadness. "Morrigan spoke true, young mistress. I *am* dead."

"Umm...what?" Will said.

"After the witch extracted Marell's missing piece, she granted me a surprising mercy. A quick death."

"You have a strange idea of mercy," Case said.

"I witnessed your noble attempt to avenge me. Thank you, but my death was inevitable. Its manner was not. Morrigan spared me certain torture at Marell's hands."

Case was confused. "You saw me go after Morrigan? After you died? How? And how are you here?"

Will nodded. "Yeah. What she said."

"My *body* died. My astral spirit—what you see before you—still clings to the physical plane."

"So that's why you're all glowy hover-boy?" she asked.

"I am pure spirit now. Before, some of my spirit always remained in my physical and mortal body. Now, it resides fully here, in my astral body. A pure spirit shines brighter."

"I thought a spirit couldn't stick around without a physical body," Will said.

"My years of astral travel allow me to stay connected to the physical world longer than most."

"Well, I'm glad you're here. And glad you found us when you did," Case said, looking at the black hole then quickly turning away.

"I sensed you entering Dream and followed your journey up the River to here. Your ship is beautiful, by the way, young master," he said, eyes twinkling. "You did not need my help until you encountered the Nothing." He nodded towards the hole.

"The *Nothing*?" she asked, struggling *not* to look at it again.

"The void. The emptiness beyond space and time. The Nothing was here before time began. It will remain when time ends."

Will scanned the bleak gray landscape. "We're walking through...nothing?"

"In a way. As Dreamers strive to reach the River of Souls, their cords create the Gray Lands, a bridge through the Nothing connecting the waking world and Dream. A brittle bridge, as you have seen."

"Are we safe, Yeshe?" Case asked.

"Yes, but tread lightly as you go. And go we should." Yeshe pointed to where Brian trotted ahead of them again, following Case's silver cord. "In a few hours, my spirit must depart this plane. Before that happens, we must reach the door through which the young mistress entered Dream tonight."

Will fell in beside Yeshe's floating form. Case walked on the monk's other side, now conscious of every step. The Hollow Boys once more encircled them as they traveled.

The grief that had seized Case at seeing Yeshe's body in the Weave room returned to her. "Yeshe, last night in Dream, why didn't you tell us right away you were dying?"

"Yeah," Will said. "I could've ordered the raid sooner."

"If I had told you, you would have ended that Dream journey to begin the raid. Morrigan's magical protections were in place weeks ago. Your raid would still have failed. I would still have died. No, I needed to guide you to the River of Souls last night, so you could devise a way to reach the Gray Lands tonight. As you have done. Now you have a chance to find the door tonight. As you must."

"And then?" Will asked.

"This is our last time together, my young friends. The last lesson I will give. After this, my spirit begins its journey to the Realms of the Dead."

"But you lived this long," Case said. "Can't you keep going somehow?"

"I owed my long life to an ability I developed. When we first met, you joked I was a vampire because I slept during the day. You struck near the truth. I became adept at draining astral energy from others. Never enough to endanger them. They recovered after a night's sleep."

"Our sleepy accountants," Will said. "That was you. You're an *astral* vampire."

"I had to be. To stay alive, to keep ahead of Morrigan and Marell. The witch extends her life with magicks. Marell by stealing bodies. I had no magicks. And I refused to take Marell's path."

"But can't you, you know, *borrow* a body for a while?" Will asked.

"No!" Yeshe said, his image flaring brighter. "I will not become a monster like Marell. I will not violate another person. I will not send their spirit to this place."

Will fell silent, the hope that had returned with Yeshe's appearance draining from his face. Case understood. Soon Will would be alone again, alone in his upcoming battle with Marell.

No. He wasn't alone. She and Fader were in this fight, too. And now they had the Hollow Boys on their side, though she couldn't imagine how they'd help.

She considered the silent boys surrounding them. "That's why they're here, isn't it? This is where Marell sends people he takes over." *Where he almost sent me.*

"Yes," Yeshe said. "Where he sends their spirits. And where those poor spirits remain forever."

"But I met them in Dream," Will said.

"They can travel to Dream," Yeshe replied, "but always they return here. Here and no farther. Never to their bodies in the waking world."

"Never?" Case related Link's attempt to communicate with her in the hospital. "Maybe he's finding his way back. Out of the Gray Lands. Could he recover from what Marell did to him? Could all of them?"

"I must confess ignorance," Yeshe said. "Marell is unique. So, therefore, are his victims. Could they recover?" He frowned. "Perhaps. But each would need to find their own door. The door through which Marell sent them here."

Will remained silent, seeming deep in thought.

"Yeshe, I was here today," Case said. "In the Gray Lands." She described her battle with Marell.

When she reached the vision of the boy on the litter, Will stopped walking. "Better idea," he said, waving his hand. A white rectangle appeared, her height and twice as wide. Brian trotted back to sit in front of the screen.

"Look at the screen—" Will said.

"And concentrate on what I saw. Yeah, you did this with Fader."

Images danced on the screen and sound came from invisible speakers as they watched the man and woman leaving the boy on the mountain, ignoring his cries. The screen disappeared.

She turned to Yeshe. "Was that him? The boy on the litter? Was that Marell?"

Yeshe frowned. "If so, why choose the body of a cripple?"

"I wondered that, too," she said. "Could that have been his *original* body? The one he was born into?"

Yeshe raised his eyebrows. "It would then be a very early memory for him and, therefore, a powerful one. Formative."

"And horrible," she said. "Abandoned by your own parents? Left to die..." She stopped. Will looked at her. She could almost read his mind. *Guess we're not the only ones with parent issues.*

"Wonder why they did it," Will said.

"They were terrified," she said. "Of him. I saw it in their faces."

"Perhaps," Yeshe offered, "his powers had begun to manifest. Perhaps he attempted taking over someone in their village, possibly even his parents. Self-preservation may have driven their actions."

Will nodded ahead. "Speaking of self-preservation..."

Fifty steps away, something big and black scrambled over the faceted landscape towards them. It was the size of a bear. But it wasn't a bear. It was a rat. A rat with blood-red eyes.

"A Mara," Yeshe said. "Marell has sent a Mara."

❧

"Nyx," Will said, "bring my sword—"

Yeshe stopped him with a raised hand. "Stay still. Stay silent," he whispered.

Will stopped talking. Beside him, Case held her breath. She tried to see the rat thing, but the Hollow Boys now blocked her view. The Boys had tightened their protective circle around the four travelers, facing outwards.

She heard the scrabbling of claws and a snuffling sound. She held her breath. The Mara began a slow circuit of the Hollow Boys, sniffing as it went. Through gaps between the Boys, she caught glimpses of the beast. Black snout and steel gray whiskers. Yellow incisors peeking from beneath a blood-red nose. And human hands on its front feet. She shivered.

The Mara finished circling the Boys. With a final sniff, it turned away, continuing in the direction it had been heading. Toward the River of Souls.

She let out the breath she'd been holding. The Hollow Boys expanded their circle again. Brian trotted ahead, following her silver cord once more. They fell into step behind the Doogle.

"What just happened?" she asked. "Why'd it ignore us?"

"A Mara feeds on astral spirits stolen from the bodies of Dreamers," Yeshe said.

"Yeah, well, it had a spirit snack box right here," Will said.

"For a Mara to feed, it must track a spirit back to its body. To do so, a silver cord must connect the spirit to a living body. My body is dead, so I have no cord. The bodies of the Hollow Boys still live, but Marell has broken their silver cords. That is why their spirits remain trapped here in the Gray Lands."

"They can't find their way back to their bodies," she said. "So neither can a Mara."

"But what about me and Case?"

"A Mara would seize on you—if it sensed your presence. Maras hunt by an astral sense of smell. To a Mara, a spirit disconnected from its body emits a foul odor. Much like a rotting corpse."

"So to a Mara, the Hollow Boys...stink?" Case said.

"Yes. By surrounding us, they prevented the creature from smelling you."

"Who do you think that Mara was after?" Will asked.

"Myself, I would guess," Yeshe said. "Marell wants you alive, young master. Yes, I overheard your tale of his letter. Until then, he also needs the young mistress alive. Plus, if he wishes to kill her, he can do so physically."

"Thanks for the reminder," Case muttered.

"But he knows you're dead, Yeshe. He has your body."

"I suspect he fears I have done what he would do in my situation. Take over another body. Force another poor soul into the Gray Lands." Yeshe's face was as grim as Case had ever seen it. "But I will not become the monster he is."

"Even to stop him?" Will asked. "You think I stand a chance against him without you? Alone? Outside? In a crowded public square? I don't even know how to astral project yet."

Yeshe's eyes narrowed. "I will *not* become Marell."

"Wait a minute," Case said. "Something's been bothering me about Marell's letter. Marell can attack anyone anywhere, right? Why does he need to *physically* meet Will? Why not use his astral voodoo to attack Will in his tower?"

Will turned to Yeshe. "Did you tell Marell about my problem? He'd *want* me outside then. I'll be easier to fight if I'm a quivering pile of jelly."

"But then he'd know you *can't* go outside," Case said. "Especially somewhere as public as City Hall. It makes no sense."

"I never told him of your challenges, young master. I do not believe he knows."

"Then like Case says, why not attack me in my tower?"

"Because he cannot," Yeshe replied. "I myself could not enter your tower home in my astral form. Something—or someone—inside your building *prevented* me."

Chapter 49

Spirit in the Night

"Wait...what?" Will said, his face showing the same shock Case felt at Yeshe's revelation.

"I assumed," Yeshe said, "you used your abilities to erect an astral shield for protection."

"I can't even astral project, let alone make some force-field thingy. And you *did* astral project into my building. You showed up in my bedroom that first night."

"And on the roof the next day," Case added.

"Both times, my body was *inside* your tower," Yeshe said. "I was not projecting from outside."

"But if Will isn't stopping Marell or you from projecting into his building, then who is?"

"Perhaps not who, but *what*. It is not the young master, and he is the only person with astral abilities in the Tower. I therefore propose that the effect is not emanating from a person, but rather an object."

"You do have an awful lot of stuff on all those floors, Home Boy."

"More than you know," Will said. "Ten floors are warehouses, packed with crates of artifacts from my parents' expeditions. Stuff they hadn't—" He stopped. "—*haven't* disposed of yet. Adi wants to give it to museums, sell it to collectors. Or something. I keep saying Mom and Dad will handle it when they..." He swallowed. "They'll handle it."

When they return. She knew talking about his parents was hard for him. But this was important. "Will, if something in your tower can block Marell, we can use it against him."

"If we can find it. Big if. I've lived there for years and never sensed anything force-fieldy."

"Maybe you need to be close. Like touching or holding it."

"If it's strong enough to shield an entire building, I'm guessing closeness is not required. But I'd still have to find it. Adi said Dad cataloged over a hundred thousand items."

"Holy crap, dude."

"Yeah. And I have until noon today."

"Can you narrow the search? Maybe it's tied to when you got your Dream powers. Something that came back from Peru."

"From my parents' last expedition? No luck there. I'm the only thing that came back."

"Yeah. Right. Sorry," she said, angry with herself for mentioning that trip. "Well, maybe you'll sense it when you can astral project."

"I do not think so," Yeshe said. "I could not detect the source of the shield from outside your tower. And once inside, I sensed no shield or astral force."

Will sighed. "We're back to me against Marell. Alone. Outside. In front of City Hall."

"But now we know *why* he needs you outside your building," she said. "And he doesn't know of your, uh, challenges." Which was the real problem. How would Will even show up at City Hall? And if he did, what condition would he be in? For sure, not ready to defeat a power like Marell.

She expected Will to raise those fears himself. But instead, he just nodded, seeming distracted. *Probably thinking about his parents, thanks to you, idiot.*

Beside and behind them, the Hollow Boys stopped. The Boys ahead of them parted, moving to the left and right, giving a view of what lay ahead.

Brian the Doogle now sat staring at a door. A door standing by itself in the gray faceted landscape. A black door, inside a white frame, decorated with posters of musical groups. Linkin Park. Alicia Keys. Rihanna. She recognized that door, those posters.

"Yours?" Will asked.

She nodded. This was her bedroom door in the apartment where she and Fader had lived with their mom. Her mom had let her paint it black, just before her mom—

She pushed that memory away. This had been her bedroom door...before. That's all. Before. A door that still sat in her subconscious as her gateway to Dream. What did that say about how important those memories were to her?

The Hollow Boys enclosed them again, circling the travelers and the door. Case walked around the door, Will behind her. The other side was identical. Same black paint. Same posters.

"Two sides?" Will asked Yeshe.

"One side. Step through either, and you will emerge where the young mistress sleeps."

"I'll be astral projecting."

"Yes, young master. But my time on this plane runs short. We must take that step now."

"We? You're coming with me?"

"Certainly. I will use my remaining time to begin teaching control of your astral form."

Case expected Will to be pleased at that, but he just nodded, still seeming distracted. "You'll both be stepping into the hospital, right?" she said. "Where Marell is? What if he attacks Will?"

Yeshe looked grim. "Then I will confront Marell, delay him while the young master returns to his own body."

"How do I do that?"

"Follow your silver cord. Back to where you lie sleeping in the white tower."

"Won't that shield thing stop Will, too?" she asked.

Yeshe hesitated. "Nothing can block a silver cord."

"You sure?" she said. "Because you don't sound sure."

"If I am wrong, the young master can wake himself, returning to his body in that manner."

And if Yeshe was wrong, Will would face Marell. Right now, having just learned to astral project. "Will, you don't have to do this."

Will shook his head. "No, I have to." He turned to Yeshe. "I'm stepping through the door."

"And I will be right behind you, young master."

"No, you won't," Will said. "You're staying here."

"*What?*" Case said. "Are you insane? You can't face Marell alone. With no training."

"Trained or not trained, I have no chance against him. He's fully restored, with over a century of experience." Will shrugged. "I'm a kid learning to drive."

She couldn't believe this. "So you're just giving up? Do you need the inspirational speech again? I'll even do the Rocky theme this time. Will, you can't quit."

He stepped closer to her. "I'm not quitting."

"I don't understand."

"I have a plan. For when I meet Marell."

"So share."

"I can't."

Now she was angry. She shoved him hard in the chest, pushing him away. "Why not? I'm in this, too, remember? So is Fader. Don't you trust me?"

"With my life. But if I tell you, and Marell pulls his your-body-is-my-body trick with you again..."

She understood. "Then he'd learn your big plan. Right. Sorry." She studied him, searching his face for hope. "Your plan—is it a good one?"

He grinned. "Good? It is freaking awesome! If, you know, it works."

"Great."

"And you and Fader are part of it. I need you to destroy Morrigan's rug."

"Count on it." She didn't know how she'd do that, let alone before Will faced Marell and Morrigan. Or if destroying the rug would even weaken Morrigan, but she didn't say that.

"Young master, I cannot advise this. Even in the short time I have left, I can still teach you much."

"How much time *do* you have left?" Will asked.

"Without a body, two hours perhaps. At most three."

"Perfect, because I do still need your help. But not for teaching me. Come over here, so Case can't hear." Will walked away, Yeshe following.

Unable to hear their words, she followed the discussion by body language. Whatever Will was selling, Yeshe wasn't buying. The monk kept shaking his head and waving his arms as if trying to shoo Will away. She'd never seen Yeshe that agitated.

But as Will continued to talk, Yeshe became still. Will stopped talking. He waited, watching the monk, biting his lip. Yeshe stood head down, wringing his hands, a rare display of inner turmoil for the placid monk.

Yeshe gave a great sigh. Pulling himself up tall, he regarded Will. And nodded. Will broke into a huge grin. He tried to hug the monk, but his arms passed through him again. Will stepped back. Yeshe bowed to Will, closed his eyes...

...and disappeared, winking out as if someone had flicked a light switch.

Case remembered seeing Yeshe's body, feeling her grief, hating herself for not saving him. Now he was gone again. Never to come back, he said. And he hadn't even said goodbye to her.

But she put on a tough face as Will walked over to her. "Dude knows how to make an exit."

"Hopefully, that wasn't his last."

She so wanted to know what Will had asked Yeshe to do, what his great plan was. But she bit back her questions. Instead, she tried to be Hard Case. "So? Later?"

He looked away, then at her. "Yeah. Later."

"Yeah."

"We can go out to a movie."

"Go *out*?"

"Hey, if I manage to face Marell, going out after should be a snap."

If you don't die, Home Boy. But she nodded, playing along. "Yeah, sure."

She let him pull her close. "I love you," he whispered.

Surprised, she leaned back, looking into his face.

He shook his head. "Sorry. Stupid thing to say. Stupid time to say it. But..." He took a breath. "But I may not have another chance to tell you."

"No. It's not stupid." She put her arms around his neck. "I love you, too." They kissed, a kiss that lasted forever, the way things can in a dream.

Then it was over.

He walked to the door. Nodding at the posters, he grinned at her. "We had very different taste in bands." Then he opened the door, stepped through...

And was gone.

I don't know if I'll have another chance to tell you.

She realized his earlier confidence about his "awesome plan" had been for her benefit. "You jerk. You probably don't even *have* a plan." She hugged herself. "Damn you, Home Boy, you're going to die." And she could do nothing about it.

No, that wasn't true. She could keep her promise. She could destroy Morrigan's rug.

Brian had disappeared when Will had. Only the Hollow Boys remained, encircling her in eerie silence.

"Sorry to cut this stimulating conversation short, guys, but I think I'll be going." She willed herself to wake up. As the Gray Lands faded from her dream vision, she caught a final image.

The Hollow Boys, their fingers all making the same twitching motions. A message for her. A message she knew from the streets.

Help us.

Will floated in the air, just below the ceiling of a room. A room in the abandoned hospital. He recognized it from the failed raid, but the room's occupant confirmed it. In a hospital bed along the far wall, Case lay curled up and sleeping. He stared down at his body. He glowed, not as brightly as Yeshe had in Dream this night, but a definite glow.

He'd done it. He was astral projecting. In the real world. His silver cord floated before him, disappearing through a wall. That, he assumed, was the direction of the Dream Rider tower where he himself lay sleeping.

He gazed at Case. A sudden longing seized him, pushing aside the thrill of his success. The hardest part of his plan had been leaving her in Dream. He'd wanted to stay there, stay with her. What he'd said had been true. They might never see each other again. His "awesome" plan was a long shot. He guessed she knew that.

He wanted to get closer. To see her face one more time. Perhaps for the last time. But he had no idea how to move.

Or maybe he did. No sooner had he formed the wish than he hovered above her. She stirred. Had she sensed him? That would be wonderful. He could go outside with her, be with her on the streets, in the city.

Assuming Marell didn't kill him today.

Case rubbed her eyes. She sat up, looking right at him. "Will," she said, shaking her head.

His heart leaped. She saw him! *Case! I'm here! I did it.*

She rose from the bed. And walked right through him.

At the boarded window, she peeked through a crack where early sunlight glowed. "Home Boy, wherever you are, your freaking awesome plan better work." She hugged herself. "Or I'll never talk to you again, dumbass."

His heart sank. She couldn't see him. She didn't know he was there. They wouldn't spend time outside together. *No big. I'll probably die today, anyway.*

With one last look at Case, he willed his astral form to turn away. Hovering before the door, he imagined himself on the other side.

And found himself in the hallway.

Man, this astral projection stuff is a snap. Who needs training or—

Pain seared his shoulder, like twin knives piercing his astral body. Something had seized him. He hurtled backwards down the hallway, pulled by the unrelenting grip on his shoulder.

He stopped. Or rather, whatever had grabbed him stopped. The pain ceased, and he dropped to the floor. He looked up.

A huge snake lay coiled in the corridor, its head swaying above him. The serpent glowed as he did. An astral spirit.

Marell.

Chapter 50

I Don't Want to Wake Up

F acing Marell again, Will's last remaining shred of confidence shriveled and died. Astral power radiated from the snake like heat from a blast furnace, a physical palpable force beating down on him. Beating him into submission.

Gazing at the beast, buffeted by its power, he knew he'd been right. He could never win in a fight against Marell.

Child, Marell whispered in his head, *we meet again.*

Will rose. He looked up to where the snake swayed above him. *Seriously? That's your opening line? Well, greetings, Captain Obvious.*

The beast reared, poised to strike. *You dare mock me? I can kill you where you stand. Seize your astral spirit. Rip it from your body. Expel it from this plane forever.*

Then rip away, Slither Belly. What're you waiting for?

The snake lowered its head. It coiled back as if now uncertain.

Will nodded. *Thought so. Killing my spirit's not the play, is it?*

Why not, child?

Because if you rip my spirit from my body, then my body dies. Where you can never reach it. Locked away in my tower behind my shield. He didn't know what Marell knew about the barrier Yeshe had described. But it couldn't hurt to let his enemy believe he'd created it. *And that's what you want, right? My body.*

Marell didn't answer.

It makes sense, Will said. *I have mountains of moola. A mind that comes pre-tuned to astral radio. And I'm young and healthy. And totally hot.*

He paused, waiting for a reaction to his claim of health. None came. Case was right. Marell didn't know about his problem. *Plus, if you take me over, you remove your last threat. I'm your perfect choice. It's the smart play.*

The snake moved closer. *Did you expect less? Did you truly think you could defeat me?*

Once, maybe. But not now. I feel your power. I can never fight you like this and win. Will shrugged. *Like you said, I'm just a kid.*

Then you will surrender yourself to me? Today? In the public square?

What choice did he have? *Yes. But only if you free Case and Fader. Unharmed.*

That miserable girl and her brother? The snake swayed. *Once you surrender, they will go free.*

Marell was lying. It was in the way he'd said "girl," as if spitting it. As if he detested even the word. Will remembered Case's vision of the boy left on the mountainside. If she *had* seen a hidden memory of Marell's, he'd never let her live. And Morrigan would never let Fader go.

But he nodded. *Then we have a deal. I'll see you at noon.*

If you do not appear, the girl and boy both die.

I'll be there.

The snake reared as if to strike. Will jumped back. Marell chuckled. *Not yet, boy.* The beast vanished. He was alone.

He glanced back toward Case's room. One last look? No. Seeing her but being unable to interact would only add to the helplessness that now filled him. Besides, he'd feel like a peeping tom.

Instead, he summoned his silver cord. The slim ribbon appeared again, sprouting from his chest. As he focused, his astral body rose, following the cord. In the next second, he passed through the hospital walls and found himself...

Outside.

Outside, hovering in an early morning June sky high above the hospital. The kid who couldn't take a step onto the street without collapsing into a trembling heap.

He was outside. And it was wonderful.

The sun colored the eastern sky. The sky. His rooftop park let him see sky, but not like this, not from horizon to horizon. The sky was so...*big*. The *world* was so big.

He drifted along, thrilling to being outside for the first time in eight years. Sure, he was in his astral body, not his real one, but that brought a bonus.

Flying.

He swooped and soared, circled and tumbled. Rose to the clouds and dove to skim the sparkling waves. Then he did it again.

Until he remembered what lay ahead that day. He let the pull of his cord take him. In an eyeblink, he flew from the hospital's suburban landscape to the edge of the Toronto skyline.

His Dream Rider tower came into sight, white and bright in the early daylight. Stretching his astral senses, he searched for the barrier Yeshe had encountered. But as the building loomed closer, he detected nothing. He flew up the outside of the tower to the penthouse floor. Still encountering no resistance, he passed through his bedroom windows. Inside, he lowered himself onto his sleeping form on his round bed.

And woke up.

The bedside clock showed 6:18 AM. Under six hours before he had to face Marell. A meeting that would decide not just his fate, but the fates of Case, Fader, and the entire world. Fates that depended on a kid who hadn't left home in eight years, two more kids who were prisoners, and a dead monk. Lying there, he realized how crazy his plan was. Long shot was an understatement.

But crazy was all he had.

One task remained. Closing his eyes, he rolled over...and tried to go back to sleep.

Case paced her hospital room. From the sunlight hitting her boarded window, she knew it was late morning, past eleven o'clock. Will was meeting Marell at noon, and she still needed to destroy Morrigan's rug.

At least Fader had done his job. She'd found a bottle of isopropyl alcohol under her pillow after Morrigan returned her here yesterday. Now she just had to escape her locked room.

And sneak into the Weave room. While avoiding Stayne and Stryke. And Morrigan. And Marell. In under an hour.

Sure. No problem.

And where was Fader? He had free run of the hospital, so why hadn't he come yet?

A key turned in the lock. That had to be Fader. She started towards the door as it swung open. She stopped. It wasn't Fader.

Morrigan entered. The witch wore high-waisted, narrow-legged, gray-green slacks and stiletto heels. Her arms were bare in a sleeveless white silk blouse, her dark green cape thrown back over her shoulders. Around her neck, she wore the triskelion amulet on its gold chain.

Case stepped back, then cursed herself for showing fear. Stopping two paces away, Morrigan folded her arms and smiled. For once, the smile seemed genuine.

Her heart fell. A happy Morrigan was bad news. "Why so cheerful? Did a puppy die?"

Morrigan chuckled. "Dreadful child, I smile because we will never meet again."

"Works for me."

"We're leaving this hovel. We will not return."

Leaving to meet Will. "We?"

Another smile. "Not you. Myself, Marell..." She paused, and her smile grew even broader. "...and your darling brother."

"No!" She stepped towards the witch. Morrigan's left arm flashed out, rune characters glowing on her pale skin. Case stopped. "You can't take him."

Inclining her head, Morrigan raised an eyebrow. "But I can. And I will. I am fond of the child. Now I will have him. And you will never see him again. But don't worry. I won't neglect you. I'll send Mister Stayne and Mister Stryke to play. Won't that be fun?"

Case stood there helpless, wanting to strike the witch but knowing better. The delicate hope to which she'd clung shattered against hard reality. She couldn't save the world. She couldn't save her brother. She couldn't even save herself.

When she remained silent, Morrigan shrugged. Walking to the door, she turned back. "Oh, one more thing. We will soon kill your boyfriend, too."

"Yeah? Good luck with that."

Morrigan smiled. She began to close the door.

"Wait!" Case cried.

The witch looked at her, one hand on the door.

Case couldn't say the words at first. She didn't want to say them. To say them meant admitting she'd lost. Will had lost. Morrigan and Marell had won. But she had no choice. She forced the words past her lips. "Take care of him," she whispered. "Fader. Take care of him."

Morrigan's eyes widened. A softness came over her features, the same look she'd worn standing beside Yeshe's body. She nodded, an almost invisible gesture, as if reluctant to acknowledge this connection they shared. "I give you my word."

With that, she turned and left, locking the door behind her. The clicking of her heels echoed down the hallway, fading into nothingness.

Case heard a car pull up. Running to the boarded window, she tried to peer through the cracks. She grabbed a board and yanked hard. It gave a little. Putting a leg up on the wall, she pulled with all her strength.

With a sudden squeal of nails, the board came free. She crashed back onto the floor. But she was on her feet again in a heartbeat, leaping to the window.

An orange and green taxi waited outside. Three figures walked toward it. Marell-Karmalov, Morrigan...

And Fader.

She screamed his name. Screamed it as loud as she could, screamed it until she was hoarse. But the window was closed behind the boards. Fader didn't hear. Or was bewitched again. Her brother slid into the rear seat without even a backwards glance. Marell and Morrigan got in on either side of him. The taxi drove away.

She sat on the bed, not remembering walking back to it. Fader was gone. She'd failed him again, as their mother had failed them. Fear ran icy fingers up her spine. She was alone now, truly alone. Stayne and Stryke were coming. This time, no one would stop them. She would die. Slowly. In agony. Alone.

A memory came to her. Of being five years old. Of being lost in a department store, separated from her mother. Lost and alone, surrounded by strangers. Lost and alone. She'd started crying. Then warm arms had surrounded her. Her mother had found her. She'd been only steps away at a clothes rack. But that moment of fear had stayed with Case to this day. That fear of being lost and alone. As she was now.

Slipping from the bed onto the floor, she hugged her knees to her chest. She rocked back and forth, whispering one word. "Mommy."

Footsteps sounded in the hall. Her head snapped up. The footsteps stopped outside her door. A key slid into the lock. Her guts clenched. She hadn't thought it would be so soon.

Stayne and Stryke had come to play.

William Jonathan Dreycott, seventeen years old, legendary Dream Rider, owner of one of the largest corporate empires on the planet, lay on his bed. It was 11:29 AM. He wore black jeans, a Springsteen t-shirt, and his favorite high tops.

He'd risen earlier to shower, shave, dress, and eat a light breakfast. He'd then lain down to wait. Wait for the time when he must leave the safety of his tower home. Leave to venture outside, into the streets to face a maniac who planned to steal his body.

His alarm sounded. 11:30 AM.

He rose and went downstairs to his studio. Passing his design table, he paused. The screen displayed the cover of the new Dream Rider issue, released into the world last night.

Released not by the normal distribution channels, shut down by Lawrence Kinland. Released instead by Will, in all popular downloadable formats. Released to the Dream Rider website and mailing list. To Rider online fan pages. To reviewers. To every online retailer and social media site that existed. To online newspapers.

Prominently displayed on the cover was the issue's price: *FREE*.

The screen also displayed the download totals for the issue, updating in real time. Will Dreycott watched expressionless as the total ticked upwards. Over one billion downloads since last night. One billion. And still rising.

On the wall, the video display showed the hospital room of Adrienne Ar-chambeault. She sat up in her bed, finally awake. She talked with a nurse, Laura at her side smiling.

Adi, his friend and confidante, his surrogate mother since his parents' disappearance. Adi, whose life had hovered on the gray borderland of death for the past two days. She was back.

His phone sat on his desk, the video app displayed. He needed only to tap it for her to see him, to talk to her. He ignored the phone. He ignored the video screen. He ignored Adi. Turning his back on her, he left his studio.

He took an elevator to his private underground garage. His driver, Jimmy, greeted him and held open the back door of the limousine. Will Dreycott did not reply. He got in. Jimmy drove out of the underground and onto the city streets.

Back in the studio, the Dream Rider download count continued to display. The total ticked higher and higher, flashing now unseen on the screen below the title of the issue:

Final Issue!

THE DEATH OF THE DREAM RIDER

Chapter 51

Brilliant Disguise

Case stood frozen, watching the door handle turn. *Snap out of it*, she swore at herself. She had only one chance, and it wasn't waiting to die.

Grabbing the bottle of alcohol, she shoved it into her back pocket. She ran to the door, stopping three paces away. Close enough for surprise but far enough to get up speed. Dropping into a crouch, she tensed to charge when the door opened. Charge past the two ghouls before they could stop her. She hoped.

The door swung open. She charged.

Straight into a pack of Hollow Boys.

She slammed into the boy at the front, throwing him into the ones behind. They all collapsed in a heap in the hallway, Case on top.

Her mind raced. These boys were bringing her to Stayne and Stryke so they could torture and kill her. She had to get up. She had to get away.

A hand grabbed her as she tried to stand. She smashed a fist hard into the boy's face. He cried out and let go. Jumping up, she leaped over more grasping hands, landing clear of the pile of bodies. She sprinted away down the corridor.

"Case! Wait!" a voice called from behind her.

A Hollow Boy speaking? Calling her by name? She stopped running. She turned but kept backing away.

Outside her room, six—no, seven—Hollow Boys stood rubbing various body parts. Link, the one she'd punched, rubbed his jaw. But he was grinning. "Hey, Hard Case, hold up. We're here to rescue you."

Jimmy pulled the limo up in front of City Hall behind a line of food trucks. Lowering the privacy partition, he looked back to where his employer, Will Dreycott, sat. "We're here, sir," he said, knowing he stated the obvious.

Will just nodded, expressionless and silent. Staring out the tinted windows at the crowds flowing across the square, he made no move to get out.

Nor did Jimmy expect him to. He knew of Will's struggle with going outside.

Which made this destination even more unusual.

Nathan Phillips Square was the largest public square in Canada, a twelve-acre rectangle in the middle of downtown. Driving Will wasn't a full-time job. Jimmy also gave city tours to visitors. The square was a popular destination, so he'd studied up on it.

Directly opposite the limo in the south-east corner sat a rectangular reflecting pool. The pool was a favorite lunch spot for office workers in the summer and a skating rink in the winter. Beside the pool stood the huge TORONTO sign, a popular photo site for tourists.

A permanent stage in the far corner hosted free concerts. One was happening today, judging from the music and crowd. Nearby, a tranquil peace garden offered a cool green respite from the white concrete covering most of the space.

The higher buildings of that area of downtown surrounded the entire square. To Jimmy, this place felt like a small village nestled amidst mountain peaks of steel and glass.

The square always had something going on. It was busy day and night, year-round. Just as it was now. The weather today, sunny but mild for mid-June, made the square even busier than usual.

In short, the square was the last place he'd expect Will to visit.

Jimmy shrugged mentally. He figured the kid just wanted to get outside for a change, even if it was inside a car. He figured Will wanted to see how normal people lived.

What he hadn't figured on was Will opening the limo door and stepping outside.

Panicked, Jimmy fumbled at his door handle. If the kid had a meltdown on his watch, he'd lose his job. But more than that, he liked Will. He didn't want something bad happening to him. Jumping out of the limo, he yelled over the car roof. "Mr. Dreycott!"

Will was halfway across the grass strip bordering the square on this side. Stopping, he stared back at Jimmy. The kid didn't look scared. He didn't look like he was having a panic attack.

Jimmy swallowed. The kid didn't look like he felt anything. Will's face was blank, devoid of any emotion.

"Should I wait, sir?" Jimmy asked, at a loss for what else to say. Not that he could wait here. A cop would move him along any minute now.

Will shook his head.

Shit. What was wrong? Why wasn't Will talking? And how was he handling being outside in such a busy place? "Do you want me to pick you up later?"

Will nodded. He pointed one finger down, then flashed ten fingers. Once.

Twice.

"Pick you up here in twenty minutes?"

Will nodded again, then walked into the mass of people swarming the square.

Jimmy watched him disappear into the crowd. He checked the time, noting when he needed to return. He shrugged and got back into the car. The kid was managing. Maybe he was testing out a new anxiety drug.

Sure. That had to be it. Jimmy pulled away from the curb. *Well, kid, I hope things work out for you here.*

Case walked back to the boys. She knew most of them—Link, Slip, Tumble, Riddle, Zapper. She stopped two paces away, scanning their faces. No one made any move towards her. They just stood there grinning.

"You're here to *rescue* me?"

Link shrugged. "Yeah, well, that was the plan. But you kind of rescued yourself."

"Hey, we opened the door," Slip added. "We should get props for that."

"Wait. Back up," she said. "How are you guys...you again? Marell took you over."

"Is that the creep's name?" Link said. "That guy in our heads? Yeah, he did. Each of us."

Link said all the boys had the same story. Snatched off the streets by Stayne and Stryke. Held prisoner until Marell took them over, one by one. "Next thing I knew, I wasn't..." Link frowned. "I wasn't *me* anymore. I was, like, split in two. Half of me was still in my body, but I couldn't control it. And my other half was in this weird gray place."

"We were all there," Slip said. "Together."

The Gray Lands, she thought. "But how are you back to normal?" She kept looking around, alert for Stayne or Stryke.

The boys exchanged glances. "Last night," Link said, "we were in that gray place, and we met *you* and—" He hesitated. "You won't believe me."

"Try me."

"The Dream Rider. You know—"

"The comic book guy," Slip interrupted.

"We'd met him before," Link said.

"You got a superhero boyfriend now, Hard Case?" Slip asked with a grin.

"Focus, Slip," she said. "Yeah, I know him. And, yeah, we met you last night in that place."

"He's real?" Link said.

"Long story, and we don't have time. What happened?"

"That old dude in the robes. The one with you and the Rider last night."

Yeshe, she thought.

"After you and the Rider disappeared, that old guy came back. He led each of us to…" Link hesitated again. "To a door." He shrugged. "When we went through our doors, we woke up. And we were back. Back to normal."

They each would need to find their own door. The door through which Marell sent them into these lands. Yeshe's words last night.

Yeshe had led them to their doors. Was that what Will had asked him to do? Or was there more?

"He told us to help you escape," Link said. "That you'd know what to do next."

She nodded, pretending she'd expected to command her own army today.

"So… what do we do?" Slip asked.

"Case, let's blow this pop stand," Link pleaded. "Let's get out of here."

She shook her head. "I'm not leaving. Something I gotta do. I can't make you stay, but I could use your help."

"With what?" Link asked.

"Stopping Marell."

Link looked at the rest of the boys. They all nodded. "We're in. What's the plan?"

"Arson."

They grinned. "Cool," Slip said. "Where do we start?"

"We need to get to the room with Morrigan's rug—" She broke off.

At the far end of the corridor in which they stood, a movement caught her eye. A tall figure in black turned the corner from the shorter hall leading to the Weave Room.

Stayne's eyes went wide. Screaming a wordless scream, he ran towards them, gleaming blades slipping into his hands.

"Run!" she cried.

Morrigan stood in the center of the square, between Marell in Karmalov's body and young Fader. Together, they waited for the boy from the white tower. She smiled down at Fader, and he smiled back. She'd redrawn her runes on him, after discovering they'd again disappeared from his skin. He seemed under her complete control once more.

People scurried past them, oblivious. What did they see when they regarded the three strangers standing in their midst? Father, mother, and child? A family? Posing for a photograph, perhaps?

She smiled at that. A family. Finally, she would have her family. A real one. She stroked Fader's hair. With a real child this time, not those empty Hollow Boys.

"It's past noon," Marell rasped, scanning the crowds, his fingers tapping against his legs. "Where is he?"

Her hand strayed to her amulet, a sudden fear arising. Was the boy not going to show? She should not have given that horrid girl to Stayne and Stryke yet. What if Marell needed the waif to draw out the Dreycott boy?

Wait. There. She caught a glimpse through the passing throngs. Yes.

The boy walked toward them from the street. He walked slowly. Understandable. He walked to his death. But he had come.

She had a momentary thought. Marell had faced the Dreycott boy's astral spirit twice now. Why had he not sensed the boy's approach, considering how close he was? The boy drew closer, and the thought flew away as she focused on the cloaking spell to hide their little party from passersby.

This would end soon. Stayne and Stryke would join them, bringing the Weave and having disposed of the girl.

And then she would start a new life. She squeezed Fader's shoulder. With her family.

Case ran, the recovered Hollow Boys behind her. Her prisoner room sat on the long south hall, near the middle. The Weave Room with Morrigan's rug was in the north-west corner.

Three steps brought her to the middle hall. She took the corner at full speed, racing toward the long north side corridor, the boys on her heels, Slip the closest. They had to keep ahead of Stayne. None of them stood a chance against those knives. And Stryke was somewhere.

Stryke. Crap.

She pulled up at the corner to the long hall.

Slip didn't. "C'mon," he cried, running past her into the corridor. "I know the way!"

"Slip, stop!" she cried, grabbing for him and missing. Swearing, she jumped into the hall to pull him back.

Too late. Slip grunted, then crumpled to the floor. Halfway down the corridor, Stryke lowered his slingshot, chuckling.

Case knelt beside Slip. She shook him. Slip didn't move. Blood ran from his ruined right eye. Slip was dead.

"Didn't miss, did I?" Stryke called, grinning.

Behind him, at the far end of the hall, Stayne appeared. The taller man positioned himself outside the Weave Room.

Shoving away Slip's death and her own fury, she forced herself to think. She had to destroy the rug before time ran out for Will. The two ghouls were guarding the rug, probably on orders from Morrigan. Or their own self-interest—the thing had restored a dead Stayne. At least Stayne couldn't ambush them from behind. But now she had to get through both creeps to reach the rug.

Stryke pulled another steel ball from his pocket.

Get up! Her Voice was back.

She got up.

Run!

Case looked at Slip's dead body. She looked at the Hollow Boys peering around the corner. She looked at Stryke slipping the steel ball into his sling.

Run!

She ran.

Not that way!

Ignoring her Voice, Case charged Stryke. The little man's mouth went wide. His slingshot flashed up, aimed at her head.

In the public square, the man who called himself Marell watched the boy from the white tower approach. Coming to surrender himself to his master.

Many, many years ago, Marell had worn another name, another body. That name he had long forgotten. That body he never had.

A cripple's body. A body drugged and left to die on a mountain in the winter's snow. Left by his own parents. Because of his power. A power he had tried to use to escape that broken vessel. A power that had made his parents and their entire village fear him. And try to kill him.

But he did not die that day. The approach of death on that mountain brought him new strength. That day, he learned how to let his spirit fully roam free. And roam he had.

His spirit caught his parents as they descended the mountain. Attacking his father, he expelled the old man's spirit and seized his body. A body he then used to strangle his own mother. He returned to the village in his father's body, a vessel he soon discarded for a younger one.

And so his new life had begun.

A life that had led him here, to this place, to this moment. The moment when he would become supreme. In a young strong body attuned to the astral planes and with riches and power.

The boy stopped before him. Morrigan muttered something, no doubt activating her cloaking spell. Marell stepped forward, considering this child. Odd. He knew the taste of the boy's astral spirit, yet he could barely sense it. Perhaps the boy had taken opiates, to quell his fear, to dull his senses to his coming death.

Marell shrugged. No matter. Drugs could not save the child. Focusing his astral form, he leaped from Karmalov.

And into the boy from the white tower.

Case's Voice was not happy with her. *Idiot!* her Voice cried as she charged Stryke.

Just help me! she cried back. She was ten steps from the little man.

Left!

She ducked left. Stryke's shot ticked her right ear. He fumbled another ball into his sling. She was six steps away.

Right!

She dodged right. Another miss. He raised the sling again.

Dive!

She dove, slamming into Stryke even as his third shot grazed her cheek. They hit the floor hard, her on top. Screaming, Stryke dropped his slingshot and clawed at her eyes. She drove the heel of her right hand up into his chin, snapping his head back. His skull smashed into the tiled floor with a sickening crunch. Stryke went limp, his head lolling to one side.

She leaped up. Stayne leaned against the wall outside the Weave Room, shaking his head. Sighing, he straightened, his knives dropping into his hands again.

Now run away!

Not happening. I have to get into that room.

I can't help you fight him.

Her heart sank. She understood. Her mysterious Voice couldn't help in a fight with Stayne and his knives. She couldn't dodge that close. Not in time.

Footsteps behind her made her turn. The Hollow Boys stood there. Link knelt beside Slip's body. Standing, he started forward, his face grim.

She held up a hand. "No! Stay back. Let me handle this." She wouldn't let anyone else die.

Stayne smiled, strolling toward her. He was twenty paces away. "Handle this?

Handle *me*? Ah, my pretty, you cannot save yourself. And those children cannot save you. At last, you and I will play."

She nodded at Stryke's still form. "Yeah? Your buddy didn't much enjoy the way I play."

Stayne sneered. "It requires no skill to defeat that fool. Come. Let us see how you fare against my darlings." He beckoned to her with his knives. "Or do you think you can defeat me, too? A girl? Unarmed?" He smiled. "I do not like your chances."

Unarmed? She scanned the floor. There. And there.

Snatching up both objects, she straightened. Ten paces away, Stayne stopped. His face fell. He stepped back.

She slipped the steel ball into the slingshot. "How do you like my chances now, creep?"

Marell's astral spirit encountered no resistance entering the Dreycott boy. That was unexpected. But stranger still, once inside he could still not detect the child's spirit. He could not detect *any* spirit. Which was impossible. How had the boy come here? Every physical body needed an astral body to activate it. So where was the spirit controlling this body?

There.

Marell received another shock. A hidden spirit. One lying quiescent, so still, so calm that even he, Marell, had not detected it. Only one person he'd ever known could hide like that. But that was impossible.

The spirit took shape, took a form. A familiar form—that of an aged Tibetan monk in maroon robes.

Marell cried out. *But you are dead. How...?*

Yeshe's astral form smiled. *A parting gift from the young master—the use of his body so I might remain on this plane a while longer. In return, I have brought his body here, now, as you so ordered.*

Marell understood. He chuckled. *You took over the boy, killed his spirit, and stole his body. Now you come to battle me. Old fool, you cannot defeat me.*

The young master is very much alive. And neither he nor I plan to fight you.

I do not understand. Where is the boy? Where is his spirit?

Another smile. *Elsewhere.*

Marell lost patience. *Enough! Wherever he is, I will destroy him. Just as I will finish you. This is my body, old man.*

And we wish you to have it. And so, I will say...goodbye.

Startled, Marell watched as Yeshe's astral form faded. The monk was leaving this body. Leaving it to him. He had won.

But even as he thrilled in his victory, a disembodied voice reached him. The voice of the monk.

Now, young master! Yeshe called. *Step through your door!*

Chapter 52

He Dreams He's Awake

Will was in Dream. He'd been in Dream since just after six o'clock that morning. He'd purposely fallen back to sleep after returning to his body from his first astral projection. After facing Marell, who he would soon face in the flesh.

Assuming Yeshe kept his promise.

Once asleep, Will had sailed the River of Souls again, following his own silver cord this time, not Case's. He'd journeyed through the Gray Lands once more, to the destination that stood before him now.

His own door. The door leading from Dream to his body in the waking world. To where he was sleeping.

Well, no. If his plan was working, he wasn't *sleeping*.

He was sleep*walking*.

His door was a deep blue and covered with July Talk and Metric posters. Beside it, Nyx floated in her swirling cloud. "You're insane," she said.

"Why? I've done this a zillion times. I memorize something, then pull it up from my subconscious by using a keyword. That's how my Doogles work. My sword, my shield. The big cool sailing ship. You."

"You mean *I* pull it from your subconscious. But in all your examples, I pull things *into* Dream that you memorized while *awake*."

"So?"

"So you're planning the *reverse*, dumbass. Pulling something into your waking mind that you memorized in Dream. And you'll be trying that as your waking mind goes into Mister Meltdown mode."

He shifted his feet, not looking at her. "It'll work." He hoped he sounded more confident than he felt.

"You can't bluff your own subconscious. Will, I'm worried."

He swallowed. "You've never called me Will."

"I've never been this worried."

"All that means is, subconsciously, *I'm* worried."

Nyx snorted. "You should be. It's a stupid plan."

"Thank you *so* much. You're helping a bunch. Now shut up."

"Tsk, tsk. Is that any way to speak—" Nyx broke off, her head cocked as if listening. "Incoming call. I think the one you're expecting."

Yeshe's glowing astral form appeared beside Will's door. "Now, young master!" Yeshe cried. "Step through the door!"

Running to the door, Will yanked it open.

"Don't forget the keyword!" Nyx called.

"I won't!" He stepped through the doorway.

As Dream faded from his mind, he whispered the keyword. The word to pull the memorized scene from his subconscious into his about-to-be-awake mind.

"Mountainside," he whispered.

And woke up.

＊

Will woke to find himself outside. Outside in the most public place he could imagine, surrounded by more people than he'd seen in years.

He also woke to find Marell in his mind, coiled like a serpent.

Having expected both situations did not stop his mind reacting to them. A full-blown panic attack hit him. His heart raced. He gasped for breath. Sweat drenched him. He wanted to throw up. Tremors shook his whole body.

Perfect. So far, everything was going according to plan.

Through his panic, he battled to keep one thought filling his waking mind. A vision brought back from Dream. A vision stronger than any he'd ever had in Dream. Strengthened by the millions of people who had now read the free copy of the final Dream Rider issue. People around the world, in places where millions slept and dreamed of the Rider even now.

Making the Rider stronger. Making this vision stronger.

A vision of a lonely mountainside where a crippled boy lay abandoned in the snow.

His hold on his mind and body slipped away, the battle lost against both Marell and his panic attack. He collapsed to the white concrete of the square. But as he lay there, with his last bit of free will, he turned his head.

Turned it *just* so.

Turned it so his view of the square aligned with the vision in his mind.

＊

Marell sensed Yeshe's astral spirit leave the boy even as he sensed the boy's spirit appear. Where had the boy been hiding? Why this charade with the monk? Marell steeled himself, expecting an attack. But none came.

He had won. This body was his. This mind was his. Now to expel the boy's spirit—

He reeled back, losing his grip on both this mind and body. The boy was having a breakdown. And now inside the child, he was experiencing it, too. Sweat poured from him. He shook. He trembled. He gasped for breath. His heart pounded. He collapsed to the concrete. Desperate, he grasped for the boy's mind, trying to seize control again. But this mind thrashed like an animal in its death throes, its panicked gyrations so violent he could find no grip.

The boy turned his head—*their* head.

A view of the square swam before him. Across the bright white concrete, a pool of water lay. Beyond that stood evergreens of a garden space. And behind them all, a backdrop of skyscrapers rose towering into a clouded sky.

But overlaying that view was another. And as that vision came into focus, the boy's panic became Marell's own.

"No!" he screamed, recoiling in sudden terror.

For this vision was from his past, a past he had tried to forget for all his long existence. In this vision, the white concrete on which he lay became snow. The reflecting pool became a mountain lake, the garden space a forest of evergreens. And the office towers became the mountain peaks of his home. The home where he'd been born into a broken body. Where his own parents had left him to die in the place that now lay before his vision.

The horror of that night flooded back to him. Overcome by both his own terror and the panic consuming the boy, Marell fled. Fled from the body and mind he had planned to make his own.

But although his spirit escaped the boy, both fears still gripped him. He now carried the boy's fear of this open space in which his spirit now hovered. And the mountainside vision of his past still hung before his astral mind.

Panicked, desperate, seized by terror, he sought a haven.

Karmalov's body stood beside Morrigan. Yes! He knew that vessel. And it was empty, ready for his return. He would be safe there. But as he tried to enter, another spirit repulsed him.

I hold this body now, Marell, Yeshe said. *You cannot enter.*

Marell's spirit screamed in frustration. Had he been in control of himself, he could have expelled the monk as if brushing away a fly. But terror and panic still consumed him, the boy's and his own. He fled from Karmalov and from Yeshe.

But to where? Where lay safety?

Morrigan's amulet hung around her pale neck. He had mocked her when she'd worn it today in case he might need it as a refuge. Now she no longer seemed so foolish.

Still fighting the panic threatening to overwhelm him, he flew toward the amulet.

Case crept forward, slingshot raised. Stryke backed away, his knives still in his hands.

Hey, Voice! she called in her mind. *Could use some help here.*

I told you. I can't help against him.

If you can tell me when to dodge, *then you can tell me when to* shoot.

Silence. Had her Voice disappeared again? Then it answered. *Oh! Yeah! That's brilliant.*

Just focus!

Get ready to fire. Pull the sling back more. Harder. Aim at his head.

She brought the slingshot to bear on Stayne's head. His eyebrows shot up. Still backing away, he danced left and right, bobbing and weaving.

She continued to advance. *He'll reach the Weave Room soon. Once he's inside, he'll lock the door.*

Wait, her Voice replied.

Stayne danced left. Then right. Then left. He was almost at the Weave Room. Her arm ached from holding the sling back.

Wait...

I can't wait!

Stayne danced left. Left again. Right. Left. The door was now beside him.

Now!

Case let her shot go. Stayne danced right...

Right into her shot.

The ball bearing caught Stayne between his eyes. His head snapped back. He stiffened. The knives dropped from his hands. For a breath, his body stood rigid as if frozen to the spot. Then the ghoul collapsed to the floor and lay still.

Case ran forward.

Be careful! cried her Voice.

No time for careful. Will needs me. Fader needs me.

She leaped over Stayne's body and into the Weave room. The rug still lay between the two hospital beds. The nearest bed was empty, but Yeshe's body remained on the other. She ran to the rug, trying to ignore the dead monk. Torches burned in sconces on the walls.

The former Hollow Boys poured into the room. "Bring me a torch," she called, pulling the bottle of alcohol from her back pocket. She poured it onto the rug, back and forth, up and down, praying there was enough.

Link brought a torch. He stared at Yeshe. "Hey, that's the old dude from our dream."

"Long story." Grabbing the torch, she touched it to the corner of the rug.

Nothing happened. The fire didn't catch. She swore, running the torch over the rug. How could she destroy it if it wouldn't burn? Maybe if she—

Flames exploded from the rug with a deafening roar, leaping straight up to the ceiling. She and the boys jumped back, from both the sudden blaze...and what emerged from it.

Human figures. Translucent, floating in the air. Women. Women dressed in long white robes, their hoods thrown back, chanting. Case counted them. Twelve women, each standing with their back to a tall pole, their hands clasped behind them.

Case swallowed. No. Not clasped. Tied. The women were bound to those poles. A thirteenth pole stood empty.

As she watched, flames licked the women's robes. Not the flames of the burning rug. Flames from this vision. The robes caught fire. The women's chants became screams. They were burning. Burning alive.

Case turned away, unable to watch. The screaming stopped. She looked back. The women were gone. The fire was gone. Of the rug, only a charred circle on the floor remained. What had she seen? A vision from the past? The scene had carried the weight of time. And truth.

The wail of police sirens reached her. Had the cops finally realized their mistake from yesterday? She hurried back to the hallway. Where Stayne and Stryke had fallen lay two piles of ashes. Both dead, and for real this time. *Good riddance*.

She thought of Will. *Okay, Home Boy. I've done what I can.*

She prayed that destroying the rug would hurt Morrigan's magic. Hurt Morrigan, too. Hurt her bad. Then she remembered the women in the vision burning, screaming. No, she wouldn't wish that on anyone.

Not even Morrigan.

The sirens were outside now. Leading the restored Hollow Boys, she ran outside, for once happy to see the police. She needed a ride.

Morrigan screamed. The Weave was burning. She felt it. In her flesh. In her bones. In her soul.

Though half the city away, she remained connected to the rug, attached to the spells written in it. Written centuries ago in runes sewn with thread. Sewn by her mother and her coven into the wool they used to weave the rug.

Now the Weave was burning. Hundreds of spells destroyed. Destroyed, too, the last traces of her sisters, the small part of them that had lived on in their woven spells.

The Weave burned. And Morrigan felt as if she burned, too. As her coven had burned. "My sisters," she whispered. "I have failed you again."

As the rug and its stored magicks died, her power drained from her. She looked down. The skin on her hands and arms was drying, wrinkling, splotching. Pain stabbed her heart. Gasping for breath, she collapsed onto the concrete.

The spells of the Weave that had sustained her long life were gone. She was dying.

But she had another source of stored magicks. Fighting her own death throes, she forced her dying body to respond. A withered hand crawled up her chest to the triskelion amulet. She touched it, croaking the release spell in Manx.

The spells in the amulet flowed into her like a river filling a lake. Her strength returned. Her skin smoothed, cleared, tightened.

She pushed herself to her knees. Several people nearby stared. She swore. Her cloaking spell had died with the Weave. If her falling hadn't attracted attention, the boy from the white tower would have. He lay on the concrete, sweat-soaked and trembling.

Hands gripped her arm, helping her stand. Fader stood beside her, worry on his face. "Are you okay?"

She stroked his hair. "I'm fine, child. I—"

Marell's cries brought her back to the moment. She had tracked his spirit when he entered the Dreycott boy. But the burning of the Weave had broken her focus.

Marell's spirit now hung in the air before her. What had happened? Why had he not seized the Dreycott boy? If not the boy, why had he not returned to Karmalov? Stranger still, Marell's spirit no longer radiated his customary aura of power. Instead, it exuded only terror. Pure terror.

Morrigan! he screamed in her mind. *I need the amulet. Take me into it.*

The amulet he had mocked her for bringing? The amulet without which she would have died just now? Now he cried for her amulet?

The Weave is gone. The amulet is empty. I need its magicks myself.

Woman, return its spells! Now!

Anger flared in her. All Marell's slights rose in her memory, cutting her again like fresh wounds. For years, she had followed him, sustained him, procured his hosts, aided him in his quest. She had found Yeshe, recovered the lost fragment, made Marell complete again. And what had she received in return? His arrogance. His contempt. His orders.

I am not your servant, Marell. I am your equal.

Return the spells, witch! Or I die.

Return them, and I die. Of your life or mine, I choose mine.

Marell gave an impotent scream of rage. *Then I choose another vessel.*

Another vessel? Her? Did he mean to take her over? She began a protection spell, feeling the runes tingle on her skin. But no attack came.

Beside her, Fader stiffened, his eyes wide.

Fury seized her. "No! Not the child!" She summoned the lioness spell, still fresh in her mind from its use on the monk. She cast it into Fader. Inside the boy, the lioness hunted the same spirit it had sought in Yeshe.

It hunted Marell.

And when it found Marell in Fader, it performed the same task it had in Yeshe. It seized that spirit in its magical jaws and leaped from the boy.

Morrigan caught the lioness mid-leap in the air between her and Fader. Cupping the spell beast in one hand, she raised it to her eyes. Marell's astral spirit, a coiled black serpent, writhed in the lioness's grip. Touching the empty amulet with her other hand, she spoke a command. The lioness leaped into the amulet, carrying Marell's spirit with it.

Thank you, my love! Marell cried from inside the amulet.

I warned you, she replied. *Many times, I warned you. Not the child!* Ripping the amulet from around her neck, she dropped it to the concrete.

And crushed it under her heel.

Marell screamed in her head. Before her magical vision, a cloud of smoke rose from the pieces of the broken amulet. The cloud coalesced into a face. Marell's face. The one he had worn as a crippled child. And then the cloud blew away. A voice called her name, then that too was gone.

Sirens wailed behind her. She turned. Police poured from cars at the south end of the square. They ran towards where she stood with Fader, Karmalov, and the boy from the white tower, who still lay on the concrete.

Grabbing Fader by his arm, Morrigan ran into City Hall.

❧

With Fader in tow, Morrigan strode through the lobby, seeking escape. In front of her, open stairs led down to, according to a sign, an underground parking garage.

She scrambled down the steps, pulling Fader with her. At the bottom, they followed more signs to the door to the parking garage. Shouts echoed behind her, followed by several pairs of feet descending the same stairs.

Wrenching open the door, she ran into the garage, still dragging Fader along. At least the boy was not resisting. Her spells still held.

They ran.

The parking garage was huge, stretching as far as she could see in all directions. The police would see her if she kept running. And she needed time to recast a cloaking spell. She had to hide.

She stopped before a large van. That should offer enough cover. She slipped along the side of the van, pulling Fader after her. But the boy wrenched his hand free and stepped back out into the open.

"Child!" she rasped, trying to keep her voice low. "Come!"

Shaking his head, Fader stayed where he was. She heard a door open, voices calling, running footsteps. Cursing, she slid behind the van and huddled on the ground.

The footsteps stopped in front of the van. "Kid, you okay?" a male voice asked.

"Yeah, I'm fine. I got away."

"From the redhead? Where is she?"

Morrigan held her breath. She had no spell ready to defeat several armed men.

"She drove out that way."

Morrigan almost let out a gasp, so great was her surprise.

"What kind of car, kid?" asked another male voice.

"White. Four doors."

The first voice called instructions in on his radio to intercept any white car leaving the garage.

"C'mon, kid. A squad car's coming with a girl who says she's your sister."

She listened as their footsteps faded into the distance. A door opened and closed. Silence. She closed her eyes, fighting back a sob. She was safe.

But she had lost him.

"You can come out now," came Fader's voice. "They're gone."

She leaped up, not believing her ears. Emerging from behind the van, she walked up to him. They stared at each other, the witch and the boy.

"How did you get away?" she asked.

He shrugged. "People forget I'm around, especially if I want them to."

She smiled. "I have noticed. My spells are gone from you, aren't they?"

"Yeah."

"Then why did you save me?"

He kicked the ground with a toe. "Because I like you."

She swallowed. "And I like you, too, little one."

He nodded. "I know." He looked back the way they had come. "My sister is waiting for me. I'm gonna find her. She'll be worried." He turned to her. "But I wanted to say goodbye."

He is leaving me. For her. She summoned a spell to bind him again.

His eyes widened as the runes tingled on her face. "Please, don't."

She hesitated...then surprised herself once again.

Letting the runes fade, she opened her arms. They hugged each other, long and hard. "Go to your sister, little one," she whispered. "Live your life. Be happy." Releasing him, she watched him walk away from her.

At the door to the garage, he stopped and looked back. "There's good in you," he called.

Startled, she said nothing.

"I know there is," he said. "You just have to find it." Then he stepped through the door. And out of her life.

She stared at the empty doorway for several moments. Then Morrigan the Bright, last of the white coven of Ellan Vannin, turned and walked away.

Chapter 53

Cover Me

W ill lay trembling on the ground, soaked in sweat. Too bright. Too open. Too many people. People surrounding him, crowding him, touching him, asking questions he couldn't answer. His heart wanted to burst from his chest. Each breath was a battle. He wondered when his body would let him die and escape this horror.

As his last grip on consciousness began to slip away, a voice beat through his fog of terror. "Get back! Let me through. Get away from him." A familiar voice. A wonderful voice.

"Case," he croaked.

And then the crowd and sky and square disappeared. The babble of voices hushed. Darkness settled over him. He smelled her beside him, felt the warmth of her body as she held him, cradling his head in her lap.

"It's dark," he said. "Why is it dark?"

"Got a blanket from the cops."

He understood. She'd thrown a blanket over them both. Hiding him from the open space. Making their own space here. Inside. Not outside anymore.

His breathing slowed. His heart rate dropped. She stroked his temple, and the tension in his limbs melted away. He still felt sick and weak, but he could manage this until he got home. As control of his body and mind returned, so did his memory of recent events. "You're okay. Oh god, you're okay. Stayne and Stryke? What happened?"

"Long story. They're dead. And I was awesome."

"Marell?" he asked.

"According to Yeshe, who's somehow in that big Russian guy, Marell was destroyed. Forever. By Morrigan, if you can believe it. How'd you manage that?"

"Also a long story. Not sure I did. But I was equally awesome. Morrigan?"

"The cops are looking for her, but Fader says she escaped."

"Fader! He's okay?"

"On the other side of this blanket."

"Are you two smooching in there?" Fader called.

"No," they answered. They looked at each other.

He sat up, grinning. "Which raises the question..."

"Why aren't we?" she said, grinning back.

He kissed her. She returned it eagerly, and he'd never known anything so wonderful. The nightmare was over. It was finally over. And they were together.

When they ended the kiss, she stroked his cheek with a finger. "So, Home Boy, still want to go out tonight?"

Closing his eyes, he leaned against her shoulder. "If it's all the same to you, I'd rather stay in."

Epilogue: Loose Ends

Two days later, Will pushed Adi in her wheelchair onto the Ancient Greece floor in the Dream Rider tower. Dr. Jin had assured Will that Adi, while still weak, would make a full recovery. For now, he was just happy she was alive and back in his life. He was also happy to have someone *else* back in his life.

A few steps away, Case stood with an architect at a dust-covered table examining a large sketch she'd drawn. This floor housed a huge collection of Greek sculpture and pottery. Workers were moving those items to warehouse levels in the tower. Once done, a construction crew would reconfigure this floor into several corridors of small apartments.

"Guys on the west side, girls on the east," Case said, pointing at her sketch. "And that's a common room in the middle. They need a sense of community as much as a place to stay."

"No problem with that layout," the architect replied. "Plumbing's the issue. Shared washrooms and showers on each side would be easier. We'd fit more rooms, too. Or bigger ones."

Case chewed her lip, then nodded. "Okay, but private shower stalls."

Will watched Case, smiling. He didn't know if they could make it work. Him and her. He and she. Maybe they could. Maybe not. But right now, things were great between them. For now, that was enough.

"What are you and your girlfriend up to?" Adi asked, watching Case with narrowed eyes.

"Case's idea. A free shelter for street kids. One where they're safe. They'll each have their own apartment and can come and go as they please."

"Wandering through our lobby where your clients are waiting?"

"We'll make a separate entrance to the elevators. Each kid's handprint will give them access to this floor and their own room."

"Giving them a place to stay won't solve all their problems. They're on the street for a reason. No money, no jobs, no prospects. Some have addiction or mental health issues."

"Yeah, but it's a start. Case has other ideas. If they want a permanent room, they'll have to enroll in high school classes or training for a trade. Paid tuition for anybody who wants to go on further. And we're setting up access to a health clinic, including counseling and addiction help."

"Why should these kids trust us?"

"Us? As in you and me? They won't. But they trust Case. They know her. The H-Boys are helping—"

"H-Boys?"

"The Hollow Boys. The survivors. Yeah, they're calling themselves that. And they're talking this up on the streets. Talking Case up, too. She always had a good rep. Now, she's like a freakin' goddess. If she says this place is cool and safe, it'll catch on."

"And how much will this cost us?"

He shrugged. "Am I running out of money?"

"If you keep giving away your comic—"

"Graphic novel."

"—for free, then possibly."

"Just the last issue was free. And orders for the next one are off the charts."

"Which is interesting, seeing you called the last issue exactly that. The *last*."

"Last issue of *The Dream Rider*."

"Meaning?"

He grinned. "Not telling. You'll have to wait until it comes out."

"You're lucky you'll have a next issue. Or a company, after Lawrence Kinland's efforts."

Oops. Back in the principal's office. "Adi, I'm sorry. I should never have signed that paper."

She shook her head. "That document had no legal value."

He frowned at her. "Excuse me?"

"You are still underage, William. Your signature meant nothing. However, people believed it did, which let him operate as if he had the power he claimed."

"What are you doing about him?"

"You leave Kinland to me."

"With pleasure." He remembered something else. "Adi, when you were stabbed, you said you had something important to tell me."

She shrugged. "Probably not to sign documents without reading them first."

"Ouch," he said. He knew Adi was avoiding the question, but pushing her to talk before she was ready never worked. "What about Stone and his team? What will happen to them?"

She raised an eyebrow. "He lets you call him Stone? You two got quite chummy while I was away. What else did he tell you?"

He shrugged. "Nothing." *Except that* your *nickname is Archie.*

"Hmm. The police released him and his men. Some enterprising officer reviewed the SWAT team's video from that hospital."

"But I watched the raid. The video didn't show a thing."

"It did when the police watched it."

"Wait, what—oh!" He understood. "Away from the hospital and Morrigan's magic, I'll bet it showed what was really there."

Adi nodded. "The missing boys. And your girlfriend and her brother as prisoners."

Case joined them. "So *that's* why the cops came back to the hospital."

"Nice of them to give you a lift to City Hall," Will said. "And loan you a blanket."

"Told them the Big Bads were there. Not that you needed any help against them."

"I needed your blanket," he said.

She slipped an arm around his waist. "Yeah? Was that the only thing you needed?"

"Nope," he said, pulling her close, breathing in her smell. They kissed until Adi cleared her throat.

"Adi," Case said. "I'm, uh, glad you're back."

"No, you're not," Adi replied.

"No, I'm not. But I *am* glad you're not, you know, dead."

"How kind."

"Ladies, can you please *not?*" Will pleaded. "I could use some peace and quiet after battling super villains."

"And kicking their butts," Case said, doing a fist bump with him. She crossed her arms and faced Adi. "A butt-kicking where Fader and *I* played a major part."

Adi nodded. "William told me of the events that transpired while I was in hospital—"

"*The events that transpired?*" Case said. "Seriously? Can't you talk like normal people?"

"I am not *normal people*—" Adi began.

"You think?"

"Ladies!"

"Sorry," Case said.

Adi glared at her. "I was about to say you *all* handled yourselves brilliantly. Against terrible odds."

Will shrugged. "Case took out two baddies single-handed. Fader dealt with a witch—"

"Somehow," Case muttered.

"All *I* did was melt down in public before hundreds of people."

"But that was your plan," Case said. "So, you know, you were awesome, too."

Adi squeezed his arm. "There is no greater courage than to face your worst fear. I'm very proud of you, William."

Will swallowed, unable to speak. Praise was as rare as a smile from Adi. Case winked at him.

Adi turned to Case. "I suppose I need to grow accustomed to your presence, Ms. Cootes."

"*Cootes?*" Will said.

Case stared at Adi wide-eyed. "How did you find out my name?"

"*Cootes?*" Will repeated.

Adi sighed. "I had Mr. Zhang investigate you and your brother. To determine if you represented a threat to my ward." She held up a hand. "No, it was not William's idea. He was not pleased when he found out."

"*And* I told you to stop," Will said.

"I did," Adi said, turning to Case. "Mr. Zhang is now focusing on locating your mother." Case straightened, but Adi shook her head. "I'm sorry. So far, we've had no success."

"But you'll keep trying, right?" Case said. "I mean...please?"

"You have my word."

Case bit her lip, then stuck out her hand. "Thank you."

Adi's eyebrows shot up. She hesitated, then shook Case's hand. "You're welcome—William, put that away!"

"Too late." Will grinned, lowering his phone. "You two shaking hands? That's like a photo op at a peace treaty."

Adi's phone beeped. She checked it. "And now, I'm meeting with Lawrence Kinland."

"And we're going to see Fader. He's binge reading DR comics in my studio," Will said.

They walked to the elevators, Will pushing Adi in the wheelchair. Adi's downbound car came first.

"Make sure you call him Larry," Will said as Adi wheeled herself in. "He hates that."

"And you can call your girlfriend by her real name— Cassiopeia," Adi said with a ghost of a smile. The doors closed on her.

He looked at Case. "*Cassiopeia?*"

"I really hate her," she said, glaring at the elevator door.

"*Cassiopeia?*"

"Shut up. Mom was an astrophysicist. She named us after constellations."

"What's Fader?"

"Perseus."

"Ouch."

"He went by Percy. I was Casey."

"Can't say I blame you. Bet they called you 'Cooties' in school. Casey Cooties. Or a "Case" of the Cooties."

She turned to him, arms folded, icicles shooting from her eyes.

"I'll stop talking now," he said.

"Good call."

Case walked beside Will on the running track, on their way to his studio. Will was talking, but she wasn't listening. She was thinking about what Adi had promised. To find her mother.

"You haven't heard a word I said, have you?" Will said.

"Sorry. No. Thinking about my mom. What'd you say?"

"Same topic. Your mom. Now that we don't have super villains to fill our time, I'll search for her in Dream. As well as still searching for my own parents. With your memories of your mom, we'll have a good shot, assuming..." He broke off. "I mean, we'll have a good shot."

"Assuming she's still alive. It's okay. You can say it. And thanks," she said, squeezing his hand. She didn't remind him he'd never found his own missing parents in Dream in eight years.

Will stopped walking. Looking up, she did the same. Ahead, a translucent glowing figure dressed in maroon robes floated above the running track.

"Yeshe!" they both cried.

The monk smiled. "My friends."

"You're still alive?" Case said.

"My spirit resides in the body of the soldier Karmalov, who enjoys the hospitality of your local police. But I have now led that man back from the Gray Lands. Soon I will leave that vessel—just as I will be leaving you."

"Leaving?" Case said. "You mean dying, don't you?"

"My body died three days ago," Yeshe said. "After I assisted the Hollow Boys with their return, the use of the young master's body and the soldier's allowed my spirit to stay connected to this physical world. But now, I must move on to the Realms of the Dead."

"Can't you stay in Karmalov?" Will asked.

"Aside from Mr. Karmalov's probable jail term, I will not choose Marell's path. No, I had a long life, one dedicated to destroying Marell. That has come to pass, thanks to you both. So, now I must say goodbye. I say this with great sadness, for we will not meet again, at least not in this realm."

He floated closer. "My young friends, my spirit has grown from knowing your own. Yours are bright flames. Long may they light this world." He reached out his glowing hands to touch Will and Case on their foreheads.

Yeshe's touch in pure spirit form was like cuddling before a crackling fire on a cold winter's night. All warmth and coziness and safety. Case tried to fight back a sob, but then let it out. She couldn't think of anything to say, and the sob expressed her feelings better than any words might.

Yeshe bowed to them both. "One day, may you forgive my frailties. I tried to do the right thing."

"Nothing to forgive," Will said.

She wiped at her eyes. "What he said."

"Thank you for that kindness. Now...goodbye." Yeshe stepped back. And kept stepping. His glowing form receded into the distance, growing smaller and smaller until it disappeared into a point.

And was gone.

She and Will stared at where he had been.

"So..." she began.

"So?" Will said, still staring.

"So, he's really dead this time, right?"

He looked at her.

"Well, I mean, this is like the zillionth time I've said goodbye to him."

"Oh, sure. Kill the touching moment."

She shrugged. "Just checking. Okay, I'll be sad now."

"Don't play Hard Case. I heard that sob."

She smiled. "Yeah. I'll miss him."

"Me, too." He hugged her, and they stood there, holding each other.

She had no idea where they'd go from here. He was still Everything Guy, and she was still...

Nothing Girl? Was she? Something had changed in her over the past week. She felt different. She felt...

She felt good. She felt happy. She felt strong. For now, that was enough. She took Will's hand. "Let's go see my brother."

"You mean Percy?"

"Don't. Just...don't."

<hr/>

Adi sat in her office behind her kidney-shaped maple desk. The desktop was bare except for a photo of her with an eight-year-old Will and his parents. She sat in her chair, her wheelchair in a nearby office. She didn't want Lawrence

Kinland to know how weak she was. A knock sounded on her door.

"Come," she called.

Stone stepped inside. "He's here."

"Bring him in. And I want you to stay."

Stone nodded and opened the door. Kinland entered. Straightening the jacket of his dark navy suit, he took a chair in front of Adi's desk. Stone remained standing at the door. Kinland glanced back at him, raised his eyebrows, then turned to Adi. "Adrienne, how nice to see you back."

"You're off the Board. I'm severing all connections between you and this firm."

He pursed his lips as he considered her, then shrugged and rose. "Well, thank you for being so efficient with my time."

"That's it?" she asked, surprised. She'd anticipated a fight.

"I expected no less," he said. "It's merely an advisory board. We serve at your pleasure." He smiled. "A pleasure I lost, I'm sure, with my treatment of your ward."

"What were you thinking, Lawrence?" Adi said. "What game were you playing?"

Kinland chuckled. "Poor Adrienne. You don't know the game. You don't even know the players. Rather hard to win in that situation." He walked to the door, which Stone still blocked. Stone looked at Adi. She nodded. Stone moved aside. Kinland stepped into the hall, where two of Stone's men waited. The door closed behind him.

Stone slid into the vacated chair. "My people will escort him from the building. And we've deactivated his security rights. What was he talking about?"

"I've no idea. Have you found out what he's been doing these past days? Beyond canceling the Rider comic and restricting Will's powers?"

"I'm just back myself. But as far as I've checked, he didn't interfere further in the operations of the company."

"No attempt to access or divert funds?"

Stone shook his head. "He spent all his time here in the building with a team from a local art appraisal firm. Laporte & Associates."

Adi frowned. "Never heard of them—and I know every appraiser in the city. A team? How big? And when did he bring them in?"

"Twenty-four people arrived the same day he restricted Will's powers. And, Archie, I checked the security logs. Once Kinland brought them in, they never left. They stayed day and night."

"Two dozen people here for three solid days? My god. Are they still here?"

"No. We escorted them from the tower an hour ago. And canceled their access."

Adi touched her wounded side, remembering the last unauthorized entry into the building. "Do we know where they went in the tower?"

Stone nodded. "From the security system logs. They spent all their time in the Warehouse."

The "Warehouse" spanned ten floors in the tower, crammed with artifacts from Will's parents' expeditions. Anything not sold to a museum or collector. "What the hell were they doing there?"

Stone tapped his phone. The wall screen came to life. "See for yourself."

Adi watched the security video playing on her wall screen. "When was this taken?"

"This morning."

The video showed a high shot of one of the ten Warehouse floors. Corridors of ceiling-high shelving filled the floor, crates and boxes of various sizes jamming each shelf. In the middle of the floor, statues and larger crates too big for the shelves sat on pallets.

A pair of figures, a man and a woman, stood in the nearest corridor. They wore long white coats, like lab technicians. The man passed a wand-like device over the contents of the closest shelf while the woman examined a handheld screen. She shook her head. Climbing a wheeled ladder, the man repeated the procedure on the next higher shelf. In adjacent corridors, other pairs performed similar actions.

"They were looking for something," she said. "Did they remove anything from the tower?"

"No. We searched them before escorting them out. And the loading dock said nothing's gone through there all week."

She sat back, tapping a finger on the arm of her chair. "Any of those crates would bring a small fortune."

"Then this wasn't about money."

"And they were still at it this morning."

Stone nodded. "Whatever they were searching for—"

"They didn't find. Which means it's still there."

"But what is *it*?"

Not answering, she considered the gang of white-coated invaders of her tower displayed on the screen. Instinctively, she touched her side again. "Have your people review all the security footage from the past three days. Minute by minute. And find out everything you can about Laporte & Associates."

Stone stood. "On it." He left the room.

Leaning back, Adi stared at the photograph on her desk. In it, her old friends, Jon Dreycott and Terri Yurikami, smiled back at her. *You bloody idiots. What did you get us into?*

When Case and Will entered the studio, Fader lay on the leather couch reading, a stack of comics on the floor beside him. Jumping up, he ran to Will, clutching the "Death of the Dream Rider" issue in his hand. "Please tell me he doesn't really die!"

Case smiled, happy to see Fader being himself again. Obsessed with the Rider—and free of Morrigan.

"The Rider?" Will said.

"Yeah," Fader said. "I mean, in the last panel, he's wounded and surrounded by monsters and the church ceiling is collapsing and it's on fire and..."

"Dude, take a breath," Case said.

"Well, does he? Die?" Fader asked, looking at Will.

Will grinned. "See for yourself." He led Fader to his design table and tapped on its surface. "Here's the cover for the next issue."

Fader's eyes went wide and his mouth flew open. "Omigod! Omigod! Omigod!" He turned to Case, a huge smile on his face. "Case! Look at this."

She joined them. The comic's cover displayed on the table, blown up large. In it, the hooded figure of the Rider crouched with sword raised, surrounded by a horde of giant black rats with human hands. She shivered, remembering their encounter with a Mara. But what drew her attention was the thing she knew was prompting Fader's joy.

Beside the Rider, two other figures crouched in fighting stances. One was a boy about Fader's size. His costume reminded her of gray mist drifting across a landscape, everything out of focus. A yellow "F" glowed on his chest. The other figure was female, about the Rider's size. Her costume was skin-tight and all black except for a red "V" that followed her cleavage.

The title of the issue ran across the top:

Astral Realms #1
Rise of the Astral Warriors!
Introducing the Voice and the Fade

Fader beamed up at her. "We're superheroes!"

Case grinned as Fader began leaping around the room, striking fighting pose after pose. And with each, he'd shout, "The Fade!"

"The Fade? The Voice?" she said, turning to Will.

He shrugged. "We can talk about the names."

"Based on my current costume, mine should be 'Astounding Cleavage.'"

"You want a new costume?"

"I want a costume period. One with more fabric than skin."

"You obviously don't understand my readership of teenage boys."

"You're saying that to a teenage girl?"

"Point. Okay, new costume. And you can approve it."

"But, Case, we're superheroes!" Fader said, running to her side.

"And what does every new superhero need?" Will said.

"A better name and costume," Case said.

"An origin story," Will said, turning to her.

She knew where this was going. "I get it. Time to explain how the weirdness started. My Voice. Fader's fading."

"Our super powers," Fader corrected.

"But tomorrow," she said. "Gotta meet with the architect again today about the hostel floor." Which was true, but mostly she wanted to put off the discussion as long as possible.

He kissed her forehead. "Tomorrow. A picnic on the roof, and you guys can tell your tales. And we'll plan how to search for your mom."

"And for that thingy, too," she added.

"Don't go all technical on me."

"You know, whatever's shielding this tower. Yeshe figured it was something inside this building."

"Right. The Mysterious Shield Thingy. Well, at least there's no rush on that anymore. I mean, Marell's gone, and no one *else* is looking for it, right?"

"Yeah, I guess," she said, uneasy and not knowing why.

Fader was staring at the *Astral Realms* cover displayed on the table, frowning.

Will walked over. "Something wrong, dude?"

Fader looked up at him. "Can I have a cape?"

The End

Afterword

Get the Next Book in *The Dream Rider Saga* Now!

I hope you enjoyed reading *The Hollow Boys*! To find out what happens next to Will and Case, visit the website below (or scan the QR code) to find *The Crystal Key*, book 2 in the trilogy, on your favorite book retailer:

https://books2read.com/TheCrystalKey

The Crystal Key

Will Dreycott is the Dream Rider, the agoraphobic teenage superhero who can walk in our dreams but never in the streets of his city. Case is his girlfriend, a survivor of those streets who hears voices. Fader is her brother, who is *very* good at disappearing. Together, they defeated a body swapper and a witch to save the world (*The Hollow Boys*).

Now, Case battles guilt over living sheltered in Will's tower home while her street friends still struggle. Blaming his affliction for Case's sadness, Will searches for a way to live a normal life with the girl he loves—a way to go outside.

But his efforts draw the attention of dark forces. Sinister figures hunt Will in Dream. Intruders scour the vast warehouse of antiquities "acquired" by Will's missing parents. And a masked swordswoman attacks Will, demanding "the Crystal Key" before disappearing into thin air.

Are they all searching for the same thing? Something from Will's parents' shady past? For the swordswoman leaves behind a flowery scent, Will's only memory from the lost expedition eight years ago that gave him powers in Dream but cost him his parents and his freedom.

A trail of dark secrets leads Will, Case, and Fader to a mysterious world. Trapped between warring cults willing to kill for the Crystal Key, the three friends must master strange new powers that grow stronger and wilder the closer they draw to the truth.

This time it's not just the fate of the world at stake...but the multiverse.

Indiana Jones meets *Teen Titans* in *The Dream Rider Saga*, the multi-award-winning urban fantasy trilogy from "one of Canada's most original writers of speculative fiction" (*Library Journal*).

Visit the website below (or scan the QR code) to find *The Crystal Key*, book 2 in the trilogy, on your favorite book retailer:

https://books2read.com/TheCrystalKey

Please Review This Book!

Reviews really do help authors. If you enjoyed *The Hollow Boys*, please help other readers discover *The Dream Rider Saga* by posting a review. A line or two is all you need to write to help me out. Just visit the website below (or scan the QR code) to review *The Hollow Boys* on your preferred retailer. Thanks!

Post your review of *The Hollow Boys:*

https://books2read.com/thehollowboys

Be the First to Hear of My New Releases

Visit the websites below (or scan the QR codes) to keep updated on my writing:

Signup for my newsletter:

https://smithwriter.com/newsletter-signup

Follow me on BookBub:

https://www.bookbub.com/authors/douglas-smith

Like me on FaceBook:

https://www.facebook.com/WritingtheFantastic

Visit my website:

https://smithwriter.com

Follow me on Twitter:

https://twitter.com/smithwritr

About the Author

Douglas Smith is a multi-award-winning author described by *Library Journal* as "one of Canada's most original writers of speculative fiction."

Published in twenty-seven languages, Doug is a three-time winner of Canada's Aurora Award and has been a finalist for the Astounding Award, the Canadian Broadcasting Corporation's Bookies Award, Canada's juried Sunburst Award, and France's juried Prix Masterton and Prix Bob Morane.

His works include the young adult urban fantasy trilogy, *The Dream Rider Saga* (*The Hollow Boys*, *The Crystal Key*, and *The Lost Expedition*); the Heroka shapeshifter novels, *The Wolf at the End of the World* and *The Wolf and the Phoenix* (in progress); the collections, *Chimerascope* and *Impossibilia*; the writer's guide, *Playing the Short Game: How to Market & Sell Short Fiction*; and numerous short stories.

Doug lives near Toronto, Ontario, Canada.

~~

"The man is Sturgeon good. Zelazny good. I don't give those up easy." —*Spider Robinson, Hugo and Nebula Awards winner*

"A great storyteller with a gifted and individual voice." —*Charles de Lint, World Fantasy Award winner*

"His stories are a treasure trove of riches that will touch your heart while making you think." —*Robert J. Sawyer, Hugo and Nebula Awards winner*

"Stories you can't forget, even years later." —*Julie Czerneda, multi-award-winning author and editor*

~~

Find all of Doug's books at your favorite retailer here:

https://books2read.com/DouglasSmith

Also By Douglas Smith

The Dream Rider Saga:
The Hollow Boys (Book 1)
The Crystal Key (Book 2)
The Lost Expedition (Book 3)

The Heroka Novels:
The Wolf at the End of the World
The Wolf and the Phoenix (coming soon)

The Heroka Short Stories:
"Spirit Dance"
"A Bird in the Hand"
"Dream Flight"

Short Story Collections:
Chimerascope
Impossibilia

Writing Guides:
Playing the Short Game: How to Market & Sell Short Fiction

~~

All titles are available in both print and ebook editions from your favorite book retailer. Just visit the website (or scan the QR code) below:

https://books2read.com/DouglasSmith

Acknowledgments

The Dream Rider books would not have been possible without the time, effort, support, and advice of the following people:

My writing critique group, the Ink*Specs:

Melissa Gold, Susan Qrose, Rebecca Simkin, and Maaja Wentz

My Beta Readers:

Ami Agner, Emily P Bloch, Laura Rainbow Dragon, Kerstin Langer, and Daria Rydzaj

My editors:

Susan Forest and Adrienne Kerr

~~

My sincere thanks to all of you.

Songs Used for Chapter Titles

You may have noticed I used popular (mostly) song titles for the chapter titles in the book. If you didn't, don't worry about it. It was just something I enjoyed doing. However, if you did notice, I thought you might enjoy seeing the whole list of songs and their associated artists.

The artists reflect many of my favorites, such as Springsteen and Bowie and the Canadian bands, Metric and The Tragically Hip. Others were picked to add even more Canadian flavor, so we have Arcade Fire, Neil Young, Brighid Fry (of the band, Housewife), and Stars.

Sometimes I took liberty with the title to make a play on words that better fit the chapter (see chapters 7, 15, 22, and 40), but always the main reason I picked a song was for how its title fit to the chapter action.

ACT ONE: City with No Children — Arcade Fire

Chapter 1: Planet of Dreams — David Bowie
Chapter 2: In the Streets of the Jungle Toronto — Brighid Fry
Chapter 3: Welcome to the Jungle — Guns N' Roses
Chapter 4: My City of Ruins — Bruce Springsteen
Chapter 5: Man at the Top — Bruce Springsteen
Chapter 6: Chasing Something in the Night — Bruce Springsteen
Chapter 7: Blinded by the Dark (Blinded by the Light) — Bruce Springsteen
Chapter 8: Over the Wall We Go — David Bowie
Chapter 9: Sister Midnight — David Bowie / Carlos Alomar / Iggy Pop
Chapter 10: Crush on You — Bruce Springsteen
Chapter 11: Darkness on the Edge of Town — Bruce Springsteen
Chapter 12: Psychedelic Ramblings of Rich Kids — Tragically Hip
Chapter 13: Monster Hospital — Metric
Chapter 14: I Know You're Out There Somewhere — Moody Blues
Chapter 15: Street Fighting (Wo)man — Rolling Stones

Chapter 16: Dreams So Real — Metric
Chapter 17: Rat Men — Metric

ACT TWO: You've Haunted Me All My Life — Death Cab for Cutie

Chapter 18: Glass Ceiling — Metric
Chapter 19: Escape Is at Hand — Tragically Hip
Chapter 20: Follow the Yellow Brick Road — The Wizard of Oz movie
Chapter 21: Ahead by a Century — Tragically Hip
Chapter 22: Seven Years (or So) in Tibet — David Bowie
Chapter 23: The Ties That Bind — Bruce Springsteen
Chapter 24: Lie Lie Lie — Metric
Chapter 25: Jungleland — Bruce Springsteen
Chapter 26: You and Me — Brighid Fry
Chapter 27: Sick Muse — Metric
Chapter 28: Satellite Mind — Metric
Chapter 29: Gold Guns Girls — Metric
Chapter 30: Combat Baby — Metric
Chapter 31: The Price You Pay — Bruce Springsteen

ACT THREE: As the World Falls Down — David Bowie

Chapter 32: Helpless — Neil Young
Chapter 33: Miss You — Rolling Stones
Chapter 34: Hit Me with Your Best Shot — Pat Benatar
Chapter 35: Surprise, Surprise — Bruce Springsteen
Chapter 36: Into Your Arms — Nick Cave
Chapter 37: A Big Hurt — David Bowie
Chapter 38: Save the Planet — Tragically Hip
Chapter 39: The River — Bruce Springsteen
Chapter 40: Dead Disco, Dead Monk (Funk), Dead Rock 'n Roll — Metric
Chapter 41: Chant of the Ever Circling Skeletal Family — David Bowie
Chapter 42: Youth Without Youth — Metric
Chapter 43: We Exist — Arcade Fire
Chapter 44: My Body is a Cage — Arcade Fire
Chapter 45: Scary Monsters (and Super Creeps) — David Bowie
Chapter 46: Dead Man Walking — Bruce Springsteen
Chapter 47: Meeting across the River — Bruce Springsteen
Chapter 48: I Died So I Could Haunt You — Stars
Chapter 49: Spirit in the Night — Bruce Springsteen

Made in the USA
Coppell, TX
08 May 2024

32129794R00225